TWILIGHT IMPERIUM

Intergalactic empires fall, but one faction will rise from the ashes to conquer the galaxy.

Once the mighty Lazax Empire ruled all the known galaxy from its capital planet of Mecatol Rex, before treachery and war erased the Lazax from history, plunging a thousand star systems into conflict and uncertainty.

Now the Great Races who span the galaxy look upon their former capital hungrily – the power and secrets of the Lazax await a new emperor...

To lay claim to the throne is a destiny sought by many, yet the shadows of the past serve as a grim warning to those who would follow in their footsteps.

T0112575

ALSO AVAILABLE

TWILIGHT IMPERIUM™

The
NECROPOLIS
EMPIRE

TIM PRATT

ACONYTE®

First published by Aconyte Books in 2021

ISBN 978 1 83908 076 0

Ebook ISBN 978 1 83908 077 7

Copyright © 2021 Fantasy Flight Games

All rights reserved. Aconyte and the Aconyte icon are registered trademarks of Asmodee Group SA. Twilight Imperium and the FFG logo are trademarks or registered trademarks of Fantasy Flight Games.

This novel is entirely a work of fiction. Names, characters, places, and incidents are the products of the author's imagination or are used fictitiously. Any resemblance to actual events, locales, organizations or persons, living or dead, is entirely coincidental.

Sales of this book without a front cover may be unauthorized. If this book is coverless, it may have been reported to the publisher as "unsold and destroyed" and neither the author nor the publisher may have received payment for it.

Cover art by Scott Schomburg

Distributed in North America by Simon & Schuster Inc, New York, USA

Printed in the United States of America

9 8 7 6 5 4 3 2 1

ACONYTE BOOKS

An imprint of Asmodee Entertainment Ltd

Mercury House, Shipstones Business Centre

North Gate, Nottingham NG7 7FN, UK

aconytebooks.com // twitter.com/aconytebooks

*For Aleister, off to make his
own way in the universe.*

PROLOGUE

On a scientific outpost clinging to an icy moon, orbiting a world of mud, jungle, and abominable light, Doctor Archambelle worked to change the galaxy.

She gazed at her screen, at an array of images found in scores of archaeological sites – including the most recent, in a crumbling metal temple on the planet below. Isolated glyphs and symbols lit up on the screen as her system collated, cross-referenced, and attempted translations. They'd found these same ideograms and symbols over and over, in samples taken from planets, moons, and technological ruins scattered throughout the galaxy. None of these symbols belonged to any known culture, but they clearly belonged to *one* culture – something ancient, that had spread throughout all of inhabited space, and perhaps beyond, an incalculably long time ago.

Over and over in these fragments, Archambelle had found references to a secret world, a hidden place, a paradise, a promised land: Ixth.

That was a place she *had* heard of before, in the prophecies of her own people, the Letnev, who imagined that paradise as a hollow world full of caverns crammed with weapons and treasure. But Ixth appeared in the legends of most of the other species in the galaxy, too. For the Muaat, Ixth was a place of volcanic forges and endless geological riches. To the Hylar, it was a teeming temperate sea, with dormant alien factories waiting in the depths. To the humans, Ixth was all cities of gold and fountains of liquor. Every culture had their own idea about the nature of that paradise, but all agreed that anyone who found it would be granted immeasurable wealth and power. If *everyone* had stories about that place, however varied, those stories had to be rooted in some fundamental truth, didn't they?

If Archambelle's theory was right, Ixth was *much* more than a story. It was the homeworld of an ancient race, almost totally forgotten, but once rulers of the galaxy. Those people were gone, but she believed their treasures remained, and that even the memory of those treasures was great enough to inspire songs, stories, and prophecies all these millennia later.

There had to be a way to find Ixth. Archambelle would be the one to–

Her computer purred, and several items on the screen rushed to the forefront and fitted themselves together into a whole, though their source materials came from millions of kilometers apart. There were small sections missing, yes, but there was enough for her to discern a star map, and a spot marked, a *world*, could this be Ixth? Surely it couldn't be that simple?

She ran the image against the astronomical database and found the coordinates. To her surprise, the fragments depicted a known system, though not a very interesting one, and the planet was definitely not Ixth. That world was nobody's promised land. It was, if anything, a planet that anyone with sense would try to get *away* from.

It was something, though. A clue. A stepping stone.

The computer hummed again, translating another reference to this unimpressive little world: *"the key to the key"*.

That was promising. "I'll step on you soon, little world," Archambelle said, and went to call in the necessary favors.

CHAPTER 1

The night before the aliens came, Bianca Xing stood in the south meadow and gazed up at the dark. As always, her eyes were drawn to one particular part of the night sky: a blank space at the center of an irregular triangle formed by three stars. That seemingly arbitrary point drifted around the sky as the seasons progressed – dipping low, rising high, sometimes hidden behind the horizon – but since she'd been old enough to look up, something about those three stars and the dark they surrounded had fascinated her. After nearly twenty years here on Darit, her whole life defined by cliffs and meadows and forests (and the flock of caprids, horns and dirty wool and all), she was no closer to understanding why that spot in the sky drew her attention.

"Maybe because it's the most faraway place I can imagine," she said aloud. "A place so far away even the stars they have there aren't visible from here." The wind blew her long white-blonde hair back from her brow in a way she hoped looked romantic and tragic, even though no one was watching. Bianca had a dramatic streak, to the bemusement of her parents, and was known to wear a flowing nightgown and walk the fields at night while lamenting the state of her life. She was too self-aware to do so entirely seriously, but it helped to pass the time.

There was no real danger in her nightly wanders. Predators were kept out by the scramble-fence – meant to protect the caprid flock, but equally good at protecting her – and the nearest human was kilometers away. Even that was just Torvald at the mech farm, and he didn't mean her any harm. He was so old he couldn't chase her across the fields anyway, with ill intent or otherwise.

Nobody ever chased her across the fields, with murder *or* romance on their minds. She was very put out by it. On her family's rare visits to town, to trade or attend the monthly Halemeetings, she sometimes saw other village youths making eyes at her, but there weren't any she wanted to make eyes *back* at, except maybe Mallory Zeen (her biceps!) or Compton Sadler (his eyelashes!), but they were already dating each other, and rich besides, not a farm girl on the outskirts like her. Bianca steadfastly ignored the occasional flirtations from the sons and daughters and androgynes of the outskirters who visited the farm; she'd given her neighbor Grandly a little too much encouragement one summer when she was bored, and he'd clung to her like a tick for ages. Grandly was nice enough, and both sets of parents thought they'd make a good match, but Grandly's life was just like Bianca's, give or take a biteweed patch or a bigger root cellar. She wanted *more* out of life, not more of the same.

Her mother, Willen, said she set her sights too high: "You're always looking at the stars, Bianca, but there are wonderful things down here all around your feet." Her father, Keon, would just puff his pipe and say, "Mmmm, ayuh." Parents.

Bianca was about to turn twenty, though, and the hints had become more explicit lately. She needed to figure out what she was doing with her life, because mooning around in the fields every night wasn't sustainable, even if she did always make sure to do her chores first. Her options were just all horrible. Pair-bond with Grandly? No, thank you. Go work for Torvald at the scrapyard? Better, but still too small. Steal a sack full of food and set off to seek her fortune? Much better, but she could walk the circumference of Darit and never get any closer to the stars, where she *really* wanted to be. She'd read stories about space travel, but no one on Darit could do it.

A new light appeared in the sky. At first, Bianca thought it was a stray reflection from one of the orbital mirrors. Darit was a rocky, frigid, inhospitable place, but the long-dead original colonists had taken steps to make regions of the planet habitable, chiefly orbital mirrors that focused light to raise the surface temperature in dozens of zones. There were also the perpetually floating rainmakers, bulbous pale-gray shapes that drifted high above, collected water, and stimulated the clouds to make rain. Old Torvald speculated that there were other ancient technologies at work – atmospheric engines disguised as mountains, carbon sequestration devices in the guise of trees, buried soil-enriching technology – but who knew for sure? The ancients had possessed great power, but no one knew the extents or the limits, or why they'd bothered to make parts of an iceball like Darit habitable in the first place.

She squinted and decided the light couldn't be a mirror-glint, because it was moving too fast. Just a shooting star, then? No, because its streak slowed and stopped, and it became a fixed point, not twinkling. It looked like a star now, but Bianca knew every star in her part of the sky, and she wasn't fooled.

She stared at the light for a long time, but it didn't do anything interesting. Maybe it was a ship? A real, actual starship? Torvald had pieces of what he *claimed* were ships at the mech farm, but those were broken, rusting, and cracked. This starship would be sleek, shimmering, and powerful, like those in the stories.

Maybe it was an envoy from the emperor of the galaxy! She'd read about the empire in books scavenged from the vault under the Halemeeting hall, and old Torvald had a lot of stories about wars and battles and intrigue, though they didn't add up to a consistent history, as he was the first to admit. What could the emperor want with a place like this anyway? Maybe Darit had some rare resource the empire needed – there were empty mines everywhere, so perhaps there was an ore you couldn't obtain anywhere else? Or maybe a rare plant, or perhaps the caprids were the source of some miracle drug that granted immortality, and the emperor was going to build a spaceport here, and bring in new people from all over the galaxy.

Or, maybe they'd come for *her*. That was the start of an old fantasy, one she'd refined carefully over the years: she was secretly a princess, hidden away on a backwater planet for her own safety, but, when the time came, she'd be rescued and restored to the glory of her birthright.

It wasn't *that* farfetched. Bianca was adopted, and her real parents were unknown: that much was true. Her father had found her in the forest when she was a baby, squalling and helpless, and her parents had raised her as their own ever since. The truth of her origins was the mystery at the center of her life – in a small community like hers, the appearance of an unknown child was genuinely baffling. What if she was secretly the emperor's daughter, born of a mistress, and the emperor's wife would have killed her, so her father sent her away to this remote planet where she'd be safe, because no one would ever look for her *here*? Maybe that new light in the sky belonged to a ship full of assassins, come to murder her before she could take the throne?

Bianca frowned. No, too dark. Better: the emperor's mean wife was dead, and the emperor was sick, and since there were no other heirs, they needed her, because without her presence on the throne, the empire would crumble! They were here to whisk her away on an imperial pleasure ship, to dress her in shimmering gowns, to crown her with rare jewels, and to teach her proper manners and comportment. When she landed on the imperial homeworld – she forgot what Torvald called it, Mehibatel Rocks or something? – her loyal subjects would shout her name and scatter flowers at her feet. She'd get to meet her *real* parents then, her mother promoted from mistress to queen (or empress, or whatever), the emperor recovered from his illness but ready to embrace his long-lost daughter, and teach her the ways of battle and diplomacy and culture and–

A caprid, shaggy and blunt-horned, head-butted Bianca in the rump and bleated at her.

Bianca sighed, patted the caprid on the head, and trudged back to the farmhouse, the new light in the sky already forgotten as thoughts of tomorrow morning's chores filled her mind.

The next day Bianca rolled out of her small bed at dawn and lit the house fires. Her mother had done that for most of Bianca's life, but Willen was getting older and didn't move as well as she used to, and Bianca was keenly aware that she herself was aging out of being a responsibility and into being a burden, so helping out was more important than ever.

Her father emerged while she was heating the water, and kissed her on top of her head, bending down to do it. Bianca was the shortest person in her family by nearly half a meter. That was just one of the things that marked her out as a child of fortune rather than blood: she also had hair so pale it was nearly white, compared to her mother's bushy red exuberance and her father's curly black; her skin was golden and unlike either her mother's paleness or her father's deep brown; and while Willen and Keon were both broad and thick-limbed, Bianca was more petite, though you couldn't spend your life working on a farm without putting on muscle. Her mother had blue eyes, and her father's were a hypnotic green, while hers were so dark they were nearly black, and – well, she could go on.

The sense that she didn't fit in with her family was just the start of her outsider feelings. The people on this part of Darit were a varied bunch, but almost all of them were taller than her, and heartier-looking, and she'd often heard people say she looked "sickly" , though she'd never been sick a day in her life. In the books she read, people with unusual qualities were objects of speculation and attention, but around here, people just frowned and looked at her like she was a problem someone else should work on solving. That was when they looked at all, which wasn't often.

"Could you go over to Torvald's and get a new power cell for us today?" her father said.

"He doesn't have anything *new*," Bianca muttered, warming up a pot of grain mush for family breakfast.

"New to us is good enough," Keon said affably. "The well pump is drawing water real sluggish, and the lights in the barn are getting dim. We can limp along a few more days on the cell we have, I reckon, but I'd like a new one on hand when the lights go out."

Bianca sighed and said, "The journey will be long, and perilous, but if my family needs me, I'll brave the–"

"Much appreciated."

Her father was impossible to annoy. That didn't stop Bianca from trying. She didn't mind going to the mech farm, honestly. It would be a nice break from the routine farm work. But it was the principle of the thing: all chores were abhorrent, all errands were wastes of her time, and her whole life on the farm just an obstacle standing in the way of... well. That was the problem. Her parents would have supported most anything she wanted to do. But what was there *to* do? She just couldn't bear to settle down with Grandly and have some kids and spend her life feeding babies and caprids. Not yet. There had to be more to life than this, or she wouldn't feel like she'd lived a life at all.

She put on a short yellow dress – her mother grumbled that those were for Halemeetings, and weren't practical for farm work, but Bianca could at least have style, couldn't she? She put on trousers and boots underneath the dress, and added a dark brown canvas jacket because it was a little crisp today, which sort of spoiled the light effect she was going for, but again: it was the principle of the thing.

Bianca had a bicycle with nice fat tires for getting around the property, and there were trails that would take her all the way to town if she wanted, but the mech farm was on the other side of a few kilometers of uneven uphill ground, perched on a bluff overlooking the bay, and since she didn't have mechanized transport, the easiest way to get there was on foot.

She set out, a walking stick in one hand, good for fending off bandits, she liked to imagine. Not that there were any bandits hereabouts. In books, cutthroat marauders lived in the forest, but anything that tried to live in the forest here would be lucky to survive a week. After dark, the nightclimbers came out, and they'd carry off a person just as promptly as any other prey. Even during the day, there were dangers in those woods. Old things were buried in the forest, ancient machines from Darit's mysterious past, and some of them weren't buried very deep. Bianca had grown up hearing stories of glowing stones, shining pillars, and buzzing wires twined around trees like ivy, all remnants of an older age. Some of those remnants would kill you faster than a nightclimber would... or much slower, which was worse.

The sky was mostly blue that day, with a few fat clouds and one rainmaker drifting aimlessly along. The sun was sending out light but not much in the way of real heat, and of Darit's three moons, only a pale crescent of Child was visible, Father and Mother hidden by the horizon. Torvald said he'd once visited a distant valley where the people called the moons Mum and Pop and Babe. How silly was that?

She followed the trail over a ridge and paused at the top to take in the view. Off to the south, she could just see the jeweled sparkle of the sea, its true vastness hidden in distant haze. To the west, the spire of the Halemeeting hall was the only visible sign of her village, though the road to the next nearest settlement was that way too. To the east and north, there was only the forest. From here it was a brown blur, but up close it was a dense world of towering trees and twining vines (and the delicious mushrooms the brave, the foolish, or the well-armed went in to harvest). The northern part of the forest was less menacing, since the foresters picked away at the edges there, but the eastern expanse was purely wild.

Bianca turned and looked back the way she'd come. Her house was there, surrounded by fields and pasture. Smoke rose from the fire she'd lit. In the nearest meadow, the tiny speck of her father walked around their caprid flock. The animals made milk and they made wool and, every once in a while, they made meat, but mainly what they made was dung and noise and mud.

Bianca wanted so desperately to get out of the mud. There was no mud among the stars.

She continued along the ridgeline until she reached the dry streambed that led her at last to the proper trail, almost a road, that meandered from Torvald's gates down to the town. The last part of the road was steep, though, and in poor repair. She'd asked Torvald once, "Why don't you fix it? Surely you could cobble together a road-building mech."

"Ah," he'd said, "but since the road is bad, and people can't get carts or wagons up here, that means they usually rent one of my cargo mechs to carry things to and from their transport, and that's good for old Torvald, innit?"

She'd snorted, knowing he was full of it – half the people he dealt with bought on credit that Torvald wasn't too zealous about collecting, and many of the others paid him with a portion of the harvests his mechs made so much easier. He just liked pretending to be a canny trader sitting on a hoard of treasure. In a way, he was as prone to fancy as Bianca was. That was probably why they got along so well.

She stood before the tall gates of the mech farm, made of welded-together scrap, and pounded on the metal with her walking stick.

"State your name and business," the gate said, its mechanical voice harsh and grating.

"My name is Empress Bianca, and I'm here to kill the old man."

"Enter," the gate said. The small door set into the left gate clicked unlocked for her. The big gates only opened when something *really* large had to come in or out.

"I mean it," she said. "I am here on a mission of murder."

"Enter," the gate said again, this time buzzing afterward, as if for emphasis. During business hours, the gate opened and closed for visitors, but that voice didn't actually understand or care what you said. Torvald said he'd read about intelligent machines, but there weren't any of those on Darit, and he didn't know if those stories were any more real than the tales of forest demons or alien sorcerers or sea monsters he'd collected over the years.

Once inside, Bianca gazed around the chaos of the mech farm to see if there was anything new. Mostly she just saw piles of scrap junk, some merely as tall as her, others three times as high, all waiting to be repaired or repurposed or melted down. Some of those piles had been waiting for decades. There were wheels, and rods, and sheets of metal; mysterious cylinders, and spheres, and cubes; and messy coils of wire, cable, and conduit. The predominant colors were gray and dull silver, but there were flashes of bright paint or peculiar iridescence. There were bits of things that *might* have been automated transports or even spacecraft, once upon a time, but they were all jumbled in with iron bedframes and rusty farm implements, metal drums and busted appliances. Grandly's family had a working icebox, courtesy of Torvald; that had halfway tempted Bianca to accept Grandly's last proposal, during the hottest part of the summer.

There were also countless busted-up mechs, ranging from ones half her size to behemoths as big as her house. Once upon a time, Torvald said, Darit had been a mining planet, a colony of the empire, and there'd been legions of mechs to work the seams and serve the inhabitants. Of course, that was so long ago nobody even knew if the empire still existed, and most people didn't know it had ever existed in the first place. There were still remnants aplenty buried all over, though, and Torvald's family had been experts at salvage and repair for generations. People found things in their fields sometimes, and more often in the forest (when they dared to venture in), and brought those curiosities to Torvald for trade. Bianca had earned enough money for a few dresses over the years with her own lucky finds while stone-picking in the fields – just bits of colored glass and mud-packed springs and fist-sized bolts, but Torvald could get them shiny and useful again.

Torvald emerged from his shack, wiping his greasy hands on his perpetually stained overalls. He grinned, his wrinkled face lighting up. "Bee! Did you bring me something nice?"

"I brought myself. What's nicer than that?"

"I'd trade you for a broken rheostat, but I suppose you'll do, if that's all you've got." Torvald had never pair-bonded or had children of his own – rumors were that exposure to some of the more exotic items in the depths of the mech farm had made him infertile, but Bianca was pretty sure he'd just never bothered – and she wondered, sometimes, what would happen to this place when he eventually died. He'd pretty much told her she could sign on as his apprentice if she wanted, and that was currently at the top of a mental list titled "The Least Terrible of All the Terrible Options I Hate," just above "Run Away from Home" and "Pair-Bond with Grandly And At Least Have Ice All Summer." (Running away from home would have been higher up, but this habitable zone was only so big, and the places she could reach without transport and cold-weather gear to navigate the tundra in between weren't much different from her own.)

"What can I do for you, if you didn't come bearing gifts?" he asked.

"Pa says our power cell is running down. I came to see how bad you'd cheat us for a new one."

He rolled a toothpick around in his mouth. "Oh, only medium bad. One of the foresters tripped over a rock that turned out to be the corner of an autonomous cargo container buried in a dry streambed. I don't even care to guess how long it's been there. He used a stump-puller mech to clear the ground around it until he found a hatch, and do you know what he found inside?"

"Certain death?" Bianca was seething with jealousy. She'd never found anything bigger than she could pick up in both hands.

"He mostly found a bunch of crates that used to hold rations, probably, before they got filled with mold instead. He *did* recover fully half a dozen power cells, hardly even drained. They were slow to wake up, of course, but I got them refreshed. I can let you have one if you'll butcher down a caprid for me before the year turns."

That was a good deal. She sighed heavily and shook her head. "You're a bandit, Torvald. If I take that offer back to Pa, he'll butcher *me*."

"You have to invite me over for Turnsday dinner, too," he said placidly. "I've been missing your ma's root mash."

They always invited him to that anyway. "I'm just a humble farm girl, and no match for your cruel and avaricious big city wiles," Bianca said. "It's a–"

Something came howling across the sky from the direction of the sea. Bianca screamed and clapped her hands over her ears as the horrible roar vibrated her from skullbones to toes. The – ship? – passed over them in a moment, the wind of its passage so ferocious that it kicked up a huge cloud of dust and sent a pile of sheet metal falling over with a crash.

"What *was* that?" Bianca shouted, her ears still ringing from the din.

"Aliens, I reckon," Torvald shouted back. "And they're headed for the forest."

CHAPTER 2

"Why would they go to the forest?" Bianca said. "Why not land in town?"

"Where they go depends on what they came for, I suppose," Torvald said. "Come on into the shack with me. I need to look at something."

She stared at him. "What are you talking about? There're aliens here! From *space*!"

"Probably not from space, Bee. People – even alien people – don't usually live in space. Not too hospitable up there. Cold, nothing to breathe, lots of radiation. They're aliens from a planet or a moon, more likely, or a space station, or just possibly an asteroid."

"What do you know about it?" She spun to face him, fists clenched, unsure why she was suddenly so furious. "You always talk like you know the secrets of the galaxy, but you were born on this dirt ball just like I was, and you don't *know* anything!"

"I don't know much about anything *currently*, that's true."

Torvald wasn't unflappable like her pa, but he tended to react to her outbursts with a sort of distant amusement. He led her toward his little shack. "I couldn't tell you who sits on the throne on Mecatol Rex these days, if anyone even does. But I know a lot about how things *used* to be. I have a… family heirloom, you could say, in my shack. Or under it. A keeper of secrets, except mostly they're secrets nobody on this planet would care about even if I got up in the middle of a Halemeeting and gave them all away. I think *you* might care, and if you'd accepted my offer to sign on as an apprentice, I was going to show you. But today…" He paused a moment and looked at the sky. "Today might be the beginning of a whole new world. Suddenly the idea of hoarding my secrets seems silly, especially since ancient history might just have some bearing on current events. Now will you come on, so I can expand your understanding of the universe and our little place in it?"

She nodded, her fury draining out of her. Secrets? She did like those. Or she thought she would. She'd never really known any worthy of the name.

Torvald opened the flimsy door and gestured her inside. She'd been into his home a few times, but there wasn't much to see: it was one big room with a bed, a couple of chairs and a table, a desk, a screen that mostly just flickered, and shelves of books. There was a kitchen with all the appliances she'd ever heard of (most of them even worked, though a couple were purely decorative, like the one that was supposed to make toast). There was a little dome-headed serving mech that did a bad job of cleaning up when it even worked, currently switched off in the corner. The shack only had one door, and that led to a small tidy bathroom with a toilet and a shower.

This time, though, Torvald lifted up the faded old rug, revealing... more stone floor. She'd been hoping for a secret hatch or a trapdoor or something. "Stand beside me," he said. She obeyed, and he cleared his throat. "Two friendlies, coming down."

The floor lurched, and she stumbled against Torvald as the ceiling receded above them. A square section of the floor, two meters to a side, was dropping down a smooth-walled shaft, and it was dropping fast. "What *is* this?"

"An elevator," he said.

She let go of him, straightened up, and refused to be impressed. "Stupid name. We're going down. It should be called a descender."

"It goes back up too, Bianca."

She looked up at the growing distance above her head. "That's good. It would be a long climb otherwise."

After a few moments, they thumped to a stop. "Good job," Bianca said. "We're at the bottom of a dry well–"

The wall in front of her split in two, one side sliding to the left, the other to the right. She grabbed Torvald again. She'd seen automatic doors before – in Torvald's gate, of course, and the Halemeeting hall had one – but those just swung in and out! They didn't disappear into the walls!

"Come on." Torvald stepped into darkness, and recessed white lights switched on, revealing a space roughly the size of the living quarters above, though there was a metal door on the far wall, suggesting deeper recesses beyond. The walls, floor, and ceiling were all gray metal, and there were only a few pieces of furniture – a simple bunk, a chair on a swivel, a table.

One of the walls held a huge blank screen. The burgher in town had a working screen, one that showed a ten-minute loop of bizarre birds like no one had ever seen in real life flying over a purple ocean, but this screen was easily twice as big. Bianca could have walked right up to it and stretched her arms out and not quite touched the edges. "What *is* this place?"

"We call it the bunker," Torvald said. "It's been in the family so long nobody remembers who originally found it. My parents told me there are probably chambers like this scattered across Darit, but I've never found one, or met anybody else who has. I sure wish I could, because if they held treasures like *this* one does, I'd be a rich man. Of course, I don't know what I'd do if I was a rich man. Buy more junk, probably. It's all I know."

"Go back. You said treasure. What kind of treasure?" There were no chests full of gold coins, no racks of alien weapons, no shining crowns or bolts of rare cloth or works of art.

"Information, Bee. Knowledge." He approached the screen. "Access local surveillance." The screen lit up and showed a view of the mech farm, and his shack, seen from a strange angle – what you'd see if you stood on top of one of the vertical posts on one side of the gate, she thought. "Roll back to, hmm, ten minutes ago."

The screen flickered, and now showed Bianca and Torvald standing among the scrap heaps, talking. "That's us!" she said.

"There are cameras up there, recording. Here it comes."

The ship streaked across the screen, and Torvald said, "Freeze."

The ship hung frozen on the screen, just barely in the top of the frame. The vessel was bigger than Bianca's house, and made of dark metal, with spikes and spines all over it, like some sort of airborne cactus. "Analyze ship to determine origin," Torvald said. The wall began to hum.

"Who are you talking to?" Bianca said. "You said there weren't any smart machines on this planet."

"Oh, well. The bunker isn't smart, exactly. It doesn't actually know things – it just contains knowledge. Sort of like a book. The bunker can't think, any more than a book can, but imagine if you had a book where you could say, 'Turn to the page with that kissing scene I like,' and it would flip right to it? Or where you could say, 'What's the name of the character who killed the hero's daughter,' and the book could answer you? It's like that."

"Sounds pretty smart to me," Bianca said.

"Could be the lines between smart and not-smart get a little blurry with some machines," Torvald conceded. "The bunker isn't much of a conversationalist, let's say that much at least. But what it does have is a long memory, full of the history of this planet from the days when it was an imperial mining colony, mostly in the form of records kept by a woman called the 'interim provincial governor.' I couldn't tell you what's happened outside Darit for the past three thousand years, but if you want to know what was going on in the galaxy before that, I know at least part of it."

"Ship unknown," the wall said, in a warm, womanly voice.

Torvald sighed. "I was afraid of that. I didn't figure

the aliens would be flying a ship so old my bunker would recognize it, but it was worth a try. Hmm. Bunker, what's the closest known vessel to the ship we just saw?"

"The closest comparable vessel is a Barony of Letnev light cruiser." A drawing appeared on the screen, and it did share a lot in common with the ship they'd seen, especially the way the hull bristled with hostile-looking protuberances. "There are multiple points of structural and design overlap, but the ship most recently recorded is far smaller."

"That's because it's some kind of shuttle," Torvald muttered. "But if the design and the aesthetics and such are that similar, then maybe it's a Barony vessel."

"What are all those spikes for?"

"Maybe they're sensors," Torvald said. "Or weapons. Maybe the Letnev just like how they look, the way Milt Karnecki painted flames on the side of his auto-cart. I couldn't tell you."

"You're the one with the secret database of hidden knowledge!" Bianca was so frustrated. Torvald had been sitting on a talking encyclopedia of the outside world all this time. "You knew about everything outside Darit, *real* things, instead of just hints and forgotten stories! You could have… have…" She slumped. "You could have done… something for me."

"The bunker doesn't have directions to the nearest spaceport, Bee." He said it kindly, and that was worse. "Nor does it know any special radio frequency to hail a passing ship to take you out into the stars. I know you've always set your sights higher than the next shearing or harvest, Bianca, and I admire that. My own interest in what lies beyond our atmosphere is more about the knowledge than the experience. But if I could have cobbled a working spacecraft together from the junk on my mech farm, you would have flown out of here three years ago on your sixteenth birthday, and you can believe that."

"Sixteenth birthday observed," she muttered. Her birthday was a guess, since she was a forest foundling, but based on how new she was when her pa found her, it was probably right to within a day or two. "But thank you. I still wish you'd told me."

Torvald nodded, perfunctory. "Maybe I should have. What's done is done. The reason I brought you down here now is because aliens have come to Darit. Even if they're human, they're aliens to *us*. They might be your ticket off this planet, or they could be trouble for all of us. My database is thousands of years out of date, but it's all we've got to go on, unless the aliens start talking. If those visitors really are from the Barony of Letnev, and the Barony still bears any resemblance to the one that was part of the empire way back when… Well. It could be worse, but it could be better, too."

"What do you mean?"

"I mean, the Letnev aren't human, but they're enough like us that we can talk to them. They aren't giant murderous spiders, or hungry slime mold, or a burning cloud that's mad at you for some reason and you don't know why. They aren't here to literally *eat* us, at least, though I suppose they might have come for the caprids. Seems a long way to go for stringy meat, though. The Barony was – let me see, it's been a while since I read about them – a militaristic, bureaucratic society, big on rules and shiny boots. They spent a lot of time in caverns and tunnels underground. They were involved in some unpleasantness that kicked off a big war, according to the journal the interim governor kept. Something about blockading a wormhole and making a whole lot of people mad."

"A wormhole." The very word was magical to Bianca. When she was little, before she'd read enough to understand what wormholes were exactly, she'd poked her arm (and sometimes head) into every hole she found, thinking one might lead her to another world. All they ever led to was dirty faces and the occasional insect bite.

"The Letnev enjoyed their rules, but didn't worry much about following anyone else's, because theirs were the only ones that mattered. They were also the type to invent new rules to punish people if the old rules weren't doing a good enough job." Torvald sighed. "The Barony is fairly high on the list of alien cultures I would hesitate to invite over for a slice of cake and a cup of tea. You might be able to use them as your stepping stone to the stars, but it won't be as easy as politely asking them for a ride."

"It's worth a try," she said. "If they even land. Maybe they're just here to see if there's anything interesting on the planet, and when they see there's *not*, they'll fly away again."

"That might be the best thing for all of us," Torvald said. "I–"

The screen flickered to a view of the junkyard again. "New environmental stimulus detected," the bodiless voice said. A loud, high-pitched keening filled the room, until Torvald said, "Lower volume eighty percent!" and it became a distant whine again.

"What *is* that?" Bianca cried.

"Emergency siren. The one in the burgher's house. I haven't heard it since the big fire, and that was, what, five years before you were born? The village elders don't like using it because they don't know how many charges the thing has left, and they're afraid one of these days there will be a *real* emergency and they'll hit the button and it won't make a sound at all. I guess this must be a real emergency. Everyone within the sound of that siren is supposed to go to the village immediately."

"We have to go!"

Torvald nodded. "We should. But I'll tell you what. I want to do a little more research here. You go down and see what's going on, and you can fill me in later. There's a power cell on the table upstairs. Take that with you. Aliens or not, your parents will still want what they sent you for."

Bianca nodded, then scowled. "It will take me forever to get to town, I'll have to run home and get my bicycle–"

"Take the trailrunner," Torvald said. "Just be careful and don't break your head. It's not a very good head, but I've gotten used to it."

Bianca grinned, threw her arms around his neck, and kissed his whiskery cheek.

"Thank you! I'll bring it back and tell you everything. I bet they're calling us to talk about the aliens."

"I doubt it's about traders come in from Upper Creek, or somebody who needs a new barn put up," Torvald said.

He led her to the elevator and sent her back up to the surface. When she arrived in his shack, alone, she allowed herself a whoop of excitement. Alien spaceships! Emergency sirens! Things were *happening*! She grabbed up the power cell – about the size of a book, but much denser – and shoved it into her pack. Probably a waste of time. The aliens would probably offer them limitless power and spaceships and all the other wonders of the galaxy soon anyhow.

Bianca went out into the mech farm. The trailrunner was parked behind the shack, as usual. Torvald had allowed her to ride it around his property, but never beyond the walls. "That thing will be my legs when my legs don't work anymore," he said. "I can't risk you running it off a cliff just because you want to feel the wind in your hair as you fall." He used the trailrunner when he came to town, or went on scavenging expeditions himself, which he didn't do nearly as often as he had in his younger days. "You can ride the trailrunner to my funeral, Bee, but I won't risk you taking it off the mech farm before that," he'd said once, and no amount of pleading would change his mind.

This was an unprecedented day in a lot of ways, though.

The trailrunner was a mech of Torvald's own design, cobbled together from pieces of mining robots, broken-down transports, and miscellaneous junk. The machine consisted of a padded metal chair surrounded by a set of multi-jointed legs, each as long as Bianca was tall, with a little control panel you could reach while seated. The controls were just used for inputting directions and preferred speed, though; the trailrunner mostly drove itself, thanks to the computer brain and cluster of sensors underneath the seat. Torvald had taught her to use it, and she'd even helped him tinker with it a bit over the years to improve its performance.

Bianca got her pack situated in the little cargo crate behind the seat and made sure it was secure and well padded. Power cells could crack if they took a fall, and sometimes when that happened there was a flash of light, and sometimes they leaked goo that smoked and ate holes in the ground… but at least once a dropped power cell had caused an explosion that blew off both a roof and a local boy's head.

She climbed into the chair, fitted on the straps, and punched in the eighteen-digit code required to unlock the controls, a level of security she thought was a bit much, but it made Torvald happy. He'd been surprised she could remember the code after he rattled it off just once, but Bianca had always been good at remembering important things. It was just boring things she forgot.

The trailrunner hummed to life and stood up tall on its six legs. She punched in a course to the center of the village and set speed to "maximum." The vehicle *jumped*, leaping over the shack in a single bound, but Bianca stayed steady in her seat; there were things called "gimbals" and "shock absorbers" and "gyroscopic balancing mechanisms" to ensure that even if the trailrunner tilted sharply or landed with a hard thump, she'd still keep her head pointed at the sky, her feet at the ground, and wouldn't get whiplash. Unless the landing was hard enough to smash the whole apparatus, but the trailrunner was programmed with preset tolerances, and its computer brain translated "maximum speed" as "maximum *safe* speed." Too bad. Sometimes it was fun to be a little unsafe.

Bianca didn't bother with opening the gates, just leapt nimbly from junkheap to junkheap and sailed over the top of the wall. The sensors it used to detect the environment could tell which structures made stable launching points, and which would collapse under its weight. Bianca whooped when they cleared the wall, full of the joy of motion, but she did wish she'd thought to put on goggles. She'd never been in the trailrunner when it was going this fast before, and her eyes were watering. She kept her mouth firmly shut against the possibility of swallowing bugs. She *did* like the feeling of the wind streaming through her hair, though.

She landed on the path outside the gates and didn't even slow down, just rushed toward the village, legs a whirring blur. There was that meandering road, but the trailrunner didn't bother to stay on that for long: it had a local survey map and a compass, and it took the most direct possible route instead. Bianca raced across the high meadows, leaping over rock walls and fences, dancing down rocky slopes, never stepping on a field under cultivation (Torvald knew better) but ducking low and hurtling through the trees of the orchard on the Glinnis farm. The trailrunner reconnected with the road not far from town, startling groups of people walking or riding on bikes or trundling along in various forms of transport, come down from their own scattered farms and holdings to answer the call. Some people shouted at her: "Torvald, slow down," and, "I wish I had one of those," and, gratifyingly, "Is that Bianca *Xing*?"

Bianca leaned hard to the right, as the trailrunner dashed off to the side of the road to avoid the traffic, picking up speed, so she arrived well ahead of the other newcomers. The mech slowed down a bit as it approached the central square, an open green space surrounded by the village's largest buildings: the elegant arched roof of the Halemeeting hall, the imposing two stories of the burgher's house, the general store with its wide porch full of chairs, and the dusty and neglected façade of the Traveler's Rest, an inn and way station hardly ever used since they didn't attract many visitors, and weren't on the way to anywhere in particular. At least the alarm wasn't going off anymore. As loud as it had been up at the mech farm, she couldn't imagine how ear-splitting it would have been right here at the source.

The mech stopped at the edge of the square, since Bianca hadn't specified a particular destination. The trailrunner hummed quietly to itself as Bianca stared at the Halemeeting hall. Something had changed. It was a small change, but it felt big.

Someone had climbed up to the roof of the hall and put a pole up there, and on top of the pole there was a big flag now, all black and trimmed with silver, with a red circle in the center, like a planet hanging in a starless void.

CHAPTER 3

"Bianca!" Her mother hurried over from the porch of the general store. Her hair was pulled back in a hurry, and she was wearing trousers and a work shirt – she'd never come to town looking so disheveled, but *things were happening*, weren't they? "What are you doing on that thing?"

Bianca directed the trailrunner to park itself on the side of the road and shut down, then clambered out of the seat. "Torvald let me borrow it." She hated how sulky and defensive her voice got around her ma. Bianca was old enough to be pair-bonded, so why did she always feel like a child when the two of them talked? *Maybe because I still live in her house and eat her food and mostly wear clothes she made me,* Bianca thought. Could you really grow up when you were still in the same place, and in the same context, where you'd spent so long as a child?

"Torvald isn't coming?" Her mother seemed distracted, her eyes skittering up to the flag and then back down to Bianca's face again.

"He said he had too much work to do. He said I should go, and tell him what happened. We… we saw a ship go by overhead, and–"

"We did too," she said. "I did, anyway, your father just heard it. Oh, Bianca." She put a hand on her daughter's arm. "I'm so nervous. What does it mean? What does that *flag* mean?"

"I don't know." Bianca squeezed her hand. "Let's go in and find out." She looked around. "Where's Dad?"

"He couldn't leave the caprids – they were all out grazing."

"How can he think about livestock right now?" Bianca said. "There are *aliens* here!"

Her mother looked at her like she'd grown an extra head. "Aliens or not, we still have chores to do, don't we?"

"I guess so." It seemed like something this big should transform the whole world, all at once, but that wasn't how things worked, was it?

By now others were drifting toward the Halemeeting hall. The interior was one big room, with ranks of benches arranged in curving rows to face the stage at the far end. This was the place where weddings and wakes were held, dances and festivals, auctions and trials (not that there'd been a crime worthy of a trial in Bianca's lifetime). There was also a small weekly fellowship meeting and a big monthly one, just so people on the far-flung farms and orchards could remember they were part of a community, with people around to help them through the hard times and celebrate the good. In theory, the Halemeeting hall could hold just about everyone within fifty kilometers, though Bianca had seldom seen it more than a third full. She thought it might get a lot closer to capacity today.

Bianca and her mother took seats near the front; her mother's eyesight wasn't very good anymore. The burgher was there, fine yellow sash across her chest. Her family was charged with maintaining the Halemeeting hall, and they owned the general store, too, and were in more frequent contact with neighboring communities than anyone else. The burgher helped organize the Five-Year's Fair, when everyone from the six nearest villages gathered in a distant field and built a temporary festival city, trading food and art and fine goods and, quite often, mingling and falling in love and bonding with strangers. A few people almost always left the Fair to make their homes in other settlements, and before today it was the most exciting thing in Bianca's world. The next Five-Year's Fair was in the spring, and she'd been toying with the idea of falling in love with someone from as far away as possible, or convincing herself she had, just for an excuse to live in a new place... but she knew the other settlements were much like her own, just in a slightly different configuration of hills and valleys, so what was the point? That fear that every place would look the same was the same thing that kept her from putting on her best shoes and filling a sack with food and setting out on her own. Darit was just *Darit*, and how could it satisfy her when there was so much more beyond? Wherever she went, her eyes would still be drawn to that dark spot in the sky and the wonders it promised.

"So many people," her mother said. Bianca looked behind her and goggled. Every bench was full, and there were other people *standing*, lining the walls! There must have been three hundred people there! She'd only seen that many at once at the Fair, and even there they weren't all jammed in together, breathing and shuffling and muttering. The sound of the crowd was like the susurration of waves against rocks.

The burgher stood up on stage and cleared her throat. "Everyone!" she said. "Thank you for coming to the call." The acoustics of the hall were perfect, and Bianca could hear the strain in the woman's voice. She was the richest person in town, and she'd always seemed effortlessly in control, but today... *Things are happening.* "Some of you may have noticed, ah, something strange in the sky earlier..."

Someone stepped out of the wings and onto the stage. He was not just a stranger, but *strange* – wearing shiny black clothes, his skin an unhealthy-looking bluish hue, his mouth set in a hard line. He walked across the stage, stiff-backed, boot heels clicking on the boards. He stood beside the burgher, then turned his head to stare at her. He was half a meter taller than her, and she was not a small woman. She shrank away, then hurried to a seat behind him on the stage. The man followed her with his gaze until she was seated, then looked back at the crowd.

He sniffed. "I am Undercommandant Voyou." He spoke in the local language, but his accent made it sound like he was building a wall of rough stones. "It is my privilege to welcome... what is the name of this charming settlement again?" This last to the burgher.

"We – this is Lowcliff, it's–"

He returned his attention to the room. "Lowcliff. Welcome, denizens of Lowcliff, to the glorious and eternal Barony of Letnev. No longer will you suffer lives of lawless anarchy. The Barony has returned to reclaim Darit. You are home."

"What do you mean *reclaim*?" someone shouted.

"I did not intend to take questions," Voyou said. "Impertinence is not appreciated in the Barony. But, because this is new to you, and you are simple country folk, unaccustomed to the uses of power, I will answer. This planet was once a mining colony, a cherished possession of the Barony of Letnev. We lost track of you for a little while – as you can imagine, we had more pressing concerns than this place – but the Baron remembers you now. He has reached out his hand, and gathered you to his bosom. Your... burgher, is it? She will explain to you what this means in terms of taxes and so on. Glory to the Barony." He turned smartly and walked off the stage.

The audience waited until he was out of sight before they erupted.

The burgher stood and called for silence. "I know!" she said. "I know. I was just as surprised as you are. I've heard from Highcliff and Midcliff and some of the other towns we trade with on the wireless, and they've all had visits like this too. I think these, ah, Letnev are visiting every settlement on the whole planet."

"Why are they here?" someone called.

"We're still figuring that out," she said. "They don't seem to *want* much, apart from making us put up a flag, though they said they're doing a survey and will announce any, ah, necessary reallocations of resources."

"We've always governed ourselves just fine!" That was Bianca's mother, and Bianca was almost proud of her.

"I agree," the burgher said. "My hope, my *expectation*, is that these Letnev won't care much about us in particular, or how we run things here. We can go on as we always have, more or less, with some… some small changes. They're imposing a tax, to be collected twice a year, from every household. They want a tenth part of whatever we produce."

The crowd roared at *that*, with shouts, curses, and, "Let them come and take it!"

"They will come and take it," the burgher said grimly. "I have no doubt of that. They… showed me some of their weapons."

"They're just bandits!"

"Worse," the burgher said. "They're the government."

"What do *we* get out of this?" someone called. "If they're our new leaders, what are they offering us?"

"Protection," the burgher said. "From the Barony's many enemies. Who are now our enemies, since we're a Barony colony world. I *know*!" She held out her hands, trying vainly to quell the uproar. "I don't like this any more than you do! Maybe they'll lose interest and go away! Maybe they won't even bother to *send* tax collectors for a few bushels of wool and baskets of apples! They…" She closed her eyes. "They wanted me to tell you, specifically, that they are forgiving all of our back taxes. Meaning, they won't try to collect what they say we owe from all the years we've been out of their control." She gave a jagged, broken little laugh. "Which is good, because as near as I can tell, that's been *thousands* of years, and that's… that's a lot of taxes. It could be worse, people. They could have burned our farms. Or even just nudged the orbital mirrors out of true by a few degrees, and turned our little bubble of green into frozen tundra. They could kill us all without even firing a shot–"

"Why would they do *that*?" Bianca called. "Why slaughter a caprid when you can get milk and wool from it for years? We're just livestock for the Barony now!"

"Better to be alive than dead, Bianca Xing," the burgher snapped. "What did you want me to do? Tell them *no*? I hear the burgher of Reachway did that, and they cut off his head and put it on top of their flagpole!"

The crowd had no reply to that. The burgher contained herself. "I'll… I'll send word if there's any more news. For now, just… go on as you have. And hope this all blows over." She slumped and went backstage, instead of walking out down the aisle and shaking hands and slapping backs like she did at Halemeetings.

"So," Bianca's mother said, "that's that, then. You'd better get that mech back to old Torvald and fill him in on how things are, I reckon. I'll see you at the house after."

"Yes, Ma."

She put a hand on her daughter's knee. "Be careful, Bianca. I know I always say that, but this time, really, be careful. There are strangers out there."

"Reclaimed?" Torvald shook his head. They were sitting in his bunker, him in the chair, Bianca sprawled on her back on the hard bunk. "No, this world of ours was a colony all right, but it belonged to the Federation of Sol, not the Barony of Letnev. The Federation, that's where most of the humans are, or at least were, back in the old days. Just look around – we're *humans*, not Letnev. Sure, we look similar, blue skin and odd proportions aside, but they're *aliens*. Who are they trying to fool?"

"Everybody," Bianca said. "They're trying to fool everybody. I can't believe I saw an alien for the first time and it wasn't even amazing. It was just awful. Why couldn't this Federation have come here? I bet *they* would have offered me a ticket to the stars."

Torvald went *hmm*. "As I recall, the Barony and the Federation didn't get along too well. When things fell apart, they did some of the fiercest fighting just amongst themselves. Maybe the Barony beat the Federation, and think that gives them some rightful claim to this place? Not that they need a claim, really, if they've got ships and guns." He sighed.

"I don't understand." Bianca stared at the ceiling. She couldn't see the sky, but she knew right where her triangle of stars was. "I thought there was an empire, one big community, back then. Why would they fight each other?"

"An emperor is a king of kings, and an empire is a bunch of nations all stuck together under a single ruler. That doesn't mean they all *like* being together. You like some of your neighbors more than others, don't you? Same thing. Just on a bigger scale. Some of those nations joined the empire because they wanted to share in the power, or they wanted to be protected, but some of them were forced to join, or threatened into joining. Any system that big and complicated and full of tensions is bound to fall apart eventually, and when it falls, it makes a mess." He swiveled back and forth in his chair. "But knowing a little bit of history doesn't change the price of wool, does it? I'm the only person on the whole planet, maybe, with evidence that Darit wasn't really a Barony colony world, and even if I told the world, it wouldn't make a difference. The Barony would just mark me as a troublemaker, and that wouldn't be good for me."

"Ships and guns," Bianca said. "I can't believe we got invaded by aliens. That we got conquered. And that the invasion is so boring and stupid! I've read stories about this sort of thing, but it's not like there's a resistance I can join or anything."

"We'd be flies resisting the swatter, I'm afraid," Torvald said. "You're sitting in the most technologically advanced place on all of Darit, maybe, and I wouldn't be a match for even one of their shuttles."

"Maybe there's some sort of super-weapon, buried out in the forest? Something to let us fight back?"

"Maybe," Torvald said. "This was an important place, once. I guess that's why the Barony is here – there's still precious metal in those mines, just too deep for us to reach with our technology. If you find some super-weapon, though, keep it to yourself, or you'll get a lot of people killed. We don't have any tactical genius generals around here. We don't even have any soldiers. In a situation like this... we mostly just have to hope the boot on our neck doesn't get too heavy."

"I don't want to be a coward, Torvald."

"You aren't, Bianca. You're brave, and you're a romantic, and I want you to stay alive so you can keep being both."

"The world has changed, though. Doesn't that mean we have to change too?"

He looked at the ceiling for a long moment, then sighed. "Probably so, Bianca. Whether we want to or not."

Nothing *did* change, though, apart from that flag on the

Halemeeting hall. Occasionally a ship flew overhead, but none landed, and no more alien visitors came to the village. There was a lot of shouting at the next few Halemeetings, but after six weeks without any contact from the Barony of Letnev, people mostly settled back into their old patterns, and hoped they'd been forgotten by the new masters. Bianca's hope and excitement at seeing the first ship go by had turned to fear and then, to her great annoyance, back into boredom.

Until the day a Barony ship landed at her parents' farm.

CHAPTER 4

Heuvelt Angriff – former treasure hunter, lapsed gentleperson adventurer, current reluctant criminal – was trying to get drunk, but he wasn't having much luck. He shook a fistful of coins at the bartender, a sorrowful-looking Winnaran. He squinted. Maybe the bartender wasn't sorrowful. Maybe Heuvelt was just projecting again. "Look, these coins are from the Xxlan system, and according to the treaty the Hylar government has with the Xxcha Kingdom, that means they're also legal tender on Jol-Nar and any associated colony worlds, and since Elekayne is a Hylar colony world, that means you have to–"

"No cash," the Winnaran bartender repeated, then pointed to a sign behind her that presumably said "No cash" in whatever language it appeared in. The bartender glanced around the bar, which was deserted at this time of day, and apparently decided to take pity on Heuvelt, because she placed a small glass on the bar before him.

Heuvelt tossed the contents back eagerly, expecting the burn of liquor, but it was just water. He sighed. "Thank you."

The bartender leaned forward and said, "I think the cash prohibition is stupid too, but we had a gene-plague last year. One of the ways it got spread around was through infected surfaces, and everyone is still being careful about unnecessary contact. Don't you have a credit account? Doesn't have to be with the Universities of Jol-Nar. We're hooked into all the major data systems, and we even have decent exchange rates for Letnev or Naalu currency."

"I am having… difficulty accessing my accounts." Heuvelt stared at the luminous, worthless discs in his hand. Xxcha money was pretty, but you couldn't eat beauty. "I was the victim of identity theft. I returned from a deep space exploration several months ago and promptly found myself arrested and accused of various horrible crimes. Only the fact that I don't resemble the perpetrator who used my name kept me from being thrown into a prison camp."

The Winnaran wiped the bar with a rag. "That's a real sad story."

Heuvelt nodded enthusiastically. "It *is*. Thank you for appreciating that. If you find yourself moved by sympathy, you could–"

"The real bad guy didn't have that big scar down his face, I take it?"

Heuvelt winced. He'd been reckoned a handsome man – almost *too* handsome, some of his lovers had told him: how could you trust a man with those teeth and that hairline and a chin like that all at the same time? But his former best friend and former first mate, Dob Ell, had left him with a long knife scar that started just under his right eye and took a wandering path down his cheek and over his jawline toward his neck. He was lucky to have both eyes in his head and all his blood inside him. "He didn't, no. One of the Hylar prosecutors said all humans look alike and I'd scarred my face as a disguise, but there was DNA evidence to exonerate me, fortunately."

"You could get that scar fixed," the bartender said. "I know a Hylar surgeon who does top-notch reconstructive work. Though, now that I think of it, yeah, all her humans *do* kind of come out looking the same."

Heuvelt bowed his head, hoping to make the scar less noticeable. "I tried. I wasted some of the proceeds from selling my old ship on a plastic surgeon. I looked like my old self... for a day. Then the scar came back. It seems I was cut by an Yssaril shame-blade. Have you ever heard of those?"

"Can't say I have."

Heuvelt slumped lower on his stool. "Some of the Yssaril tribes use them back on their homeworld, during their feuds. Sometimes it isn't enough to kill an enemy, you see. You want them to carry the mark of their defeat with them for the rest of their lives instead. So they take the sap from some horrible swamp plant and boil it and mix it with the venom from some reptile and coat a blade with it, and any wounds given with that blade create a scar that has *memory*. I don't know how it works. Something about the toxins on the blade promoting collagen degradation. The surgeon said I should be grateful. Without his intervention, the wound would have just kept opening up on its own, never quite healing, for the rest of my life. This bright meandering line across my face is the best medical science can do for me."

The Winnaran chuckled. "I'm sure some people will find it

appealing, though they'll wonder why you don't get it fixed, and assume you *want* to look dangerous. Wearing a scar is, in its own way, a weird kind of vanity, don't you think?"

"I hadn't thought about it. So now I'm scarred *and* vain. I used to just be vain."

"And broke, apparently. If you were cleared of wrongdoing, why didn't you get access to your accounts back?"

"An excellent question," he said. "It turns out, once your accounts are frozen, they take a long time to get *unfrozen* again." There had been precious little in the accounts anyway, since Heuvelt's parents had cut him off for "being an incorrigible wastrel" and stopped replenishing his funds. "As a further complication, I was wanted by both the Universities of Jor-Nal and the Barony of Letnev. Their different alliances and reciprocal business arrangements, taken together, encompass most of the systems where a human is likely to visit or do business. I'm having trouble establishing new accounts – there's a flag on my name, apparently. I'm told a fancy Hacan lawyer could sort it all out for me, if I could afford one, but I can't."

The Winnaran looked to the left, and looked to the right, and confirmed once again that the bar was empty, except for a human sleeping with his head on a table in the back. "Give me the coins. I'll buy your drinks on my account."

Heuvelt was moved by the kindness, even though he suspected the bartender drank for free, and would simply pocket the coins as profit, but as long as the end result was booze inside him, he was happy. "Thank you."

"We have a range of alcoholic beverages safe for human consumption. What are you drinking?"

"Do you have anything that started out life as corn?"

"That's one of those plants humans like, isn't it? I thought they made syrup out of it."

"You can make *lots* of things out of it. Including sweet, brown liquor."

"I have sweet brown liquor," the Winnaran said. "Well. Brown-ish. I think it's made of algae. That's the best I can do."

"I'm sure it will suffice."

The Winnaran poured him a small glass of something too dark and syrupy to be mistaken for bourbon, but it *was* brown-ish. Heuvelt took a sip and winced; it was sweet, too, repulsively so, with a distinct hint of cinnamon. It tasted like something that should be poured over pancakes. "This is alcohol?"

"It's fifty-five percent alcohol, according to the label on the bottle."

A hundred and ten proof, then. That cheered him up. "Thank you. Maybe something… less sweet for my next round."

The bartender nodded and wandered off down the bar, busily attending to nothing much, probably just tired of his company. Heuvelt was getting used to that. When had he become a bore? Probably when his stories stopped being about recent adventures and became about old grievances instead. "Rotten thieves," he muttered into his glass. "Ruined my life." That was a comforting idea, though it wasn't true. Having his identity stolen hadn't made his old friend and family retainer Dob Ell attack him with a knife. His fortunes had been circling a black hole even before his accounts were frozen, after the ruinous expense of his failed deep-space exploration. He'd had visions of discovering new rich worlds, ancient alien artifacts, perhaps a previously unknown species of alien, and returning a hero. Instead he'd found radiation, rocks, and betrayal, and he'd returned the next best thing to a pauper.

Dob Ell had stabbed him the *very day* her scheduled monthly stipend failed to arrive: as soon as she was off the payroll, the illusion of friendship and the reality of a lifetime of resentment had become manifest. His parents had hired her to watch over him when he was a mere child, and he'd assumed a bond of love had grown between them. He'd called his parents to tell them about the attack, hoping they could take some vengeance on his behalf, but they weren't talking to him anymore. The second underbutler who took the message had laughed at him and said, "Of *course* she attacked you. She was paid to guard your body, and I can't imagine a more thankless or tedious job."

And so, scarred and betrayed, he'd been forced to sell his pride and joy, *The Lady of Misrule*, an exceptionally beautiful long-range cruiser he'd emptied his trust fund to buy as a university graduation gift to himself. (He hadn't technically graduated from university, but he'd stopped going, which was close enough.) Oh, the times he'd had in that ship, plying the spaceways with Dob Ell and a series of attractive humanoids! He could have lived the life of a dashing adventurer for decades if he hadn't decided to get so ambitious. "Ambition is poison!" he called to the bartender.

She ignored him. Perhaps she couldn't relate. She worked the morning shift in a dingy bar on a Hylar colony world that was mostly desert (and as the Hylar were mainly an aquatic species, that meant it wasn't a colony world held in high esteem), so it was possible she'd never sipped the poison of ambition, personally.

He'd gotten a lot of money for the *Lady of Misrule*, and used the proceeds for living expenses and to purchase a far less beautiful ship, the *Show and Tell*. It was a fast courier retrofitted with extra cargo space, and Heuvelt had planned to use it to establish a business for himself as a high-end transporter of luxury goods. He'd even hired a crew. Why not? He knew *lots* of rich people from the Federation of Sol, the Jol-Nar, the Emirates, even the Mentak Coalition and the Yin Brotherhood, because his parents were well connected in those circles. He might as well exploit their good name.

He hadn't counted on the difficulties his not-fully-expunged criminal record would cause when it came to getting licensed and insured, though. No one would hire him for legitimate work, so he was forced to take on less savory jobs. The sort that paid in cash, and brought him to planets like *this*.

Where the hell was his contact, anyway? His crew – sorry, his *partners* – Ashont and Clec were waiting for him back on the ship, and while he didn't think they'd steal the *Show and Tell* and leave without him, he had trouble trusting anyone fully after his experience with Dob Ell.

The door swung open, and a Hylar came clomping in on six mechanical legs, its real body a tangle of tentacles floating in a dingy soup of fluid inside a translucent tank. The alien approached the bar and stood beside Heuvelt.

The bartender started toward them, then thought better

Twilight Imperium

of it and withdrew. Oh, good, so the illicit nature of their business was *that* obvious. What a comfort.

"You are Mr Scar?" The Hylar's voice grated out of a metal box on the front of the containment suit.

Heuvelt sighed. He certainly hadn't chosen that *nom de crim*, but some Saar drug dealer had called him that, and it stuck. People didn't have much trouble identifying him, at least, though it wasn't like there were a lot of potential criminal contacts in this particular dingy bar at this particular dingy hour. "That's me. You're Mr Slosh?"

The artificial voicebox gave a harsh, uninflected series of ha-ha-ha sounds. "I chose my name when I heard yours."

"Most clever," Heuvelt said. "You have my money?"

"You have my data-stick?"

"Right here." He reached down for the briefcase by his stool and opened it up. There were dozens of data-sticks inside, all different colors, jumbled together. "It's one of these."

"Which one?"

"Give me the money and I'll show you."

The Hylar grabbed the briefcase instead and tried to run for the door. Annoying, but not unprecedented. None of the data-sticks were the one Mr Slosh's employers actually wanted, and once they figured that out, they'd have to slink back to Heuvelt and pay a "we're sorry we tried to screw you over" premium to get the *real* one–

"Stop right there!" The sleeping human in the corner leapt up and became very much an awake human, and one armed with a long and complex energy rifle. "Jol-Nar Data Enforcement Agency!"

Oh, no. The last thing Heuvelt needed was an *actual* criminal record on top of his accidental one. He dropped to the floor and started looking for a likely table to hide under as more agents came rushing in through the door, humanoid and Hylar both.

That's when Mr Slosh triggered some kind of smoke bomb. The bar filled with thick, inky black clouds, but there was still a little clear air near the floor, so Heuvelt crawled along on his belly toward the restrooms.

The cloud really was thick and blinding, but didn't seem to be nerve gas, or at least, not one that did anything untoward to humans. He knew some Hylar had ink sacs, used in the old days to release clouds in the water to let them evade predators, and it seemed Mr Slosh had replicated the effect for use on dry land. The data enforcement agents weren't shooting blindly, at least. They must be pretty well trained.

Heuvelt stuck close to the walls while he crawled, so no one stepped on him, though he saw some boots and mechanical feet go by. He reached the restroom door and slipped inside. The air was clear here, relatively speaking, though it didn't exactly smell *good*; this was a multicultural colony world, and various sorts of aliens had relieved themselves of waste here since the place had been cleaned last. In deference to the stench, though, there was a small window, and since this bar made you pay in advance for drinks, there weren't even bars on said window to stop patrons from escaping without paying their tabs.

After glancing behind him to make sure no one was watching, Heuvelt climbed up on a trash bin and peered out at a tantalizing strip of horrible arid desert ground. There were various data enforcement agency vehicles parked here and there, but no actual agents in sight, so he might just wriggle out of this.

He got his head through the window okay, but his shoulders gave him a bit of trouble until he twisted himself around at just the right angle, and wriggled a bit. Hadn't he possessed considerable dignity once upon a time? Better undignified than imprisoned, though.

He was halfway through the window when someone grabbed his ankles and hauled him out. He managed to cover his head so he didn't get a concussion when he slammed into the trash bin and bounced onto the ground. He landed on his back, groaned, and looked up at the Winnaran bartender, who stood over him, aiming a slim black kinetic sidearm at his chest. "Did I not tip you well enough?" he croaked.

She reached into her shirt and pulled out a badge hanging on a chain.

"Ah," he said. "As my father used to say when mother caught him canoodling with one of the gardeners, 'All right then, it's a fair cop.'"

"I'm sorry," she said. "It really *was* a very sad story."

"And getting sadder all the time, don't you think?" Heuvelt said.

CHAPTER 5

Bianca and her family had just settled down to supper when they heard the sounds: first the terrified bleatings of the caprids out back, followed by a roar-like gale force wind rushing through trees. Bianca's parents looked at one another, wide-eyed, across their small wooden table, but Bianca leapt to her feet and rushed for the door. She did grab a heavy walking stick on her way out – curiosity didn't entirely override good sense.

The ship she'd seen fly over the mech farm (or one just like it) was settling down in front of her house. Its presence in her front yard was as incongruous and disturbing as seeing a snake on her pillow. In the course of landing, the ship crushed the metal watering trough and obliterated an ornamental flowerbed her mother had put in during some of her rare free time.

Up close and unmoving, the ship was, if anything, *more* menacing: gleaming black with silver highlights, and covered in cruel barbs, hooks, spikes, and spines, as if it meant to tear apart the very air as it flew. In general shape, it reminded her of a diving predator bird, and its lowered, beaked head was pointed right at her front door.

That beak dropped open, and a ramp extended to the ground. The man from the Halemeeting hall, Undercommandant Voyou, walked slowly down the ramp, looking around as if inventorying the farm for auction. His eyes marked Bianca, but he seemed to take no more notice of her than he did of the house, the barn, or the trees. When he reached the bottom of the ramp, he adjusted his black gloves, wrinkled his nose like he smelled something foul, and opened his mouth.

"You're going to have to pay for that," Bianca said. She stood with the walking stick leaning over her shoulder in a deliberately casual way.

"What?" Voyou seemed as baffled as he would have been had a tree stump or a caprid talked to him.

Bianca was pleased to see him taken aback. She pointed with her stick, and Voyou turned to look where she indicated: at the water trough, crumpled under one of the ship's legs, and the flowers ground to mud and mush. "You should have looked where you landed." She clucked her tongue. "That's going to cost you."

He narrowed his eyes. "You–" He stopped, took a breath, and said, "On behalf of the Barony of Letnev, please accept my apologies. Be assured, your parents will receive recompense. If it's any consolation, the only other nearby landing zone my pilot deemed acceptable was the field near your... livestock... and I chose this location instead, since I did not wish to risk upsetting your animals."

Now it was Bianca's turn to be taken aback. "Oh. Ah. That's… thank you. Why are you here?"

Her parents emerged then – they'd taken the time to change clothes, Bianca saw, her father in a clean shirt, her mother with a Halemeeting day dress pulled hastily on. "Don't be rude, Bianca." Her father's voice seemed calm, but she knew him well enough to detect the undercurrent of anxiety. "How may we help you, Undercommandant Voyou?"

He puffed up. "I am – ah. You recall my name. Yes."

Bianca was pleased to see him bumped off his equilibrium again. These Barony people certainly had shiny tech, and Torvald said they were a major galactic power (or had been), but if things didn't go the way they expected, they wobbled like newborn caprids. Or maybe she was overgeneralizing about their species. She'd only met the one, after all.

The alien said, "You are Keon and Willen Xing, Bianca's parents?"

Bianca felt a chill. She didn't like this man knowing her parents' names. Her mother and father shared a glance, then nodded mute confirmation.

"Excellent," Voyou said. "You ask how you can help me, but in fact, I am here to help you. May I come inside? I'm afraid it's all rather complex."

"Are we in any trouble?" her mother said.

"Trouble, Madame Xing? Absolutely not. Indeed, you may be the luckiest people on this planet. Except, perhaps, for your darling daughter."

Kind words and compliments. They just seemed wrong, coming from the undercommandant. Bianca thought of a snake on a pillow again.

Her parents exchanged one of their infuriating pair-bonded-people-telepathy glances. When Bianca was little, she'd thought they could *really* read each other's minds, and only realized later that they'd simply been together so long they knew one another's habits of thought. "You'd better come in," her mother said. "Can we get anything for your crew?"

"No, they are amply provisioned." Voyou made a gracious half-bow and gestured that they should lead the way.

"Why are we lucky?" Bianca fell into step behind him.

He leaned a little closer to her, and spoke low. "Your parents are lucky because we are going to give them a great deal of money. *You* are lucky because you get to leave this latrine of a planet."

"What–"

"All will be explained." He patted her arm. In a friendly way! Looking at him, you'd think his only interaction with a peasant like her would be hitting her in the face with a riding crop if she got in his way while he was crossing the street.

Having an extra adult in the house made the small space seem terribly crowded, but the undercommandant said, "What a charming home you have," and took a seat on the long wooden bench at the table like he was settling onto a cushioned settee. "I see I interrupted your dinner. I am terribly sorry. Please, feel free to eat while we talk."

Her mother hurriedly set a plate before him – root mash, a few thin slices of dried caprid meat, a sorghum cake – but he demurred. "I am so sorry, the biology of my people, it's just different enough from humans that your food tends not to agree with us. It looks and smells delectable, however, I assure you. I would welcome a glass of water, though, if such is available?" Her father rushed to comply.

Bianca pulled his plate toward herself and chewed on some of the dried caprid while staring at him directly. That seemed to make him nervous, which she found exceedingly interesting and wished to know why.

Her parents didn't eat. They just stared at Voyou, like they were waiting to see if he might do a trick, or bite someone. "We've heard some interesting stories, about your daughter," the undercommandant said. He picked up the cup of water, gazed into it, and then put it back down without drinking. Bianca couldn't imagine what the problem was. That water was fresh from the rain barrel. There hadn't even been any bugs in it last time she checked, and they always picked those out anyway. "Would you tell me a little bit about how Bianca became part of your family?"

Her father glanced at Bianca, coughed, and said, "Ah. Well. It was almost nineteen turns ago now, I think, right, Willen?"

Her mother nodded silently. What was that look on her face? Bianca thought she'd seen every possible expression either of her parents was capable of producing, but the way Ma looked now was calculating? Speculative?

"I was out in the eastern forest," her father went on. "We were having a real hard go of things that year. Lost half our flock to heartstone, and the crops were only just middling. I went out to gather mushrooms, hoping for some to eat, maybe a few to sell. There's always good foraging, bird-of-the-wood, green lady, witch fingers, especially after a hard rain–"

"This was soon after a hard rain?" The undercommandant's attention was fixed on her father like a laser tracking sight.

"Hmm? Oh, yes, a big storm, blew over trees that had stood for two hundred years. There was flooding down the valley, a bridge even washed out, and I mean a good bridge, stone and all, not a plank someone had thrown across a gap. We haven't seen a storm like that since, thank the moons."

Voyou nodded like this was confirmation of something he'd suspected. Who cared about the weather twenty years ago? "You were gathering mushrooms, in the forest, you say. But aren't those forests dangerous for a man alone?"

Her father nodded. "They can be. But I went in the middle of the day, when the nightclimbers are deep sleeping in their holes and boles."

"I'd heard there were other dangers in these woods," the undercommandant said. "Relics of a past time, that can cause people to sicken and die, or suffer more immediate hardships."

"That sort of thing happens," her mother said. "And none of us wants to see it happen to our children, so we make sure they know how dangerous the woods can be. But…" She looked at her husband.

He picked up the thread. "When someone digs up something dangerous, it's the talk of the town for years afterward. Such things are rare, is what I mean. It could be we overstate how likely the danger is. In truth, I can't remember the last time someone picked up a glowing piece of glass and died puking with their hair falling out. Not since I was a child myself." He looked at his daughter. "We didn't really mean to mislead you, Bianca, it's just–"

"I know," Bianca said. "I know you made the forest sound scarier than it is. I've been halfway an apprentice to old Torvald for years now, and half the stock at his mech farm was scavenged from the forest. I've even gone foraging with him once or twice, but just on the edges – don't worry."

"Please go on," the undercommandant murmured, apparently fascinated by this familial back-and-forth.

Bianca's father blinked. "Ah. I just mean, I felt fairly safe going to gather mushrooms. Back then I had a walking stick with a jolt-tip on it. Do you know what that is?"

"I would assume some sort of electrical discharge weapon."

"That right," he said. "Torvald fixed it up for me. I figured if I ran into anything nasty, I'd give it a spark and drive it away. As for the other dangers... I know well enough not to pick up glass that shines all blue or yellow or green on its own, or to go digging around the edges of any bit of metal I see poking up out of the ground."

"Did you see any metal poking up out of the ground that particular day?"

"Oh, no, no." He shook his head and held up his hands and Bianca thought, *Wait. He's* lying! He'd looked flustered in exactly the same way when he tried to convince her that her pet felid had run away, when really she'd been eaten by a nightclimber. "No, nothing out of the ordinary happened. I just filled my basket with bird-of-the-wood and such, and then I heard this squalling. Sounded like a child in trouble, so I followed the sound. There she was, baby Bianca, just laying naked on the forest floor, crying her lungs out, and it's lucky I found her before a predator did–"

"I am offering you an opportunity to revise your account,"

the undercommandant said. The worst part was, he didn't even sound menacing. He sounded *kind*. "I understand, this is the story you've told for so long, perhaps it has come to replace the truth, even in your own mind. But I'm afraid the truth is what I must have."

"I don't know what you mean." Her father twisted a napkin in his hands. "I found Bianca in the forest, just like I said."

"You did find her in the forest. That I believe." The undercommandant had one hand under the table. It emerged, holding a sleek black weapon, some kind of sidearm, an energy pistol or flechette gun or something else Bianca had only read about and never seen. He rested it on the table, not pointed at anyone. "You did not find her 'just like you said,' however. The truth, please."

He glanced at his wife, and the undercommandant barked, "You need not look at her! Look at *me*!"

Bianca gripped the knife by her plate, but the undercommandant noticed the movement, and his weapon shifted – pointed now at her mother. "Mademoiselle Xing, I would not advise that. You might very well bury that blade in my throat – you seem to me to possess the will, and I respect you for it. But I would surely discharge my weapon in my dying moments, and then there would be two bodies here, instead of none. Listen. Your parents have not told you the truth about your origins. Aren't you curious?"

Bianca didn't release the knife, but she did glance toward the end of the table where her parents sat. "What is he talking about?"

"We… we just didn't want you to feel different, Bee," her mother said.

She'd always felt different, in a hundred ways. "Different *how*?"

"You're a very special young woman," Voyou said. "More special even than your parents know. Why don't you tell us the *true* story, Monsieur Xing? Then, when you're done, I can fill you in on some context you might be missing."

Her father looked down at his plate for a moment. When he looked up, there were tears shining in his eyes. "Bee, it doesn't matter where you come from. You're our daughter, and you always will be. You're *ours*."

"The story, please." The undercommandant put the gun back in his lap and returned his hands to the tabletop. Bianca carefully put her knife back down beside her plate. Even when she exhaled, she still felt somehow like she was holding her breath, every muscle tensed in anticipation. There was some secret in her life, and it was about to be revealed.

"As best I remember," her father began, "it happened like this."

CHAPTER 6

Keon Xing was a man with only a few things to call his own:
he had a little house, a half-sick flock, a few fields of crops
all torn up from a storm, and a wife who'd once been happy
and beaming and full of life, but who spent more and more
time now crying, or just gazing off into space. She loved him,
and she loved the farm, but most of all she wanted to share
that love by starting a family... and try as they might, they
couldn't seem to have a child.

She blamed herself, though Keon told her she shouldn't.
He'd done a fair bit of scavenging in his youth, going deep
into the forest in search of ancient remnants to sell to the
mech farm, and he thought he might have been exposed to
something that made him sterile, or at least diminished the
likelihood of having children. The wise woman said it might
be that, or "Maybe just bad luck." The life of a small farmer
on Darit certainly had enough of that.

Keon went out that morning to forage for mushrooms,
yes – with the crops beat up by the storm, they needed all

the food they could get – but he also went out because he needed some time alone, and thought his wife might like some as well. Willen had been so excited just a few days before, thinking they'd finally hit lucky, and they'd start a family at last… but it turned out she was just late on her monthlies, and there was no baby on the way. She'd put on a brave face, but he'd seen her shoulders move up and down with silent sobbing as she pulled weeds in her little flowerbed. He couldn't stand to see that, so he fled, and in his own sadness and distraction, he looked up and realized he'd gone much deeper into the woods than he'd intended. Subconsciously trying to put distance between himself and his troubles, maybe.

Now that he was in the forest, though, beneath the dense and dripping trees, he felt guilty about leaving Willen alone in her grief. *What kind of man am I?* he thought. *I can't give her a child, can't comfort her in her sadness, can't–*

He shook it off. Keon was a practical man, and he could at least bring home supper. There was some bird-of-the-wood right there, yellowy-orange shelves of fungus clinging to a tree that had fallen over in the storm. There must have been a kilogram or more of the mushrooms, and they really did taste a lot like poultry when you cooked them right. He filled the basket he carried on his back, and, somewhat cheered, continued to forage.

He climbed up a hill, slow and careful because the slope was muddy and partly washed out, but the erosion had exposed a lot of roots he could use as handholds. When he got to the top he found a patch of green lady mushrooms, bright and still damp from the rainwater sifting down from the trees above. He hummed happily as he plucked the stems and caps and put them in the basket. Once he was done, he straightened up, stretched his back, and looked across the gully before him–

Something was buried in the hillside across the way. He caught a flash of light on glass, and the gleam of metal. That hillside had also been torn up by the storm, but even more so: a tangle of uprooted trees lay at the base, tumbled down from the ridge, resting now amid piles of mud. The root system of those trees had been holding all the soil in place, and with so much washed away, the secret at the heart of the hill was revealed.

Keon's own heart fluttered. He wasn't sure what he was looking at, what kind of forgotten tech, but whatever it was, it was *big*. Size wasn't everything – power cells weren't very large, and they were about the most valuable thing you could find – but Torvald over at the mech farm paid for scavenged metal by weight. A find like this might not save the farm, but it sure would slow the rate of failure considerably.

Keon set his basket down and carefully picked his way toward the metal gleam. A stream of water still ran along the bottom of the gully between the hills, about a meter across and shallow, the remnant of what must have been a great flood the day before. He stepped across, climbed over the mess of fallen trees, and finally reached the exposed hillside. Using both hands, he brushed away the mud from the surface, trying to reveal the full extent of his find.

He uncovered a rectangle of shining metal, two and a half meters high by a meter and a half wide, with a plate of square glass set in the middle, just above his head height. The glass was milky, and he couldn't see anything behind it, but he realized with surprise that there might *be* something behind it, because this surely did look like a door, didn't it?

People found ancient vehicles sometimes, shuttles and trucks, and maybe this was an unusually large example. Or maybe... maybe it was something else. There were always rumors of hidden spaces below the forest, secret tombs or vaults in the more fanciful stories, or just rooms the long-ago inhabitants of Darit had built to keep supplies dry or hide from storms, in the more plausible legends. There were ancient tales of plucky youths finding caves full of treasure and making their fortune, though no one knew anybody it had actually happened to.

Keon looked for a handle and couldn't find one, but he did find a crack where the door didn't quite sit true in its frame. Even the best-built artifact of the olden days would fail when left out in the weather for hundreds or thousands of years. That crack could mean everything inside would be buried in mud, but metal was metal, dirty or not, and Keon was up for the hard work of excavation if it meant saving his farm.

Keon's jolt-stick was made of stout metal, and would serve as a pry bar. He hesitated, thinking of the dangers that sometimes accompanied old tech, but he was an experienced if out-of-practice salvager. If he saw anything glowing or oozing mysterious liquids, he'd back away fast and just sell Torvald the location of the place instead. He'd make less money that way, but it was an adequate fallback plan.

Settled in his mind, Keon worked the end of his bar into the crack beside the door and heaved, then moved the stick a few centimeters down and heaved again. He worked his way along that seam, using all his weight and strength and leverage, and when he'd worked his way through about three-fourths down the crack, he heard the *pop* of a seal breaking and a hiss of air. Maybe the inside wasn't going to be so muddy after all; the door was loose but not broken.

After that, he was able to work the bar deeper into the crack, and a few more hard, grunting heaves got the door open enough for him to squeeze through the gap. He peered through first though. The space beyond was dark, and he was nervous – he didn't have anything with him to make a light – but no animals could have gotten in to make their lairs inside, and it wasn't like whoever'd lived in this place hundreds or thousands of years ago would still be lurking around. Nothing could live *that* long, no matter how good their tech was. He didn't believe in ghosts, either, not since he was young.

My eyes will adjust, he thought, and squeezed into the hill.

Adjustment proved unnecessary, because when he entered, lights came on, and hidden machinery hummed to life. Keon froze, overwhelmed first by the sudden brightness and then by all the things it revealed.

The room was as big as his whole cottage, and the first thing he noticed was the skeleton on the floor. Keon had seen such remains before – a flood had unearthed sections of the old graveyard when he was a boy, and there'd been bones strewn for a kilometer afterward – but never one all together like this, still in the shape of a person... or something like a person. This one was on its belly, one arm down by its side, the other reaching over its head, legs cocked at funny angles. Whoever it was had fallen down and never gotten up again.

There were metal straps and bits of old cloth crisscrossing the skeleton – the remnants of clothes or jewelry, or both, maybe? How long had this body been here? And what kind of body *was* it? The shape of the head was all wrong for a human, too thin and too bulbous, and something about the proportion of the limbs was strange too. There were aliens in the galaxy, everyone knew that, but Keon never expected to see one on Darit, alive *or* dead.

I'm a grave robber, Keon thought with something like horror. He stepped around the skeleton and took in the rest of the space. The room contained a metal table, with a stone bowl and cup on top, all coated in a layer of dust. There was a metal frame in the corner, low and rectangular, and after a moment Keon realized it was a cot, its sleeping surface long since turned to dust. There were crates full of cans and tins, probably food, but Keon would never be hungry enough to risk opening something *that* ancient. There was probably nothing inside except dust by now anyway.

All that was basically ordinary. The back wall of the chamber was something else, though. It was covered from the ceiling halfway to the floor in shiny black surfaces, screens like the one in the burgher's house, each a meter long on each side. Beneath the screens there was a sort of ledge, or maybe desktop, covered in switches, dials, knobs, and lights. Those lights were all lit up now, some steady green, most pulsing orange, a few red and flashing rapidly. As he watched, some of the oranges turned green, and some of the reds went orange. Were they changing because of him? He hadn't touched anything!

There were eight screens in three rows: three along the

top, three along the bottom, and in the center, just one on the left, and one on the right. That left a space right in the center, and it was glass, too, but instead of being blank and black like the screens, it was transparent. At first Keon thought it was just a different kind of screen, but when he stepped close, he saw it was more like a window. There was a chamber beyond, the same dimensions as the window, and maybe two meters deep. There were things protruding from the walls and ceiling of that little compartment: nozzles, maybe, and shining rods that came to sharp points, and oily-looking eyeball-sized hemispheres. Keon couldn't even begin to imagine what any of it was for. Even Torvald would scratch his head, Keon reckoned. He'd never even heard tell of such things.

Keon glanced down at the console. All the red lights were gone now, and as he watched, the last orange one turned to green.

Then all the screens lit up, some scrolling with symbols that were meaningless to him, others displaying colored bars, a few showing the progress of zig-zagging lines. The machinery behind the clear glass started to move, rods turning slowly, hemispheres emerging from the walls to reveal themselves as spheres, nozzles sliding back and forth on hidden tracks. Keon leaned forward, hands on the ledge, to get a closer look–

Something gave beneath the palm of his hand, and he leapt back, horrified. A panel had slid open on the console, revealing a square button, and he'd put his hand *right on it* – he'd pushed the button down! What had he done? What if this was some kind of weapon?

A bright drop of blood shone on the end of his fingertip, and he put it in his mouth and sucked it instinctively, then pulled his finger out and stared at it, a sick feeling roiling in his guts. What if he'd just been poisoned?

Nothing happened, though. The lights continued to pulse green, and the other screens continued to display data that was entirely incomprehensible to him. One of the colored bars started to rise, and one of the others shrank, which suggested something was happening, but he couldn't know what. The blood was troubling. Maybe he'd just brushed his finger on a sharp burr of metal, a little accidental lancet too small to see. He'd wash the wound out with icewort when he got home and wrap it up good and hope it didn't get infected, or worse.

Assuming he didn't die from that little prick, this was a life-changing find. Whatever this place was, it was unimaginably valuable. He'd gone way beyond making up for a bad harvest and a sick flock. Once he brought this out, and started selling it to Torvald… he'd be wealthy by the time he was done. Indeed, he'd have to sell it in bits and pieces, because otherwise Torvald wouldn't be able to afford it all. This place could set Keon and Willen up for life.

For an undertaking like this, though, he'd need tools, and equipment. He could borrow a drone from the mech farm – he'd been meaning to do that anyway, to pull some stumps and expand the back field, so no one would think twice about it. He would come back here tomorrow and start taking this place apart, breaking it down into components he could transport.

Back outside, he dragged some of the smaller fallen

branches around until he'd covered up the door in the hillside. He was pretty far out in the woods, and thought it unlikely anyone else would stumble on this place. On the way out, he carved a few discreet markings on tree trunks so he'd be able to find it again, his head spinning with visions of his glorious future.

When he got home, Willen didn't notice his good spirits, absorbed as she was in her own troubles. He couldn't give her a child, maybe, but he could give her a better life, of plenty and comfort. Maybe they could afford a journey to distant Tallmount, where they were supposed to have all manner of fancy medical machines – could be the doctors there could sort out this whole fertility thing once and for all.

He decided not to tell her about what he'd found. He was being superstitious, not counting his caprids before they were lambed, because he didn't want to risk handing his poor wife another disappointment. He made a big show of cooking up the bird-of-the-wood just the way Willen liked it, hoping that would explain his irrepressible smiles. *We won't have to eat forage anymore after this*, he thought.

The next day, he borrowed a mech and went out to the woods. The machine walked along after him on its four nimble legs, pincer-arms dangling at its sides until it was time to pull or lift something, its body nothing but storage space and a few sensors to keep it from walking into things.

Keon made his way back to the bunker, only consulting his trail signs once or twice to confirm he was on the right track – the path was burned into his memory. He had a tool satchel, and he was already planning out how to take apart the console to get at all the valuable wire that must be inside, and to remove the screens without cracking them. Maybe he'd even hang one in his *own* house, and be as fancy as the burgher was–

When he stepped inside, the screens looked different. Now some of them showed different views of a newborn baby – her puffy red face on one, her body as a whole on a second, her curled fist on a third. Three other screens showed the *inside* of her body: the shape of her bones, her organs, her brain. The remaining two screens were just those incomprehensible symbols, scrolling by.

Keon walked forward, baffled. Who was that girl? He leaned over the console and peered through the little window at the center of the screen, careful not to touch anything this time.

The machine somehow sensed his approach anyway, though, because the window turned out to be a door, and slid aside into the wall.

The tiny baby girl in the compartment there sucked in her first breath of Darit's air, and let out a great whooping cry.

CHAPTER 7

"You found me inside a *machine*?" Bianca said.

"It was a miracle," Willen said. "*You're* a miracle."

"You never told anyone about this place you found?" Voyou said to Keon.

Her pa shook his head. "When I found the baby… Bianca… I knew I couldn't tell. People would ask questions, wouldn't they, if I found a baby *and* a bunch of old tech on the selfsame day, or even in the same year? Plus, I don't know how to explain it, it seemed ungrateful to tear apart the place that gave me a daughter. Breaking up a miracle to sell it for scrap. Does that make sense? I just took Bianca home… I showed her to Willen, I showed her our *daughter*… and the next day I went back. I stepped inside the bunker again, but the lights were off, the screens dark, the chamber where I found Bianca empty. I was a little afraid there'd be a new baby in there every day."

"No," Voyou said. "The machine was made to incubate just a single child. What did you do next?"

Keon shrugged. "I used the mech to jam the door shut, then I made it shift about a ton of dirt and buried the hillside again. I shoved all the fallen trees up against the hill, and turned that place back into the grave it used to be. Before I left, though, I said 'thank you' to that alien skeleton. I don't know who he was, or what he was doing there, but if he's the one who made it possible for me to have a family, I'll give him thanks every day."

Voyou nodded, once, apparently satisfied. "This version of events accords with our own analysis. I needed to hear your story, in case there were unexpected elements, but I am pleased to say there was nothing of concern."

"Why is no one talking about the fact that I was *made* by a *machine*?" Bianca's mind spun with horror and wonder, confusion and dismay. "Does this mean I'm not even *human*, am I even a person, am I some kind of machine?"

"You are biological," the undercommandant said. "That machine was a sort of incubator. You were tucked away inside it, nearly ready to be born, frozen in a sort of stasis field. You would be there still, if your father had not activated the machine and completed the process of your birth."

Bianca frowned. Her father hadn't described an incubator – they had one of those for caprids who were born too early. The thing he described had machine components, nozzles and manipulators, and what were *those* for? But she didn't have any other explanation. What was the alternative? That the chamber had somehow *made* her? Printed her out? What kind of technology could, what, *fabricate* a baby, and in the course of a single night? She'd never heard of technology like that, even in the stories she'd read.

She'd ask old Torvald about it, though. Wow, would *he* be astonished by all this!

"You know about the machine?" Keon asked Voyou.

"Of course I do," the Letnev said. "My people built it, after all, when they first ruled this planet."

Bianca opened her mouth to say, "But you never ruled Darit," and only just stopped herself in time. She knew the Barony had never controlled this world, but only because Torvald's database knew, and he'd never forgive her if she revealed that secret, especially to their new alien overlords. Was Voyou lying, or confused? Or was he right, and Torvald's database wrong?

"I bring you glad tidings," Voyou said. "Your daughter is very special. She is, to put it in simple terms, a princess of the Barony of Letnev."

That astonishing assertion was met by a long beat of total silence, and then Willen said, "*What*?"

Voyou sat back in the chair and laced his long fingers over his stomach. "It is an interesting tale, and one with deep roots in the history of our people. As you may know – though perhaps not, given how remote this world is – there was once a single galactic empire, ruled by a race of cruel oppressors known as the Lazax. My people rebelled under the yoke of their rule and fought for our freedom, inspiring many other worlds and peoples to do the same. The Lazax empire did not fall quickly, but it *did* fall, and even now we continue to rebuild what was lost in that time of turmoil. That's why we've reclaimed your planet. The Barony of Letnev is positioned to found a *new* empire, and gathering in all of our lost worlds is an important part of that process."

"What does any of this have to do with me?" Bianca said.

Voyou gazed at her with a benevolent smile. "During those tumultuous days, there were, of course, factions, even within the Barony. Some people remained loyal to the Lazax emperors – contemptible lapdogs, unworthy even to be called Letnev, but they possessed power and influence. These divisions expanded into the aristocracy, with some nobles siding with the empire, and others with the revolutionaries. The nobles fought with the tools they always had: private armies, assassination, hostage-taking. There happened to be one nobleman, highly placed in our society, who was also a brilliant scientist, adept at all matters biological. He was loyal to the revolution – indeed, he was a hero of that war. His wife was pregnant, and very nearly ready to give birth to the family's only heir, when he was attacked by his cowardly enemies. He fled, his wife dying from her wounds, his unborn child's life in grave danger as well. He vanished from our history then, and we all believed he was dead, his line and legacy extinguished... until we reached this planet and began our survey. Our sensors picked up the same bunker your father found – fortunately, it was close to the surface and its seal was broken, or else we might have missed it entirely. Such places are often shielded from detection, you see, when their systems are intact." Voyou leaned forward, smiling at Bianca with his small, even teeth. "We found the skeleton. We found the incubation chamber. We accessed the computer systems there, and have spent the last weeks analyzing the data. That skeleton belongs to your *true* father, the nobleman and scientist Ranulph Malladoc – we have confirmed this definitively. You are also the daughter of Adeliza Malladoc, a noblewoman in her own right, who must, sadly, have passed away en route to this remote place, where your true father took refuge. Your father took you from her dying body and placed you in stasis."

"I waited in that cavern to be born for thousands of years?" Bianca said.

Voyou nodded. "So it seems. Your father was a scientist beyond compare, even for one who lived in that age of wonders – his brilliance is what made him a target for his enemies, of course."

Bianca shook her head. "I don't understand. Why did he keep me locked away in some machine? Why not just let me be born, and raise me?"

"These are excellent questions, and display the sort of keen mind I would expect the heir to the Malladoc name to have. Sadly, the records we found were incomplete, and partially corrupted. Based on what we could read, and our own extrapolations, I suspect your father intended to wait until things were safe for him at home before bringing you fully to term. Doubtless he wished to raise you in the Barony, rather than in this savage place. Before he could return home, though, some tragedy befell him. We do not know how he died. His remains were far too old to provide useful information. Perhaps he suffered wounds himself in the escape. Perhaps it was something as simple as an infection. Or–"

"She doesn't look anything like the Letnev," Willen broke in. "Her skin isn't blue. This doesn't make any sense!"

"That skeleton didn't look much like you either," Keon said with a frown.

"Do not humans come in a variety of hues and shapes?" Voyou smiled. "The Letnev are the same. Oh, most of us have a bluish tint these days, but some are far paler. The Lady Malladoc doesn't resemble *you* much more than she resembles *me*, does she? Why, to an alien eye, you might not even seem the same species – she is smaller, her skin and hair differs from yours, and so on. Over the course of so many thousands of years, a species must be expected to change its appearance somewhat. I assure you, your adopted daughter is the very epitome of beauty, by the standards of imperial-era Letnev."

"So, she's a princess." Keon crossed his arms. "Fine. What does that mean?"

The undercommandant spread his hands. "It means her life is about to change, and infinitely for the better. While the noble families no longer possess the absolute power they once held in Letnev society, the Lady Malladoc *is* the heir to great estates and wealth."

"Surely after thousands of years there'd be nothing left," Willen said.

"You too show a keen mind!" Voyou said. "The Malladoc assets were indeed dispersed, when their line was believed to be finished, but Barony inheritance law is complex, and your daughter had many other powerful relatives. Portions of at least a dozen assorted estates have been held in escrow while a legitimate heir is sought. Those will be hers. I have also mentioned the Barony's ongoing attempts to recover *old* property and holdings, like the planet Darit. Some of the properties scheduled for reclamation are the rightful property of your daughter."

Bianca stared at him. "Wait… do you mean I'll own houses, and fields, and things?"

"My lady," Voyou said. "I do mean that, but I don't mean *just* that. I mean you'll own islands. I mean you'll own continents. I mean you'll own *moons.*"

Moons. "If I were reading this in a story," Bianca said, "this is the part where I would 'faint dead away in shock.' But I've never felt more awake in my life."

"You want to take Bee away from us?" Willen said. She took Keon's hand and squeezed it tight.

Voyou shook his head. "I would not dream of *taking* a lady of her stature anywhere she did not wish to go. But, yes, she does have the option, if she wishes, to join me on my ship. I have informed my superiors of her presence, and they have authorized me to take her to one of her ancestral properties."

One of my properties. "Undercommandant," she said. "This is a lot to think about. If I go, can I take my parents with me?"

They looked even more terrified at the prospect of *that* than they had at the possibility of losing her, she realized, but then, they actually liked the rhythms of life here, and found the sameness comforting in a way Bianca never had.

But Voyou was shaking his head. "We cannot accommodate your parents on our ship, I'm afraid. Normally we wouldn't take on any passengers at all – the *Grim Countenance* is a Barony military ship, not a transport vessel – but these are special circumstances. An exception has been made for you, my lady, but only for you. Once you are settled, of course, you can send for your parents if you like. You'll have ample resources to send more comfortable transport for them." He looked around the room. "Or, if your parents prefer to stay here, you can make sure they are amply provided for, and live in comfort forever."

Bianca leaned forward. "I'm going to need an advance."

Voyou looked at her blankly. "I'm sorry?"

"You're proposing to take away one-third of the labor force of a working farm," Bianca said. "My parents will have to hire help if I leave. They'll need to be compensated for that." Her mother and father looked from her to the undercommandant and back again like they were watching a spirited game of bounceball.

"Surely you're of marriageable age, and would be leaving the farm soon anyway?" There was a gleam in Voyou's eyes that made her think, improbably, that he was *enjoying* this, but then, you probably didn't get to run a planetary annexation team if you didn't enjoy sparring, even of the verbal kind.

"Any pair-bonding arrangement would involve a reciprocal work exchange," Bianca said. "My partner's family would provide labor or tangible goods to balance the benefits of me joining their family. That's simple economics. Surely if I have such vast resources coming to me soon, compensating my family for the cost of my departure should be trivial?"

Voyou leaned back and crossed one leg over the other, then laced his fingers together over the knee. "I am authorized to make such arrangements. I must say, you're very practical and level-headed for someone who just had her entire understanding of her world and her self transformed."

"I grew up on a farm," Bianca said. "You can look up at the stars as much as you want, as long as you remember to shovel all the dung first." She glanced at her parents. "We'll need to talk this over as a family."

"Would, say, ten minutes suffice? The *Grim Countenance* is leaving shortly."

Bianca snorted. "Don't be ridiculous. Even if I decide to go, I'd have to make arrangements, say my goodbyes, pack–"

"There is nothing here that you *need*, believe me. We can provide all–"

"Even if you'll feed and clothe me, there are matters of sentimental value."

Voyou sniffed. "Sentimental? That's not a very Letnev thing to say, but then, you weren't raised among your people, so it's understandable." He rose. "I can give you, mmm, seven local hours, and even then, you'll have to come to town to catch the shuttle."

"You want her to leave home in the middle of the night?" her father burst out.

"Where I am from, Monsieur Xing, it is *always* the middle of the night. And yes. That is when the *Grim Countenance* is departing this system." He smiled faintly. "Don't worry, there will be Letnev officials stationed in all the villages. The Lowcliff governor will be moving into your burgher's house, I believe. If you wish to send a message to your daughter, you may contact him, and receive any replies in the same way." He bowed smartly to Bianca, turned, and walked out of the house.

The Xings sat, silently, as they listened to the shuttle spin up its engine, roar, rise, and gradually fade to silence, except for the distant bleating of the caprids.

After a beat of quiet, her father burst out, "Bianca, you can't go!"

Bianca looked at him, an almost physical pain in her chest.

"Pa…" she began, but her mother put her hand on his arm instead.

"Our little Bee was always going to fly away, Keon," she said. "I half expected to wake up some morning and find her gone a-wandering, with just a note left behind."

Bianca reached across the table and took their hands. "I love you both. But… I think I need to see what all this means. If I really am what he says, then I can help the family, help the farm, help all of Darit, even. And if the truth is something else, if this story he told us is *just* a story, I should find out why they lied."

"Maybe it's true," Keon said. "What that man said, it does explain things, about the… birthing chamber, or whatever it was. I'm sorry we never told you the truth about how we found you, Bianca. We just, we wanted you to feel like you *belonged*."

She'd never felt like she belonged, but not because of anything her parents had done. There was just something waiting for her out there in the stars. She'd always known it. Now she might find out what. "You did make me feel that way," she said. "You always did."

"What will you do with your last hours?" her mother said. "Say goodbye to Grandly?"

Bianca had never been as attached to Grandly as everyone else, including Grandly, wanted her to be. "Maybe," she said. "But I have to go see someone else first."

CHAPTER 8

"Your majesty." Torvald puffed on a foul-smelling pipe, the stench of which not even the advanced air filters in his bunker could fully neutralize. "Your *Baronic* majesty? Is that the adjective?"

"They didn't give me a book of protocol." Bianca flopped back on Torvald's cot. Her parents had fussed over her and cried and put together a care package of her favorite jerky and dried fruit and so forth for hours, and Bianca didn't have much time left before she had to go to the village to catch her ride off the planet. "What do you make of all this?"

"Hmm?" Torvald said. "Oh, you mean their story, and you being a princess and all? Total nonsense."

Bianca stared at the shiny metal curve of the ceiling and sighed. "Yeah. I thought so, too."

"For one thing, Darit was never a Barony holding. I dug deep enough into the database to confirm my recollection for real and for sure. We were part of the Federation of Sol, the bitterest enemies the Barony of Letnev had. There's no way an aristocrat from the Barony would have hidden out on a planet full of humans, even in the midst of a civil war, unless he was some kind of traitor who'd allied himself with the humans, and then the Barony would hardly be welcoming you back, now would they? If that part of the story is a lie, and it is…" He shrugged.

"Then there's no reason to believe any of it," Bianca said. "But if I'm *not* a secret princess, why do they really want me?"

"Something to do with the non-standard nature of your birth, I'd guess," Torvald said. "Could you do me a favor, Bee?"

"What?"

"Stand up there and lift up your shirt, just enough to show me your belly."

She sat up on the bunk and glared at him. "The last person who asked me to lift my shirt was Grandly, Torvald, and I was fool enough to do it for him, though I didn't get much out of the experience myself. Why do *you* want me to do it? You've never been creepy before."

Torvald burst out laughing, which she found reassuring. "Bianca, you don't have to worry about that. For one thing, you're an ill-tempered irritant, and for another, you're an infant, but the main thing is – have you ever wondered why I don't have a wife and a whole mess of children around here? My romantic preferences lie in *other directions*, if you see what I mean."

Bianca's face warmed up. She herself was attracted to men and women and androgynes, but she'd never thought of old Torvald being attracted to *anyone*, because he was *old*. "Gross. Fine. You'd better have a good reason, though." She lifted up her shirt, just enough to show her stomach.

Torvald peered at her, then nodded and puffed his pipe. "You've got a navel."

"*Everyone* has a navel," she said.

He shrugged. "It suggests their story isn't entirely caprid-shit, is all. The database says it is indeed possible to grow a baby from scratch in a laboratory, but if you never spent time in a person's womb, that means you never had an umbilical cord, and then you wouldn't have that little dimple full of lint on your stomach. That suggests you *were* inside a mother at some point, even if that mother wasn't a Letnev aristocrat." He cocked his head. "Unless."

"Unless what?"

"Oh, nothing, I've always had a twisty and treacherous sort of mind."

"Out with it, old man. I can't go into space wondering what you're not telling me."

"I keep thinking about the way your pa cut his hand," Torvald said. "A drop of blood on his fingertip, and the next day there's a baby. A *human* baby, as far as we can tell, though skin color aside, our species does look enough like the Letnev that's it's hard to tell."

"You think the machine, what, took a sample of my father's blood and used that as a blueprint to make me?"

Torvald shook his head. "You'd look more like your ma and pa if that was the case. That skeleton watching over the machinery *wasn't* human, though, and it doesn't sound like it was Letnev, either. Why would you turn out to look so human, in that case? What I'm wondering is, did the machine take a sample of your pa to find out what the local people are made of? What if the birthing chamber used that information to tweak your design parameters, to make sure you'd conform to local norms, physiologically speaking? If that's the case, you looking like a human is just a good disguise, and that belly button you've got there might just be a convincing detail the machine added on."

Bianca frowned. "That seems like a stretch. You're always telling me the simpler explanation is usually the right one."

Torvald shrugged. "I'm just wondering out loud, that's all. But Bianca, whatever you're caught up in now, it's not simple, so maybe my old saws don't cut as well in this situation. This whole thing is so strange, there's not a simple explanation to cover it. I sure wish we could run a test or two, though, maybe peek into your genetic code and see what's going on there, but I don't have that capability down here. The nearest place with decent medical facilities is days away, too."

"I wish I could just believe them." Bianca slumped. "It's such a *nice* story. I'd love to be a secret princess. What if they want to cut me open or something? Maybe I should run away and hide."

"If they really wanted to find you, they would," Torvald said. "They wouldn't even have to look that hard, would they? They could just burn your parents' farm, or kill one of them and broadcast word that they'd kill the other if you didn't come home."

Bianca shuddered. "Would they really do that?"

"The head they put on a spike a few villages over wasn't a cultural anomaly, unless the Letnev have become a more peaceful and relaxed race since my database was last updated. But as for cutting you open... I think you can rest easy there,

Bee. If they wanted to hurt you, they'd have just snatched you and been done with it. Nobody here could stop them, after all. If they wanted to look at your genetic code, they could have plucked a hair or come up with some excuse to take a blood sample. No, whatever they want from you, they need your cooperation to do it, or they wouldn't have spun you such a tempting tale."

"Maybe I'm the daughter of a *human* aristocrat, and they want to ransom me back, or something."

"Maybe," Torvald said. "Maybe someone in the Federation of Sol, if it even still exists, gives enough of a damn about family history from thousands of years ago to make that worth the Barony's while." He took another puff. "I'd enjoy reading a novel about something like that, sure enough. No matter what the truth turns out to be, though, you're getting what you always wanted, albeit in something of a roundabout way. You're leaving all the caprids and mud behind and going to the stars."

Bianca nodded, but with a sour face. "I never thought about everything I'd *miss!*" she cried. "Pa's cooking, Ma's songs, nights sitting around the fire reading, even visiting *you*, old man. I'll even miss Grandly, a little, looking at me with those big eyes like he's a caprid hoping I'll give him something to eat. He made me feel special and important, anyway."

"Grandly won't be the last one to look at you that way, Bee. And you're some kind of special and important anyway, it seems. You just have to find out what. I've got a little gift for you." He reached into the front pocket of his overalls and fished out something that glittered: a ring of some moon-bright polished metal. "Why don't you slip this on? And if the Barony people ask about it, tell them it's a promise ring from your beau or something of the sort."

Bianca took the ring and held it up to the light. Pretty, in a plain way. "I'm not sure we're ready to get engaged, Torvald. I have some concerns about your ability to support our inevitable brood."

"Me, support you? I was thinking the other way around. Why else would I want to marry a princess? You can keep me in the manner to which I wish to become accustomed." He grinned. "That ring's a piece of old tech, taken off a skeleton found beneath a tree uprooted in the last real big storm. Damnedest thing I've ever seen. That skeleton had been in the ground so long the roots of the tree had grown all through the ribs. I thought the ring was just a bit of shiny and took to wearing it myself, and I'd fiddle with it sometimes, twist it this way and that. One day, I twisted it just right, and fried the insides of a mech I was repairing." He leaned forward. "I assume the ring was used for self-defense. Wear it on your finger, and twist it *all* the way around, counterclockwise, exactly three-hundred-sixty degrees, no more and no less. I put a little scratch in it on the side there so it's easier to tell when you've gone all the way around. Do that, and the next thing you touch with that hand will get one hell of an electric shock. Enough to overload a machine or paralyze a person, according to my voltmeter. Somehow the ring shields the wearer from its effects, so don't worry about hurting yourself, just others. It has a little integrated battery that I have no idea how to recharge, and think it only has a jolt or two left in it. I hope you'll never need to use it, but if there's ever a proper emergency, maybe it'll give you an edge the cause of that emergency won't see coming."

A piece of tech like that, a remnant of a lost age, was worth a year's supply of food at least, and Torvald was just giving it to her. Tears welled in Bianca's eyes, and she dashed them away, then slipped the treasure onto her finger. She held out her hand and tilted it to and fro, as if she was a girl admiring a real promise ring. "In that case, sir, I accept your proposal." She frowned. "Torvald, you've got such treasures down here… this ring, that database… if the Letnev found the bunker where I was born, or made, or whatever, won't they find this one?"

"I asked the database that, too," he said. "There are working countermeasures in place to keep this bunker shielded from detection, and the tons of junk upstairs should baffle their sensors even further. They only found the chamber where you were born so easily because it was cracked open and exposed to the air. I don't think they'll notice me down here." He shrugged. "Which isn't to say I don't *worry* about them noticing, but the Letnev were so excited about finding the place you came from I hope they got distracted from looking too closely for anything more."

"You should clear out anyway," Bianca said. "Pour concrete in the opening to the elevator, so if they *do* find the bunker you can pretend you didn't even know it was under your house all this time."

"That is a wise proposal, and if it makes you feel better, I can tell you I'll consider it." Torvald rose. "I reckon you should be on your way to the up-and-out. It's been nice knowing you, Bianca Xing. I'll give you the same advice my father gave me the first time he sent me out to the woods to search for salvage on my own: 'Be careful, but not too careful; be bold, but not too bold.'"

She stood up too, and started to twist the ring, then stopped herself. *That* was a habit of fidgeting she'd better not fall into. "You talk like I'm never coming back, Torvald. Of course I will. Whether I'm a princess or something else, I'll come back."

"I believe you intend to, and I hope you will, Bee. But the world is big, and you're going beyond the world, into something a whole lot bigger. You don't need to make me any promises, except to take care of yourself as best you can." He embraced her and kissed her on the cheek, his whiskery chin tickling her. He'd never done that before. Torvald pulled back and winked. "Go on, then. Make a name for yourself, earn your fortune, conquer the galaxy, or whatever other damnfool thing you've got a mind to do."

The ride back up in the elevator was long, and the walk over the dark hills to her house was longer still. All three moons were up, so it was bright, but she knew the way well enough to traverse what obstacles there were even in total darkness. She wouldn't be traveling paths that familiar again for a long time – if ever. She was going where everything was new.

When she reached the field closest to her house, and saw the lights still burning there, waiting for her, she stopped, and looked up at the sky, and the black patch between that triangle of stars. *I'm on my way*, she thought.

Her parents went with her to the village – there was no

stopping that – but otherwise there was no seeing-off party. They'd acceded to her wishes and promised not to tell Grandly or anyone else she was gone until tomorrow at the earliest. The village was sleeping, except for the shuttle from the *Grim Countenance*, crouched like a predatory insect in the clear space behind the Halemeeting hall. They had wrestling matches and dances in that spot when the weather was fair. Everything really had changed.

Voyou emerged from the shuttle, strolling down the ramp to meet them. "Right on time, even though as far as I can tell no one has an accurate clock on this entire planet. The punctuality is appreciated. Perhaps it's your Letnev heritage asserting itself."

I'm no Letnev, Bianca thought, but she only smiled. "I learned to be on time from my parents. It's only polite. And we don't need clocks. We have the sun, the moons, the stars, the animals, and our bellies, after all."

"All quite alien to my experience, I'm afraid," Voyou said. "Except for my belly. We should really get going. Say your farewells and come aboard."

Bianca hugged and kissed her parents, and admired them for not breaking down; they'd done plenty of breaking down earlier, but it wasn't as if they would exhaust their supply of worry anytime soon. They bore up, though, and soon Bianca lifted her small knapsack, waved, and walked up the ramp to whatever her future held.

CHAPTER 9

Heuvelt sat in his cell and contemplated his dinner. There was a mound of something gray that smelled like fish, and a mound of something green that smelled like brine, and a mound of something yellow and gelatinous that smelled acidic. He had his doubts about whether any of it was meant for human consumption. The tray itself honestly seemed more edible than anything on top of it.

The Winnaran bartender-turned-officer walked in and peered at him through the bars, her arms folded across her chest. She still wore her pull-tab necklace, which he'd assumed was an affectation for her undercover role, but now she was dressed in a sleek, black, well-fitted uniform.

"Hello," Heuvelt said. "Have you come to bring me my change? I paid *far* too much for that drink."

She smiled. "Your story checked out, Mr Angriff. You really did have a run of terrible luck, though it seems a rich kid like you could have bought your way out by now."

"I am in my thirties, officer," he said. "In human terms, that no longer qualifies as a 'kid.' I also no longer qualify as 'rich.'"

"How did you get mixed up with a data smuggling operation?"

"I have no idea what you're talking about," Heuvelt said. "I merely went to a bar to have a drink, and a strange Hylar tried to steal my briefcase full of empty data sticks. I tried to get away from the chaos that ensued, and you hit me in the head with a sink. Be glad I'm not a rich kid anymore. Rich kids have voracious lawyers."

She nodded. "You're right. We checked all those data sticks, and there's nothing on any of them, so we don't have any legal grounds to keep you."

He stood up. "I'll be going, then?"

She smiled. "We were *going* to process your release, but it's all a bit complicated, because of how muddled your history is. It seems you're still technically a wanted criminal in the Barony of Letnev – their bureaucracy takes forever to update their records, and they really hate admitting they were wrong about anything. While we don't have an extradition arrangement with them, my superiors think this could be a good opportunity for a trade. We give them something they want, and we get something we want, like that."

Heuvelt slumped. "I see. Please, tell me what action I can take to inspire your superiors to release me instead of handing me over to a notoriously punitive militaristic nation."

"You're pretty smart, for a rich kid. If you happened to know the location of a data stick with stolen cryptographic keys on it, the sort of thing that a criminal consortium might pay medium-good money for, why, we'd be so busy and excited by the news that we'd probably forget all about handing you over to the Letnev."

"Perhaps there might even be a reward for this information?"

"I've always found that freedom is its own reward, Mr Angriff."

"Have you really?" Heuvelt knew when he was beaten. He had lots of practice. He gave her the coordinates of the buried data stick, and she went away. Four hours later she returned and personally escorted him out of the facility, into the cold, dark, desert night.

"You're free to go, Mr Angriff."

He looked around. "Go *where*? What happened to my sand-skidder?"

"Your vehicle was impounded. It won't be processed and ready for release for eight or ten weeks. But it's a lovely night for walking, isn't it?"

"A lovely night for many things." He gave her his most charming grin, which was a shadow of its former self, but not without some lingering potency. "What's your name, officer?" She really was quite attractive, and perhaps *something* could be salvaged from this disaster.

"My name is Sergeant Get Off My Planet and Never Come Back."

"I suppose that means you won't let me buy you a drink?"

"You already bought me a drink, rich kid. I kept all your coins, remember?" She sauntered back into the long, low building, and Heuvelt was alone.

The authorities had returned his comm bracelet, at least, so he called the *Show and Tell*, half expecting an "out of range" error message. That would be a suitable new chapter in the saga of Heuvelt Angriff, outcast scion of the Angriff Industries fortune, gentleperson adventurer turned scurrilous rascal: stranded on a desert planet controlled by an aquatic race, with the local criminal element doubtless highly motivated to show him the opposite of hospitality.

To his pleasant surprise, the growling voice of Ashont, his Rokha first mate, said, "Heuvelt? Are you all right?"

"I am alive," he said. "I suppose that counts. Can you come pick me up?"

Once he was back on board the *Show and Tell*, Heuvelt just wanted to retreat to his cabin with his last bottle of sorghum whiskey, but he had to debrief his crew first. Ashont and Clec were waiting for him in the galley – together, of course, because they were *always* together.

Ashont was Rokha, and Clec was Naaz, but of course the species were seldom spoken of as individuals: they were the Naaz-Rokha Alliance, physically dissimilar aliens who shared a culture and history as well as a symbiotic relationship that Heuvelt sometimes envied, when he wasn't feeling too misanthropic: the Naaz-Rokha never had to be alone. Oh, it wasn't like they were physically or psychically bound together, but by culture and preference they seldom spent much time or distance apart, and it must have been a comfort, knowing you could really trust someone like that. Heuvelt absently touched the scar on his face.

Ashont was a panther-like humanoid, all sleek black fur and round green eyes and bright white canines. Heuvelt's family had pet cats growing up, and it was tempting to think of Ashont as a giant housecat... but her eyes had round pupils, not slit ones. Ashont had helpfully explained that cats with slit pupils were ambush predators, and cats with round eyes were "Active predators. We chase down our prey." The Rokha were relatives of the lion-like Hacan, but evolved in the jungle rather than desert or savannah climes, and the two species had diverged countless millennia before and didn't share much in the way of culture anymore. The Rokha were known as mercenaries, and for most of their history had been nomadic wanderers, traveling from place to place and job to job, without a homeworld to call their own. That changed when they met the Naaz.

Clec often rode around in a sort of open-weave harness Ashont wore on her back, but at that moment, the Naaz was perched on her shoulder. Clec was diminutive, smaller than a human toddler, with four arms, a bulbous head, and large eyes. Two of the arms clung to Ashont, and the other two were busily disassembling some small engine component. Clec was Heuvelt's first mate *too* – they'd insisted on sharing the rank equally, as their peoples shared everything – but in practice Ashont was the pilot and navigator and Clec was the ship's engineer. The Naaz were a highly intelligent race, adept at science and engineering, but they had a long history of falling prey to powerful oppressors. In ancient times their homeworld had been invaded by a Winnu corporation, then conquered by deserters from the Federation of Sol, and so on, changing hands countless times over the centuries, their people always under the heel of a new overlord who wanted to exploit their world and their population, until the Naaz finally had enough, and hired the vast Rokha military army.

With the help of those famous soldiers, the Naaz finally won their freedom, and they offered the nomadic Rokha a place on their homeworld in exchange. Their reasons had doubtless been practical: a way to keep the army without paying mercenary prices, and to make the Rokha more invested in defending their now-shared homeworld. Yet, somehow, that pragmatic arrangement had blossomed over the centuries into a true shared culture.

Heuvelt found their history astonishing. The Naaz looked like something the Rokha would hunt for sport, but the two species were by now so closely associated that if you saw one without the other, you knew a terrible tragedy must have occurred. Even on their homeworld, they lived in mixed households, a Naaz couple and a Rokha couple cohabiting together and rearing one another's young collectively. Heuvelt didn't like to imagine what it was like for such a species to *date*, but maybe it was all arranged marriages or something. He'd deliberately never inquired about the details of Naaz-Rokha love lives.

"I take it things went badly?" Clec said.

"It could have gone worse, but it went bad enough." He sat down and told them the tale of woe.

Once he was finished, Ashont clucked her tongue and put a bowl of protein mush in front of him. "Eat. They never feed you right in jail." She treated Heuvelt like he was one of her cubs, sometimes, but right now he didn't mind.

"We have the half of the payment we were given up front for the delivery," Clec said. "So we can, at least, afford the fuel to get off this planet. We need to line up another job, though, and soon."

"We should be transporting a hold full of ice-mink furs, or sun-spice, or the singing beads of Halcyon-IV," Heuvelt said. "Not grubbing around like lowly smugglers."

"We are smugglers," Clec said. "Not lowly ones, though. Excellent ones. I'll point out, you did your job exactly as you were hired to do, except for the last bit, and that was outside your control."

"Carrying any cargo at all is a waste of our time and talents," Heuvelt grumbled. "We should be exploring new worlds in search of treasure, seeking our fortune among uncharted stars!"

"It's hard to seek your fortune that way if you don't already have a fortune to start with," Clec pointed out. "Financing that kind of expedition isn't cheap. How about we make some more money this way, and then we can go... out there." She waved one of her nimble-fingered hands vaguely skyward.

"Or not," Ashont said. "Treasure-hunting didn't work out so well for you last time, Mr Scar. Making an honestly dishonest living will be good for you. It builds character."

"I have quite enough character already, thank you. If anything, I have too much." He looked up from his bowl. "I was a day late returning, and didn't send you any messages. Why didn't you two leave me?"

Clec and Ashont glanced at each other, and Heuvelt sensed that a vast quantity of information was silently shared in that look. Ashont was the one who spoke. "Our people understand loyalty, Heuvelt. We aren't like Dob Ell. We won't betray you."

"We also won't spend your entire life pretending to be

your best friend when, in reality, we were just paid to do that by your parents," Clec added. "So we won't have any pent-up decades of grudges to take out on you when those payments stop coming. See the difference?"

"Now that you point it out, the distinction does seem clear."

"We are *partners*," Ashont said. "We own half the ship, and you own the other half, and we are stronger together. There was no question of us leaving you."

Clec made a noise of agreement. "We were already tracking down your location and planning a jailbreak, in fact. I'm glad we didn't have to follow through. Even my best calculations showed only a seventy-three percent chance of success. But we would have tried."

Heuvelt lowered his head so they wouldn't see the tears welling in his eyes. They were a fine crew, and more than that, they would be his friends, if he let them. Did he dare hope they might someday become… family? His own family had always been cold, until they cut him off, and then that cold had plunged further, to absolute zero. His closest other relationship, with Dob Ell, had proven to be a sham. "I don't have much practice with this sort of thing," Heuvelt said. "But I will try to be worthy of your loyalty."

"Good," Clec said. "You can start by not arguing when we tell you what we have to do next."

"What's that?"

"We need to take that job from Sagasa," Ashont said.

Heuvelt groaned. Sagasa was a Hacan who ran a shady shipyard, scrap, and salvage operation near Vega Major. Nicknamed "The Disciplinarian" , Sagasa was trustworthy as far as criminals went, but he was also famously unforgiving when it came to failure. Ashont was connected to him vaguely through a series of cousins, and an offer for a high-speed transport job had come through recently. Clec and Ashont had argued in favor of accepting the job, but Heuvelt had resisted, because working for the Disciplinarian meant fully immersing himself in the criminal world, a fate he still half-hoped to avoid. "There has to be another job we can take."

"Not one this simple and lucrative," Clec said. "More importantly, this job would lead to *more* jobs."

"It's basically the work you planned to do when you first bought this ship," Ashont added. "We'd just be transporting high-end goods for wealthy clients."

"I meant wealthy *legitimate* clients."

"Legitimate rich people are just criminals successful enough to manipulate governments and bribe lawmakers," Clec said. "Sagasa is practically a government of his own."

"We could take a vote," Ashont said.

"You two always vote together," Heuvelt said. "You only own half the ship, so you should only get one vote anyway."

"Then we'd always have ties," Clec said. "We'd never get anything done. This way is much better."

"I vote yes," Ashont said.

"Me too," Clec said.

Heuvelt sighed. "I suppose it's unanimous, then."

"I do so like it when we're unified in purpose," Clec said.

A basic tenet of the freight business held that there was nothing worse than traveling with an empty hold, so they picked up some replacement parts for decommissioned Hylar vessels from a nearby wholesaler trying to clear out a warehouse. If nothing else, Sagasa would pay them *slightly* more than the parts had cost – enough to cover the fuel it took to get to his scrapyard, anyway.

The trip to Vega Major required a jump through a wormhole, and Heuvelt always got nauseated during those – space-time distortions were bad for his digestion – so he hunkered down in his cabin while Ashont and Clec handled the transit.

Heuvelt stared at the bulkhead above his bunk and thought about the future. He didn't want to be a smuggler. He wanted to see *new* things, stand on planets that no human had ever seen before, smash open alien crypts and plunder the contents, make first contact with new species – do something important, exciting, and meaningful. As a child he'd had every material comfort, but he'd grown up feeling empty and without purpose. Losing those material comforts hadn't suddenly imbued him with any sort of suffering-based enlightenment, though; now he was just empty and purposeless and *poor*, which was even worse. Was it so much to ask, to be rich *and* feel like your life had a purpose?

Ashont and Clec never seemed to worry about such things. They just got on with the job at hand. Heuvelt would have to try and do that too. Focus on the now, and the future would come… or maybe, at least, he could stop thinking about it so much.

"We're here," Clec called on the comms.

Heuvelt made his way to the front of the ship and gazed out at what appeared to be the aftermath of a vast space battle, but was, in fact, just Sagasa's scrapyard: hundreds of ships ranging from seemingly intact to blackened wrecks and every state in between. He'd never seen so much broken metal in one place. "There's a space station in the middle of all that?" he said.

"Quite a nice one, too, from what I hear," Clec said. "But we won't be visiting it today. Sagasa is sending a ship out to meet us, take our spare parts away, and deliver our package."

"There's one interesting thing," Ashont said. "When Sagasa heard we were traveling with you, he said he'd throw in a complimentary refuel, 'as a way of making things square between us.'"

"What does *that* mean?" Heuvelt said. He'd never had any dealings with the Disciplinarian.

Clec replied. "He also said, 'Tell Angriff I thought he was dead when I sold his ID to those pirates.'"

Heuvelt widened his eyes. "*Sagasa* stole my identity?"

"We told him the whole identity theft issue was still causing you problems," Clec said. "Sagasa offered to purge your name from the remaining criminal databases as a bonus if we complete this mission early, and with the fuel he's giving us, that shouldn't be a problem."

"Oh, I see," Heuvelt said. "He ruins my good name, but he offers to *fix* it, as a reward! Isn't *that* nice."

"By the standards of Sagasa the Disciplinarian, that is beyond nice," Ashont said. "I told him we would be most grateful to accept his offer."

"Your name wasn't all that good to start with anyway," Clec said. "At least you'll be able to get a proper credit account again."

"Then I could begin my legitimate courier business!" That was a happy thought.

"There's more money to be made being illegitimate," Clec said. "Especially if we get more jobs from Sagasa."

"Which means we could go on a treasure-hunting adventure that much sooner," Ashont added.

"But whatever you want," Clec said.

"We're easy," Ashont said.

Heuvelt recalled his recent decision to focus on the present. "Let's just complete the job in front of us. What are we delivering, anyway?"

"Sagasa just said 'biological materials,'" Clec said. "We're taking them to a space station run by a member of the Yin Brotherhood."

"Huh," Heuvelt said. "'Biological materials' could be a euphemism for so *many* horrible things. And as for the Yin, I have to confess, I know it's an irrational prejudice, but I find clones a little bit creepy. Don't you?"

They shared another one of those information-rich glances, mostly inscrutable to Heuvelt. "You should probably let us handle client relations on this one, then," Ashont said.

CHAPTER 10

The interior of the shuttle was just one long room, with a pilot and co-pilot seated up front, two rows of three seats each in the middle, and bulky storage lockers running along the walls on either side. Voyou was already seated in the front row, strapping himself in. "Stow your gear there." He pointed to an open locker. "I'm pleased to see you didn't bring any livestock with you."

"You seem very cheerful, Undercommandant." She put her bag into the bin and secured the compartment – it latched just like the feed bins at home – and then sat down in the same row, with the middle seat empty between them. The straps here were different from those used in the trailrunner, of course, but the design was intuitive enough: you slipped a metal tab into a slot and there was a click when it locked, with a simple button-push to release it.

Voyou nodded. "Have you noticed it's never properly dark on your planet, Lady Malladoc? The sun... well, I was prepared for the sun. We have a special lotion to protect us from its rays, my uniform hat has a brim, and I have lenses in my eyes that adjust to keep me from being blinded. But I thought, when the sun went down, there would be something resembling *darkness* – not the case. Those moons! Three of them. Far too many moons, and all shining, all night long."

"Sometimes just one or two are visible, and there are a few nights when they're all below the horizon at once," Bianca said.

"Do your people revel in blessed peace then?"

She shook her head. "Those are festival nights. We light big fires. Part of an old ritual, I think, meant to call the moons back? But now it's just an excuse for a party."

Voyou shuddered. "I cannot understand such an impulse. To be surrounded by darkness is to be safe and secure and home. Do *you* like the dark, my lady?"

She was neutral about the dark. There were times it was nice, and times it was inconvenient. "My favorite part of the sky is the blackness between the stars."

The undercommandant was quiet for a moment, and then he barked out a laugh. "Perhaps you really *are* Letnev."

"So I'm told." The shuttle began to hum, far more muffled from the inside than the outside. She looked around, wishing for windows – the only ones in the ship were those up front. It would be nice to see the world shrink beneath her. The Letnev, it seemed, were not keen on looking outward. The shuttle lurched, but after that there was no sensation at all.

After (presumably) rising in silence for a few moments, she said, "Is it true there's no sun on your world? A friend of mine told me he'd heard that."

"The homeworld of the Barony, Arc Prime, has no star. We are not bound to a single system, locked in orbit, as other planets are. We are free to go wherever our ambitions take us."

"How do you live on a planet with no star? Isn't it cold?"

"Rather," he said. "We do not live on the surface, as a rule – it is inhospitable, even for a people as hardy as ours. We live in vast caverns underground, warmed by our planet's core."

"What do you eat? How do you *breathe*?"

"Oh, we have immense fungus farms, of course, and these days we have colony worlds to supply other resources. As for breathing, there is a plant called Ao, a blessed wonder, that grows in great profusion throughout the tunnels and caverns, supplying ample oxygen."

"I can't imagine living in such a place," Bianca said.

"You needn't necessarily settle on Arc Prime, my lady. There are many colony worlds under the Baron's care, and while I find most of them inhospitable, they might be more to your liking. You don't even have to live in the Barony, though once you see all we have to offer, I can't imagine why you'd want to live anywhere else."

"Where are we going now?" Bianca asked.

"Our immediate destination is known only to the captain," he said. "But I gather we'll be returning to civilization soon, and the restoration of your birthright will shortly follow."

"So, you aren't in charge of the ship, the *Grim Countenance*?"

He grimaced. "You flatter me, lady. No, I am merely one of several undercommandants sent to ensure a smooth transition of power during the annexation. I was given stewardship of the eastern half of this continent, though I have been reassigned to assist you instead. Perhaps I might someday command a vessel as fine as the *Grim Countenance*. Bringing you home should help my career immeasurably."

"What's the captain like?"

"Complicated," the undercommandant said. "Only a few members of the crew, the senior officers, have even seen her. She relays her orders remotely, or through subordinates. She prefers a level of anonymity. Some say she likes to dress as a common soldier and mingle with the crew, so she can see what's *really* happening on the ship."

"Wouldn't that sort of thing make everyone nervous and paranoid?" Bianca asked.

"I prefer to think it fosters an atmosphere of continual excellence." He craned his head, apparently checking to see if the pilot and co-pilot were paying attention, and then leaned over to whisper in Bianca's ear. "We hear rumors about her, though. They say she once ran a research facility, and when a leading scientist tried to defect to the humans she led a commando team to recover the traitor. When recovery proved impossible, the captain killed the traitor personally, and then kidnapped a scientist from the Federation of Sol to replace her. They say her favorite training exercise is to clear an entire deck of a ship and lock herself down there with a soldier, one armed with the best in Letnev technology, while the captain has only a knife. If you survive the experience, she puts in a good word for you with her superiors. As far as I know she hasn't organized any such exercises since I joined her command, but then, the annexation schedule has been very demanding."

"She sounds... formidable," Bianca said.

"All the Letnev are formidable. The captain is something else again, if the stories are true."

"I don't suppose I'll meet her?"

"I wouldn't count on it. She did instruct me to tell you that you are most welcome on board. That's not a sentiment she ever extended to me."

"How kind of her." Bianca's curiosity was piqued, but life would probably be easier if she *didn't* meet someone Voyou clearly found intimidating.

Voyou pointed toward the front of the ship. "There, look through the viewport, and you'll see the *Grim Countenance*, one of the many glories of the Barony."

Bianca turned her head and watched as a large, dark shape loomed larger still against a backdrop of blackness. "It looks like a muddy caprid," she blurted, and Voyou reared back as if she'd slapped him.

"Why in the dark do you say *that*?"

Bianca put a hand to her mouth to stifle a laugh. "I'm sorry, I just – it has all those, what, those curly bits–"

"Those are spikes." His voice was as cold as winter mud. "Our thorn ships strike terror into our enemies and ensure proper respect from our vassals."

"I'm sorry, I didn't mean anything, it's just, well, our caprids have that curly wool, you know, and sometimes there's a storm and they get all muddy, and then the sun comes out and the mud dries, and they end up covered with all these curving spiky sort of things and… well… it just struck me, that's all. The resemblance."

"I would refrain from mentioning that comparison to anyone else, my lady." Voyou sounded less affronted now, and more resigned. "The rest of the crew might not understand your charming country ways. Oh! Speaking of which. When we dock, I'll throw a cloak over you, and we'll rush you to your room, hidden from sight."

That sounded like something you'd do to a criminal, not a princess. "Why?"

"You are a lady of the Letnev aristocracy, a distant cousin to Baron Daz Emmicial Werqan III himself, and when the officers first get a glimpse of you, you should appear suitably regal, don't you think?"

Bianca looked down at herself. She was in her best Halemeeting dress, flowy white with little blue flowers stitched around the hem, and it was as clean as it could be. "What's wrong with what I'm wearing?"

"Nothing at all, from the local perspective. But you are now entering a world where the perspective is different. Wider. Unless you don't want new dresses and jewels and shoes?" He gazed at her with wide-eyed innocence, not an expression his face was suited for.

"I suppose I can at least *look* at them," she said.

Because of the cloak – it was more of a blanket, really – thrown over her head, she didn't get to see much of the *Grim Countenance's* hangar bay, which was too bad, since her knowledge of spacecraft came largely from novels and most of those were extremely old. As Voyou and the co-pilot guided her blindly along, each holding one of her elbows, she could hear banging, thumping, sizzling, grinding, and shouting, which suggested the hangar bay was a busy place, and not much fun.

Then again, maybe there was no fun to be had on the whole ship. She had delivered herself into the hands of people who put heads on spikes to make a point. She'd seen the Letnev as a means to an end, a way to escape Darit and set off into the galaxy (and, eventually, reach that dark spot in the sky that called to her), but she hadn't dwelled on the fact that she'd be in their custody and care for an indefinite interval. The Letnev were less a stepping stone and more of a way station. She'd just have to keep her head down and her eyes open, learn what she could, and wait for her moment to leap free if their true plans for her turned out to be unacceptable.

A tiny part of her hoped against hope that they *were* going to take her to a palace on her very own moon. Surely the world could be like stories *sometimes*, couldn't it?

Her escorts led her into a quieter portion of the ship. She hoped they'd reach their destination soon and that it wouldn't turn out to be a dungeon or something. It was hot under the cloak, which smelled like engine oil. "I must say, you're navigating the gravity here very well," Voyou said, his voice only a little muffled.

"What do you mean?"

"The artificial gravity on the ship is set at a slightly higher intensity than Darit's. I was afraid you'd find it uncomfortable."

Now that he mentioned it, she supposed she was working a little harder to walk than usual, but it was no more strenuous than making her way uphill, and she tended to leap up slopes anyway. "I've always been in good shape. Ma says I have enough energy for two girls."

"Oh, to be so young." Voyou was puffing a little. "Those

weeks on your planet made me soft, and *I* certainly feel the extra weight. I'll have to get back to the gym soon. My exercise regime has suffered lately."

"I've heard of exercising," Bianca said. "I think the burgher's son used to stretch, and lift buckets of rocks and things? The rest of us… we just work, mostly. That seems like exercise enough."

"You need never work again, my lady," he said. "You can simply relax in splendor and comfort for the rest of your days."

That sounded awful. Bianca liked having things to do. Oh, it would be nice to be able to *choose* which things she did, and if she never had to shovel another heap of dung that would be fine, but a lifetime of indolence didn't appeal. She wanted to go places and do things. "How nice," she said.

"We've arrived." The co-pilot whipped the cloak off her. They stood before a gray metal door set in a gray metal wall. The light here was grim, with a lot more red in the spectrum than she was used to. She looked left and right, and saw more doors set at intervals along a narrow corridor in both directions. The overall effect of the place was claustrophobic. *They live in caverns,* she thought. *Being all squeezed and cramped probably makes them feel at home.*

"Touch the door, please – just press your hand against it, anywhere at all," Voyou said.

Bianca did as she was bid, the metal cold beneath her skin. The door made a grinding sound and then gave off a chime.

"There, now it's keyed to you," Voyou said. "Simply touch the door, and it will open to you."

"No one else?" Bianca said.

"*Almost* no one else. The security team has access, and the political officers, and of course the captain, but none of them would come in uninvited unless there was an emergency. Why don't you go in, familiarize yourself with your room, and get some rest? I'll be along to fetch you when it's time for breakfast. I'll bring your bag to you then too."

"Why can't I have it now?" There was nothing in the bag she really needed, but on the other hand it contained literally everything she owned.

"Luggage from the surface is subject to mandatory inspection. Your planet is full of filth and parasites and such, after all." Voyou bowed, then turned and walked away, co-pilot at his heels.

Bianca touched the door again. It swung open, and she stepped into a dim chamber of unknown dimensions. The door shut behind her, turning the dim into total darkness. Bianca swore softly. Could the Letnev see in the dark? Probably. Where were the lights?

"Hello, Bianca," a voice said in her ear, and Bianca screamed and swung her fist.

CHAPTER 11

Far from Darit, far from Elekayne, far from the path of the *Grim Countenance* or the course of the *Show and Tell*, far from any other inhabited or even habitable place in the galaxy, someone stirred in his slumber, deep underground. This was only the second time in two decades the sleeper had moved toward wakefulness, and before that he had not stirred for millennia. Things were *happening* now. A quickening was underway.

The sleeper's shrouded world was remote, but not unreachable. A series of relays hidden in asteroids, comets, and dead stars formed an invisible chain between his world and Darit; a chain that existed for the sole purpose of delivering simple supraluminal messages to the sleeper.

Two decades earlier the first message had arrived, and it said simply: *The child is born.* The sleeper swam up from the depths of his stasis to think, *Oh? Already?* Though he'd been awaiting that signal for millennia, his sleep was deep, and dreamless, and the passage of time was irrelevant to him in almost every way. Nothing that happened in the galaxy while the sleeper still slumbered had any meaning at all, of course. Because none of it would last for long after he woke again.

Now, nineteen years later, a second message came: *The child is on her way.*

The sleeper was not capable of smiling, but he felt pleasure.

There would be no more messages from distant Darit. The next alert would come from somewhere much closer to his silent world.

It was not yet time to wake, so the sleeper sank back into his long slumber, but as the darkness closed in around him, he thought: *Soon.*

CHAPTER 12

Bianca's fist didn't connect with anything, which was disappointing. She crouched and held up her hands. "Who's there?"

"I am Ayla," the voice said, smooth and uninflected. "Your artificial learning assistant. Would you like to turn on the lights?"

"Yes."

"Say 'lights.'"

"Lights?"

The room was hardly flooded with brightness, but it was illuminated by a red-tinged wash, revealing a space slightly smaller than her bedroom back home. There were storage cabinets just above head-height, a seat that folded down from the wall, and a door as long as she was tall set into the far wall. She didn't see a bed. That wasn't promising. Did the Letnev sleep standing up, like caprids, or was she expected to bunk on the floor?

There was no sign of whoever had spoken to her. Was this something like Torvald's database, then? A voice in the wall? "You said you're a… learning assistant?"

"That is correct. I am programmed to answer your questions and begin teaching you the rudiments of the Letnev language."

"Are you a mechanical intelligence, then? I've read about such things."

"True machine intelligences are rare in Barony space," the voice said. "Artificial intelligences often develop goals that are in opposition to the glory of the Barony. I am programmed to answer your questions and begin teaching you the rudiments of the Letnev language, as well as the most common trading argot."

"Yeah, you said," Bianca muttered. Ah, well. So much for making a mechanical friend. She'd sometimes talked to the caprids in the fields when she was lonely or needed to work things out in her mind, and talking to a robot wouldn't be any stranger than that. Although… she thought of Torvald telling her to be careful. A robot that could talk could also listen, couldn't it? It could even record what she said, or transmit her words in real time to a listening Letnev soldier. She'd have to watch her tongue. "Where am I supposed to sleep?"

"Your bunk folds down from the wall automatically during the designated rest interval. The Letnev are an industrious people, and do not require constant access to a bed, as some of the lazier races in the galaxy do."

"How about a bathroom? Or is the elimination of waste also something only lazier races do?"

"Hygiene facilities are located behind a wall panel, and may be accessed at will."

"That's something. Are there any other hidden amenities?"

"A desk with a terminal can also extend from the wall. The information accessible by the terminal is primarily in the Letnev language, however. Machine translation options are available, but since Letnev is the most sophisticated and nuanced tongue in the known galaxy, such translations are inherently inferior."

"I see." Bianca sat on the hard chair. The benches in the Halemeeting hall were more comfortable. "This room is pretty small. Is it some kind of jail cell?"

"This is the second-best cabin on the *Grim Countenance*," Ayla said. "Only the captain's is more spacious and luxurious."

Ah. She would have to adjust her interpretation of "palatial splendor" to fit Letnev standards. Her supposed estates were probably holes in the ground. Still, if this really was the second-best cabin, they were treating her like she mattered. "I was promised dresses," she said.

That long door on the wall swung open, and revealed a closet half again the size of the rest of the cabin. Bianca doubted it was intended as a closet – it was probably a guest bedroom or office or something – but she approved of the transformation. The closet held racks of hanging garments in rich dark colors, and a shelf full of shoes in similar hues. The inside of the door was studded with pegs that held necklaces, earrings, and bracelets, all glistening with gems in red and black and a blue so dark it was *almost* black.

Bianca's lips parted and she said "Ooohhhh," quite involuntarily. She reached out to touch one of the dresses – it was deep red, and shimmered like flowing water – and then stopped. "I need a shower before I touch clothes this nice."

A section of the wall slid aside, revealing a tiny pod with a showerhead on the ceiling and a drain on the floor. That thing off to the side must have been some kind of toilet. She hoped Letnev anatomy was roughly congruent with her own when it came to using *that*. Bianca slipped off her dress, which suddenly seemed very shabby, and stepped into the pod. "How does this work–"

Water – not freezing, but also not warm – beat down on her from above in tiny stinging streams, and soap or something like it sprayed her from all sides. She shrieked and spun as jets of water started coming from the sides, too, and even up from the floor. Okay. This wasn't some horrible malfunction. This was just how the thing *worked*.

She stopped, closed her eyes, and let the water pound her – it was invigorating, once she got over the surprise. After a few moments the water stopped, and warm air blew on her from all directions. "A *hot* shower, I should have said!" she shouted, just as the drying wind cut off.

"Hot showers are an indulgence," Ayla said. "The Letnev are a practical people, and this is a warship."

Bianca opened her eyes, and screamed again, because someone was in here with her–

No, it was just *her*, reflected in a wall that had become a mirror. Except, looking closer, she realized it was a screen, because it didn't show her reversed, the way a mirror would.

"I need to brush my hair," she said, annoyed that her luggage was being pawed over by Barony lackeys. A panel in her reflection slid open, and a tray emerged, holding the most beautiful hairbrush she'd ever seen, its silver back elaborately engraved with swirling designs. Bianca took the brush and ran it through her hair, meeting far less resistance than she usually did. "Is this some sort of magic brush?" she said.

"It has an auto-detangler setting," Ayla said. "It works by creating tiny bursts of sonic energy. The Letnev take proper grooming very seriously. An orderly appearance reflects an orderly mind."

"Everything is going to be a lesson on the nature of the Letnev with you, isn't it?"

"I am programmed to–"

"Yes, yes, I know." Bianca stepped out of the shower and considered her new wardrobe. She found a drawer that contained undergarments – they, at least, were simple and familiar, though of higher quality than her own – and gazed at the dresses. "Am I really supposed to dress like this all the time? These are nicer than bonding ceremony dresses back home. A ball gown every moment of every day seems excessive."

"You also have access to crew-standard clothing, stripped of uniform insignia, if you would prefer."

"Well… maybe tomorrow. It can't hurt to try something on for now." She selected the deep red dress and wriggled into it. The cloth seemed to shift and adjust to fit her better. "Is this stuff *alive*?"

"The Letnev value efficiency," Ayla said. She then spoke in some language Bianca didn't understand, full of harsh glottal stops and noises like throat clearing. "Taking measurements and creating bespoke garments tailored for an individual is needlessly time-consuming. Instead, that dress is made of smartcloth, capable of adapting to your particular needs." More incomprehensible phrases. "The skirt can divide itself and become leggings, if that is preferable." More guttural talk.

"Are you repeating everything you say in Letnev?"

"Yes." Then: Something like *Yechh*. "We have begun your language instruction." More Letnev followed. Bianca recognized the word for "we" this time, assuming word order worked the way in Letnev it did in her own tongue, which was probably a big assumption. She actually didn't know how other languages worked; she'd never been exposed to any.

"Carry on, then," Bianca said. Ayla made another wall into a mirror and Bianca played around with the dress. Stroking the cloth in a certain way could make the sleeves extend from caps to full-length, and smoothing the skirt just right could turn it into leggings, as promised, and with a little more effort she could even make leggings beneath a shorter skirt. The bodice was adjustable, too, from low-cut to so modest it made it hard to breathe. The cloth wasn't totally mutable – the fall of the skirt and the nature of the hem were limited, and there were only a few styles she could coax the rest of it into; nothing asymmetrical, for one thing. "This dress has weird limitations."

"It is smartcloth designed for Letnev aristocracy," Ayla explained. "It is programmed to always adhere to current fashions, or timeless elegance." Her repetition of her statements in the Letnev language continued.

"So I won't be able to look like a fool, no matter how hard I try. That's comforting. Show me the shoes."

The shelf slid forward, and she chose a pair of pumps that matched her dress. "These heels are absurd." They were easily six inches high. The burgher back home had a pair of heels; she'd worn them in her bonding ceremony, and still talked about how bad her feet hurt at the end of the night.

These heels were adjustable, it turned out: they shrank down to a mere inch, and Bianca laughed. "That's handy."

"They can be any length you choose, or even become flats," Ayla said. "But they are equally easy to walk in at all heights, with auto-stabilizers built in, and they will make constant micro-adjustments to ensure you do not blister or experience discomfort."

Bianca strapped the shoes on, and even though they looked wonderfully impractical they were the most comfortable things she'd ever had on her feet. She did a few twirls, as best she could in the small space, then admired her legs in the mirror. "I guess the life of an aristocrat isn't so bad. Tell me about the ways of the Letnev elite, Ayla."

"We are a true meritocracy, where the strongest and smartest inevitably rise to great heights in the Baron's service."

Bianca frowned. "That doesn't sound like a system with much room for hereditary aristocrats, which is what I'm supposed to be."

"While even those from humble origins may rise to great heights through diligence or brilliance, it is no surprise that the most prominent families produce the most impressive offspring, and so the great families of the Barony maintain their positions and justify their power through the continued excellence of their–"

"Right," Bianca said. "The burgher's son back home always has time to study, and plenty to eat, and he's the healthiest and best-educated person in the village. That kind of excellence just runs in the blood, huh, Ayla?"

"I am afraid I do not understand the question."

"That's all right. I understand the answer." Bianca's belly rumbled. "When do we eat?"

"Breakfast is in approximately one standard hour."

"How long is that in Darit time?"

"I do not understand the question. There are twenty-five standard hours in a standard day, and ten standard days in a standard week, and four standard weeks in a standard month, and ten standard months in a standard year–"

Her door chimed, and a screen appeared on its inner surface, revealing Voyou. He was smiling, and it still looked out of place on him. "Are you ready, Bianca?"

"Almost." With a few smoothing touches and tugs she turned the dress into the leggings-and-short skirt arrangement, and clicked her heels together to turn the shoes into flats. She was a lot shorter than the Letnev around her, but she refused to compensate. She glanced at the jewels, thinking it would be silly to wear something like that to breakfast, though it would probably be good to get into the habit of wearing the jewelry all the time, wouldn't it? Then she'd have some ready wealth at her disposal if she had to strike out on her own unexpectedly. She plucked a bracelet of dark red stones from the wall and closed it around her wrist, then went to the door. Voyou's eyes widened when he saw her. "I clean up all right, don't I?" she said.

"The style suits you, my lady," he said, offering a half-bow. "Are the accommodations satisfactory?"

"They're as good as it gets, aren't they? Unless you're planning to kick out the captain and give me *her* room."

"I would hesitate to make such a suggestion."

"Is it breakfast time already?" she said.

"Soon. Will you accompany me?"

"I don't know how to find my way around on my own yet, so yes." He set off down the corridor, and she fell into step beside him. "Did the lights get brighter?" They seemed less red, somehow, and she could see more clearly now.

Voyou glanced at her. "The illumination level is set to Letnev military standards, and is unchanging."

"Maybe my eyes are adjusting, or something." She was getting used to the gravity difference, too. It no longer felt like walking uphill – just taking a stroll down to the village.

"That must be it," Voyou said. They turned down more identical corridors, and finally reached a door twice the size of her cabin's. The door slid open as they approached, revealing a gleaming white room, with pedestal beds and mechanical manipulator arms clustered along the ceiling and poking out of the walls, all folded up and waiting. She thought of her pa's description of the birthing chamber.

"What's this place?" Bianca said.

"The medical bay." A Letnev wearing a transparent face mask and a white uniform emerged. She was taller, thinner, and paler than Voyou, and her eyes were bright and avid. The overall impression was that of a predatory insect adapted to hide in the snow. "I am Doctor Archambelle. I will perform your medical assessment. Disrobe now."

Before Bianca could object, Voyou snapped, "Show some respect, doctor. This is the lady Malladoc."

The doctor cocked her head, then bowed. "My apologies, lady. *Please* disrobe now."

"Why do I need a medical test? I feel fine."

"You come from a backward planet, lady. Your body doubtless contains countless parasites, viruses, bacteria, toxins, and other harmful elements. You may have a genetic predisposition toward disease or organ failure. We will scan for, and correct, any such problems."

Bianca looked at Voyou, who was, she realized with mild horror, the closest thing she had to a friend here, unless you counted Ayla, who was no more a person than old Torvald's database was. "Don't worry," he said. "Doctor Archambelle is the head of our medical team, and the captain's own personal physician."

She sighed. She could kick up a fuss and argue, but she was enmeshed in the might of the Letnev military now, and she wanted them to *keep* being nice to her, after all. A medical examination made sense. They'd even inspected her bag for foreign contaminants; of course they'd want to inspect her too. She slipped off her shoes and began to pull at the straps of her garment.

"I'll be back to pick you up for breakfast." Voyou retreated from the room, leaving her alone with the doctor.

Bianca had never really been subject to a doctor's care before – there was a woman who set broken bones and another who knew the herbs that broke fevers and soothed nausea, but Bianca had never been sick or injured a day in her life. She had a sense from her novel reading that doctors were aloof and dispassionate, but this woman wasn't that; she looked positively eager to start poking and prodding and scanning Bianca. *She probably just loves her work*, Bianca thought, and climbed up on the pedestal bed as the doctor directed. "Will this hurt?" Bianca said.

"Letnev medical science is the greatest in the galaxy," Archambelle said, which didn't really answer the question, did it?

CHAPTER 13

Severyne Joelle Dampierre, captain of the *Grim Countenance* and provisional governor of the newly annexed planet Darit, was watching Bianca Xing's medical examination on a screen when her door chimed with Undercommandant Voyou's pattern.

"Enter," she snapped, and the undercommandant came slinking in, overly deferential as always. "My *personal physician*?" she said. "As if I'd let Archambelle touch me." The woman was a doctor, and an entirely competent one, but healing wasn't really her specialty. "She'd probably start vivisecting me out of habit."

"I was trying to set the girl at ease."

Voyou stood at attention, and Severyne didn't bother to set *him* at ease. "I must admit, you do seem to have a rapport with the creature."

He shrugged infinitesimally. "I am a slightly familiar face in a wildly unfamiliar place, captain. Someone surrounded by the unknown will cling to the known, however scant the connection."

"A reasonably astute observation," Severyne acknowledged. Voyou was really quite capable – he'd run his portion of the annexation flawlessly, and even dealt with this… unexpected side mission… with aplomb. Severyne wasn't in the habit of doling out compliments to underlings, however. Negative reinforcement was much more effective, in her experience. "I just hope Archambelle can turn up something useful about this girl. Did you see the way she reacted to the gravity here?"

"More the way she failed to react, captain, but yes."

Severyne had deliberately cranked up the artificial gravity several percentage points above normal – not in her own cabin, of course, but everywhere else – in an attempt to make the girl feel weak and overwhelmed and dependent upon her arrival… but Bianca Xing had skipped along the corridors like she didn't even notice, even as Severyne's own crew visibly sagged under the strain. "That thing she said earlier, about the lights changing – are her eyes *actually* adjusting to conditions here? That quickly?"

"It would seem so, captain."

Severyne leaned back in her chair. "I don't like it when my tools are so unpredictable."

"The entire situation is unprecedented, captain. But I have no doubt you will handle it with grace and efficiency. You certainly worked out the best way to get her here without any complications."

Severyne turned back to the screen, where Archambelle was poking the girl with needles, presumably not just for her own amusement. "However unusual her origins, Xing is still just a young woman with big dreams from a backward place. Once you gathered some data regarding her personality, it was easy to tailor a story that would appeal to her. Of course she wants to believe she's the lost heir to a great fortune, with the whole galaxy her playground. Who in her circumstances wouldn't want that?" Severyne touched her terminal, pulling up the preliminary results of the medical exam as the machines hidden in the medical bay's walls scanned their patient. The Xing girl seemed entirely human so far, but she had to be more than that, didn't she? "The map and the key," Severyne muttered.

"What's that, captain?"

"Nothing," Severyne said. "Dismissed. See that she's treated with all due pomp and honor when you feed her."

"Captain." He clicked his heels, turned smartly, and exited.

Severyne rubbed her temples, a show of exhaustion and weariness she would have never indulged in while a subordinate was present – or a superior, for that matter. This was her first mission as captain of the *Grim Countenance*, and it should have been relatively simple. Her brief was to subjugate one of the old colonies of the Federation of Sol as a way of sticking a metaphorical thumb into the eye of their human rivals. Severyne was happy enough to comply. During her career, Severyne had met only a single human she didn't entirely loathe, and even her, Severyne had *partly* loathed. As a result, she had the same instinctive antipathy toward Bianca Xing that she did for the rest of the population of Darit… but she wasn't even sure the girl *was* human, or not entirely. Severyne was curious to see what Archambelle found. The doctor wasn't Severyne's superior, but she wasn't her subordinate either, and the latest orders from Barony high command were to "aid the doctor in her researches." They were, the captain had to admit, very *interesting* researches, with significant implications if Archambelle's suspicions were true.

The *human* factor was troubling, though. So much depended on that young woman with her head full of dreams.

"The map and the key," Severyne said again, louder this time since she was alone, and gazed at the sleeping girl on the screen.

The call that changed Severyne's mission came from one of the survey ships, out searching for ancient human weapons hidden on Darit. The locals might choose to stage an uprising, after all, and it would be preferable if they didn't come armed with anything more deadly than sticks, rocks, and gunpowder. There was always the chance of finding buried treasure on these colony worlds, too – caches of wealth or resources, embarrassing old secrets – though the Federation of Sol hadn't been present here for millennia, and the odds of turning up anything interesting were low.

Severyne's first officer, Richeline, buzzed her private comms. "Captain, one of the survey ships found something unusual in Undercommandant Voyou's sector."

A two-headed sheep, perhaps? Severyne thought. *A gourd of astonishing size?* "Brief me in person," she said, on the off chance that it was something relevant.

Richeline sidled into the room; she always moved like an assassin creeping up on her target, even when in plain sight.

Severyne liked her as much as she liked anyone: Richeline was poisonously ambitious, but her ambitions didn't overlap much with Severyne's. She wanted to lead covert specialist kill teams, and had only requested a post on a pacification ship to polish the "leadership skills" section of her file. Severyne had no interest in being an assassin. She wanted to be the person gathering intelligence and *dispatching* the kill teams. Why get blood all over her own boots?

"Take a seat." Severyne gestured at the chair on the other side of her desk, which was, she knew, the single most uncomfortable seat on the ship.

Richeline perched on the edge of the chair (the least painful option), her uniform perfect, a tiny scarlet teardrop insignia on the collar her only deviation from the standard: only survivors of the Battle of Three Lions were permitted to display that pin. Severyne had looked into her file and knew Richeline had been knocked unconscious by the first sonic bombardment at that battle, and had awakened on a hospital ship with no memory of the previous three days, but she *had* survived the engagement, which technically entitled her to the pin, and suggested she was lucky, at least. "Thank you, captain. I know you didn't want to go down to Darit at all, but… this might benefit from your personal involvement."

Severyne's exact words had been, "I don't intend to set foot on that human-infested ball of excrement," and she'd meant it, but now she was intrigued. "Do tell."

"May I?" Severyne granted Richeline access to one of her screens, and bright clear footage appeared: someone walking through a dreary forest, toward a steep, muddy hill.

"This is from one of our surveyors? Why did they land?" The survey ships were supposed to fly low, scanning the ground for signs of buried technology, with search teams to follow. They weren't supposed to land and poke around personally.

"Extraordinary circumstances," Richeline said. "I authorized it."

Severyne grunted. That level of initiative was within her remit as first officer. Severyne didn't want to be bothered by every little thing, after all. Nevertheless, she paused the playback. "Why?"

"The surveyors picked up readings inconsistent with human technology... inconsistent, indeed, with *any* known technology. What they found is older than the human colonization of this planet."

"What do you mean? I thought Darit had no native sapients?"

"It didn't," Richeline said. "Someone else came here, a long time ago, and built... a sort of laboratory."

"Who? Do you mean... the Lazax?" Those aliens were the former rulers of the galaxy, now degenerate and debased, but at their height they'd possessed incomprehensible powers.

Richeline licked her lips. "Ah. No. Older."

"Older? Who are you talking about?"

"Have you ever heard of the Prophecy of Ixth, captain?"

Severyne frowned. "Ixth? That's the promised land, where the Letnev will someday dwell in blissful, perfect darkness? Why are you talking about children's stories, Richeline?"

Richeline cleared her throat. "It's more than just the Letnev. Almost every culture in the galaxy has legends about the lost paradise world of Ixth. The tales are older than the Lazax, and they pop up *everywhere*."

"That's because people everywhere are fools, Richeline, and would rather imagine a paradise waiting for them in the future than do the hard work of creating their own paradise here and now."

Richeline seemed to change tack. "How much do you know about Doctor Archambelle, captain?"

"I know she asked me to get her human test subjects from Darit so she could vivisect them and see how they'd diverged anatomically and genetically from their cousins in the Federation of Sol," Severyne replied. "That told me everything I *need* to know about her."

"I served with her on a prior mission," Richeline said. "She is a scholar of the body, yes, but also of antiquity, and a believer in the powers of ancient, lost science – technology so advanced that its users would seem like gods to us. She believes Ixth is a real place, and a treasure trove of technological wonders powerful enough to transform the balance of power in the galaxy."

"Oh. She's a lunatic, then."

"I'm… not sure, captain. Archambelle's studies have led her to remote dig sites on forgotten worlds, and she has pored over old scrolls, tablets, databases, and drives that expand on the prophecy of Ixth. She has even, she says, seen some remnants of their technology. Before we began our survey, she took me aside and asked me to report any *peculiarities* we found to her. When I asked what sort of peculiarities, she specified exactly the sort of readings we found in that forest."

Severyne didn't allow herself to react. So, Archambelle had a secret mission, hidden within Severyne's own. That was irritating, though hardly unprecedented among her people. Wheels within wheels was the norm. "And you promptly shared your discovery with the good doctor?" Severyne didn't try to keep the ice from her voice.

"No, captain." Richeline shook her head firmly. "This is your ship. You decide who receives information, and why. I just wanted to place what you're about to see in context. This place... it may be a relic of a truly forgotten age. Archambelle says she believes an ancient, almost forgotten alien race *created* Ixth, and that they may have also come to Darit."

Why would ancient powerful aliens ever come here? Severyne silently resumed the video playback. The surveyor approached the hillside, and directed a many-armed utility drone bobbing along on anti-gravity thrusters to clear the dirt and mud away. The machine worked furiously, scooping and scraping, until a portion of a metal doorway was revealed. Bright metal was overlapped by duller sheets of steel, crudely welded on. "Someone tried to seal this place up," Severyne said. "One of the locals must have found your ancient relic before you. There won't be anything of value inside by now, I'm sure. It's all picked over by grave robbers."

Richeline didn't answer, just inclined her head at the screen, as if to say: *keep watching*.

The utility drone tore away the metal patch and hauled the door open, metal bending with a grinding squeal. The camera view moved in, with the surveyor shining a light into the space beyond. The light was swiftly made redundant, though – when the surveyor stepped inside, the chamber illuminated, revealing a wall of screens and dials and lights, a control console... and a skeleton on the floor.

"Interesting," Severyne said. "Are the remains human? No, I can see they're not." The surveyor ducked down to look at the body, and its head was bulbous and misshapen, its limbs oddly proportioned. "What is it?"

"I don't know," Richeline said. "We can ask Archambelle, if you like. Anatomy is one of her passions."

Severyne grunted. The surveyor stepped over the body, moving closer to the console. If he *touched* anything in there, she would have his skin peeled off–

But he knew his work. He merely panned his camera slowly around, taking in the whole room. "What is that little window?" Severyne said. "In the center of all the screens?"

"We don't know," Richeline said. "But look, here it comes–" The screens lit up and began to scroll unfamiliar glyphs, startling the surveyor, who hastily retreated from the hidden lab, if that's what it was, and back to the forest. The video ended.

"Was that gibberish on the screens supposed to mean something to me?"

"When I was with Doctor Archambelle on that other mission, at a remote dig site... we saw screens with glyphs a lot like those, captain. I can't be sure, we'd have to check with the doctor, but... I think it's a language used by these ancient aliens Archambelle talks about."

Severyne grunted. "I will go to the surface in one hour. The site is to be secured until my arrival. Tell Archambelle I require her company for a visit to Darit, but don't give her any further information. You will have command of the *Grim*

Countenance while I am gone. Do not use that command to do anything at all."

Richeline bowed her head. "Yes, captain."

Severyne flicked her fingers. "Dismissed." Richeline departed, and Severyne sat in the dimness of her office for a long moment, thinking about the deep past and the uncertain future.

CHAPTER 14

Not long after her meeting with Richeline, Severyne set foot on the surface of her colony world for the first, and, she hoped, last time. Darit smelled, and it was much too bright, and the gravity was different, and there were bugs. Severyne hated each new problem she noticed slightly more than the last, due to the cumulative effects.

Her shuttle landed as close to the mystery site as possible, but reaching the location still required a long slog through leaf mold and mud, beneath spindly trees that made ominous whispering sounds in the wind. The whole place would have benefited greatly from a raging forest fire. Severyne could have piloted an all-terrain vehicle through the filth instead of walking – there were numerous forms of ground transportation available, fast-moving nimble things designed for putting down all the insurrections that hadn't happened – but she refused to show anything like weakness.

Besides, Archambelle clearly hated walking through the dirt even more than Severyne did, so that was a pleasure. *Her* uniform was bright white, and showed the muck rather more starkly than Severyne's blacks. They had four armed guards with them, faceless in their reflective dark helmets, and the soldiers formed a square with the doctor and the captain in the center. In theory, the locals could use their knowledge of local terrain to wage effective guerilla warfare, and such precautions were standard for an officer visiting a newly annexed area. In practice, the natives seemed more baffled by the arrival of their new masters than combative. They'd never really been ruled before, apparently. They didn't know what to make of the experience.

They reached the hillside – Severyne recognized it from the video – and there were two surveyors there, armed with energy weapons, a utility drone patrolling around them. Archambelle started to rush forward, and Severyne cleared her throat. The doctor paused, looked at her, and sighed. "Really, captain, I am eager to look inside."

"I can't imagine why," Severyne said. "All I told you was the survey team had discovered something anomalous, and I wanted you to take a look. It's almost like you expected to find something here."

"Isn't it?" Archambelle said brightly.

"I wondered why someone of your standing and experience was sent along on an annexation mission. I assumed you'd done something to enrage one of your superiors, and once I spent a little time with you, I was confident I'd guessed correctly. But you came to Darit for a reason. You were expecting to find something like this."

Archambelle stared at Severyne for a moment, sucking her teeth. It was a disgusting habit. "Expecting is too strong a word," she said at last. "*Hoping*, perhaps. Fortunately, I have enough influence in the right circles that hope was enough for me to secure the assignment."

"What are we walking into?" Severyne said.

"I am not entirely sure," Archambelle said. "But if we're lucky... we might just find the keys to paradise."

"Someone else gave me a vague and poetic answer to a serious question, once," Severyne mused. "He had twice as many kneecaps before he did that as he did afterward. Try again. If you don't answer me to my satisfaction, you aren't setting foot inside that chamber."

Archambelle scowled. "One call to my friends in the Barony–"

"How would you place such a call?" Severyne said. "Not from the surface of this planet, certainly, and I'm afraid you may need to stay here indefinitely. I understand some of the locals have parasites and fungal infections, things like that. Your skills are definitely needed. Try again."

"You are *not* my superior officer, Severyne. I don't take orders from you."

Severyne picked up a stick and whipped it viciously through the air a few times. "That's true. Of course, everyone in a position to get you off this planet *does* take orders from me. Or were you going to walk back to the *Grim Countenance*? Try. Again."

The doctor sighed. The guards and surveyors were stoically pretending to ignore the friction between their superior officers. "Fine," Archambelle said. "Have you heard of the prophecy of Ixth?"

"Of course. Hasn't everyone?" The entirety of her knowledge, apart from the half-remembered fairy stories she'd mentioned to Richeline, had been acquired from a database query earlier that day, but Severyne hadn't attained her rank by showing weakness.

"I have a theory about Ixth. I think it belonged to, or was at least somehow associated with, an ancient race known as the Mahact. It may even have been their homeworld."

Severyne kept her face impassive. To profess belief in one outlandish imaginary thing was an eccentricity; to believe in two was pathology. "The Mahact are just a story, Archambelle. They were supposed to be, what, ancient wizards or something? They're no more real than the Ebon Witches or cave ghosts or the Strangleman."

"I believe the stories of the Mahact are rooted in fact," Archambelle said. "They were powerful gene-sorcerers. Mad tyrants. Terrors of the galaxy in ancient times, long before the Lazax empire rose. They twisted the bodies of their enemies to amuse themselves, and did the same to their servants to make them more useful. They could enslave other species with a glance. The Mahact hated everyone, and hated each other, and released horrific technologies into the galaxy in pursuit of incomprehensible feuds, or just for fun. Then the Lazax stepped in, an upstart race full of ambition and ferocity. The Lazax defeated the Mahact, killed every last one of them, and took control of what remained of their dominion, including the imperial seat on Mecatol Rex."

"Or so they claimed," Severyne said. "Sounds like propaganda to me – 'Oh, be grateful, citizens, we saved you from the scary star wizards.' It's nonsense."

Archambelle sighed. "Many scholars share your view, but I believe the Mahact were real. I think it's safe to say they were terrors, and that any single member of that strange race possessed more technological power than the entire Barony does today."

"You'd better hope one of these guards isn't secretly a political informant," Severyne said. "Good citizens, like myself, know that *no one* could be greater than the Barony."

Archambelle waved that away. "You must rise above such concerns, captain. Some things are beyond politics, and the stakes are much higher than personal ambition now. Not that personal ambitions can't be satisfied in the process." She gazed at the broken door of the ancient chamber.

"The Mahact are long dead… but the wonders they created remain, waiting for worthy successors to claim them, and use that power to found a new empire."

"On Ixth, you mean?"

"Yes. If I'm right about Ixth being the homeworld of the Mahact, it is a graveyard now, a monument to a dead race… but there are treasures in those tombs. If we can locate Ixth, and loot that technology, the Barony will become what we always claim to be: the most powerful faction in the galaxy, rightful inheritors of the throne of Mecatol Rex, destined to be the new rulers of a single galactic empire."

"Ruling a single galactic empire didn't work out well for the Mahact *or* the Lazax," Severyne pointed out.

"True," Archambelle said. "But the Letnev are superior to those filthy aliens in every respect except technological might. We would run the empire *properly*." The doctor *was* a patriot, then – just one whose loyalty was so unquestioned by the higher echelons that she could indulge in petty critiques of the regime.

"You have some plan to find Ixth, then?" Severyne said. "A plan that, inexplicably, has something to do with an old Federation of Sol colony world like Darit?"

"The Mahact were secretive, paranoid, covetous – we can't expect to find a map leading straight to Ixth. They would have hidden any such map, broken it into pieces, disguised it with a cipher. But if someone very smart, and very dedicated, put enough pieces together, followed enough clues… they might find the way."

"You think there's such a clue here?" Severyne slapped at a bug on her neck. Biospheres were repulsive. She couldn't wait to get back to space.

Archambelle smiled. "Oh, yes. I have found certain artifacts I believe to be of Mahact origin, and fragmented files, largely corrupted, but with suggestive lines of code intact. Mentions of a map that could lead to a hidden treasure planet – a planet that *must* be Ixth. My colleagues and I have been gathering those hints for more than a decade, translating them, and looking for clues. One such clue pointed to this world, Darit, as 'the key to the key.'"

"I thought we were looking for a map. Now we're looking for a key?"

"We're looking for both. And sometimes, instead of a map, there's mention of a 'navigation system,' or simply 'a compass.' Maybe we're looking for all three. Or one thing that serves all three functions. Perhaps we need a map or a compass or both to find Ixth, and a key to open it. I don't know. But… I think the secret might be there." Archambelle pointed to the door in the hill. "May I *please* take a look?"

"Fine," Severyne said. "Since the future of the Barony and

the fate of the galaxy is at stake." She glared around at the guards and surveyors. "None of you heard *any* of that, all right?"

"Yes, captain!" they chorused, with acceptable levels of zeal. Severyne decided not to have them all executed to keep the secret safe. Likely there was no secret at all. This was probably just a vault full of mud and crawling things.

Archambelle slipped through the crack in the door, and light spilled out. Severyne followed, more carefully. She looked around the interior, and found it much as it had appeared on the video. The only notable difference was the scent, which was rather musty and stale. She crouched and looked at the skeleton on the ground. "What manner of creature was this?"

The doctor spared it barely a glance. "The physiology is unfamiliar to me. Some unknown species, then. Almost certainly one of the many slave races of the Mahact, sent here to hide the key. But where is it? *What* is it?" She went to the console and began manipulating knobs and dials, causing the incomprehensible characters on the screen to change.

"What am I looking at?" Severyne peered into the square compartment at the center of the screen array, with its odd nozzles and manipulator arms, some with crusts of organic effluvia on the tips. "Is this some kind of... biomatter printer?"

Archambelle groaned, staring at the streaming characters on the screen. "That's exactly what it is. I'm looking at the logs, and this machine... it made an organism. I shouldn't be surprised – that's what the Mahact *did*. They were wizards with flesh, gods of genetic engineering. Some say they could even create life from non-life. Our scientists can't even create living *wood* from raw chemical components, let alone animal life, but this machine made... wait. It sampled a dominant local species, which based on a glance at this DNA code is clearly human, and then created an organism based on that template, with... frankly incomprehensible additions, hidden inside the genome. Lines of dormant code, strange strings of RNA, chemical signatures that make no sense inside a living creature. They should be totally inert. Though I suppose if they combined with some sort of catalyst, internal or environmental... or maybe there's a kind of internal timer, counting down..."

"What are you talking about?" Severyne demanded. "You're saying this machine created a person? A human person?"

"It created something that *looks* human," Archambelle said. "But only because it sampled a human's DNA to create a template. If the machine had sampled a Letnev instead, the child would look Letnev, and if it had sampled a Hylar, the child would have fins instead of legs."

Severyne looked into the compartment. "This machine built a child?"

"It would have been an infant, at the beginning," Archambelle said. "Something small, showing perfectly ordinary human development, most likely. I wonder if it's a sort of camouflage, so the child would blend in with the local population? But underneath, the child would be... something other than human. I don't *know* what, but – wait. There's a message in the archive. A brief note that was apparently displayed, hmm, approximately nineteen standard years ago, when the child was first... printed? Decanted?"

"Settle on the nomenclature later," Severyne said. "What did the message say?"

"This a loose translation, mind you, but it says, 'The child is the map and the key.'" Archambelle slammed her fist on the console. "The map and the key! The path to Ixth must be hidden in the child, probably written in its genetic code!"

"Mmm," Severyne said. "Can you make the machine print us another child?"

Archambelle shook her head. "This device was meant to do one thing, and it has done it. The reserves of organic material are spent, and I can't begin to imagine what to refill them with. I suppose the Mahact who created this chamber expected one of their operatives to find it and decant the child. I'm sure one of *them* would know how to decipher the secrets hidden in the child's blood."

"It all seems a bit involved," Severyne said. "You'd think they could just write the directions down."

Archambelle shrugged. "Maybe it's not that simple. There could be complicating factors we can't imagine or hope to understand. The ways of the Mahact can be incomprehensible. They were as gods to us, captain." Archambelle's eyes were wide, and she gazed around the chamber with a reverent intensity Severyne found troubling. Zealotry had its uses, but Severyne preferred not to be so close to it, in case it exploded and made a mess. "You can't expect to understand everything the gods do." She sagged. "But some stupid human found this place, nearly twenty years ago, and triggered the machinery. The child is lost. The map, and the key, lost."

Severyne sniffed. "I imagine we can find it. The number of humans in the immediate area numbers in the hundreds, not the thousands. Small communities gossip, and everyone knows everyone else's business. The human who discovered this place probably burst into the nearest tavern and shouted 'Who wants to buy a mechanical baby?' Even if she showed more discretion than that, there would still be rumors. Mystery infants appearing in the absence of pregnancies always start people talking – such things are either a scandal or a miracle, and people love both. I'll have Voyou make some inquiries, and see what we can find out."

Archambelle perked up. "Yes, captain, it's of the utmost importance, this supersedes all other elements of your mission–"

"The child could be dead, of course," Severyne mused. "Is that a problem? I think they bury their dead here, instead of sensible, efficient cremation, so we might be able to recover bones with some viable DNA inside."

"If it comes to digging up a corpse, I'll wield the shovel myself," Archambelle said. "But alive is better. Alive and cooperative is *much* better. I don't know exactly what form the code will take, and the message says the child is the key as well as the map – what if it has to be alive to activate the wormhole, perhaps via some sort of sophisticated biometrics? What if the child has to speak some phrase, something programmed deep in its memory, that will come to mind only when the child reaches the appointed place? We simply can't know until we arrive... wherever it is we're going."

"So we need to find a local mysterious foundling, now a young adult, and convince them to accompany us to an unknown destination, ideally of their own free will, since if the child decides to fight us, they could ruin everything?"

"Yes," Archambelle said. "When you put it that way… it sounds like rather a difficult challenge."

"Nonsense," Severyne said. "Once Voyou tracks down this human compass of yours, and does a little research, I'm sure I can come up with the right lie to elicit the desired outcome."

Severyne's comms buzzed with Archambelle's priority call, and Severyne shook off her memories and answered. "Well? Have you completed your preliminary examination of the girl?"

"I have." Archambelle's voice was dull. "There's nothing in her blood. Nothing in her tissue. I examined her hairs under an electron microscope. I looked at every inch of her body, in case her freckles and moles formed some kind of star chart. I examined her fingernail clippings and the underside of her tongue and every other part of her, inside and out. I found no code. No sign. No ciphers, no secrets, no coordinates. Nothing at all."

"That's not good," Severyne said. "Did you ask her about the yearning?"

"What?" Archambelle said. "What yearning?"

Severyne sighed. "You didn't read the dossier I compiled on her, did you?"

"Why would I? I was interested in *her genetics*, not the details of her life or the psychological profile you used to concoct your silly secret space princess story!"

"If you'd read the file, then you'd know about our princess's yearning, so I suggest you take a look, doctor." Severyne shut down the comms and sat smiling in the dark. She knew she should focus on the success of the mission, especially since Archambelle's very powerful friends back home had called to make it *Severyne's* mission too... but seeing Archambelle frustrated was still something to savor. "Speaking of the secret space princess," she said to herself, and switched on the hidden cameras in Bianca's room.

CHAPTER 15

Bianca repeated the Letnev words Ayla had just spoken. She couldn't imagine why she'd ever *need* to say "These mushrooms are too pungent," but the phrase was now lodged in her mind, along with hundreds of others. She'd never tried to learn a foreign language before – everyone she'd ever met spoke *hers*, though people from the most distant valleys rounded their vowels in a peculiar way – and, it turned out, she had a knack for it. At least, she assumed so, judging by the fact that she was already doing what Ayla called "third-year lessons" just a few days into her studies. Maybe the program was intended for small children? The machine didn't show any surprise at her progress, but then, surprise was probably beyond the scope of Ayla's programming. Bianca was also, simultaneously, learning the trading tongue used by most of the species who used spoken language at all when they had to deal with one another; that language was far simpler, with logical rules and a more limited vocabulary, and she'd basically mastered it already.

Bianca had been back to the doctor three times, and had every fluid she could produce drawn out of her (including some she'd never even heard of – what was a lymph, anyway, and who knew she had fluid in her *spine*? That one had pinched a little). She'd been prodded, poked, scraped, scanned, exposed to various wavelengths of light, and endured having every inch of her body examined through a hand-held magnifying glass, wielded by Doctor Archambelle personally. "What are you doing that for?" Bianca had asked.

"Looking for unusual moles," the doctor said. "You've been on a planet, under a sun, and people of Letnev heritage are vulnerable to skin cancer in such conditions. Your health seems perfect, however." The doctor didn't sound very happy about the good news, but then, the Letnev, as a rule, were not a joyful people. They had so many wondrous things – high technology, the freedom of the stars, citizenship in one of the great societies of the galaxy – but as a group they seemed less cheerful than the humblest farmer on Darit.

Ayla said, "You have progressed to the year four curriculum. At current rates of language acquisition, you will achieve full fluency in Baronic Letnev in two days. Would you like to begin the next lesson?"

"No, not right now." Bianca flung herself down on the bunk and looked up at the ceiling. She was *bored*. She was sick of studying languages, the Letnev "entertainment" videos and texts available didn't merit the name (it was all patriotism and shooting, with very little kissing and cleverness), and she'd already written two letters to her parents and three to old Torvald, which Ayla assured her were being transmitted. At this point, she'd even welcome another round of medical tests, just to get out of her cabin.

She was free to walk around the ship, but guards trailed her everywhere, because "elites must be protected," which made her feel awkward, and the ship was pretty dull anyway. She'd been to the engineering deck and the bridge and the navigation room and all of them sparked a million questions, but no one would *teach* her anything, except the hydroponic gardener, who'd been happy to talk to her for an hour or so yesterday about farming techniques on a spaceship versus a planet. Bianca had made one or two obvious-seeming suggestions for improving crop yields and the gardener had acted genuinely stunned by her ideas, though she supposed he was just being nice and humoring her; if it was obvious to *her*, it must be obvious to everyone, right?

Funny how she'd never had any ideas about farming back home, but maybe the change of scenery had inspired her mind to look at things from a different angle.

She'd also discovered a knack for computers. With a little digging around, she discovered there *was* surveillance in her room, though it was intermittent and usually brief – spot checks rather than constant vigilance. Maybe the Letnev spied on *everyone* that way. Even so, she managed to create a loop of her napping under the covers that she could run while she did things she doubted the captain would approve of. She'd had a lot of fun exploring the ship's various databases, learning all sorts of fascinating technical details about spacecraft, though there were restricted areas where the security defeated her efforts to explore... at least so far.

The officer files in particular were heavily encrypted, and her attempts to satisfy her curiosity about Voyou, Archambelle, and the captain were stymied at every turn. She was getting better and better at understanding the architecture of the Letnev systems, though, so in time–

Someone knocked at her door, and Bianca sat up and said, "Come in!"

Doctor Archambelle entered, wearing the strained expression that passed for a smile with her. "Greetings. May I sit?" Bianca gestured grandly to the fold-down seat, and Archambelle perched on its edge.

"Is everything all right?" Bianca said. "Did the tests show something wrong?"

"No, nothing we didn't expect," she said. "Your health is excellent. But I was perusing your file recently, and read something I wished to ask you about."

"You have a file on me?"

"Yes, of course. When we began to suspect your true identity, Undercommandant Voyou made certain inquiries on Darit. While many people were understandably reluctant to talk to a member of the Letnev military, he managed to glean some information about you through diligent efforts."

Bianca felt a chill. "Did he threaten people?"

"I believe his chief motivational tool was bribery, actually. Don't worry, we didn't learn anything embarrassing or salacious. Several people he interviewed did mention your, ah – 'yearning'?"

Bianca couldn't help it: she blushed to her roots. She'd stopped talking about her obsession with the sky when she got older, of course, but as a child she hadn't realized her fixation was strange, or that other people *didn't* feel the way she did. In a small community, hungry for any gossip, people remembered, and they talked. "Yearning. It sounds like something from a love story when you put it that way."

Archambelle looked at her, alert and attentive. "Could you describe the experience to me?"

Bianca looked down at her hands, twisting the edge of her blanket. "Oh, it's just, ever since I was little, I sometimes find myself looking at the sky. Day or night, it doesn't matter, and my eye is drawn to different parts of the sky at different times. I feel this... well, 'yearning' is a good enough way to put it. Like I was supposed to *go* to the place where I was looking. Like I belonged there. My parents said I just had wanderlust, itchy feet, things like that. But when I got old enough, I realized I *wasn't* looking at different parts of the sky. I was looking at one particular spot in the sky – it just moved around throughout the year. It was easiest to point out on summer nights, because there's a triangle of three stars, not especially bright or useful for navigation, and as far as I know we don't even have special names for them. When I see those stars, I just feel this need to go there." Some nights she would stand and stare so intently that she lost track of time, only blinking herself back to true consciousness when dawn arrived. She wasn't even looking at the stars, exactly, but at the center of the triangle they formed, where there was nothing to see at all... but that sounded too ridiculous to admit. "Do you think that yearning means something?"

"We'll do a neurological workup," Archambelle said.

"Sometimes compulsions to go to a particular place are caused by parasites."

"*Parasites?*" Bianca was aghast.

She nodded enthusiastically. "On Darit there is a parasite that lives inside small insects. It gives those insects an overpowering desire to climb *up*, and so the insects trundle up a blade of grass, to the very tip." She made a little walking motion with her fingers. "Of course, once they're on the end of a blade of grass, your caprids come along to munch the grass, and eat the insect along the way. That suits the parasite fine, because it needs to continue its life cycle in the belly of a caprid. The parasite lays its eggs inside the animal, and when the caprid defecates, those eggs are evacuated as well. Insects crawl through the fecal matter, and in so doing, they pick up the parasites, which infect the insects, and compel them to climb, and so the cycle continues."

Bianca made a gagging face. "You think I'm drawn to those stars because there's some kind of parasite inside me? What kind of parasite needs to complete its life cycle in a distant star system?"

"Do you have a better theory?" Archambelle snapped. Bianca narrowed her eyes, and the doctor winced. "Apologies, Lady Maladroit."

"It's Malladoc," Bianca said frostily.

Archambelle blinked. "Isn't that what I said? We'll do a few more tests, just to rule out anything dangerous, and if we do find a parasite, we'll deal with it. You're in good hands." The doctor hurried out, and Bianca flopped down on her bunk again.

Then she stared at a spot on the bulkhead, beyond which,

she knew – she just *knew* – those three stars shone. They were getting closer. She knew that, too.

"There you have it," Severyne said. "Find out where those stars are and set a course for them. I'm sure you'll find your wormhole gate there."

"I will investigate the issue," the doctor said. "Perhaps this yearning of hers is relevant, though more likely it's a meaningless epiphenomenon. Even if she is being guided to those stars, there's nothing to say they're our actual destination – they may be merely signposts or markers."

Severyne shrugged. "At least now you're *fully* informed." She chuckled. "I did like the bit about the parasite."

Archambelle grinned back, and for a moment Severyne very nearly liked her. Then the doctor remembered herself and scowled. "I did see something new in the girl's medical records."

"Oh? What's that?"

"As I said, there was no cipher in her genome that we could detect. One part of her genetic code is particularly rife with incomprehensible data, though, and while perusing her latest scans, the sequencing looked *wrong* to me. Still baffling, but in a different way than I remembered. I assumed I was simply mistaken, but that's rarely the case, so I compared her newest genetic sample to the first one we collected." Archambelle clenched her fists. "The code was *different.*"

"Your latest sample was corrupted, then?"

"No! I double-checked, and triple-checked, I *octuple*-checked, and the sample was fine. The girl's genetic code is actually changing."

"By the endless dark, what does that even mean?"

"I have no idea what it means," Archambelle said. "But it makes me think, perhaps the secret hidden in her genes is not a static message, but something dynamic. Maybe it's a timer, or a counter. Or the secret could be hidden in the nature of the *change* – a message being revealed only gradually."

"I see. Does this insight bring you any closer to deciphering that message?"

Archambelle opened her mouth, closed it, opened it again, then sighed. "No. I hate to admit no, but I think we need to contact an outside consultant."

"Outside, doctor? As in, not Letnev? But we are the best, the brightest, the greatest, without equal–"

"All true," Archambelle said. "But there are certain individuals outside the Barony with highly specific skill sets that could prove useful."

"Who are we consulting, then?"

"His name is Brother Errin."

"Ah. One of the Yin Brotherhood, I assume?"

Archambelle nodded.

"Why do they call themselves 'Brother This' and 'Brother That'?" Severyne complained. "They're all male anyway, and I never heard of one who claimed a gender other than 'man', I assume because of their odd religion. You'd think the 'Brother' bit could just be taken as read."

"Every culture has its oddities," the doctor said. "Except for the Letnev, of course. Brother Errin is something of an outcast among his people – a brother exiled from the brotherhood, as it were. You are aware of the Yin's deep preoccupation with genetic matters, I assume?"

Severyne nodded. The Yin Brotherhood were all clones of the founder of their order, a human named Darien Van Hauge. Cloning was frowned upon even now, and in that scientist's time, under the Lazax empire, it had been outright illegal. That hadn't stopped his research, and he became a master of the forbidden craft. When his family died, Van Hauge went mad with grief and made a child from his own seed and one of his dead wife's eggs, and then proceeded to clone that egg. The cloning process had two flaws, though: one caused a genetic predisposition to Greyfire, a disease that disfigured the flesh before killing the victim, and the other resulted in a total inability to create female clones. Over the centuries, the clones in what became the Brotherhood of Yin had continued tinkering with their own genome, but so far they'd failed to solve *either* problem, though they'd managed to make the Greyfire less lethal, if no less disfiguring. These days the Brothers most grotesquely altered by the disease were considered "blessed," and formed the ruling councils of their people, while the "untouched" went out to deal with the other races of the galaxy, since their presence was considered *slightly* less off-putting.

Severyne didn't have any issues with the disfigured – that sort of thing couldn't be helped, and a physical infirmity reflected nothing meaningful about the affected individual. Ideals of "beauty" or "normality" were culture-bound and subjective anyway. Severyne found zealotry off-putting, however, and every time she'd met a member of the Brotherhood they'd gone on about the wonders of their founder and the majesty of the egg they called "Yin" and considered the embodiment of some kind of "feminine principle," and *that* was tiresome and repulsive.

"This Errin knows more about genetics than you do?" Severyne asked.

"Oh, yes. Does it surprise you to hear me admit that? There are only half a dozen people in the galaxy who can rival my expertise in these matters. Errin happens to be one of them, and he's the one who's easiest to reach. His quest to remove the flaws in the Brotherhood's cloning process led him to study ancient accounts of the gene-sorcery of the Mahact." She leaned forward, clearly fascinated by her own knowledge. "One story says the Lazax forbade cloning under their rule *because* the Mahact made such extensive use of the technology. Others say that propensity for clones led to the downfall of the Mahact. They were so jealous and selfish they didn't like to have children, but instead made cloned thralls of themselves. Some legends say the Mahact could even move their minds into the bodies of their clones, though that strikes me as an *actual* fairy tale. Errin's studies strayed into areas the Brotherhood found unsavory, his experiments were denounced, and he was cast out... which didn't stop him from doing his research. He continued his studies, just more unfettered than before. He still wants to help his people, whether they want that help or not."

"That's zealots for you," Severyne said.

"Errin's work may give him a special insight into the nature of the girl's changing genetic code. Perhaps he can decipher what I cannot."

"Fine. Give me the details, and I'll have Richeline set a

course for his doubtless horrifying bio-lab. You can meet with him by yourself, though. The last time I encountered one of the Brotherhood, he wouldn't stop talking about how 'ineluctably feminine' I was, and I don't need any more of *that*."

CHAPTER 16

The direction of Bianca's yearning changed, suddenly and dramatically, which meant the ship was charting a new course. She wondered where they were going, and why they were going somewhere other than wherever they'd been going *before*, but her guards were uncommunicative, Archambelle wasn't answering her messages, and Ayla had no insight, of course.

Bianca passed the morning doing years five and six of the Letnev language study. Apparently, she'd attained fluency. Languages weren't that hard, really. It was all just sounds paired with meanings. Now she was learning to read the Letnev language, which was even simpler, despite the unfamiliar alphabet, since there were far fewer characters than phonemes. The sound each character represented changed according to the context of the characters around it, that was all, just like the language she'd grown up speaking. Maybe next time she'd learn the written and spoken versions of a language (or two) at the same time, just to give herself a *bit* of a challenge–

Ayla spoke up, unprompted: "I have received permission to share the star charts you inquired about," she said.

That made Bianca sit up. She'd asked for the charts ages ago, and been refused, because "navigational data is classified," which was baffling – how could a simple map of the sky be a secret, when anyone could look up and see it? She'd tried and failed to hack into the navigation system herself, though she thought in another day or two she'd get in – now it wasn't necessary.

Why had the Letnev changed their minds? She wondered if her odd conversation with Archambelle about her "yearning" had something to do with the sudden reversal of policy. "Show me."

One wall became a screen, depicting a night sky that was at first just a profusion of stars but that she soon recognized as the view from her own farm. "Those stars." She pointed to the trio of lights that always drew her attention when she looked up – and to the space between them, where she so desperately wanted to go. "What are those?"

The screen zoomed in closer, though they just remained points of light. "Those stars are known as Burgis-A, Burgis-B, and Eekhout."

"What's out there?"

"Nothing of note," Ayla said. "The Burgis star systems include no habitable planets, and the gas giants there were deemed poor candidates for resource extraction. Eekhout has never been formally surveyed, but imaging indicates no planets of any kind in its orbit, only asteroids."

"What about right *there*?" She pressed her finger into the center of the triangle. "What's in that empty space?"

"Only more empty space, Lady Malladoc."

Bianca shook her head. "There has to be something!"

"There are no objects noted in my database, though there are presumably uncharted areas."

"That's not very helpful, Ayla."

"I always try to be helpful, my lady."

"Try harder." Bianca slumped on the bunk, frustrated. For all her yearning, she still didn't know what she was yearning *for*, and it troubled her that the ship was no longer moving in the direction of those stars.

She was tired of all this "Lady Malladoc" business too – she'd gone from "wouldn't it be wonderful if it were true" to accepting the whole thing was total nonsense. The Barony doctor had done so many medical tests on her it was clear they were trying to figure something out, not just assess her health, but what? She hadn't left her family, her planet, and everything she knew just to be kept in the dark and fed shit, like one of the Letnev's beloved mushrooms. If they needed her for something, they could at least tell her *what*, if they expected her cooperation.

"Message Doctor Archambelle, Ayla. Tell her I want to know what all these tests are really for. Tell her, if she isn't honest with me, I won't help her anymore."

"Message sent, my lady."

"Let's see what she has to say to *that*," Bianca said.

"The girl has grown suspicious," Archambelle said. "She no longer believes your space-princess story."

Severyne yawned. She didn't require much sleep, but she needed some, and the doctor had interrupted her scheduled downtime with an urgent request for a meeting. "So? The story was only meant to entice her on board and into our control anyway."

"You don't understand. She has threatened to stop cooperating. If I just needed access to her blood and tissue her cooperation would be irrelevant, but we don't know what reaching Ixth will require from her. If she refuses to help us, she could make our mission difficult or impossible. She is demanding answers, captain."

Severyne yawned again, more widely. "Then give her answers."

"You want me to tell her the *truth*? That her genetic code contains a treasure map hidden by ancient alien gene-sorcerers?"

The captain rolled her eyes. "I didn't say give her *correct* answers. Or complete ones. She's seen through our lie. Admit to that, and tell her a *new* lie, and she'll believe that's the truth, because of course we wouldn't try to deceive her twice. The names Ixth and Mahact won't mean anything to her, but you can tell her... oh, tell her that Darit was never really Letnev territory at all. Hide the lie inside as much truth as possible. Tell her... Darit was a Federation of Sol territory, and the humans hid the location of some great treasure cache in her genetic code. Say we need her to lead us there and breathe on a biometric lock or something, and that we'll split the treasure with her. Do I have to think of everything?"

"That might work," Archambelle said. "I don't think the girl considers me trustworthy, though."

"Send Voyou. He's the closest thing she has to a friend

here, and he's excellent at lying to humans. He did an admirable job of that on Darit."

"So there you have it." Voyou spread his hands. "I know my superiors misled you, Bianca. That was wrong, and now the captain *knows* it was wrong. They were afraid you'd be unwilling to travel with us if you knew the truth, and concocted a story to gain your trust. They tricked me too. I can only offer my sincere apologies on their behalf, and convey their promise to be truthful with you in the future. While you aren't, technically, a princess of the Letnev, once you take possession of your share of the Federation treasure we hope to recover you might as *well* be – you will possess wealth beyond imagining."

"I'm going to need something in writing." Bianca crossed her arms and glared. "The Letnev are great believers in law and rules and order, aren't they? That's what my language-and-culture bot tells me. So, I'll require a contract, specifying the terms of this split, and the rights and responsibilities of *both* parties." She wanted to say all that in Voyou's native language – Letnev was almost poetic when it came to the subject of binding agreements – but she'd decided to keep her degree of fluency a secret, just in case. Sometimes the Letnev spoke in their own tongue within her hearing, and they might be more discreet if they knew she understood them.

"I'll take your request to the captain," Voyou said.

He rose and departed, and Bianca made her way to the gym. She'd started working out recently, using the weights and resistance machines, and she could feel herself getting stronger and more flexible. This time, in her frustration, annoyance, and anger, she piled more and more weight on the bar as she did deadlifts. She grunted, lowering the bar, and noticed a gargantuan Letnev staring at her. "How someone so small lift thing so big?" he sputtered in the trading tongue, accent heavy and diction broken.

She grinned. "I grew up on a farm. When one of the caprids had a kid, I lifted the baby over my head. I kept lifting that kid over my head every day and when it was full grown I could still lift it, as easily as I had that first day." That was a lie, of course, but it was a story she'd heard about a muscle-bound boy she'd seen at one of the festivals, and she'd always found it delightful in its unlikeliness.

"I must find one of this kid," the bodybuilder said.

Bianca returned to her room so she could shower in private – the Letnev tended to sneak glances at her when she used the communal showers in the gym, which was probably because she was *human*, a completely different *species* than them, and not because they were in awe of her royal nature. Although to be fair, she didn't know what the crew had been told about her – Voyou claimed he'd been deceived about her nature too. They probably thought she *was* some kind of elite. It was much easier to tell hundreds of people the same story than to expect all of the people on board to keep a secret, after all. Or perhaps the captain hadn't told them anything at all. The Letnev weren't big on sharing information, she'd come to learn. They were an elitist military hierarchy with a strong streak of bureaucracy. She smiled. Those were all terms that would have been mostly meaningless to her a month ago, since none of them had much bearing on her life on Darit.

It was amazing the things you picked up in the course of learning a new language, since you couldn't achieve true fluency without understanding the cultural context of the tongue. For instance, the Letnev *liked* darkness, and they found tunnels and caverns comforting, and those qualities were reflected in their idioms – instead of "over the horizon" they said "beyond the chasm," and instead of "the sky's the limit" they said "we venture into the endless dark," and other things like that – "bright stars" was a mild curse. It was odd how she'd never thought about the nature of language this way before. Like so many things lately, the insights just came naturally the moment she gave a subject any thought at all.

When she got to her cabin, Voyou was waiting outside with a woman Bianca hadn't met before. "This is First Officer Richeline," Voyou said. "She is the captain's right hand, and she came to bring the contract personally."

"Are those *paper*?" Bianca had seen paper books at the Halemeeting hall, but they weren't common. Almost everything was digital, even on Darit.

"They will be scanned and entered into the central database, of course," Richeline said. "But we begin with paper. We are traditionalists in the Barony. Shall we go over the terms?"

Bianca showed them into her cabin, and they folded down her desk and clustered around it. The documents were printed on thick, heavy paper, festooned with seals and sigils. The text was in her own language, alongside the Letnev tongue, and Voyou assured her the words were as identical as possible. Bianca could read Letnev well enough by now to spot-check and confirm that for herself, fortunately. "What's this about a seventeen percent split?" Bianca said. "That seems impossibly low."

"I am authorized to go up to twenty-one percent."

"How about twenty-one percent for *you*," Bianca said.

Voyou and Richeline conferred furiously in Letnev, and Bianca listened in; they were arguing about what the captain would accept, and what the *Baron* would accept, and finally Richeline said, "Twenty-five percent, and you get to keep all the clothes and jewelry you have received. Understand, twenty-five percent of the treasure we expect to acquire will be enough for you to buy your own *system*."

"What if the vault is empty, though?" Bianca said. "We're going to need to set a minimum floor for my compensation, regardless of the value of monies and goods recovered – I can't possibly do all this purely on spec."

Another furious conference, this time with expressions of shock from Richeline that a simple farm girl was so adept at negotiating, and speculation that she must have been in charge of haggling for animal feed or something back home. In truth, Bianca had never had much to do with the business side of things, but it seemed she had a knack. She was discovering all kinds of knacks lately. Anyway, even if the deal had struck her as perfect, she would have argued several points. The Letnev didn't respect anyone who didn't bargain hard and negotiate for every possible advantage. Their words for "contract negotiations" and "total war" were close cognates.

They agreed on a minimum level of compensation, and set deadlines for when she'd be released from the contract if they failed to find this treasure (she didn't want to be stuck roaming the galaxy on the *Grim Countenance* for years if the search proved fruitless). She even negotiated a better deal for Darit in terms of the colony world's tax burden, though it meant giving up some things she could have gotten for herself.

In one of their huddled conferences Richeline insulted her rather colorfully, but Bianca didn't let so much as a hint of comprehension slip. She filed away the phrases for later, though. Ayla's teachings had been remarkably short on profanity. Fortunately, the meaning was clear enough in context.

After three hours, they finally had a contract they could all agree upon, and they signed with great flourishes and then scanned the contracts and uploaded them.

Richeline's collar was undone and her hairline was sweaty. She gave Bianca a stiff bow. "That was as satisfying a duel as I have ever fought, Miss Xing. And I'd say we *both* drew a little blood."

Bianca almost said, "A battle without blood is like a day in the sunshine," but that was a Letnev idiom, so instead she said, "I think you got the best of me, but you've been doing this a lot longer."

"Your performance was more than creditable," she said. "Doctor Archambelle will be in touch about your next round of tests, and yes, she will discuss the results with you, as the contract requires." Another bow and she left, Voyou following at her heels.

Bianca flung herself down on the bed and smiled. She'd finally taken control of her destiny, and it felt good.

•••

"She believed you?" Severyne said.

Richeline nodded. "She thinks the contract is legitimate, yes."

"As a resident of a Barony colony world, she is entitled to protection under our laws. It would be a valid contract… if I sealed and witnessed it, of course." Severyne tore the sheaf of papers in two and tossed them into the matter recycler.

"It was clever of you to make sure that detail was omitted from her lessons on Barony contract law, captain," Richeline said.

"I don't need you to tell me how clever I am, Richeline."

"She's even more clever than you realize," Voyou said. "The captain had me alter the same pertinent information in the ship's legal database, even though Bianca doesn't have access to those files, just in case. We've made a few other redactions elsewhere in the system, and planted some false information here and there, too, including in the personnel files."

"Why would you bother to do all that?" Richeline said.

Severyne didn't have to explain herself, but sometimes it was useful to let your subordinates know you'd already dealt with problems they hadn't even considered yet. "The girl spends too much time in her room, using her tutoring program. Remedial schoolwork isn't that interesting. I suspect she's been using her terminal for other things, and poking her nose into places it doesn't belong."

"You think she's hacking our systems?" Richeline said. "Without leaving a trace? How? She has no training. The computers on her planet are probably made of dung and corn cobs."

"Nevertheless. Caution costs nothing. The girl has shown surprising capabilities, time and again. I'd rather not be surprised further. Speaking of... what was your assessment of her language skills, Richeline?"

The woman made a sour face. "We negotiated as if the contract were real, as instructed, even when speaking in our own language, but she showed no interest or attentiveness when we spoke Letnev. I insulted her, also as instructed, and she showed no reaction. I'm sure she has a few words of Letnev, but no one can become fluent in the great tongue so quickly, no matter what her system says. She's probably using a dictionary program to cheat on the tests she takes, or else the system is just poorly calibrated."

"Those are possibilities. She did negotiate well, though, for a human." Severyne had briefly regretted not taking part in the ruse – it would have been enjoyable to spar with the girl. Severyne was withholding direct contact with Bianca, though, in case she *really* needed to step in to fix things at some point. It was better if the captain remained a figure of shadow and menace in the girl's mind. That left more possibilities open.

"Oh, she did all right," Richeline said. "I'm sure her bargaining skills come from all those years trying to get a better price for turnips. You know what people in gravity wells are like."

"I suppose. Be discreet around her anyway, in case she understands more than you think. As I said–"

"Caution costs nothing." Richeline didn't roll her eyes, but Severyne could tell she *wanted* to.

"Remember that. Dismissed."

Once she was alone again, Severyne called up what scant information the Letnev database had about the world of Ixth. She was beginning to think they might actually see the place, and wanted to be prepared if they did. Archambelle seemed to think there would be miraculous technology and priceless artifacts lying around unattended, just waiting to be picked up by anyone who happened by, but in Severyne's experience nothing worthwhile happened *that* easily. Everything worth getting came at a cost; the key was to make sure someone *else* paid it. "I nominate Bianca Xing," she muttered.

CHAPTER 17

Bianca spent the journey to the space station mostly alone in her room, studying with Ayla, trying to find out more about the galaxy in general, and hitting a lot of "data redacted" and "that information is outside the scope of my programming" responses. The history of the Barony was officially an unbroken string of victories, and that seemed unlikely for a culture that was at least thousands of years old. Even her hacking skills didn't help – there were odd gaps wherever she looked. The Baron didn't want his own people learning the truth about their heritage either, it seemed.

She did eventually finesse the systems enough to break into the encrypted personnel and medical files, though there wasn't much of interest there – not the juicy secrets Bianca had hoped for. Archambelle's parents were doctors from the Letnev homeworld, and her life was a boring series of schools and residencies and fellowships. Voyou's first name was Orist, he'd been born on a remote outpost moon, and he was allergic to some medication Bianca had never heard. Riveting stuff.

The captain's name was Rania Jennis Dampierre. Her file was heavily redacted, full of sections blacked out and marked "classified" and "state secret," which suggested she was potentially interesting, but Bianca couldn't find out exactly how. At least now Bianca knew what the mystery woman looked like, since there was a photo in the file: the captain was at least as old as Torvald, white-haired, stone-faced, and she had a cybernetic left eye with a red pupil. Bianca didn't think she'd seen that face around, but maybe the captain wore one of those full-face masks when she secretly mingled with the crew.

There were occasional other distractions. Voyou dropped by more often than he used to, and played one of the Barony's favorite games with her – spiralstone, a strategic and tactical combat simulator traditionally played with stones on a circular board marked out with spirals, but played more often these days via holographic interface. When they first started playing Voyou warned her not to get discouraged if she lost a lot, because the game took a lifetime to master, and he was ranked in the top five thousand players in the Barony.

He was so easy to beat that Bianca soon started losing intentionally, in different ways, without him realizing she was failing on purpose, because that was more challenging than playing in a more straightforward way. She'd played some similar games back home with old Torvald, and had only beaten *him* about half the time, so she knew she wasn't some sort of unrivaled gaming savant. Maybe he was ranked in some kind of amateur league, or just bending the truth to impress her. Did he *like* her? He'd never done anything creepy or even flirtatious, so maybe not.

Occasionally Voyou accompanied her to the mess hall, a welcome change from eating alone in her room. She was still the subject of glances from the rest of the crew, but not as many as before. They'd grown more accustomed to the aristocrat – or alien – in their midst.

One day, an ensign bumped up against their table by accident and knocked Voyou's teacup off the edge. At the moment of impact Bianca's perception of time... changed. As the cup tumbled toward the floor, spilling its mushroom tea, everything seemed to slow down, the cup drifting down as slowly as a feather. Bianca reached out and effortlessly plucked the cup from the air, and even scooped up the tea in midair before it could splatter on the floor. Voyou stared at her, and some of the other officers actually applauded. "Fast reflexes, my lady."

Bianca shrugged, trying for nonchalance. Later, in her room she experimented, trying to trigger that bizarre perceptual shift by knocking small objects off her desk. She couldn't make the time dilation happen again, and wondered if it was a protective reflex, an unconscious and reactive ability, like flinching away from a blow. If it happened again, she'd try to analyze the experience more closely, because if she *could* control her perception of time, it would be all sorts of useful.

Her yearning worsened as their journey continued to take her away from those three stars, but Voyou assured her the scientist they were on their way to visit would give them the insight they needed to complete their journey. When Voyou arrived at her door that day, she booted up the game, but he shook his head. "Not this time. We're approaching Brother

Errin's station. We should be there in an hour or so, if you'd like to get dressed. Are you excited to visit your first space station?"

Bianca shrugged. "I assume it's going to be a lot like being on a spaceship, only without the engines making the deck vibrate."

He chuckled. "This is a military vessel, and short on amenities. I think you'll find the Tree of Grace rather more pleasant."

"The station is called the Tree of Grace? Why?"

"Get dressed and you can see for yourself."

Bianca put on her favorite red smartcloth dress and shoes and went out to the corridor, following Voyou down in a lift to an observation deck she'd never visited before. The room was circular, with windows on all sides. Even the floor was translucent, and she felt like she was floating in the void.

Something else floated in the void, beyond the windows, and it *did* look like a tree – a silver one, uprooted and suspended in the air. The station had a central trunk with symmetrical arrays of modules at the top and bottom, like branches above and roots below.

"Brother Errin is one of the galaxy's leading experts on biological matters," Voyou explained. "He became wealthy by treating genetic disorders in prominent members of various species. They say he helped a major Naalu leader overcome her infertility problems, and she gifted him with this crystal space station, retrofitted inside to suit human habitation."

Bianca glanced away from the vista to look at Voyou. "Brother Errin is human?"

"He's cloned from human biological material, anyway. The Yin Brotherhood consider themselves distinct as a species, though, and I imagine their biology has diverged a lot from that of baseline humans by now."

Bianca pressed her hand to the glass and gazed out at the station. "It really is beautiful."

"The Tree of Grace is hopelessly impractical and needlessly ornamental by Letnev standards, but I've spent enough time in foreign service to know that our aesthetics aren't universal. I do think it looks like it would shatter if you tapped it with a small hammer, but the Naalu build whole cities out of crystal, so I'm sure it's stronger than it looks. We should head for the shuttle."

Voyou, Richeline, and Archambelle accompanied Bianca, along with three guards in their faceless helmets. The shuttle was smaller than the one that had taken her from Darit up to the *Grim Countenance*, and Voyou explained that this one was meant strictly for ship-to-ship (or -station) transfers, and wasn't meant to land in atmosphere. One of the guards sat in the front, but apparently there was no real piloting to be done – the shuttle computer talked to the station computer, and the guidance and docking happened automatically.

They let Bianca sit in the co-pilot seat, so she had a good view as the crystal branches grew larger. Their shuttle approached one of the uppermost modules, shimmering like it was made of diamonds, and docked. There were various clanks, hisses, thumps, and whirrs, but soon enough all the connections were secure and pressures equalized, and the shuttle door opened. Two of the guards went ahead, as if they expected an ambush, and then Richeline strode out. Archambelle stuck close to Bianca's side, and Voyou brought up the rear.

The inside of the station wasn't all diamond sparkle, but it was pleasant: plush carpets on the floors, walls a soothing shade of greyish blue, corridors dotted with little niches that held flowering plants or climbing vines. The lighting was indirect but full-spectrum, a welcome relief after the dim redness of the Letnev ship. Voyou squinted, and Archambelle slipped on a pair of dark glasses.

A towering figure stepped into the corridor from a side room. She had a catlike face and long sand-colored hair in complex braids, and wore a robe intricately embellished with ornamental knotwork. "Greetings," she purred. "I am Kyrria, Brother Errin's representative."

"Why does he need a representative?" Richeline said. "We came to see the scientist, not the secretary."

Kyrria smiled, or at least, Bianca supposed it was a smile; she showed off a terrifying array of teeth, anyway, with long curving canines.

"She's a Hacan, right?" Bianca whispered to Voyou. Ayla had provided Bianca with very little information about the other inhabitants of the galaxy, but she'd been able to access a children's book called *Rivals to the Barony* that included brief descriptions of other species, including the Hacan, though the alien in the picture had been holding a curved sword and a severed head and had blood smeared all around her mouth.

"That's right," Voyou murmured. "If you shake hands with one, count your fingers afterward."

Bianca suppressed a gasp. "They eat *fingers*?"

"What? No. Or, I suppose they might – who knows what they eat? I just mean, they're famous negotiators and traders."

"Oh. I thought they went around beheading people all the time."

"Not in my experience," Voyou said. "Though it can't hurt to be watchful."

Bianca wondered what else in the children's book was inaccurate or slanted. Perhaps the Hylar weren't really building doomsday weapons on the bottom of the sea, and the Gashlai didn't destroy planets because they liked how pretty the explosions were, and the N'orr weren't desperate to lay their eggs in Letnev abdomens. The book had been rather alarming for a work aimed at children, but Bianca supposed many of them had a taste for the bloody and the macabre. She certainly would have devoured a book like that if she'd found it at the Halemeeting Hall.

Kyrria was explaining herself. "So you see, Brother Errin has little patience or interest in matters of the world, preferring to dwell wholly in the realms of science… but, alas, tissue vats and chemical printers and genomic scanners cost money, and I make sure he has all the resources necessary for his work. *That's* why I'm here. We're still waiting for your consultation, and we'll need it before you go any deeper into the Tree of Grace."

"You haven't paid them yet?" Archambelle glared at Richeline, who winced.

"I submitted all the paperwork, and the captain expedited things, but you know how the procurement office can be. Let me see what the holdup is." She stepped off into a niche beside a plant and began jabbing furiously at a hand terminal.

Bianca took a step forward and cleared her throat. "Hello," she said to Kyrria. "Why is this place called the Tree of Grace? The tree part I can see, but…"

The Hacan looked down at her from a great height, then crouched so their eyes were at the same level. "Brother Errin is a member of the Yin Brotherhood. They come from the Lael system, and Errin grew up there, in the Lucas monastery. The monastery stands on a place called the Hills of Grace, and though Brother Errin has parted ways with his fellows, he still considers himself part of their sacred order. He says if he cannot live on the Hills of Grace, he will carry the spirit of the place with him, and so he named this station in their honor."

"That's lovely," Bianca said. "Thank you for explaining."

"You have such nice manners," Kyrria said. "How did someone so polite end up in the company of the Letnev?"

"They kidnapped me under false pretenses," Bianca said. Voyou coughed so loud it sounded like he was choking.

"That sounds like the Barony," Kyrria said amiably. "I'm not in a position to rescue you, though I can reach out to the human authorities if you'd like. It's possible they might intercede, especially if it annoys the Barony."

"That's all right," Bianca said. "We worked things out. We negotiated the terms of my cooperation."

"Your contract was signed by all parties?" Kyrria said.

"Oh, yes, of course."

"And properly wit–"

Richeline stepped between them, though there was hardly space to do so, and waved her terminal in Kyrria's face. "There, the transaction is complete, if we can *please* get on with the examination?"

The Hacan showed her teeth again, then checked her own terminal. Once she was satisfied, she bowed her head. "Right this way. Brother Errin is waiting in his lab."

Properly wit? Bianca thought. *What did she mean?* She must have stood with her brow furrowed for too long, because Voyou took her elbow and guided her along the corridor.

Brother Errin's lab was all gleaming metal surfaces and white tile, and the man himself looked just like plenty of other humans Bianca had met, though his head was entirely bald and his skin was an unhealthy, grayish sort of pale.

"The clients from Letnev are here," Kyrria said.

Errin was standing at a workbench, staring into a complex device mounted beneath an array of lenses. He looked up and blinked. His eyes were large and moist-looking, he sniffed constantly, and overall he reminded her of a sick caprid. Maybe not terminally ill, but you'd want to keep him away from the rest of the flock until he got better. "What? Who?"

Doctor Archambelle pushed herself forward. "Brother Errin. You remember me, I'm sure. Araminta Allencourt Archambelle?"

"Archie?" He squinted.

Bianca couldn't *actually* hear the doctor grind her teeth, but she certainly sensed it. "That is… what you sometimes call me on the forums, yes."

"Can't remember all those other names," he said. "Too many, too long. Come and look at this, it's remarkable, a specimen recovered from a bog, have you ever been to a bog? Horrible places, squishy, look." He grabbed the doctor by the arm and manhandled her over to the scope, practically pressing her face against a set of lenses. "See, I know what you're thinking, it's just *Ascaris lumbricoides*, but look closer and it's *not*, do you see the ring pattern there, it *can't* be, doctor – what you're looking at is a worm unknown to science!"

"That is fascinating, Brother Errin." Archambelle stepped away and straightened her jacket. "I brought the woman I told you about. The one with the, ah, genetic anomaly?"

Errin cocked his head, then slowly followed her pointing finger. "Strange. Strange, strange, strange. I reviewed your samples and they are, something, what's the word. Strange." He walked in a slow circle around Bianca, the guards and other Letnev moving aside to give him room. He reached out and touched Bianca's hair, poked her shoulder, and sniffed at her elbow, and she tolerated all of that, but when he grabbed her lower lip and pulled it down and looked into her mouth, she shouted "Hey!" and he jumped backward.

"Apologies!" His voice was much too loud. "So much time in the lab, I forget myself, yes, would you believe I used to work in the diplomatic corps, ha, me? Scientific liaison, I was, they brought me to talk to the scientists when we visited other nations, so much talking." He shook his head. "Wasn't for me. Wrong path. Had some shocks. Met the Creuss! The Ghosts, you know them?"

The children's primer hadn't mentioned anyone called the Creuss, and Bianca didn't believe in ghosts, so she shook her head. Errin didn't seem to notice. "The Creuss, that was hard, I kept it together, for a while, did my job, went to parties, smiled and nodded, but I had nightmares. Every time I went to a new place, I thought, will a Ghost be there, asking me things, 'Where is music?' and 'Would you vapor?' and 'Why electric meat?' I retired. I say I retired. I was not retiring. I made a fuss, I made a scene, I was taken away, then I *went* away, and here I am."

"I see," Bianca said. "That must have been very hard for you."

Errin gave a solemn, big-eyed nod. "Now, here, I do the work. I don't go anywhere anymore. The same place every day. New people, yes, sometimes, but the same place. My Tree is solid. My Tree won't come apart. It won't turn into a ghost under me." He clapped his hands together in front of her face. "You! An interesting anomaly, hmmm, yes. Let's get you scanned and see what's happening inside you. *You* don't stay the same, oh no, you don't dissolve, or haven't yet at least, but you certainly change." He hurried over to a console and started pressing buttons, and parts of the wall slid open, revealing person-sized glass cylinders, shelves of vials, and gleaming robot arms tipped with alarming attachments.

Bianca sidled over to Archambelle. "He's insane."

"Well, yes," Archambelle said. "But within very predictable parameters, which is functionally identical to being sane. He's good at his work, the best at his work, and that's all that matters. If there's a way to decipher the secrets inside you, he'll know them."

"Take off all your clothes!" Brother Errin shouted.

CHAPTER 18

"I'll just escort the rest of you outside," Kyrria said. Archambelle started to object – "We are *colleagues*, I'm sure Brother Errin wants me here to assist" – and the Hacan simply picked her up, as easily as Bianca would have lifted a teacup, and carried the doctor, stunned and silent, out of the room.

Voyou patted Bianca on the arm, rather awkwardly. "You'll be all right," Voyou said. "He's, ah… a professional."

"Just do as you're told, Xing." Richeline beckoned to the guards, who followed her and Voyou out of the lab.

Bianca disrobed. She was chilly at first, but the lab must have warmed up or something, because a moment later she was perfectly comfortable. At least her weeks undergoing Archambelle's tests had given her lots of practice being naked around a stranger… though Brother Errin was stranger than most.

He turned, looked at her, nodded, then returned to his console. "Archie believes in fairy tales, you know. Ancient aliens, former masters of the galaxy, experts in cloning and genetic manipulation. The legends say they were experts on *everything*, super-scientists with everyday conveniences that violated the laws of physics as we understand them, and cities that soared impossibly high and delved impossibly deep. Supposedly the Mahact could make almost anything. Archie thinks they made *you*." He looked at her again, and this time there was a shrewdness and clarity in his eyes she hadn't noticed before.

"Wait. Who are the Mahact?"

Errin clucked his tongue. "What did the Letnev tell you?"

Oh, no. "Which time?"

"All the times, please. I'm curious."

Bianca told him the first story, about her being the heir to a lost fortune, and the "truth," that she was the child of a human aristocrat with a treasure map hidden in her genetics. "But I guess that's not true either?"

Errin shook his head.

"Then, what am I?"

"Something new in the galaxy, I think," Errin said. "I thought Archie was losing her grip, and believe me, I *know* about losing your grip, but I've seen your test results and who could have made you *but* the Mahact?"

"I still don't know who they are," she said.

Errin nodded. "According to old stories, ones almost no one remembers and even fewer people believe, there was once a great empire ruled by a cruel and brilliant people called the Mahact…" Errin told her about the aliens and their purported genetic mastery, and how Archambelle's research led her to Darit, and how the Letnev hoped she would lead them to the treasure world of Ixth. "Archie thinks Ixth might have been the Mahact homeworld, or maybe just one of their holdings. If you could find it, that would be remarkable. The legends of my people say that on Ixth we'll finally find the secret to cleansing our genome, and even creating female clones."

Bianca took in everything he'd told her and finally said, "Why did the Letnev lie to me? Why not just tell me the truth about this Ixth?"

"Bianca. They need you to find Ixth. You don't need *them*. If you knew the truth, there would be no reason for you to travel with them. You could make your own way, and leave the Letnev behind. They brought you here because they hoped I could tell them your secrets so they wouldn't actually need *you* anymore, either. But don't worry. They're going to be disappointed, because I don't think I can give them what they need."

"But they're supposed to work *with* me. We have a contract!"

"Oh, do you? I'm sure that's all right then. I'm sure the Letnev would never try to deceive you."

Bianca slumped. "Should you be telling me all this?"

"I was, in fact, forbidden to tell you any of this, but the Tree of Grace is *my* domain, and I think it's only fair you know the truth of your nature. You are a miracle of sorts, Bianca. And you're being exploited."

She nodded slowly, then said, "You aren't as insane as you seemed to be earlier, are you?"

He lowered his head and sighed. "When I act mad, it's not an act. My mind expands and contracts. It comes and goes. But when the wind is right, I *can* tell a knife from a nightjar.

Sometimes I think, when the Creuss made that station come apart, they made part of *me* come apart, too…"

"Who are these Creuss you keep talking about?" Bianca said.

Brother Errin shook his head rapidly. "No, no, no, that's a tale for another telling. We're not talking about *those* bogeymen this time, we're talking about the Mahact. The Creuss don't care about flesh, they care about energy, but the Mahact, they were supposed to be *sculptors* of flesh, wizards with it, gods with it, even. And yes, they did, they did make you. I didn't say so to Archie, not straight out, because she's insufferable when she knows she's right, but looking at the data she collected, and the fragments of unknown provenance she's gathered over the years, it's clearly all connected. The mark of Mahact handiwork is all through you, their little signature touches, their embellishments, their elegance. Elegances? All of those."

"If you already studied my samples, why am I standing naked in your lab?"

"Because you are not a static problem, Bianca Xing, you are a dynamic one, and I wished to see how you *changed*. But yes, come, stand here." He beckoned and gestured and led her to the wall where the tiles had slid away, indicating a circular podium only a little shorter than Bianca. "I need you to get on the scanner, I have a stepstool somewhere, wait, it's just–"

Bianca rolled her eyes, bent her knees, and jumped up onto the platform from the floor. She straightened, turned around on the podium, and resisted the urge to do a curtsy or take a bow.

Brother Errin looked at her, then at the podium, then at her again. "That is... not a record. No. Not quite a record for highest vertical leap by an unaugmented human at this level of gravity. But it is *close* to a record, and the person who set the record was *much* taller and *much* more muscular and–"

"I'm in good shape," Bianca said. "It's nothing." But she was blushing. When she'd jumped up onto the platform, it hadn't *felt* like a big deal – she'd just instinctively known she could do it – but she certainly hadn't leapt that high back on Darit. *Nobody* had. She must have cleared, what, a hundred and twenty centimeters, straight up.

"The Mahact made you well," Errin said. "You are not an unaugmented human. Not really human at all. You're something new. Or something new wrapped around a core of something very old. Please stand as still as you can. Commencing scan."

Bianca froze herself in place and held her breath, but more than that, was her heart even beating? Wouldn't she die if it didn't beat? And... shouldn't it be harder to hold her breath? Doing so wasn't even a strain, not like when she'd competed with the other children to dive to the bottom of the pond to retrieve rocks – that had been hard, and she'd come up gasping. She felt no need to gasp now.

Am I changing? The thought had occurred to her before, several times, but always in the back of her mind, always quiet, always quickly dismissed. What Errin said about her being a *dynamic* problem, though... that made the thought louder. Maybe she really was getting stronger, faster, and smarter than she had been before. But how? And why?

Violet light shone from the walls, and she hoped it wasn't

radioactive or anything. "Lift your arms, please. Hmm. What an interesting vascular system."

"People are always telling me that," Bianca said.

"I wonder, if I made a clone of *you*, if the clone would retain your polymorphic qualities. I suspect there are failsafes in place…"

"You don't have my consent to make a clone of me." Bianca crossed her arms and glared down at him.

"Noted." He put on a pair of square-rimmed glasses and began drawing in the air, probably interacting with some kind of virtual display… or else the wind was blowing the wrong way again, and he was mad.

"What are polymorphic qualities?" she said. "What does that mean?"

"I am under strict instructions to discuss my findings only with Archie and the woman who scowls so much." His eyes were unreadable behind lenses full of flickering light. Before she could object, he continued. "I refused to sign anything to that effect, of course, so I can say whatever I like. You are the subject of the examination, so you're entitled to know my findings. Most people, in most species, are born with their genetic code essentially fixed. Sometimes things can change that code – radiation and toxins can damage DNA, or dormant sequences can be activated by environmental factors, and of course individuals are born all the time with random mutations, which survive in successive generations if they turn out to be useful adaptations… or useless but not especially detrimental. Traumatic experiences can cause a change in gene *expression*, though that only alters the phenotype, not the underlying genotype – that's known as epigenetics, and allows a parent to pass certain heritable traits to their offspring. Often they're traits they wouldn't *want* to pass on, but it's not optional. And, of course, with the tools available to us, courtesy of science, we can alter DNA at will, though the results are often unpredictable. Does all that make sense?"

"It does." Ayla had been allowed to give her texts on basic biology, at least. She hadn't even needed to hack the systems for that.

"Good. Your DNA isn't like everyone else's. Your genome is changing, constantly, without recognizable environmental causes or the deliberate actions of anyone, including yourself. Your phenotype – that is, your actual observed physical characteristics – have remained fairly constant, but only on the most superficial level. You look basically the same, is what I mean: you haven't grown wings or started glowing bright green. But when I look a little deeper, I find significant changes in your bone density, muscle mass, blood volume, synaptic activity, and other systems that aren't apparent to the unaided eye. You've changed a lot since Archie first scanned you on the *Grim Countenance*."

"So I am getting stronger," Bianca said. "Thinking faster, too. Doing everything faster. Remembering things better. I thought I might be, but it just… seemed impossible."

"It is certainly unprecedented in my experience. If we could make a serum that does for others what your body does naturally for you, we'd be rich enough to buy whole systems."

"I retain the intellectual property rights to any technology derived from the study of my body," Bianca said.

"True enough in the Barony," Errin said. "Provided you aren't in a subordinate client relationship and have full legal status, which you don't. Anyway, this isn't the Barony. Not all jurisdictions have the same rules, and some places have no rules at all. Those are the places where the most interesting science gets done." Bianca glared at him, and he winced. "But don't worry. I don't care about wealth, and I don't think I could replicate the miracle of you anyway. You are the product of Mahact technology. I can look at your genetic code, and see what it does, without having the faintest idea about how to replicate that effect. A worm might sense the vibrations of a spacecraft passing overhead, but that doesn't mean the worm can invent space travel. All right, you can jump down now."

"My body started changing when I left my homeworld." Bianca leapt easily from the podium and accepted the thin white robe Errin held out for her. "Why?"

"You're being prepared for something." Errin bustled over to a console and began calling up data on several of his screens. "I have no idea what. The changes aren't just altering your physical characteristics. There's another part of the code, linked to the deepest parts of your brain, where the instincts and the autonomous systems live. Your file said something about a 'yearning'?"

Bianca nodded. "I look at the stars, and I feel a strong desire to go to a certain place."

"Hmm. Perhaps it's similar to the way some migratory species feel a need to travel when the weather changes."

"That's nicer than Archambelle's idea. She thought it was like a parasite, changing my behavior for its own purposes."

Errin smiled. "Archie does have a certain point of view, doesn't she? I have examined the mechanism of the yearning, and have reached certain conclusions. I will have to share those conclusions with the Letnev, since that is why they hired me, but I do not have to share all the other details of my examination with them. Do you understand?"

"You mean, you're not going to tell them how I'm changing?"

"I am not. I do not know their ultimate intentions for you, but I do know they're meddling with forces beyond their ability to comprehend *or* control. You have been chosen for something – no, you have been *made* for something – and Archie and the rest think they can control that process. But I'm not sure the creations of the Mahact can be controlled. They're all dead now, exterminated by the Lazax, but if the stories are to be believed the Mahact were prepared, once upon a time, to destroy the galaxy in order to demonstrate their refusal to bow to those they considered lesser races. The Letnev share the arrogance of the Mahact without as much justification. If they try to push things too far, they may bring ruin. If I tell them how strong you are, I fear they will hobble you. When the time comes, Bianca Xing, you might need your new strength and speed and cleverness to ensure your own survival."

Before she could reply, he punched a button on the console, and the lab's doors slid open. Kyrria walked in, the Letnev delegation following. "Well?" Archambelle said. "What were your findings?"

"Have you deciphered this map hidden inside her genetic code?" Richeline said.

"Are you all right, Bianca?" Voyou asked, and she smiled at him and bowed her head in assent.

The guards didn't say anything, just hung back in a little cluster, unreadable in their blank facemasks.

"There is a no map," Brother Errin said. "Bianca is more like a metal detector. Beep beep beep, yes? Or a radiation sensor. She can feel when she is going in the right direction, and when she is getting closer to her destination."

"There must be a way to extrapolate from the data and figure *out* that destination!" Archambelle said.

Errin shrugged. "There may be a sort of counter hidden inside her, or a complete set of directions, or even something like coordinates, though we don't know how to read these ancient cartographic measurements, so they wouldn't do much good. Given enough time – on the order of years – and computational power, yes, there's a chance I could find out where her yearning will take her, or perhaps I could bioengineer an organism that glows or screams or hisses when you're headed the right way... but there is a simpler solution, yes?" The Yin scientist looked around expectantly, and they all looked back at him blankly. Brother Errin sighed. "Why don't you just *ask* Bianca which way you should go, and follow her directions?"

The Letnev delegation stared at him for a long moment. Then Archambelle and Richeline burst into furious outrage at once: "Absurd," "impossible," "give control of our navigation to a *human*," "not even part of the chain of command," "you don't ask the test subject to run the test," and other objections along those lines.

Bianca cleared her throat, and then did it again, louder , and then said, "Quiet!" She smiled at them sweetly as they scowled at her. "We have an agreement, don't we? A partnership?"

"Yes," Richeline said, rather sullenly, Bianca thought.

"Then I don't see the problem. I'll talk things over with the navigators on the *Grim Countenance*, and we'll set a course." They wanted to use her? Fine. She'd use *them* instead. She'd make the Letnev take her to the source of her yearning, and when she got close to Ixth, she'd escape and make her own way to the planet, and seize the treasure for herself. Ha. She'd show them all.

"We can't go wandering all over the galaxy on the say-so of a human," Richeline said.

"We both know I'm not human," Bianca said. "Not really. You wanted a treasure map. I *am* the treasure map. Now you don't want to follow the map's directions?"

Richeline looked at her, dead-eyed and cold. "I'll have to consult with the captain."

"Of course you will," Bianca said. "I'd like to the meet the captain soon, too. As the most important person on this mission, it's really time I stopped talking to subordinates."

Kyrria made a low rumble that was probably a laugh.

Archambelle didn't care. She was arguing with Brother Errin, who was shooing them toward the door. "Yes, Archie, I'll send over my data, but it won't tell you anything I didn't – it will just illustrate the wisdom of my advice."

Kyrria led them back to the corridors. Archambelle and Richeline went first, heads together in furious conference, followed by Bianca and Voyou, with the guards at the rear. Voyou walked beside her, murmuring, "Very impressive, Bianca, it's good to see you asserting yourself and recognizing your value," and she wanted to shush him, because the doctor and the first officer were exchanging angry words in Letnev, and she wanted to hear them. Then she realized she could just split her auditory focus, taking Voyou's bland affirmations into one ear and the more interesting discussion into the other.

"It doesn't really matter," Archambelle was saying. "Let her think she's in charge – let her play the space princess again, strutting around the command deck in her fancy red dress! Once we reach our destination, you can hand her over to me for vivisection as planned. *That* will shut her up, apart from all the screaming."

"She thinks she's so smart," Richeline seethed. "But she doesn't even realize the contract she signed is a sham. As if we'd let some alien science experiment extort us that way."

"Lower your voice," Archambelle said. "She speaks a *little* Letnev, we think, after all, so better to be discreet."

Oh. Bianca's plan to use the Letnev suddenly seemed ill-advised. If she let them get close to this Ixth, they might decide they were close *enough*, and kill her. Plus, how could she travel with them as she had before, knowing the depth of their deception, and their plans? Bianca thought for a moment. She considered angles, velocities, the dimensions of the corridor, the distance to the shuttle, and, the true x factor: her body's new capabilities. A little time dilation would have been welcome, but she still couldn't enter that state deliberately, so she'd have to settle for speed, strength, and the element of surprise.

After a few milliseconds, she was satisfied with her calculations, and she spun. As she whipped around, she elbowed Voyou in the face, his nose crunching beneath the blow. She whipped an energy rifle out of the hands of a startled guard, used her momentum to strike a second guard across the face with the gun butt, then dropped and struck out with her leg, sweeping the two guards still standing off their feet.

She didn't want to fire the rifle here – what if it punched a hole in the wall and exposed them to vacuum? – but she'd always been good at throwing things, even back on Darit, before her improvements. She ejected the rifle's energy cell and then hurled the weapon at the back of Archambelle's head.

That was a tactical mistake – she hated Archambelle more, so she'd aimed for her, but Richeline was a bigger threat. When the doctor hit the floor, Richeline spun and rushed straight at Bianca, without hesitation. The look on her face was *gleeful*. Bianca tossed the energy cell at her face, but Richeline just ducked and dove for her.

Bianca did a standing vertical leap, higher even than the one she'd done in the lab, and when Richeline passed below her Bianca dropped, both feet slamming into the back of her neck. Richeline landed with a gasping cry, and Bianca bent her knees and launched herself onward, down the corridor, toward the towering form of the Hacan. Fighting *her* would be a different proposition; the Letnev were big too, but they didn't have those fangs or those claws.

But Kyrria just stepped out of the way, putting her back to the wall. "No one paid me to stop you, child. Best of luck to you."

Bianca made it to the shuttle and got inside, sealing the doors. She scanned the documentation and figured out how to take manual control. She started the engines, but the station wouldn't release its docking clamps. She could manually force the *shuttle's* clamps to release, but that was only half the issue.

People began hammering on the shuttle doors, trying to override her locks with various priority codes she had to frantically counter. There were no weapons on board, no escape pod, nowhere to go from here. Maybe if she put on an environment suit, she could spacewalk, make her way to another portion of the station, somehow get inside, hide in the service tunnels, but she couldn't get *out* of the shuttle, because there was only one door, and it led to an airlock full of angry enemies.

The Letnev, she knew, were not a very trusting people. Their technology was full of spyware, remote overrides, and countermeasures meant to enforce obedience and punish non-compliance. On the shuttle, it turned out those countermeasures consisted of anesthetic gas, triggered remotely from the *Grim Countenance*, she assumed. Once the vents began hissing, Bianca filled her lungs with clean air, and then she held her breath.

It turned out she could hold her breath for thirty-seven full minutes. *Is that a record for a human, Brother Errin?* she thought, and then she opened her mouth and inhaled, and sank into blackness.

CHAPTER 19

"We've been waiting here for over an hour!" Heuvelt shouted into the comms.

"We're terribly sorry," the Hacan's voice purred. "We've had a small… security issue. The situation is nearly resolved, and then you will be allowed to board the station."

Heuvelt cursed and stomped back to the galley, where Ashont and Clec were playing a card game. Heuvelt had no idea how that worked, because Clec was perched on Ashont's shoulder, and could see all the cards in her hands, but apparently the Naaz was scrupulously honest when it came to playing games. "They treat us like our time is worth nothing," Heuvelt said.

"'A small security issue' could be a euphemism for all sorts of horrible things," Ashont said. "A terrorist attack by genetic originalists, a lab-grown monster eating the staff, a disappointed client waving around an energy rifle… anything really."

"So you're saying I shouldn't be in such a big hurry to

climb onto the Tree of Grace," Heuvelt said. "I suppose you're right. Even if it's nothing as dramatic as you describe, there are Letnev on board, and they still want to arrest me for crimes I never committed." He paused. "Don't you want to know how I surmised there are Letnev on board?"

"The giant Barony warship floating a few klicks away, all covered with unnecessary spikes, was my first indication," Clec said. "The presence of a Barony shuttle, covered in smaller unnecessary spikes, in one of the other docking modules confirmed my initial findings."

Heuvelt picked at a peeling piece of the tabletop's laminate. "Yes, that's what gave it away for me too."

"Well spotted, though, captain," Ashont said. "You still get credit." She slammed down two cards, one depicting some kind of snake twisted into a sigil and the other a curving fang. "Serpent's Tooth! Ha! The initiative is mine!"

"I am sure you cheat," Clec said. "I don't know *how*, but you must."

Heuvelt looked at the screen in the galley, showing a map of the system. "After we finish this delivery, I say we head to that moon there and spend some of our profits."

"I didn't know we had profits," Ashont said. "I thought we were looking at offsetting some debt at best."

"We can afford a few *drinks*, Ashont."

"Mmm. That particular moon caters to medical tourists who come here to consult the Yin," Clec said. "Since he doesn't let friends and family stay on the Tree of Grace overnight, just patients, there are luxury accommodations and entertainments for all the relatives and hangers-on. The amenities on that moon are expensive, is what I mean to say."

"Then we can afford *one* drink," Heuvelt said. "I call dibs on said drink."

"Oh, there are always bars for the pilots and security staff and valets and corset-lace-tighteners and scale-polishers and mandible-cleaners," Ashont said, shuffling the cards. "We can find some affordable entertainment. The captain's right. We should celebrate our change of fortune. We'll get a lot more work from Sagasa after this job, and with the captain's record cleared we'll be able to pass through Letnev space without worrying about it more than anyone *else* does."

"Did the two of you just disagree with each other?" Heuvelt said.

"No," Clec said. "Ashont makes good points. What you just witnessed was the process of us discussing a topic and then coming to agreement. We do that a lot. You just don't usually pay attention."

Heuvelt went back to the cockpit to wait for someone to open the airlock. He had a crate full of who-knew-what grotesque biological material in his cargo hold, and he just wanted to hand it over to the mad scientist, go on his way, and reap his rewards. Working for someone like Sagasa was troubling, but if it got his record cleared and allowed him to give up this furtive half-fugitive lifestyle, and make progress toward his dreams of exploration again, it was all worthwhile.

I can't wait for life to get simpler again, he thought.

"We could threaten to torture her parents," Voyou said. "She's clearly very fond of them."

"That is an option," Severyne said. "I am certainly not

above compelling obedience, but there are drawbacks to the technique. For one thing, we'll have no idea if Bianca is telling the truth or leading us astray. Since we don't know where we're going, or what might be required from her in terms of activating mechanisms or opening vaults or what have you, she could lead us on indefinitely."

Richeline rubbed the back of her neck where Bianca had stomped on her. Severyne had watched that part of the video twice, her annoyance slightly tempered by amusement. What a leap! The young woman clearly had hidden capabilities, including fluency in Letnev, since overhearing Richeline's comments about the sham contract was the only reasonable explanation for the timing of her escape attempt.

Richeline growled. "I say we just cut off one of her hands and tell her we'll cut off the other if she doesn't take us where we want to go, and fast."

"Same problem," Severyne said. "We can't give her a ticking clock, because for all we know the journey will take years. Besides, now she knows we don't plan to let her live after we're done with her. We also don't know the extent of her physical capabilities, so torturing her effectively will be a difficult series of trials-and-errors, with more of the latter than we have time for. Especially in light of Archambelle's theory about her pain management."

"What theory?" Richeline said.

"No one reads the whole files," Severyne sighed. "Really, you can't just skim the precis." She leaned back in her desk chair and fixed Richeline with the full weight of her disappointment. "Tell her, doctor."

The doctor was still a little groggy from the meds she'd

taken after the blow to her head, but her gaze sharpened as she spoke. "I think Bianca can control her pain receptors, though perhaps not consciously. I deliberately did some painful procedures, to test her reactions, and after a brief wince she evinced no further distress, and I detected reduced conductivity in her nerves. Very targeted, very selective. Inflicting pain on her is likely to be difficult. As for maiming her, yes, that could be highly motivating, but I have also noted astonishing capabilities in terms of tissue regeneration. I have not gone so far as to cut off one of her hands, but if I did, I suspect it would grow back. I also have other concerns about compelling her cooperation through force."

"Such as?" Severyne said.

Archambelle shifted in her chair, unable to find a comfortable position, by design. No one in Severyne's presence should be too relaxed. The doctor said, "What if Bianca is developing mental powers in addition to physical ones? We know there are species who can read minds, project thoughts, even dominate the wills of others. What if the Mahact seeded those abilities in her? Perhaps she beats Voyou when they play spiralstone, not because of her superior tactical skill, but because she can sense, perhaps unconsciously, what's in his mind, and knows what moves he plans to make in advance?"

"That's certainly something new to worry about," Severyne said. "Though her tactical acumen is obviously impressive, for a farm girl. She bested a first officer, an undercommandant, a ship's doctor, and three marines in hand-to-hand combat."

"We didn't think she posed a threat!" Richeline said. "We'll be much more careful going forward, you can believe me—"

"Going forward *where*? We've already established that any attempt to compel obedience could backfire. Archambelle says the girl's genome and volatile brain chemistry mean our usual drugs to weaken human wills are unlikely to do any good."

"We keep having to switch sedatives," the doctor said glumly. "The gas that knocked her out the first time didn't work the next time, and the anesthetic we used instead failed the time after *that*. Her body is learning to shrug off everything we use against her. It won't be long before we're reduced to bashing her in the back of the head with a rock if we want her to stay unconscious, and obviously that has certain inherent dangers."

Severyne nodded. "This girl was designed by the Mahact, or whomever, to operate with independence and reach her destination. We spent all this time poking and prodding and trying to decipher her secrets, when Brother Errin has it right: we should have just asked her where she wanted to go, and gone along with her. We've spoiled any chance of that now, thanks to you two babbling fools."

"So what, then?" Archambelle demanded. "Are you saying the mission is a failure?"

"Of course not." Severyne rolled her head around on her neck, limbering up for what was likely to be a very strenuous few days. "I'm saying it's up to *me* to fix things, as usual. Here's what we're going to do."

Bianca woke up with a groan, her head all fuzzy and her eyes all blurry, but two blinks later she felt sharp and in focus again. She was stretched out on the floor in a bare, dimly lit room with some sort of flickering energy field in the place of one wall. The brig, then. And she wasn't alone.

The person she wasn't alone with was Letnev, but her hair was loose and messy around her face, a level of disarray Bianca had never witnessed in the crew before. The woman had a split lip, still a little bloody, and her close-fitting black uniform was askew, one sleeve torn. The woman sat on the floor, back against the wall, legs folded up so her knees were close to her chin. She frowned at Bianca, and spoke in the trading tongue. "What did *you* do to get locked up, princess?"

Bianca had no intention of talking to any Letnev in any language ever again, so she took a personal inventory instead. She was wearing her smartcloth dress, and she still had on her silver ring, so *that* was a surprise they wouldn't be prepared for if need be. They'd taken her shoes away for some reason, but she'd grown up running barefoot across rocky fields, so that was hardly debilitating. Otherwise, she had… well, just what she took with her everywhere. Strength and speed that wouldn't surprise her captors as much next time, and her mind. Those advantages would have to suffice.

The brig didn't have beds, just niches in the wall that were slightly more padded than the floor. Nothing she could wrench free to use as a weapon. Otherwise, the space was entirely bare. *So* bare, in fact, that, huh…

"You're wondering where you're supposed to shit?" the woman said. "That sleeping cubby in the middle isn't a sleeping cubby. You can tell by the smell. There's a hole, and suction. Crawl in there if you need to do your business. I'll avert my eyes from your aristocratic nethers, my lady." She cackled.

Bianca carefully examined the walls, looking for a seam she could pry open – she only had her bare hands, but they were strong, and her nails seemed to be unbreakable lately. There was nothing, just smooth metal. She growled in frustration.

The other prisoner was amused. "My people are apex jailers, and this is the cell where they keep enemy combatants, princess. We are secure. You aren't going to find a handy ventilation duct to crawl through. That's storybook stuff."

Bianca dropped down to the floor, thinking furiously, but her mind was like a vehicle stuck in the mud: the wheels spun, but there was nothing for them to dig into, so none of her thoughts got any purchase or took her anywhere. She cursed, elaborately, in Letnev, a combination of oaths she'd picked up from listening in on the cargo bay workers.

Her cellmate cackled again. "You swear like a toddler. You can't use *eshin* as a verb, that would be like saying, hmm, 'you assholing scum,' ha."

"Oh, shut up," Bianca said. "I know you're just a spy here to watch me."

"Watch you do what? Sit here and pout? My report back to my superiors is going to be *scintillating*." She worked her jaw, winced, and spat a tooth out onto the floor. "Seriously, princess, why are you locked up in here? What crime could *you* have possibly committed? A grievous breach of aristocratic etiquette? Did you use the wrong spoon at dinner with the captain?"

Bianca let her annoyance bubble up. "I've never even *met* the captain."

"Lucky break there. She's the worst. So what, then? Did you drop a stitch in your embroidery?"

She ground her teeth. "No. I assaulted three guards, a doctor, an undercommandant, and the ship's first officer, and tried to steal a shuttle."

The woman whistled. "Why did you do *that*? Was the thread count on your sheets too low for your tastes? Why would a princess like you–"

"I'm not a princess!" Bianca roared. "I'm a *prisoner*, and I was a prisoner *before*, but once I realized I was a prisoner and tried to get away, they made me a *real* prisoner."

The woman was silent for a long moment. "Oh. I see. You mean to tell me the officers lied to us about the aristocrat in our midst? Barony officials, bending the truth?" She smirked. "Truly unprecedented. I've never heard of such a thing before. You've shattered my worldview and dashed my illusions to splinters. Or shards. Whatever illusions break up into. I'm sad to hear you aren't a princess, though. I thought I must be pretty important if they put me in here with the likes of you."

"Why are you here?" Bianca said. "I know you're a spy, but I assume you have some elaborate cover story, and I could use the entertainment."

"Oh, yes, I really commit to my role. That's why I had to spit out a tooth just now, for *verisimilitude*. Listen to you – you think you're so important. They have cameras and microphones. Why would they need to punch me in the face and put me in here to listen to you whine? You're not the supermassive black hole at the center of the galaxy, princess – not *everything* revolves around you." The woman leaned her head back against the wall and appeared to go to sleep.

So what if she was a spy. That didn't necessarily mean Bianca shouldn't talk to her – maybe she could get *her* to let something slip, some piece of information that could help Bianca out of this situation. It wasn't like she had a lot of other avenues to pursue just now. If the woman tried to pump her for information about which way her yearning wanted them to go, Bianca simply wouldn't give her any. *I'll secretly and expertly interrogate* you, she thought. "All right," she said. "You're right. I've had a difficult day. I apologize. My name is Bianca. What's yours."

The woman cracked open one eyelid. "You can call me Sev, princess." Then she closed her eye again, and a moment later started to snore.

CHAPTER 20

It was difficult to convincingly pretend to sleep – faking the right kind of breathing was famously tricky – so Severyne didn't pretend; she actually went to sleep. She'd slept in worse circumstances, after all, and in more dangerous company.

Severyne woke up, not too much later, and smacked her dry lips. "Water!" she shouted. "Do you idiots want me to die before you get the chance to execute me?" She looked over at Bianca, who was sitting against the far wall hugging her knees to her chest, but didn't say anything to her. People didn't appreciate things that came too easily.

So far, Sev thought she'd done a good job with the girl. She didn't know if Archambelle's speculations about Bianca's possible psychic abilities were plausible or not, but for all they knew the girl could detect minute changes in breathing and heartbeat and blood pressure too, and might be able to sense when people were lying to her. Severyne had learned long ago that you could lie a lot without actually *lying*; you just said carefully chosen true things, and let people draw the conclusions you'd led them toward. You could even say some of your deep dark secrets straight out, and as long as you used a sarcastic tone, people would believe you meant the opposite. Avoiding outright lies while speaking to Bianca might not be necessary, but it couldn't hurt, and the challenge kept Severyne's mind focused.

"Will they bring us water?" Bianca said in a small voice.

Severyne yawned. "Oh, probably, eventually. As a rule, Barony officials don't let people they're planning to execute die of thirst. Why give their prisoners the easy way out? They must want to keep you alive too, if they kidnapped you and made up a whole elaborate story. Do you know why they really want you?"

Bianca ignored that. "Why are they going to execute you? What did *you* do?"

"Oh, lots of things." Severyne walked to the forcefield wall separating them from the corridor, and freedom, or at least, *relative* freedom; even if they escaped the cell, they'd still be on a Barony warship, after all. Though maybe not for much longer. "I got my start working in security – not standing by a door with a pulse rifle, my scores were too high for *that*, but managing teams of guards in a secure facility. Everything was going well, and my career was on the rise, when there was a regrettable incident and we lost a high-value asset. In the aftermath, I was reassigned to the *Grim Countenance*." All that was true. It was just that, in reality, she'd turned that regrettable incident to her own advantage, and the reassignment had been a promotion to captain of her own ship. "Once I got here, I kept clashing with high-ranking officers, especially first officer Richeline. We had a lot of disagreements and, well, today I called her a babbling fool." All true. "Do you know how the Letnev feel about insubordination?"

Bianca nodded. "Section nineteen-c, paragraph g, of Barony military code says the penalty for willful insubordination is confinement to quarters, docking one cycle's pay, and a level-three formal public apology."

Severyne blinked at her with unfeigned surprise. "You memorized the military codes?"

She shrugged. "I get bored easily. The codes were one of the only things I was allowed to read in my room that didn't have any redactions. Lately, when I read things, they sort of stick in my mind."

"Huh. Do you remember what it says about *striking* a superior officer?"

Bianca laughed. "Detention, court martial, execution. Is that what you did?"

Severyne spread out her hands. "You see me standing here in this cell, don't you?"

Bianca nearly smiled. "It looks like Richeline got a couple of hits in herself."

That she had. Richeline had definitely seemed to enjoy hitting Severyne to complete her "fellow prisoner" disguise. The captain hadn't expected to be hit hard enough to loosen a tooth, but she could get it replaced later, and it did help sell the whole story. Severyne had refused painkillers, because as a real prisoner she wouldn't have received any, and she wanted to be as convincing as possible. A little pain – all right, a medium amount of pain – was a small price to pay to win Bianca's trust and complete the mission. "Richeline is trained in combat, and it shows. I understand why she was in such a bad mood when we had our little interaction now, if you roughed her up earlier."

"I guess we're both here for the same reason, in a way," Bianca said. "Except I don't think they plan to execute me. They want something from me." She paused, and it was such a *deliberate* pause that Severyne knew it was a trap. If she started probing about *what* the Letnev wanted from her, Bianca would suspect her even more of being a spy.

But Severyne's plan didn't rely on Bianca telling her anything, really, so she ignored the bait, and dangled a little bait of her own instead. "Screw them," Severyne said. "Why should you give them anything they want? I used to think the Barony was a true meritocracy, but I've been forced to serve under enough fools to know it's not that simple." She sat down next to Bianca, leaned in close, and whispered, "I have absolutely no intention of being tried and executed. I'm getting out of here."

"I thought you people were apex jailers?"

"Oh, we are. Nobody has better prisons. But do you know the weakest part of any system?"

"People," Bianca said.

"That's right. We can't break the walls, but we can break the *people*. Like I said, I worked in security, so I have some insight into these operations. I'm familiar with the duty rosters and shift changes and security procedures down here, too. I should be. I drew them up myself."

"Wait – you were in charge of the same brig they *put* you in?"

Severyne shrugged. "I oversaw security for the whole ship, yeah." As captain, that was true; the real security chief reported to her, after all. "This is the most secure brig they've got. It's not like the guards would set me free just because they used to work for me – personal loyalty only goes so far, and once you get locked up and scheduled for execution, you tend to lose your influence."

"So what's your plan?"

Severyne looked away. "I, ah, well, I, you see, I…" She didn't have to pretend to be uncomfortable. Talking about this really did bring up all sorts of complex feelings, including but not limited to guilt and shame. "I have a sort of history. With humans. Human women. A human woman. I was on a mission once, with a woman from the Federation of Sol, and we… became close. I know, we're ancestral enemies and all that, but we had a common interest that forced us to work together for a time, and professional respect grew into something more. That sort of thing is frowned upon in the Barony. It's seen as perversion. Worse, a violation of Barony values. It's like fraternization with the enemy, but more repulsive."

"There's no regulation against interspecies intimacy in the military codes," Bianca whispered.

"There's not a specific regulation against chopping up your mother and making her into soup, either, because there doesn't *need* to be – everyone knows it's simply not done."

"So, what? You want to *fraternize* with me? This is a very elaborate way to be creepy, Sev, and I don't like it."

Severyne wrinkled her nose. "You are far too young for me, princess, among other drawbacks too numerous to list. But I know the camera angles, and we can make it look like we're getting intimate without the necessity of actual contact. Believe me, the guards will come in with stun batons to break things up quickly if they think we're kissing. Witnessing a grotesque perversion of Letnev purity will probably make them a little careless – both guards on duty tonight are especially straitlaced."

Bianca laughed. "Why not? Say we lure them in. What then?"

"We beat them up. I wouldn't rate our chances high in a fair fight, but you say you took out three guards, so maybe you'll impress me. If it doesn't work…" She shrugged. "I'm already going to be tried and executed. It's not like I can get in *more* trouble for trying to escape."

"Say we do defeat the guards. Then what?"

"Then we hope Richeline hasn't gotten around to changing my security codes yet, so I can cancel any alarms and open the security doors and get to the shuttle bay."

"What if she *has* changed your codes?"

"Then I'll use Richeline's officer-level codes." Severyne grinned. "The security officer is the one who *generates* those codes. Sure, you're not supposed to look at them, let alone memorize them, but who knows what people get up to when no one else is watching?"

"It sounds pretty risky."

"My other plan is to fake a seizure, and try to escape when the medical team comes."

"I've read about that kind of thing in stories," Bianca said. "Actually, lots of stories."

Sev scowled. "Some things are classics for a reason,

princess. Anyway, I like the first idea better, because I'd only have to punch guards instead of guards *and* medics, and you'll help with the punching, but like I said: when you're going to die anyway, every risk is an acceptable risk. If you're so valuable, they won't hurt you even if we fail. But maybe you'd prefer to stay, negotiate with the captain, try to make a deal–"

"They don't honor deals anyway." Bianca's voice shook with bitterness. Severyne felt a tiny bit bad about that. This all could have been handled differently. It had simply never crossed Severyne's mind to deal with the girl *fairly*, on an open, even-handed basis; the stakes were too high, the path too uncertain, and, after all, Bianca was just some human farm girl from a worthless mudball, not worthy of any real consideration. By the time Severyne started to respect the girl and understand her true capabilities, they'd gone too far down the road of deception, and well, here they were. But this road, however twisty, could still lead them to their destination. "Let's do it. At least this way I'll get to *hit* someone."

"Wonderful," Severyne said. "I hope you're as good at fighting as you claim to be. All right, you sit there, let me cuddle up close beside you. Good, now, lean *this* way, a little and I'll bow my head, here, and my hair will hide our faces. Go ahead and put your hand, ugh, on my hip there, all right, and the other one on the back of my neck…"

They weren't *actually* kissing, but their faces were very close together, and it still felt more intimate than Bianca had been with anyone except Grandly, a few times, when the stars were bright and the moons were high and her blood sang in her veins. "Move your hands a little," Sev whispered. "Look passionate." Bianca did her best to comply, pretending she was in the throes of lust like the heroines she'd read about, but it was hard to feel those feelings when she was nose-to-nose with an alien woman. (But, she supposed, Grandly wasn't really the same species as her either. Was anyone, since all the Mahact were dead? But she wasn't quite Mahact, either.)

"No touching!" a voice grated harshly over the loud-speaker. Sev's hand briefly left its place on Bianca's shoulder, then returned.

"What did you just do?" Bianca whispered.

"I made an obscene gesture," Sev said. "I'll teach it to you later."

Boots came thumping down the hall – *three* sets of them, Bianca could hear, not two, as Sev had expected. Maybe she didn't know the rota here as well as she claimed, or they'd changed things up to confuse her, or they'd brought an extra guard because they knew what Bianca was capable of. Ha. Probably that one.

Bianca didn't expect this plan to work, not really, but trying something was better than waiting around for someone *else* to do something.

There was a buzz as the wall of energy came down, and Sev let go of Bianca and turned her head. With her view now unobstructed by the Letnev woman's face, Bianca could see two masked guards and first officer Richeline, all three holding black batons that crackled with blue sparks of energy at the ends.

Richeline stepped forward, a bruise dark around her eye.

"A pervert as well as a violent insubordinate," Richeline said. "And you, Bianca – I thought better of you. When the guards first called me, I thought the traitor was molesting you, but no, apparently you're a willing participant!"

"It's boring in the cell, Richie," Sev said. "We had to entertain ourselves somehow. How's your eye?"

"How's your *neck*?" Bianca added, wanting to get in on the fun.

Richeline growled and stepped forward, baton at the ready.

Sev did a diving somersault, grabbing for Richeline's legs, doubtless intending to take her down – but one of the guards got a boot in, kicking her in the side and throwing her off course. Sev tried to scramble to her feet, but the guard hit her with a stun baton in the neck, and she jolted, eyes rolling back, and went limp.

So much for two against two. Now it was three against one.

Bianca almost felt bad for the three.

CHAPTER 21

Bianca still thought Sev was probably a spy and this was all a ploy to gain her trust. Participating in a doomed escape attempt would create a bond between them that would lead to shared confidences, and eventually Sev would encourage Bianca to cooperate with the Letnev... or, perhaps, Richeline would offer to spare Sev's life as a "reward" if Bianca helped them find their treasure world.

None of that mattered, though. If this was all a sham to manipulate her, Bianca would show them what a bad mistake they'd made trying to play her. While Richeline and the guards were distracted by their efforts to incapacitate Sev, she rose smoothly to her feet and kicked out Richeline's knee. The first officer squawked, dropping, leaving Bianca with a clear shot at the guards. They were impressively armored, but they needed to be able to move their heads around on their necks, so their throats weren't as well protected as the rest of them. (There weren't any body armor specs in the databases Ayla could provide, of course, but one bored afternoon Bianca had idly hacked into a security database and perused some of the technical manuals.) She stiffened the first two fingers of her right hand and jabbed straight into the most vulnerable spot. Poking the guard that way felt a lot like pushing her fingertips into a pudding. He gasped and fell down, writhing and grabbing his throat.

Richeline was slumped on the floor, but she was still conscious, and still a threat. She hit Bianca with the stun baton, jamming it right into the muscle of her calf, but apart from a faint tingle, Bianca didn't feel anything. She plucked the baton from Richeline's hand and used it like a club to smack the other guard across the facemask when he came at her, rather slowly since he was now trying not to trip over Richeline, Sev, *or* his writhing compatriot.

His mask shattered under the blow (the stun baton came apart in Bianca's hand, too), and he howled, blood running out from under the mask – a fragment must have cut his cheek. He stumbled around the cell in a very distracting fashion, so she kicked out one of his knees. She picked up his baton and zapped him in a now-exposed part of his neck, and that was him sorted out.

Fighting was pretty easy, it turned out: mostly just physics and anatomy, with a bit of psychology thrown in, and synchronizing three disciplines at once presented no particular challenge. Richeline was trying to crawl away, but Bianca looked at her and shook her head, and the first officer sank back, staring at Bianca and breathing hard.

Severyne sat up then, rubbing her face and blinking. "Wha? You took them all out yourself?"

"I am not taken *out*," Richeline spoke through clenched

teeth. "This is absurd. You're on a secure deck. There's no escape."

"Sure there is," Bianca said. "You're going to escort me to a shuttle."

"I can fly us out of here," Sev said.

"I've read the manuals," Bianca said. "I can manage. If you really are a prisoner, I'm sorry, and I wish you luck with your escape. But you could be a spy, trying to trick me, so I'm going to take Richeline as a hostage and make my own way out of here."

Sev reached over, picked up a shard of the guard's broken mask, and stabbed it into the side of Richeline's neck.

The first officer screamed, clapped a hand to the shard, and tried to drag herself away on a broken knee as blood welled out all around her fingers. Sev kicked Richeline hard in the ribs, making her roll over and curl up. She glared at Bianca. "A *spy*?" she shouted. "Do you still think I'm a spy? Would a spy do *that*?" She kicked Richeline again, and the first officer huddled into a ball at the center of a spreading pool of blood.

Bianca stared at her. "I... no. I guess not."

"Shall we go, then?"

Bianca nodded. With Richeline dying – she was really dying! Bianca had never seen a person gurgling their last like this, only livestock, and this was *very* different! – Sev was the only one with the necessary access codes to get them out of the brig.

Sev picked up a stun baton in each hand, then tore a gauntlet from Richeline's arm. The first officer made a desperate sighing sound and clawed at her with the hand, but Sev idly kicked her arm away. She stalked off down the corridor, and Bianca hurried after her, happy to leave the scene of carnage behind. Sev didn't have Bianca's strength, speed, or reflexes, but she had a will to strike hard and without mercy that Bianca knew she couldn't hope to match and that she didn't *want* to match, honestly.

"You're lucky Richeline's baton malfunctioned," Sev called over her shoulder. "If we'd *both* gone down, that would have been the end of us."

"Yes," Bianca said. "Really lucky." She wondered, though. Her body was good at lots of things, lately: that impressive Mahact handiwork. Maybe she could just ignore the effects of a stun baton now. She had no doubt a knife wielded with sufficient force would cut her, that a laser would burn her, that a ball of superheated plasma would put a hole through her body, but she suspected she could shrug off a lot more than anyone supposed.

"Here." They reached an imposingly solid door at the end of the corridor. Sev strapped the first officer's gauntlet onto her own arm and slid her fingers across it until the door slid open. "Perfect. She never changed the default code used to unlock the gauntlet. Very sloppy. She should be written up for that. Not that her permanent record matters much now, I suppose, with her dead on the floor of the brig." She tapped the gauntlet. "With this, we can get anywhere on the ship, as long as we move fast."

"Where are we going?" Bianca said.

"I haven't thought any farther than 'off the ship'," Sev said. "You don't have any contacts in the Lue-Hel system, do you?"

"I only know people on one planet, and it's a long way from here."

Sev grunted, stepping out of the corridor into some sort of security station, with a curved desk, a row of monitors, and a rack of silver and black weaponry sealed behind a forcefield like the one in their cell. "Can you use a gun?"

"My father taught me to use a kinetic rifle, a few years back, when there was a drought and the nightclimbers expanded their territory."

"Same principle." She waved her hand, and the field over the rack of guns shimmered, responding to the gauntlet. The ship thought she *was* Richeline now. Sev took down a long black gun and handed it to Bianca, then took one for herself, and tucked a sidearm into her belt, too. "These are better than a kinetic rifle, though. You don't have to account for recoil, so it won't bruise your shoulder."

I don't think I bruise so easily anymore, Bianca thought. She looked over the rifle, and its mechanisms were readily apparent to her. In fact, she saw two or three ways she could improve it to boost its power and accuracy, if she had the right tools and a few minutes to work on it, but now wasn't the time.

"The main hangar bay is too crowded." Sev tapped on a terminal at the security desk, consulting various screens. "But there's a secondary launch bay where we keep the survey ships. They aren't made for long-distance travel, but they can handle vacuum and atmosphere both. We'll need to switch ships as soon as we can, so the more flexibility the better. Let me spoof a security alert to get the guards in the secondary launch bay to leave their posts… Done. Let's move."

Sev set off without hesitation, and Bianca followed close behind, gun at port arms. "Aren't you afraid someone will see us?"

"I checked our route. There's no one along our path right now but cleaning drones. I looped the camera feeds, too. That won't fool anyone who looks closely, but we can avoid triggering any automated alerts."

"You act like you've done this before."

Sev snorted. "I was trained to *stop* this sort of thing. I've done countless simulated jailbreaks, escapes, rescues, hostage situations, you name it. There are ways to ruin my plan, but only if they've got someone smarter than me running things, and by definition, they don't. The person who's in charge of security now is no match for me."

"I've never been in this part of the ship." Bianca looked around with interest. The corridors here were more bare and austere, and more cramped too. She heard the rumble and whirr of machinery hidden by doors and access panels on all sides.

"Why would you come down here? It's where we keep the cargo, the noisy boring machines, the air scrubbers, the matter recyclers, all the unlovely infrastructure of long-haul space voyages. And the prisoners, of course. No reason to give them deluxe accommodations. Here, this way."

Sev scrambled up a ladder, and Bianca shifted the rifle on its strap so it hung on her back, then followed. She looked up, Sev's feet just inches from her face. There was blood all over one of her boots. "Did you have to kill Richeline?" Bianca said.

"You were going to take her with you instead of me," Sev

said. "That was a choice *you* made. I simply responded in the only tactically sound manner."

Bianca frowned. "Then why are you *still* with me? Once you took Richeline's wristband, you could have left me behind."

Sev emerged at the top of the ladder into an even more cramped space, some kind of service corridor, and gestured for Bianca to hurry up. When she answered, it was in a whisper. "I don't know what you are exactly, princess, but you tore through those guards like they were made of lace. Maybe you're some kind of vat-grown supersoldier who had her memory erased, or Brother Errin crammed you full of military implants, or maybe you're something else I could never hope to understand, but you are a definite asset. I forgive you for trying to leave me behind. *That* was tactically sound too, and it's why I stabbed Richeline in the neck: so you'd believe I *wasn't* a spy, and that we're in this together. How about we stay in this together, at least until we get far away from the *Grim Countenance* and Letnev space?"

Bianca considered. Sev definitely knew more about the galaxy than Bianca did – she hadn't even known this was the Lue-Hel system! – and that expertise could prove useful. Plus, if Sev didn't care where she went, and she just wanted to get *away*, then maybe she'd be amenable to traveling to the source of Bianca's yearning. She still intended to go there, and see what she was meant for. She didn't want to go on the end of a Letnev leash, but it would be easier to make her way with company than all alone. "That works for me."

"Then let's go. Through here." Sev crept forward, then waved her gauntlet at a door. It slid open, revealing a guard who stepped back in surprise. Sev launched herself forward, attempting to bowl the man over, but he was huge, and she bounced off his armored legs instead. She swung one of her stun batons, and he caught her arm with one hand and her throat with the other. Sev swung her other baton at the guard's head, but he kept his chin tucked, taking the blows on the solid back and sides of his helmet, and not the more fragile faceplate.

Amazingly, he didn't seem to notice Bianca at all, but then, he was understandably focused on choking the life out of Sev. Bianca slung her energy rifle around her body, took aim at his center mass, then shifted and squeezed the trigger.

The rifle emitted a beam of reddish light – Bianca knew no portion of the energy that emerged needed to be in the visible spectrum, but she assumed it was probably useful for soldiers to see if they were firing straight. The beam passed through the soldier's ankle, nearly detaching his foot from his body. He howled, dropped Sev, and fell backward. Sev gagged, spat, and drew her sidearm, pointing at his head.

Bianca blurred across the intervening space and batted the gun out of Severyne's hand. "He's *down*! You don't have to kill him!"

The guard wasn't even screaming, just moaning; probably going into shock, though he shouldn't bleed out since the beam had cauterized the wound on its way through.

Sev scowled at Bianca, baring her teeth, and Bianca thought she might lash out, but instead the Letnev woman nodded. She stooped to pick up her handgun and put it away. "Strangle me," she muttered, looking balefully at the fallen guard. "Yesterday he would have *saluted* me."

"A couple of months ago, the most unpleasant thing I ever had to do was shoveling caprid shit," Bianca said. "Things have changed for both of us."

"Ha. True enough." Sev strode down the hallway toward a large set of doors. She waved her wrist gauntlet, cursed, and then punched in a code. One of the doors lurched open half a meter, and Sev said, "Hurry, they're going into lockdown, I don't know how long before they cancel these codes!" She squeezed through the gap, and Bianca followed. They were in an airlock. The door behind them closed, and Sev cursed at the door on the opposite side, finally convincing it to open a crack.

Once they squeezed through that, they were in a small hangar, with three of the birdlike shuttles. The far wall was open to the stars, a shimmering forcefield standing between them and the void… and freedom.

Sev ran toward the nearest ship, punching inputs on her gauntlet, and the shuttle lowered a ramp. They raced onto the ship, and Sev slid into the pilot's seat and began punching at the controls.

Bianca sat beside her, watching the ship's external camera feeds on the co-pilot screens. A guard was trying to squeeze through the gap in the door they'd used, but in her bulky body armor, she couldn't quite make it. She stuck a sidearm through the crack instead and started firing at their ship. "They're shooting at us!" she shouted.

"Might as well throw rocks at a moon," Sev said. "Those weapons can't hurt this ship, and I locked them out of the main hangar controls, so they won't be able to scramble fighters to come after us until they untangle my code. Still,

I don't like being shot at. I could turn on the maneuvering thrusters and cook her in her armor…"

"*Don't*," Bianca said.

"I won't. I was just saying I could. See how merciful and noble I can be, princess?" The survey ship rumbled and rose up from the deck. "They'd better get back into that airlock and shut the door if they don't want to suck vacuum, though." Sev manipulated the controls, and the shimmering wall of light before them vanished. Bianca kept one eye on the external camera feed, and was relieved to see the arm pull back and the airlock door close.

The ship rumbled. Sev moved a slider on the hovering visual interface, and they shot out of the *Grim Countenance* and into the dark. The shimmering crystal beauty of the Tree of Grace floated out on their left, but they were headed the other way, toward dark, and stars… and the source of Bianca's yearning.

Sev said, "There. If we survive the next hour without being blown up by Barony fighters, I'd say we have a chance at living at least, oh, say, another week." She rose and entered the main compartment, where she began stripping off her torn and bloody clothing. Bianca averted her eyes, then thought to look at her own clothes, but her smartcloth was pristine, stain-resistant and self-cleaning. None of the blood or dirt or grease of their escape had stuck to her.

"Where are we headed?" Bianca called.

Sev returned to the cockpit, pulling on a plain gray sweatshirt over matching pants. "There's a moon nearby, where wealthy visitors to the Tree of Grace stay sometimes. I'm sure I can find another ride for us there." She pulled her messy hair back into a tight ponytail and secured it in place with an elastic band. When she was done, she still looked like someone who'd been in a couple of fights recently, but less like someone who'd *lost* them all.

"Sev, I couldn't have gotten away without you. Which isn't to say I approve of everything you did along the *way*, but... thank you."

"Mmm. You really don't like killing, do you, princess? That's odd, since you have a real knack for causing mayhem."

"I'll defend myself," Bianca said. "I'll fight for my freedom. If I had no choice, maybe I could kill. But that guard, all those guards, were just doing their jobs."

"Their *jobs* were imprisoning you. Doesn't that make you angry?"

"They had their orders," Bianca said. "If you're a Letnev, orders are all you have, and if you don't follow them... well, you know. Look at your own situation. Now, if we're talking about the people who *gave* the orders, I might not be so forgiving if I ended up in a room alone with the captain."

"It might surprise you to know captains have to follow orders, too," Sev said. "So do admirals. So do the heads of the great families. The only person in the Barony who never has to take orders from anyone is the Baron. But if he declared tomorrow that the Letnev should become a pacifist nation, devoted to doing good works for the downtrodden people of the galaxy, he might find out his rule isn't quite as absolute as he *thinks* it is, and we'd owe our fealty to a newly elevated Baron by the end of the week – one who supports the true Letnev way of life. We *all* follow someone's orders."

"I don't," Bianca said.

"Huh," Sev said. "I guess you don't. Neither do I, now. No one to answer to. No one making demands. Thinking about living that kind of life, honestly, it makes me a little dizzy."

"I hope we both have a lot of time to get used to it," Bianca said. And yet… was she really as free as she claimed? There was that yearning, wasn't there? A compulsion to visit one particular bit of the sky. Who'd given her *that* order, and why?

What if she'd escaped one tether, only to discover she was at the end of another, much longer one?

She'd just have to go and see. And if she arrived at her destination and found a hand holding the other end of that leash, she'd just have to see about biting it off.

"Do you know where you want to go?" Bianca asked. "I mean, longer term?"

Sev shook her head. "The only life I've known is the Barony military. I've got access to a little money, enough to keep me going in the short term. After that, I guess I'll try to find work as a soldier-of-fortune or something. I have some useful skills."

"I could use some help," Bianca said. "I think I could even make it worth your while, on the other side."

Sev cocked her head. "Oh? Do tell, princess."

There was a lot to tell – about the Mahact, about the compass in her head, about the fabled world of Ixth… but she started where it began. "I have this… Dr Archambelle called it a *yearning*…"

CHAPTER 22

"Are we going to steal another ship once we get to that moon?" Bianca asked.

Severyne couldn't tell if the idea excited or bothered the girl, so she chose a neutral response. "We'll assess the situation when we land. We have more immediate concerns. Help me get this panel off." Severyne pried at a part of the cockpit console that wasn't meant to be opened from this side; even jamming in a probe as hard as she could, she couldn't get it to flex more than a millimeter or two.

Bianca reached over and popped off the metal square without apparent effort. "What are you doing?" She peered inside at a tangle of wire and dull metal components.

"There's a transponder under here. Barony tracking technology. They like to know where their ships are. The tracker is integrated with the propulsion system, so if I remove it, then the ship stops flying. I can't do anything about that, but I think I can stop the tracker from *reporting* it's been tampered with, and make sure it keeps broadcasting its location even once I remove it from the ship."

"How does that help us?"

"We'll put this tracker on another ship after we land, and send the Barony chasing after *them* instead of us. Should buy us a little extra time." Severyne delicately snipped at wires. This was all theater, of course – there was a tracking chip in her body, and anyway, she wanted to be followed. But she performed the alterations as carefully and accurately as if it really mattered, because it was safest to treat Bianca as if she were omniscient and omnicognizant. It was doubtful that she could discern the workings of complex machinery from a mere glance but–

"Not that one," Bianca said. "That goes into the navigation system, but then it continues on to the communications array, see? You need to jump that wire instead, peel away the insulation and attach those clips here and here."

"I didn't realize you had an engineering background," Severyne said.

"Oh, just watching my father work on machinery around the farm. But I pick things up quickly."

A primitive tractor on a backward colony world had as much in common with a Barony starship as a candle had with a star, but no matter. It was good to know her caution had been warranted. "There," Severyne said. "That should buy us a little time later."

The luxury moon was called Glamarij, and it orbited a blackened cinder of a planet. "What happened there?"

Severyne glanced at the dead husk of a world. "War."

They glided down toward the surface of the moon without being challenged, skimming over low scrub. "This moon has an atmosphere?"

"It's a bit thin and inhospitable, but yes. The inhabitants of that planet started a terraforming process here before they destroyed themselves. We'll land soon."

"We weren't allowed to dock at the space station without permission," Bianca said.

"Oh, we can't get anywhere *good* without permission here, either," Severyne said. "We can land on the surface, but the underground galleries and pleasure domes are less accessible. This is the unfashionable side of the moon, where the servants and crews congregate, so we'll fit right in." They crested a low mountain range, and Severyne said, "Oh, good, we can set down there."

She pointed to a hexagon marked out on the ground in glowing lines. Other hexagons were scattered across the greenish-gray surface of the moon, many of them occupied by ships of varying shapes and sizes. "We're allowed to park in any open hex. The locals will impound the ship eventually, when we fail to pay our docking fees, but we don't need this shuttle anymore anyway." Once they were settled on the ground, Severyne deployed the ramp, then popped out the transponder they'd tampered with earlier. The ship blared an alarm, but only briefly, and then the vessel's lights went out.

Severyne had to suppress a gasp. In the sudden darkness, Bianca's eyes began to glow, a faint blue that quickly faded. Was it some adaptation that helped her see in the dark? What *was* she?

They walked down the ramp and stepped onto the

moon's surface. The air was breathable, if a bit astringent. "I'm so bouncy!" Bianca jumped into the air in the low gravity and did a full pirouette as she drifted back down, laughing joyously. Severyne had experienced the same joy in movement, at times... but usually those movements involved hitting people with things.

"That ship should do." Severyne nodded toward a vessel a few hexes over, larger than theirs, with a crew lugging cargo crates on board. "They look like they're on the way out. Do you want to distract them, or hide this?" She held up the transponder, still blinking its little telltale light.

Bianca frowned. "Won't the Barony shoot them when they catch up?"

Severyne sighed. "You're so concerned for others. Once the *Grim Countenance* gets within range, they'll realize it's not our ship, and shooting won't be necessary. They'll be fine."

Bianca grunted. "I'll do the distracting, then. I like meeting new people." She turned and bounded toward the workers, shouting, "Hello, I just got here, it's wonderful, can you tell me, is there anywhere good to *eat* around here?"

Severyne tuned out the prattle, slipped around the far side of the ship, and crouched by one of the landing gears. She had a small pressurized can of sealant on her belt, sufficiently strong to bind the transponder to the gear. She sprayed, attached, and counted to ten slowly for the sealant to dry. She wiggled the device. Hmm, still a little loose. She'd better–

Severyne sighed. She had to act like all these evasive maneuvers were real in front of Bianca, but she didn't have to *believe* it was real. She gave the transponder a last squirt anyway and then sauntered around the ship. "Amina, stop bothering those people, they have work to do. Forgive my hireling. She's new."

The Xxcha lugging a crate rumbled, "It's fine. She's charming. Enjoy your visit."

"They told me where to get *pie*," Bianca said. Severyne led her away, toward a cluster of low domes beyond the landing zone. Bianca leaned closer and said, "Why did you call me Amina?"

"I knew an Amina once. It's the only name, other than Bianca, that I know for sure is plausible for a human."

"Secret identities! What should I call you?"

"Whatever you like, as long as it's a Letnev name." Might as well indulge her.

"Genevieve, I think," Bianca said. "That was the name of one of the great Barony generals I read about. We'll call you 'Gen' for short."

Severyne couldn't help but be flattered. Genevieve Lamorte was a legendary general who'd crushed a dozen uprisings with effortless aplomb. She frowned. "You actually *are* charming. Where did you learn to be like that?"

"I don't know," Bianca said. "It's just… Look, I really thought you were a spy earlier. I almost left you to certain death, and I feel terrible about that. I've decided I'm going to treat people like they really are the way I wish they were. Sometimes I'll be disappointed, but you know what? I bet a lot of people will rise to the occasion."

"You're so… *human*."

"Tell that to Brother Errin," Bianca said. "What's in the domes?"

"Places that sell various intoxicants, probably. Along with places to sleep off their effects."

"Yay!" Bianca said. "But I guess we aren't getting intoxicated?"

"We are not. We are going to find intoxicated people to take advantage of instead."

Heuvelt sat drinking in a corner of a bar on Glamarij. Ashont and Clec were a few tables away, playing cards with a Winnaran and a Saar. They were only betting with toothpicks taken from the bartender, but apparently the toothpicks represented the honor of their respective species, and Heuvelt did not feel capable of representing humanity in the manner his people deserved. He stared at his hand terminal, where two windows were open. One window showed their credit balance in the ship's account Clec had opened (since accounts with Heuvelt's name on them tended to get frozen or seized), and the other displayed a Barony of Letnev fugitive bounty database.

The first window was very nice. The Disciplinarian had paid quite well for their delivery, with a bonus for swift completion. He paid so well that Heuvelt wondered what, exactly, they'd handed over to the twitchy little Yin scientist, but it was probably better not to know. The *Show and Tell* was actually operating in the black again.

The second window was... less nice. Heuvelt was still listed as a "fugitive alien of interest" with a note to "contact Barony officials immediately if you know his whereabouts." The Disciplinarian said that alert would be expunged, but it might take a few days for the system to update, Barony bureaucracy being what it was. The Letnev weren't offering a reward for him anymore, so he doubted anyone would bother to turn him in – most species didn't feel a need to do the Letnev any uncompensated favors – but the sight of those Barony vessels back at the Tree of Grace still had him twitchy and on edge.

Which is why, when a Letnev woman strode in, glaring around the bar, he froze.

Her eyes didn't linger on him for very long, though, before she stomped toward the bar, moving like she wanted to kick the floor to death with every step. *Then* Heuvelt noticed the woman she'd come in with. Young, slender, pretty, wide-eyed and smiling, and *human*. Why in the galaxy would a human and a Letnev be traveling together? The species had a long and extensive history of enmity, stretching back to the collapse of the Lazax empire, if not earlier. The human ambled over to Ashont and Clec's table and said, "Ooh, what are you playing?"

"Where I'm from, we call it Kiss-Kill," Ashont rumbled. "The Saar call it Song and Scream, and I don't know what Winnu call it."

"By its proper name," the Winnaran said. "Traitor's Tongue."

"May I watch?" the young woman said. They assented, and she sat down, perched on the edge of her chair. She wore a red dress that should have been out of place in this working-class bar, but somehow she seemed perfectly at ease, and the motley group around her was at ease with her in return.

Heuvelt couldn't stop staring at the young woman. There was something strangely captivating about her, and it wasn't just her beauty (when it came to lust, he was mostly attracted to men, though as a rich spendthrift with a taste for adventure he'd dabbled considerably more widely).

The Letnev woman walked over to the table, looked down, and said, "Are you playing for money?"

The other players exchanged glances. "We're playing for honor."

"I don't have any of that to spare," the Letnev said. She put a small glass in front of the human. "You get this one, Amina. Just *one*. Don't accept drinks from strangers, no matter how nice they are. If they're nice, in fact, be especially suspicious."

"Good advice," Ashont rumbled.

"I'm going to the bathroom," the Letnev said. "Lesson one of space travel: never pass up the chance to use a toilet someone else has to clean."

"Yes, Gen." The girl beamed at her. The Letnev scowled and stomped off toward the back of the bar.

Heuvelt watched her go. Was she really just going to the bathroom, or was it a ruse? Maybe she was a fugitive hunter, setting a trap to capture him. Or maybe she was just a loyal Barony citizen, but she'd recognized him, and gone off to call the authorities to turn him in. He looked around, scanning for the exits, so he'd know where to go if heavily armed Letnev shock troopers burst into the bar—

He shook his head and took a deep sip of his liquor. He was being paranoid.

Heuvelt went back to watching Amina as they dealt her in for their next hand. "Oh, I think I picked up the basics from watching," she said airily. Heuvelt doubted that. It was a twisty game, all bluff and double-bluff and cards that changed value depending on the placement of other cards around them. He'd been taught six times, and still made beginner's mistakes. Ah well. As long as they had fun. Everyone deserved a little fun every once in a while.

"Stop whining," Severyne snapped. "You're alive, aren't you?"

Richeline's face flickered on Severyne's stolen wrist gauntlet. The first officer – now acting captain, since she'd lived – had an immense bandage wrapped around her neck, and wires and tubes running into her body, but she was sitting upright, and she was lucid. Too lucid for Severyne's taste, honestly. "I just didn't expect you to *stab* me, captain!"

"I had to improvise. That's part of being a field operative – you should know that, since your dream is to run covert teams. I knew there were soldiers watching us, and that they'd send medical help as soon as I left. You were never in any danger." Richeline had been in a great deal of danger, of course, but Severyne could lie all she wanted while talking to *her*.

The woman wasn't done venting yet, though, apparently. "Archambelle said if you'd stayed even a minute longer, I would have bled out."

"That's why I didn't spend the extra minute, Richeline. Now, please, *focus*. Things are going perfectly on my end. The girl actually *asked* me to help her find Ixth – I didn't even have to plant the seed in her mind." She scowled. "I am curious how she knows the name of her destination, though, and how she learned about the Mahact. She is distressingly well informed."

Richeline groaned. "It must have been Brother Errin.

He refused to sign any confidentiality agreements, but Archambelle said we should go ahead with the meeting anyway. I knew it was a mistake."

"It is what it is," Severyne said. "We can only go forward. Is my new ship ready?"

"Yes. We contracted with the mercenaries through the intermediary you suggested. They had a team in the system, and they just landed on Glamarij. How did you get Sagasa the Disciplinarian to vouch for you? A Hacan crime lord and a Barony captain, it's... not a connection I'd expect."

"Oh, I have connections everywhere," Severyne said. That wasn't really true, but the connections she *did* have were valuable. "Once we give Bianca a proper scare, we'll flee toward the landing zone, 'hijack' the mercenary ship, and lock up the crew. Then we'll escape, and Bianca can set a course for us. You just hang back and follow at a discreet distance until we get wherever it is we're going. Once we've reached Archambelle's magical wonder planet and all the locks are open, the mercenaries can throw off their chains and subdue the princess for me. Understood?"

"Yes, captain."

"Good," Severyne said. "Give me two minutes, and then send in the shock troops."

CHAPTER 23

"I'm really sorry," Bianca said again, raking the last of the toothpicks toward her. "It's just beginner's luck."

"You can't be a hustler," the big teddy bear said, voice all a-growl. "We weren't playing for money, and we certainly aren't going to start *now*."

"Oh, I just enjoy games, and making new friends." Bianca picked up one of the toothpicks and began chewing on it.

Sev emerged from the bathroom, glanced around, and beckoned to Bianca.

She stood up, offering her hand to Strig (the teddy bear), and to Gretla (the Winnaran), and Ashont (the kitty with the little four-armed person on her shoulder), and to Clec (the little four-armed person). "It was lovely to meet all of you."

"Very nice to meet you, too, Amina," Ashont rumbled.

She walked to the bar, where Sev was leaning with studied casualness. "Are we leaving, Gen?"

"I hope." Sev drew Bianca in close and spoke into her ear.

"Did any of those gamblers mention plans to leave soon? We could follow them, and persuade them to let us borrow their ship." She patted her waist, where her sidearm was hidden under her sweatshirt.

"Gen, they're my *friends*. I bet they'd help us if we just asked."

Sev snorted. "Faint hope. Oh, you're charming enough to get us a ride off this rock, no doubt, but we need a ship we can take anywhere we *want*, so we can explore this... what did you call it?"

"My yearning."

"Yes. That. You're not charming enough to convince someone to give us a ship for free, I'm afraid, so we'll have to proceed by other means."

Bianca sighed. "I suppose you're right. I just hate to strand anyone here."

"This is a civilized place. If they're professionals, their ships are insured against theft. They'll be fine." She looked past Bianca, toward the door. "So, again, are any of your new friends departing Glamarij soon?"

Ashont and Clec were planning to leave shortly, she knew – they'd just landed here to refuel and resupply and "get a little R&R."

"I suppose after we find the treasure, I can repay them for the trouble," she said.

"Repay who?" Sev asked.

Bianca started to point out Ashont and Clec, and then time slowed down, the same way it had when the cup fell in the mess hall, but far more extreme. The sounds of the bar, the drinking and boasting and grousing and flirting and slurping and clattering, all elongated and stretched and dropped in pitch. The movements of the people around her stopped almost entirely, until she was surrounded by a room full of mannequins.

Last time, this power had manifested so she could prevent the very small disaster of a broken teacup. What disaster was it meant to prevent this time? What danger had her subconscious noticed, and acted to protect her from?

She looked at the open door and saw a shadow. Two shadows, actually, overlapping. The shadows were moving quickly, far quicker than anything *else* here, though they still crawled. Someone was rushing into the bar. That probably wasn't good.

Bianca stepped away from Sev, discovering that she could move at normal speed. She picked up a bottle from the bar as she went by – not glass, but a heavy metal vessel, containing some potent brew not meant for human consumption. The floor was crowded with patrons, now frozen in place, and cluttered with tables, so she just stepped onto an empty chair and used it as a launching pad to leap over the whole crowd. (Fortunately, the ceiling was high enough for such a maneuver, though the top of her head only cleared it by a few centimeters.)

She landed near the door just as the first of the Barony shock troopers cleared the entryway. Bianca dropped, spun, and swept his legs out from under him, and he fell forward in slow motion. The trooper behind him came at her, and, since Bianca was already crouching, she swung the metal vessel at his knee.

Just at the last moment, she pulled the strike, following

a quick mental calculation. Force equals mass times acceleration, after all, and her acceleration must be a *lot* faster than it currently appeared. If she hadn't pulled back, she thought she would have torn his whole lower leg off – it would have been more like blowing off his kneecap with a shotgun than hitting him with a bottle.

As it was, his knee crunched, and he began his own slow fall. Bianca stood up, and then stepped back, giving herself some room to operate. Two more guards approached, one of them raising a weapon at her – not a lethal armament, she noted, but some kind of tranquilizer gun, meant to subdue.

She threw the bottle at his gun hand, then stepped toward the other soldier while the bottle was still making its way through the air. She had to reach over the first two troopers (who were still slowly collapsing to the floor) to shove him in the chest, sending him flying back into yet another trooper beyond him.

Their bodies moved slow, slow, like drifting snow. Last time, the time dilation had stopped when the cup was saved, and the danger was done – but the danger here was ongoing, wasn't it? This state wasn't likely to end on its own anytime soon, but she needed to get Sev out of here, and that was hard when she was a statue.

Bianca turned her ever-more-powerful attention to the contours of her own mind, seeking to understand the mechanism. How could you seize control of a process that happened without thought? There were ways. Breathing was an automatic function, but you could *choose* to exert control, to hold your breath, to stop and start… or how about changing the focus of your eyes from something up close to something far away? That happened by itself too, but you could blur your vision at will if you wanted... Ah. There. The process had been opaque to her when the teacup fell, but now she could understand. Brother Errin was right. She was changing all the time. Bianca exhaled, walked over to Sev, and then bid time return...

Heuvelt jerked his head up at a sudden explosion of violence by the front door. His hand went to the knife at his belt – a gift from Dob Ell that he hadn't thrown away, because even though their friendship was over it was still a good blade. He couldn't tell what was happening exactly, but bodies were falling, and people were screaming. After a moment, his brain caught up to his eyes and made sense of what he was seeing – those were Barony of Letnev soldiers, in their terrifyingly blank face masks and black body armor.

Someone *had* seen him, and turned him in, and the Barony was coming for him! He couldn't tell what had happened to their ranks, whether they'd been attacked or if one of their weapons had gone off by mistake, but the commotion might allow him a few crucial moments to escape.

"Ashont, Clec, come on!" Heuvelt leapt up from the booth as his crewmates shoved back from their table and rushed to join them. "Through the back!" They followed as he hurried toward the doors leading to the kitchen. Heuvelt had spent enough time in bars to know that door would inevitably lead to some sort of back alley or service entrance or loading dock – they certainly didn't take the trash out or bring the kegs in through the front door, after all.

He was surprised to see the human and Letnev women –

Amina and Gen – rushing toward that exit too. What were they running from?

They all piled up in the rear of the kitchen while a human in a dirty apron shouted at them. "It's locked!" Gen shouted, hammering her fist against the door. She spun toward the cook, drawing a gun, and said, "Open this door!"

He shrieked and ran away, and Gen swore, then pointed the gun at Heuvelt. "Who the hell are you and what do you want?"

"I- I- we…" Heuvelt had never been good at expressing himself when he was figuratively under the gun, and it turned out he was even worse at doing so when the gun was literal.

"I've got it." Amina kicked the door, and it *crashed off its hinges*, banging against the wall of the hallway beyond. Was the door made of lightweight plastic or something? It had certainly *looked* solid enough. Amina rushed through, and Gen followed.

Heuvelt looked at Ashont and Clec. "Very strange," Ashont rumbled.

"They went through there!" a voice shouted from the bar behind them. Heuvelt swore and ran through the opening, his crewmates following. They pelted down the service corridor on the other side, Gen and Amina just a few steps ahead. Someone yelled at them to stop immediately, so Heuvelt ran faster. Gen looked back at him without breaking stride and shouted, "Why are you following us?"

"I'm not!" he called. "We're just running away in the same direction!"

"Why are you running away?" Amina called.

"Because there are Letnev soldiers *chasing* us!"

"They're chasing *us*, you fool!" Gen said.

Oh. Could that be possible? Surely not. Such a thing would constitute good luck, and Heuvelt no longer believed in that. "I don't think so!" he said. "I'm a wanted man in the Barony!"

"Us too!" Amina said. "Only we're wanted women!"

"Go away, leave us alone, you're slowing us down!" Gen shouted.

"How can we be slowing you down when we're behind you?"

"Stop chasing us or I'll shoot!" the Letnev howled.

"No, don't!" Amina said. "This is perfect! Ashont, Clec, strange man – let's all go to your ship!"

"*What*?" Gen shouted.

They escaped the building and slammed the external door behind them. "I don't know how to lock it!" the human (who ran pretty fast, for an old guy) cried out, furiously pushing his fingers against an access panel.

Bianca touched his shoulder and gently pushed him aside. She was learning to be gentle, now that she could so easily break things accidentally. She squinted at the panel, punched in a rapid sixteen-digit code, and then smiled as the lights went red and bolts slammed home. "There. I remembered the factory settings, and they didn't change. The door thinks there's atmospheric decompression on this side. It won't open without a command override from the station administrators now."

"There's *atmosphere* out here," the man said. "Why would there even be a code to indicate decompression?"

"This facility uses standard hardware and software," Clec said. "The same doors are used on space stations and habitats all over the galaxy. But there are dozens of manufacturers – how did you know the factory codes for *this* one?"

Bianca shrugged. They were the same sort of doors used on the *Grim Countenance*, and she'd perused a technical manual on one of her visits to the engineering department, until they chased her off. The next time she came down, the terminal with those files had been locked. It had taken her almost a full minute to unlock them. "I must have picked them up somewhere."

"Our Amina has a mind like a wastebasket that never gets emptied," Sev said. "It's been a displeasure meeting you. We'll be on our way now–"

Bianca shook her head. "They've got a ship, Gen. I'm sure they want to leave in a hurry. We should go with them, instead of taking our chances on finding a ride elsewhere."

Sev opened her mouth as if to object, then looked toward the ranks of parked spacecraft in their neat hexagons. Her shoulders slumped. "Fine. We can work with this. Take us to your ship."

"You weren't *invited*," the human said, drawing himself up and crossing his arms over his chest.

"She's the reason you aren't in Letnev custody right now, Heuvelt," Ashont said. "Even if those troopers weren't chasing us specifically, they would have been happy enough to pick you up as a bonus." The panther-woman showed off her teeth in what was surely meant to be a smile. "*I'm* inviting her."

"Seconded," Clec said from her shoulder.

Heuvelt sighed. "I–"

Something slammed hard against the door on the other side.

"Go!" Sev said. Ashont and Clec set off running, weaving through the parked ships, and the others followed. They arrowed toward one particular vessel, on the far edge of the lot, and Bianca was surprised to see it was a fast courier, though retrofitted to add extra compartments on either side of the main body – it looked like a wasp wearing saddlebags.

A signal pulsed out from Clec toward the ship, and – Wait. Bianca wondered how she knew that. Apparently, she had another new ability, bubbling up from the depths. She couldn't exactly *see* the beam of energy, but she could sense it, from its origin to its direction. Now that she knew to pay attention, she could sense a whole overlapping array of signals, crisscrossing the facility and the ships. She could pick out individual signals and trace them from source to destination. She shook her head. There would be time enough to ponder this new sense later. Clec's pulse triggered a mechanism on the ship, and a boarding ramp slid down as they approached.

"Get us out of here!" Heuvelt shouted, the last one on board, the ramp rising under his feet as he ran. Ashont and Clec were already moving to the front, the engines engaging in reply to more signals from Clec.

"We'd better strap in," Heuvelt said. "Things get a bit bumpy on the *Show and Tell* when we take off in atmosphere."

"Your ship is called the *Show and Tell*?" Sev said. "That is a ridiculous name."

Bianca smiled and turned toward her. "Your old ship was called the *Grim–*"

She stared at Sev for what felt like a long moment (it was, in fact, barely a microsecond), then snatched the knife from Heuvelt's hip, knocked Sev's legs out from under her, and leapt atop the Letnev, blade raised.

CHAPTER 24

"Report!" Richeline barked. Voyou winced, and he wasn't even on the receiving end of her bad mood.

The shock trooper's head filled the screen at an odd, tilted angle, as seen from the camera on a wrist gauntlet. "Xing disabled half a dozen of my people. We need immediate medical attention–"

Richeline pointed at the bandage bulging around her neck. "I *told* you to be careful around her."

"We didn't have time to be careful, captain. She attacked us before we even came through the door."

"Remarkable," Archambelle murmured. "If we could replicate her transformations, the military applications–"

"Shut up," Richeline said. "Not you, trooper. Continue your report."

"Xing fled, as planned, along with some bystanders from the bar, who we assume were frightened by the violence. Those few troopers capable of movement pursued her all the way to the facility's external door. The door was sealed before we could continue pursuit, but we'd chased them nearly as far as we were supposed to, anyway."

"Are you expecting congratulations? Following your orders exactly is the bare minimum I expect, squad leader, and you didn't even manage to do *that*."

If he looked chastened, Voyou couldn't tell; those full-face masks were useful for hiding emotions. He wished *he* had one. "Understood," the trooper said. "We're in some trouble, here, captain. The local security forces aren't happy with an unauthorized action on their moon—"

Richeline slapped the terminal, and the squad leader's head vanished from the screen, replaced by a map of the moon's surface, with a blinking dot moving slowly from left to right. "What in the bright stars are they doing over *there*?" Richeline said. "Their rendezvous with the mercenary ship is on the other side of the facility, but the captain is going the wrong way. No one is chasing them anymore, so they should be heading straight for the extraction point. The whole *point* of sending in those troopers was to herd Xing in the right direction and make her jump onto the first available transport."

"I'm sure the captain knows what she's doing," Voyou said loyally. He wasn't sure why he was even part of this executive team – probably because he was the first person on board to meet Bianca, and the only "friend" she'd had on board, which made him, rather laughably, the closest thing they had to an expert on her psychology. He didn't think he'd be able to add much of value, but no Letnev would turn down an opportunity to sit closer to the seat of power. In this case, *very* close: they were in Captain Dampierre's ready room, the most secure place on the ship for monitoring a clandestine operation.

"Spoken like someone the captain never stabbed in the neck," Richeline said.

"Wait. Where did her signal go?" Archambelle shoved her face close to the screen, as if perhaps the little blinking dot had merely gotten smaller and fainter, instead of completely disappearing.

Richeline hissed and pulled the doctor away. "Stop it. Maybe I just need to reboot the monitoring system." She tapped at the terminal for a moment, squinted, then shook her head. "No good. We've lost her."

"What does that mean?" Voyou asked.

"It means we can't track her anymore." Richeline sat back in her chair – the *captain's* chair, and, to be fair, she was acting captain, but Voyou still wouldn't have dared to sit there in her place. "As for *why* we can't track her... it could be a malfunction, I suppose. *You* implanted the tracker, Archambelle – what are the odds you botched the job?"

"Nil," she snarled. "That tracking device is so simple it's barely capable of failure." The doctor didn't look good, in Voyou's opinion. She'd always been pale, even by Letnev standards, but now she looked somehow waxy, too. She must not be sleeping much, or not very well when she did. "We deliberately chose the most foolproof device available. The tracker doesn't even have a separate battery. It's passively powered by Severyne's own body heat – oh." The doctor sat down and stared at the least interesting wall in the cabin.

"So that means if she died," Voyou said, "then the tracker would die too? Once she, ah, cooled off?"

"One outcome I did *not* consider was the death of Captain Severyne Joelle Dampierre," Richeline said. "I honestly thought she was too mean-spirited to die." She shook herself. "All right. The mission goes on, even if the captain doesn't. Let's scan the moon, and interdict and search any ship that leaves. Our runaway princess has to be *somewhere*–"

A Letnev face appeared on the screen, the image bordered by the flashing red that indicated an emergency override message. "Captain, the Glamarij authorities are demanding we collect our troopers and immediately leave the system."

"What? Who are they to give commands to a Letnev warship? We could bomb their moon into shards!"

"They, ah, have excellent orbital defenses, captain. They've also jammed our scanners and communications equipment – indeed, *everyone's* communications equipment – so we can't reach out to the Barony. I think they're concerned about public relations, considering their wealthy clientele, and they have the newest Hylar tech, so we can't overcome their jammers, except by traveling outside their range." The bridge officer cleared her throat. "We've also received a message from Lord Alicante's personal secretary asking, quote, 'Why are you bothering her Lordship's dear friends the Glamariji?'"

"When you say Lord Alicante…"

"The Baron's second cousin, yes, captain."

Richeline closed her eyes. Voyou was very glad he didn't have her job. "Fine. All right. Get me the Glamarij – whoever is in charge here – so I can apologize for the misunderstanding. Let them know we were pursuing a wanted terrorist, and there was no time to go through proper channels. Send a shuttle to pick up our troopers." She blanked the screen and slumped back in her chair.

"What *now*?" Archambelle said. "We can't simply give up! That girl holds the key to securing Letnev supremacy, throughout the galaxy, forevermore!"

Richeline shrugged. "I'm not the one who killed the captain. More's the pity."

"We can't follow her as planned," Voyou said. "But don't we know where she's going? Those three stars she always talked about, right?"

Richeline sat up. "That's true. Archambelle, what are the coordinates for that empty bit of nothing in the sky?"

"Coordinates? There are no coordinates! She pointed at a bit of darkness! The center of a triangle made by three stars that aren't even all that close to each other, astronomically speaking."

"So we don't have coordinates," Richeline said. "We have a direction, and that means we have a heading. What wormhole gate gets us *closest* to those stars?" She looked at Voyou. "That question was directed at you, Undercommandant. You're in charge of surveyor teams, so you're the closest thing in this room to a navigator."

Voyou wasn't flustered. The captain – could she really be dead? – had flayed him with words on a regular basis. Richeline couldn't compete. He consulted his wrist gauntlet. "There are two possible gates nearby, one controlled by the humans, the other by the Naalu. The Naalu will let us pass for a price, but the humans won't let a Letnev warship pass through for any price."

"Fine. Send word ahead to the Naalu, with a photo of Xing.

Tell them she's a wanted terrorist and we're offering a reward for her apprehension. Maybe we'll get lucky and she'll try to use that wormhole too."

"And if not?" Archambelle said. "We just, what, aim for a vague point in the distance and hope we happen to cross paths with the girl?"

"We're headed to the middle of nowhere," Richeline said. "No one goes there, because there's no *reason* to go there. If we find any ship in the vicinity, odds are it's hers."

"I detest this plan," Archambelle said. "But I cannot think of a better one."

The screen blinked on again, with the same apologetic bridge officer, bordered in override red. "The premier of Glamarij is on the line."

Richeline made a shooing gesture at Voyou and Archambelle. "Get out of here. I have to practice diplomacy now."

Voyou didn't much like Archambelle – she looked at you like she was guessing how much your organs weighed – but when engaged on a secret mission, one had to find camaraderie where one could. "It's a shame we didn't put a tracking device on Bianca," he said once they were in the corridor.

"We did. Three times. The first two were simple subcutaneous implants, placed secretly in her back. I found the first tracking chip on the floor outside her cabin. The second one, I found on the floor of the corridor, halfway between the lab and her rooms. The third time, I told her I needed a deep tissue sample, and jammed a needle in as far as I dared." She sighed. "I found that tracking chip under the examination table – it never even made it outside the lab. Her body simply expelled the devices, so quietly and efficiently that I don't think Bianca even noticed."

"She's a remarkable woman," Voyou said.

"Mmm. She is a compass and key that will lead to a world of wonders. Her only value is utilitarian and scientific."

Voyou could hardly think of a suitable reply to that, so he moved on to another topic. "Do you really think the captain is dead?"

"As a scientist, I am reluctant to draw conclusions based on a single piece of indirect evidence, but I am also capable of assigning probabilities to various explanations. There *are* other reasons the tracker could have failed, but Severyne's death is the most likely. It's a shame. She didn't believe in the mission, not the way I do, but she would have pursued our goals to the death anyway, simply because that *was* the mission."

"She did," Voyou said.

"She did what?"

"Pursue our goals. To the death. It seems."

Archambelle made a sour face. "I wish she'd pursued the mission a bit *closer* to the goal first."

"Be careful with that." Severyne scowled at the Naaz as she sewed up the shoulder gash Bianca had inflicted on her. Clec had a delicate touch, at least. "Did you stitch up that human's face, too? I don't want a big ugly scar like *he's* got."

Clec, hovering in a little anti-grav harness, made a clucking sound. "I think it gives Heuvelt's face character. And no. That wasn't my work. This shouldn't leave a mark once you've healed."

"Back on my ship they would have smeared on some medical gel and healed my wound seamlessly. You're using a needle and thread? Barbaric."

The door to the tiny medical bay – really just a closet with a reclining table, a first-aid kit, and some rudimentary medical machinery – slid open, and Bianca sidled in, eyes downcast. "Back on your ship, they were going to put you to death," she said. "No amount of medical gel would have fixed that."

"Did you *have* to tackle me, princess? Really? You could have told me what you had planned."

Bianca shook her head. "Once I realized there was a tracking device inside you, I knew we had to cut it out and destroy it right away. If the ship had actually taken off while that device was active, the *Grim Countenance* would have been able to figure out our heading, and then it would have been easy to tell what vessel we were on – I had to act immediately."

That was all true, and it was also why Severyne really wished Bianca had noticed her tracking chip ten minutes later.

"I was very careful, really, and I made the smallest incision I could."

"How did you know they were tracking me?" Severyne allowed a little of her genuine dismay to come through, since she could play it off as pain from her wound. When Bianca had leapt on her with that knife, Severyne was sure it was all over – that Bianca's psychic abilities had blossomed, and she'd seen the truth of Severyne's treachery. But then Bianca had flipped her over and cut the tracker out of her shoulder instead.

"I just… I can tell when there are signals going back and forth, from machine to machine, system to system. That's new, or anyway, I just realized I can do it. When I saw signals coming out of *you*, I knew it had to be a tracker. I'm just glad we found it. Now we've got a real chance at getting away."

Yes. Getting away on *the wrong ship*. They should have been on board a mercenary vessel, crewed by Severyne's hired freelancers, pursued at a respectable distance by the full might and majesty of the *Grim Countenance*. Instead, they were on a ship with a crew who were, apparently, fugitives from Letnev justice. Bianca really was off the leash.

Not entirely, though. Severyne was still here. She'd just have to complete the mission herself.

She reached out and snatched the hovering Naaz from the air, grasping its four flailing limbs, two in each fist. "Tell your captain we're commandeering his vessel," she said.

For the second time that day, Bianca hit her.

CHAPTER 25

Severyne rocked back when Bianca smacked her arm, and Bianca winced – she hadn't meant to apply that much force. Clec went spinning out of Severyne's grasp, and suddenly her four arms were glistening with tiny metal spikes – weapons, though Bianca wasn't sure what kind. She stepped between Clec and Severyne. "Stop! Clec, I apologize, our original plan was to hijack a ship, *but*," she turned and glared at Severyne, who was rubbing her arm. "*But*, that won't be necessary, because we can make an arrangement that benefits everyone."

Clec lowered her weapons. "If I tell Ashont what you did, she will bite your face off," Clec said. "And I tell Ashont *everything*. Amina, if you wish to have a discussion with us, you must first lock her up." She sent out a signal. Bianca watched it pass through the door.

A few moments later, Heuvelt appeared, holding a pair of shackles. "What's going on here?"

"This Letnev uses violence as a first resort," Clec said. "It is best if we curb her negative impulses before she gets hurt."

"Amina could kill you all in the space of three heartbeats," Sev said. "That's three of *your* rapid little heartbeats, Naaz."

"But I *won't*," Bianca said. "Everyone, please, calm down." She spread her hands, smiling, and to her surprise, Heuvelt and Severyne both appeared to relax, their muscles loosening, their eyes softening and then going glassy. What was happening?

"I must ask you to stop generating soporific pheromones," Clec said.

Bianca blinked. "Am I? Did I?" She stopped doing it, and only in that moment did she even realize what she'd done, or that she could control it.

"I have detected an anomaly in the atmosphere, yes. My personal filtration system prevented the chemicals from affecting me, and I'm instructing the ship's filters to do the same." The Naaz bobbed before her in the air. "How did you even *do* that? With cross-species compatibility!"

"I didn't mean to!" Bianca said. "I'm so sorry, really. Can we just... talk?"

Heuvelt snapped the shackles onto Sev's wrists. "Oh, yes. We should definitely talk."

"Why did you shackle her, Clec?" the Rokha growled.

"Because I know you won't bite someone in chains," the Naaz said.

"Using my own ethical framework against me is unfair."

"It may be reasonable to bite her later," the Naaz said. "We should try to gain a better understanding of the situation first, though." She turned, fixing her eyes on Severyne and Bianca. "Why were you fleeing the Letnev?"

Severyne placed her shackled wrists on the table. Playing the prisoner had been rather more enjoyable than actually being one. The galley was small, and five people crowded it, even when one of those people was so small they perched on another's shoulder. "Do you want to field this one, princess?"

"Sev is on the run because—"

"Who's Sev?" Heuvelt interrupted.

Severyne sighed. "I am. And the princess here is Bianca. We were using assumed names earlier, but I suppose it hardly matters now."

"I see," Heuvelt said. "I disapprove of false names, for personal reasons, but... do continue."

"Sev struck a superior officer," Bianca said, "and was sentenced to death. She helped me escape the brig on the Barony ship. I'm so sorry she grabbed you, Clec, really, we just didn't have time to discuss changing our plan, it's my fault—"

"Why were you in the brig?" Ashont said. "Does it have anything to do with your ability to dispatch half a dozen Barony shock troopers in mere seconds?"

"Yes, are you some sort of augmented soldier?" Heuvelt said. "A Barony experiment meant to infiltrate Federation society or something?"

"I'm not any kind of soldier. I'm... well... I'm a compass. And a key. But mostly I'm just a person."

"Explicate," Clec said.

To Severyne's considerable dismay, Bianca told them her entire life story, from her father discovering the secret lab up to their escape to Glamarij, and all points in between. Some of it, like Bianca's early fluency in Letnev, Brother Errin's revelations about her true nature, and her hacking her way to free rein in the *Grim Countenance* systems confirmed the worst things Severyne had suspected. She congratulated herself on her paranoia, though; Richeline had thought planting the fake personnel file was an unnecessary precaution, but if she hadn't, Bianca would have seen a photograph of the real captain, and the whole ruse would have failed.

"I do not know about these Mahact," Clec said, "but I have heard of Ixth. A world of impossible wonders."

"I've heard of Ixth too, in adventuring circles," Heuvelt said. "A world with rivers of liquor and trees made of gold. But tales of Ixth are like those stories about the lost colony world of the Hylar, filled with forgotten technology, or the Muaat City of Diamond – they're just *stories*."

"The Mahact were real," Bianca said. "They made me. They're remaking me, even now. I don't know why, but the Letnev thought I was created to lead people to Ixth. They thought following me would make them rich and powerful. If you help us get where we're going… I can make you rich, instead. Will you help me?"

"We'll have to discuss this," Heuvelt said.

Bianca nodded. "Of course! Sev and I can wait. Ah…"

"My cabin is fine," Heuvelt said. "Please don't remove her shackles."

"I don't even have the key or the code," Bianca said.

"I think we all know that would not prevent you, if you wished to set her free," the Naaz said.

Bianca blinked. "Oh. I suppose that's true. Of course I

won't." She rose, and Severyne followed her. They went into Heuvelt's room, with its unmade bed and pile of dirty clothes in one corner, and the door closed after them.

Severyne wrinkled her nose. "This place is vile." She shook her shackles. "Will you get these off me?"

"I think Ashont would hurt you if I did. I could smell she was serious."

"Oh, you can smell intent now?"

"Sometimes." Bianca sat down on the edge of the bunk. "Really, Sev, you didn't have to grab Clec like that. I listened to them while we played cards – they're doing deliveries these days, but by preference they're explorers and treasure hunters, trying to make money to outfit their next expedition. We can *be* that next expedition."

"I apologize," Severyne said. If she couldn't have her own loyal crew on hand, the next best thing was dumping *this* crew out an airlock, but it seemed that wasn't going to happen, either. What could not be changed must be accommodated. "I was acting in what I believed to be our best interest. That trick with the pheromones, did you know you could do that?"

"I really didn't." She sounded miserable. "I don't want to make *anyone* do things they don't want to do."

"I don't know much about these Mahact, princess, but you sure don't sound like you inherited your morality from them. According to the legends, they liked taking and making slaves, ruling by force, and destroying anyone who opposed them."

"Just because I have some of their power doesn't mean I have to use it the way they did. I'm afraid of my own capabilities, Sev. With all the things I can do, I have to be extra careful, don't you see? Sometimes I think it would be better for me to forget all about my yearning and go live on some little planet out of the way somewhere. But I have to know what's in that dark space behind the stars. I thought when I got closer, the need would diminish, but it's actually gotten stronger. It's like being hungry, or thirsty, or exhausted – it's a desire beyond thought, deep in my body. I know the Mahact programmed this need into me, but I need to know why."

"What if it's something bad?" Severyne hadn't thought much about that question before. She was a pragmatist. She had her orders, and knew the purpose of her mission, and she would do everything she could to fulfill it. Archambelle was irritating, but she was also brilliant, and there was no reason to doubt her theory about Bianca's provenance and purpose. But it was all speculation, based on fragments of ancient lore and assumptions that could be faulty. The only way to truly know Bianca's purpose was to follow her and watch her fulfill it.

Severyne's first field operation had gone disastrously awry, and given her a glimpse of cosmic horrors beyond her capacity to imagine. She really hoped that sort of thing wasn't going to become a pattern.

"Then I'll do my best to use it for something good instead." Bianca glanced at the closed door. "How long do you think it will take them to decide?"

Severyne snorted. "Bianca. Really. What is there to decide?"

"What is there to decide?" Clec said. "If we refuse to help her, Bianca could disable all of us, lock us in the cargo bay or jettison us from the airlock, and take our ship for her own. If we cooperate with her willingly, we might actually make a profit instead."

"I concur," Ashont said. "Working with her is the only practical approach."

"So, we believe her story?" Heuvelt said.

"It's so outlandish, it's hard to believe it's a fiction," Ashont said. "Surely a liar would have concocted something more plausible. The Letnev certainly wanted her for something. Plus, we saw what she did in that bar, and even on our ship – she *is* something more than human."

"It's all very hard to credit," Heuvelt said. "But it won't be the first time I've chased a hint of a whisper of a rumor into the depths of space." He smiled. "Let's do it."

Ashont cocked her head, and Clec made a sort of strangled sound. "Wait," the Naaz said. "You agree?"

"All I want is to be a treasure hunter," Heuvelt said. "I didn't lay awake in bed as a child and dream about transporting freight – that was simply a necessity for survival. This is a chance to get back to what I love. Seeing the light of unknown stars on new worlds. Cracking open vaults and looting the treasures within. Walking where no human has trod before. That's what I was *made* for. To be honest, I'm delighted this strange woman hijacked our ship. Otherwise, what – we'd be doing more deliveries for Sagasa, ad infinitum?"

"Helping a Letnev fugitive – *two* Letnev fugitives – isn't going to help your legal situation," Ashont said. "If they find out we're involved in this, Sagasa won't be able to scrub you from their systems."

"I have spent too long driven by fear," Heuvelt declared.

That fact had recently struck him with the force of epiphany. "Look at Bianca – barely an adult, from a nowhere planet, taken from her family and friends, used against her will, abused and experimented upon, and what did she do? Did she sulk on the outskirts of a system waiting for paperwork to go through? No. She seized control of her destiny and struck out into the unknown, to *seek* her destiny. She *inspires* me."

"Are you sure there aren't any more strange pheromones floating around?" Ashont said.

"None at all," Clec said. "This is all him."

"It's unanimous, then," Heuvelt said. "Set a course for the nearest appropriate wormhole."

"There's a Federation of Sol gate that will get us in the right direction," Clec said.

"And we won't have to worry about running into any lurking Letnev there," Ashont added.

"I'll go give our guests the good news." Heuvelt stood up, smiling. He didn't do that much anymore – smiling made the muscles in his face contract around the scar, and the skin felt tight there as a result, which usually wiped any brief sign of happiness off his face. This time, though, he didn't care. He'd resigned himself to a life of shuttling to and fro, running errands for criminal scum. But now, *now*, he was on a mission of greatness, chasing a chance at wonder once again.

Granted, things hadn't turned out very well last time he tried that, but what kind of explorer would he be if he gave up forever after the first time he got lost?

CHAPTER 26

The Federation of Sol ran an efficient port, and, according to Heuvelt's grumbles, charged accordingly. Bianca sat in the cockpit, watching the ships bustling to and fro, taking in the strange convex shape of the space-time anomaly at the center of all the traffic. "Why does the wormhole *glow* that way?"

"There is nothing I'd call a glow in any of our visual spectrums," Clec said, hovering over the pilot's chair. "I think you're seeing things we can't see again."

"That's a shame," Bianca said. "It's so beautiful."

The *Show and Tell* transited the wormhole without difficulty. Bianca slowed down her subjective time sense as they passed through – she could do that at will now – but the transition still happened almost instantaneously, and she didn't gather any useful data. She'd have to think about wormholes more. They were interesting. The whole fabric of space-time… it seemed like there were possibilities there.

They emerged on the far side of the wormhole, where there was comparatively little traffic, and all of it headed in the same direction. Heuvelt stepped into the cockpit and nodded at Bianca. He looked a little queasy. "That's step one on our journey of who knows how many steps."

Bianca pointed at the departing ships on the viewscreen. "Where are they headed?"

"Toward the Zaxony system, mainly," Clec said. "It's the nearest point of interest, a Federation of Sol colony built in the ruins of a star-shell left behind by some lost civilization. There's a joint project with the Hylar government to research the structure's origins and find new applications for the tech. Beyond that, there's a colony world called Whiteraven, which I'm told is a nice place to live, except for all the bone-colored terror birds trying to rip you to pieces. Is that where we're going?"

Bianca shook her head and pointed. "We're going that way. What's over there?"

"Nothing," Clec said. "At least, as far as anyone has noticed in any recorded survey."

The door opened again, and Ashont stood on the other side, Severyne lurking nearby, hands still shackled. They couldn't all fit in the cockpit.

"Should we resupply?" Heuvelt said. "The administrative station for the wormhole can provide most of what we need, but it would be nice if we had some idea how far we were going. I don't suppose you can be more specific than saying 'that way', Bianca?"

She considered. "We're *much* closer now. Drastically so. That wormhole really made a difference. Hmm. I know how far we've traveled, and I know how much more intense my desire to reach our destination is now, and if I plot the change in my internal state against our movement in space, I can extrapolate an end point to the curve–"

"You don't have any telemetry data," Severyne interrupted. "You don't have records of ship speeds or course headings, nor do you know *this* ship's capabilities. How can you extrapolate anything?"

"I glanced at navigation screens on the *Grim Countenance*," she said. "I perused star maps. I read through this ship's manual this morning, so I know the specs. I was sitting right here when coordinates were discussed. I remember it all well enough. It's just a question of putting the data together."

"How can anyone possibly remember that level of detail?" Heuvelt said.

"I… just can," Bianca said. "Do you trust me?"

"Trusting you is the entire basis of this expedition," Clec said. "So it doesn't seem to be optional."

She closed her eyes, and a three-dimensional map of this sector of the galaxy filled her mind. She drew curves across her vision and watched them converge. She opened her eyes. "At top speed, it will take us seventeen days to reach our destination. But I don't know if that's our *final* destination. Maybe it's just the first stepping stone."

"You're saying there might be a wormhole there," Sev said.

"There may be. Or maybe just directions, or a trail marker, pointing to another place. I just don't know. Sev, do you want to stay here? Or on the shellworld? You just wanted to escape the *Grim Countenance*, and I feel terrible asking you to risk your life this way. You never set out to be a treasure hunter."

"Though there is no more noble calling," Heuvelt said.

"Not many more interesting ones, at least," Ashont said.

Sev grinned. "Being free is one thing, princess." She rattled her shackles. "Isn't it better to be free *and* rich? Besides, now I'm curious about these Mahact of yours."

"Very well," Heuvelt said. "We'll outfit ourselves for a journey of indefinite length. I've done *that* before."

"We'll outfit ourselves for a journey of depressingly finite length, actually," Ashont said. "We didn't get paid *that* much for our last job. We did some repairs based on the assumption that we'd be getting more work from Sagasa soon, too."

"Oh, that's all right," Bianca said. "I have authorization codes. We can charge whatever we need to the Barony, or rather, to one of the officially neutral sub-accounts they use when it's necessary to make payments to organizations they don't have diplomatic ties with."

Sev made a choking noise. "*What*?"

"I hacked the ship's financial system, just to see if I could." She shrugged. "When you see something nested under ten levels of encryption and dig through those and see the words 'covert operations budget' in the metadata, well, that sort of thing grabs your interest."

"The Letnev will *know* someone defrauded them," Sev said. "They'll know we came this way. Use those accounts, and we might as well still have tracking devices on us."

Bianca cocked her head. "They'll know we came this way anyway. They know the general heading of my yearning, after all, and this is one of the obvious wormhole gates to use. A flagged transaction won't tell them anything they don't already know. They just won't know where we went *from* here. We can lay a false trail, I bet – Heuvelt, when you're getting supplies, talk about your plans to explore the uncharted regions of space beyond Whiteraven."

"That might possibly work," she said.

Bianca beamed. "Sev, coming from you, grudging admiration is like a kiss on the mouth and a whoop of joy all rolled up in one."

Bianca loved her time aboard the *Show and Tell*.

When she'd first caught sight of Heuvelt, sitting alone in the bar on Glamarij, she'd made the sort of swift (and usually accurate) assessment her mind automatically generated these days: a once-formidable man, handsome and privileged, fallen on hard times – slipping into middle age, nursing his bitterness, and fixated on his failures and scars. She didn't think her read on him was wrong, exactly, but it was incomplete. Heuvelt Angriff had simply been a man out of place, and miserable there, but now, he was back in his element: right or wrong, wise or otherwise, he was pursuing his passion again, and being on a treasure hunt animated him, made his spirit bright, and turned his whole bearing boisterous and warm.

She'd been worried, at first, that Heuvelt would be creepy – he was a human man, after all, and she'd met plenty of those on Darit who wouldn't let a little thing like a two-and-a-half-decade age difference stand in the way of flirtation or attempts at even greater liberties. Heuvelt had never even needed a brush-off, though, either because his tastes didn't run that way, or because, as seemed increasingly obvious, he looked at her more like a younger sibling than anything else.

Bianca didn't know if she reminded him of someone from his earlier life or if she was the little sister he wished he'd had, but they clicked, and spent a lot of time together laughing as they told each other stories about their homeworlds. Their upbringings could not have been more different, which made the swapping of experiences more interesting for both of them. He called her "farm girl" and she called him "rich kid" , and he told her about exploration techniques and she tried to teach him to be slightly better at cards.

Ashont and Clec were complete in themselves, but Bianca got to know both of them too: as the members of a relatively less powerful polity, they had strong opinions about all the various factions in the galactic political arena, and Bianca absorbed their perspectives as fast as they could share them. For their part, the duo was amused and amazed by Bianca, and they frequently played games to test her capabilities – throwing multiple objects for her to snatch out of the air, blindfolding her and making her identify various objects through the synergy of her other senses, cranking up computer games beyond their maximum speed settings and watching her reflexes keep up just fine anyway. Ashont liked to recite long passages of literature in a foreign language into one of her ears while Clec whispered technical specs into the other, and they'd marvel as she recited them back, one after another at first, and then alternating word-by-word, letter perfect every time. "You could make good money on the entertainment vids," Ashont said. "If the whole being-a-fake-space-princess thing doesn't work out."

"I'll keep that in mind," Bianca said.

Sev was... not blossoming, but she was, at least, not

engaged in open hostilities anymore. She sulked a bit, and didn't talk to anyone except Bianca, but *their* talks were fascinating. Sev was more than willing to answer questions about security protocols, how to exploit flaws in systems (people, Bianca knew, but Sev explained *how* to exploit people), and to share her opinions on assorted military matters. Bianca had the persistent sense – based on another synergy of senses – that Sev was hiding something, but really, a woman like that probably had *lots* of secrets.

One night, Sev loosened up sufficiently to share some of Heuvelt's liquor – Letnev biology was roughly compatible with that of humans, at least when it came to getting intoxicated. Bianca got tipsy and told her about her first time (pretty much her only time, with Grandly, which is what led to him following her around all moon-eyed).

"My first time was nothing to speak of," Sev said. "Just another girl in the dorms. Lots of us did that sort of thing, just to calm the hormonal distraction so we could focus on our studies."

"You've never been in love? I thought I was in love with Grandly, for about five minutes, but it was just the *idea* of being in love."

"The Letnev are more about strategic interpersonal alliances than love, princess. But…" She sipped brown liquor from her tumbler and grimaced. "There was one person."

"That human you fraternized with?"

She winced. "Ah, that memory of yours, princess. Yes. Her name was Azad. She was fascinating, and challenging, and profoundly irritating – she made your company positively soothing in comparison. Still. I am glad we shared what we did. Knowing her opened up my understanding of the world. But we could have never worked out. I'm glad our involvement ended before it became even more disastrous."

"Doomed romance is even *more* romantic, in a way," Bianca said.

Severyne threw her head back and laughed until tears rolled from her eyes.

"What?" Bianca said. "*What?*"

"Sometimes, princess, you're so fast, and so smart, and so strong, that I forget you're also *so young.*"

Bianca grinned despite herself. "It's nice to hear you laugh, Sev, even if you *are* laughing at me."

"It's a cold, dark universe, princess. We should all take laughter where we can find it."

It was fourteen days into the journey before Severyne felt safe making contact with her people.

Bianca was sleeping, and careful experimentation had revealed that she didn't snap instantly awake when a signal went past. Severyne wriggled her way into the ship's communication system so she could piggyback on their emergency beacon and its powerful supraluminal broadcast capabilities. She wouldn't be able to engage in an actual *conversation* with Richeline and Archambelle and Voyou, but she could update them on the ship's destination... assuming they'd had the good sense to traverse the obvious Naalu wormhole and head in the known direction of Bianca's yearning. If not, Severyne would be broadcasting to empty space. She didn't like depending on the competence of her underlings, but she had no choice.

Severyne recorded and sent her transmission, before scrubbing all evidence of the message. Then she waited, crouched in the corridor beside the access panel she'd tampered with. After ten minutes, when no one came to jettison her into space, she crept back to the hammock she'd strung in the port side cargo hold.

Heuvelt slept in the starboard hold, and if the connecting doors were open she could hear him snoring. Bianca was sleeping in the captain's bed, because Heuvelt was a polite host, but that politeness didn't extend to Severyne. She was meant to be grateful they'd taken the shackles off her a mere three days into the journey. Bianca had finally convinced them that "Sev is trustworthy, even just on the basis of her naked self-interest!" That was certainly true, to a point. She would help Bianca and her pet menagerie fulfill their mission, up to the moment it diverged from her own. There was no reason to be a treasure hunter when you could just follow the treasure hunters and steal what they found, after all.

She looked at the hammock with great distaste, and went instead to the cockpit. Clec was there, as she was most of the time. Naaz didn't sleep much, apparently, and while Ashont slept frequently she didn't do so for very long at a time. Severyne dropped into the co-pilot seat and said, "Anything going on?" Casual, casual, always casual.

"Nothing at all. No one has even tried to tear my arms off in over a week."

"I said I was sorry."

"You never did, actually."

Severyne sighed. "I meant to. That sort of thing doesn't come easily to me. So: I apologize for laying hands on you."

"Apology accepted. Why did you strike your ship's first officer?"

Severyne didn't have to watch her words as carefully with Clec – there was no reason to think the Naaz could detect a lie – but she was in the habit now. "Richeline is arrogant, self-important, and irritating."

"These are qualities you detest? In anyone other than yourself, I mean?"

It could have gone either way. Once upon a time, a jab like that would have made Severyne bare her teeth and strike back, verbally at the very least. She'd been through a lot, though, and had been jabbed more ruthlessly by experts. She was able to laugh at herself a little now, and so that's what she did: or chuckled, anyway. "I have nothing against arrogance, as long as it's justified. I don't think I'm arrogant at all. I simply have… a clear-eyed self-regard."

"You can't be all bad. Bee seems fond of you."

"The princess doesn't have many friends. She becomes overly attached to those she does have. Even if we aren't worthy of her regard."

"She's extremely pleasant, for an unstoppable, genetically engineered killing machine."

"She's not engineered for killing, I don't think." Severyne decided speaking freely here would do no harm, and might ingratiate her, a little, with Clec and thus the rest of the crew, which could be useful when the time came to betray them. "I think her capacity for violence is a side-effect. If it was just about murder, the engines in her DNA would have her spewing neurotoxins or producing biological weapons instead of bliss-inducing pheromones. She's engineered to do something *else*, and the ability to defend herself is just a way of making sure she survives long enough to do whatever that is."

"Was she always so bright and quick? She pumped me for everything I know about space flight, physics, and galactic history and culture, and it's not because she needs to know anything, she just has an endless hunger for information. I think she's read every piece of media we have in the ship's database, and the other day I caught her consuming audio-visual media at thirty-two times the standard playback speed – how can she even follow it when it plays that fast?"

"Time doesn't work for Bianca the way it does for us. That's how she took down armed shock troopers without any combat training. She's not a particularly skilled warrior. She's just so much faster than everyone else that it doesn't matter. A clumsy blow can knock you down just as well as a graceful one, if you can't dodge or block the strike."

"I hope those kind of reflexes aren't a prerequisite for survival wherever we're going."

"Me too," Severyne said. "Though we could actually trust Bianca to go in on her own, and bring back whatever treasures she finds, and share them out as agreed. Isn't that remarkable? I've never known anyone like her."

"I think you're right," Clec said. "She seems so... well, good. But I think the flip side is, she expects her allies to behave just as honorably. If someone disappoints her, and she loses her temper and acts impulsively? I wouldn't want to be on the other end of that fit of pique."

Severyne kept her breath steady. She was afraid that was a hint, and that the Naaz would casually say, "By the way, I intercepted your transmission," and then things would turn very violent very fast.

Clec didn't say anything like that, though; instead, she said, "I'm picking up something on the long-range sensors."

"A planet? A moon?"

"Can't tell. Maybe an asteroid, but there's a lot of metal in it. Could be a ship, but if so, it's derelict – no energy signatures. We'll be close enough for a visual scan in a few hours."

"I knew this trip was going too smoothly," Severyne said.

"You make a good partner for Bianca," Clec said. "Someone needs to provide a counterbalance to her optimism and good cheer."

CHAPTER 27

Another message arrived.

This time, when the sleeper woke, he remembered who he was: Kor Noq Weer. A name to inspire terror, once upon a time, even among those who trafficked in terror. A name synonymous with rogue, with renegade, with apostate, with traitor. But that name had outlasted so many others, hadn't it?

He took in the message, sent by a nearby relay. The child had passed through a wormhole, it seemed, closing the distance between them greatly, and soon she would reach the World of Stone. From there, she need only traverse the gate, and open the tomb, and fulfill her purpose.

After so many uncounted millennia spent patiently waiting, things were moving fast, now – very fast.

Soon the name Kor Noq Weer would be known and feared across all the worlds of the galaxy again.

CHAPTER 28

"A wrecked ship." Heuvelt gazed at the viewscreen with everyone else. "When I was a teenager, I went hiking in the wilderness. I forced my way through the brush, broke trail along the bottom of an overgrown ravine, climbed up a cliff face, and reached the summit of a rock tower, with absolutely breathtaking views in every direction. Except right at my feet. Do you know what I saw right at my feet?"

"A beer can," Ashont said. "You've told this story before."

He sighed. "Sev and Bee haven't heard it. The point is, there's a unique sort of disappointment in going to a place you think is wholly undiscovered and realizing someone else got there first and left their junk behind."

"The more pressing question is who *wrecked* that ship," Sev said. "I've never seen damage like that before."

The ship actually looked a bit like a crumpled can, Bianca thought. It had probably been graceful, once, shaped like an arrowhead or a predatory bird in flight, but it had been crushed. "Do you know what kind of ship that is, Clec? I didn't see anything like it in the *Show and Tell*'s database, or the *Grim Countenance*'s, either."

"Its design is unknown to me," Clec said. "Would anyone like to go over and see what's inside? Whatever destroyed the vessel doesn't seem to be lurking around at the moment."

Bianca, Heuvelt, and Sev suited up for the spacewalk. "You could probably go outside without a suit on, Bianca," Heuvelt said over their comms. "Given everything *else* you can do."

"I can hold my breath for a long time," Bianca said. "But that wouldn't help with the moisture on my eyeballs and tongue vaporizing instantly, or my lungs exploding from the pressure change, and then there's the solar radiation... let's just say I'd rather not test my capabilities that way unless I have to."

The outer airlock door opened. Bianca had never done a spacewalk before, and the experience of stepping out of the ship into the void was dizzying, exhilarating, and astonishing, but by now her yearning was so intense she had to fight her urge to use her little propulsion pack to send her off past the wreck, toward the point of her mysterious desire. She was tethered to Heuvelt and Sev, though, so they pulled her along to the ship and didn't even notice her urge to fly away alone.

They reached a huge gash in the hull of the wreck, and Heuvelt shone a light inside. Debris floated around the interior, the artificial gravity as dead as everything else. They eased into the ship. The corridors were a little larger than they were on most human or Letnev vessels, but the contents of the compartments weren't too alien – there were hammocks, even, though they seemed to be spun of some cocoonlike silk material. There was a galley, with unfamiliar foodstuffs, preserved by the airless vacuum – pale blue eggs, bits of gray meat sealed in plastic, bundles of stalks and flowers and stems.

"They were humanoid, judging by the clothes in this locker," Heuvelt said. "Let's take a look at the bridge. Maybe there's some data to be recovered."

Bianca reached the bridge first, so she was the one who found the bodies. The front of the bridge was open to vacuum, the viewscreen cracked right down the center, and a hole torn in the hull big enough to walk through upright, so the two crew members must have died quickly. Unlit consoles ringed the room, controls for systems that had been catastrophically damaged.

The floating aliens were humanoid, insofar as they were bipedal and had two arms, but they had wickedly curved beaks, and heads covered in feathers, though they seemed devoid of wings. They both wore uniforms with unfamiliar insignia at the shoulders, six jagged quadrangular segments of alternating size arranged around a central point to create a sort of starburst shape. "Bird people?" Bianca said. "I didn't know there were bird people."

"It's a big galaxy." Sev floated past the corpses, toward one of the control panels. "I wasn't aware of any avian humanoids with the capacity for space travel, but I'm no xeno-anthropologist. Unless a species is powerful enough to be a military threat, or unlucky enough to live somewhere with resources we need, the Barony isn't concerned about keeping track of every sapient species." She worked at the computer for a while, then shook her head. "Even if I understood their technological architecture, this is all hopelessly broken." She looked at the deep dents on the ceiling and the floor, where the metal had been deformed under some terrible pressure. "It looks like somebody picked up this ship and squeezed it in their fist. Have you led us to the land of spacefaring death giants, princess?"

"Your guess is as good as mine."

Sev grunted and sailed out of the bridge, down an unfamiliar corridor.

"How long ago do you think this ship was destroyed?" Bianca asked.

"It's hard to tell," Heuvelt said. "Nothing rots in vacuum, and I have no idea if this ship is state-of-the-art for bird people, or a quaint antique. I think we should probably proceed very carefully from here. If the place we're headed is as valuable as you think, it could well be protected. We might be looking at the aftermath of a security system being triggered."

"I'm supposed to be the key, though," Bianca said. "Surely they won't crush *me*?"

"Let's hope they won't crush the people standing next to you, either." Heuvelt spun around slowly, taking in the bridge. "There's nothing here for us. No information, and nothing I'd call treasure. We should continue on our way. We'll be wherever we're going in a few days now, if your calculations are correct."

It took them a while to find Severyne – she'd gone to the

engine room, she said, to see if there was anything worth salvaging, but the technology was so different from their own, she soon realized it was pointless.

The three of them returned to the *Show and Tell* and continued on their way, the crew overall more subdued, and more watchful.

But they were more watchful in the sense that they were looking *out* for potential threats from the outside, which is why none of them noticed that Severyne had a souvenir. She'd carefully wrapped an item she found on the wrecked ship in a layer of alien hammock fabric and jammed it in the crack between her back and her suit's propulsion pack. While everyone was getting out of their suits on the *Show and Tell*, she managed to slip the salvaged item out of the gap and into her waistband, and made her way to her own little corner of the ship, a hammock strung among heaps of supplies.

Nestled safely behind a pile of crates, she slid the object out of her waistband and unwrapped it.

Severyne had found a weapons locker near the engine room on the alien ship, and there had been many lovely things inside: rifles of an unfamiliar curving design, and graceful sidearms with multiple barrels, and even something like an archer's bow, but with integrated sights and no visible ammunition, which made her wonder if it fired energy bolts of some kind.

Most interesting, though, was the symbol she saw carved into all their hilts or stocks or barrels. She had no idea what the symbol *meant*, but she'd seen it before:

it was one of the glyphs Archambelle had shown her. A symbol of the Mahact. Archambelle hadn't said anything about the Mahact servants including bird people, but her information was hardly complete. Perhaps these were Mahact weapons. Or, perhaps they were the weapons used by those who *opposed* the Mahact. There were hash marks beside the symbols, three lines on one weapon, four on another, two on a third, all clearly scratched there by hand. Were they tallies, perhaps, of enemies killed by those weapons? There was no telling how old the ship was – the dead might have been soldiers in a war that ended untold eons ago. Those guns probably wouldn't work after all this time, anyway, even if Severyne could have gotten one off the ship unobserved.

But there was a knife, with a blade curved like a raptor's beak, the edge shimmering with its own faint blue light. The hilt was etched with that same symbol, and there were easily a dozen hash marks carved around it. This might be a blade that had tasted Mahact blood – or whatever they had instead of blood – many times. Best of all, the knife was small enough for Severyne to sneak it out.

Would the knife hurt Bianca? She wasn't sure, and in truth she hoped she never had to find out, given how formidable the girl had proven to be, but Severyne believed in taking advantage of opportunities when they arose, and this knife was a gift from the universe.

She found some canvas and used the blade to cut it into strips – the weapon was gratifyingly sharp, having lost none of its edge during its long interval of disuse. She used some epoxy resin to bind the canvas into a sheath, and fixed the sheath to the inner waistband of her pants. Now the knife could rest comfortably, hilt nestled into the small of her back. Maybe it would stay there.

The blade was just a contingency, but Severyne felt so much better when she had one of those at hand.

"It's today," Heuvelt said. "Isn't it today? You said it would be today."

"We're very close," Bianca said, for the third time that morning. She sat in the co-pilot's chair, while Ashont and Clec ran the ship. Their scanners were stretched to the limit of their range and sensitivity, and they revealed: nothing.

If she shuffled through the *Show and Tell*'s external cameras, Bianca could still see the three stars that had formed that triangle encompassing her yearning, but each one was off in a different direction now; one behind, one above, one below. They formed no discernible pattern from this vantage, transformed into unrelated points of light. Everything was a matter of perspective, wasn't it?

They *were* close – she could feel that. Doubt crept in, though. What if she was being drawn to a place that had *once* held something of value, but now held nothing at all? What if her yearning led her to a wormhole that had been disabled millennia ago by the victors in a forgotten war? The lab her father Keon found her in was so *old*. Maybe her whole existence was meaningless. She could be a compass leading them to a city that was not just ruins but entirely vanished. A distress beacon on a dead ship, still pointlessly beaming out a cry for help. A key to a door that had turned to dust in some forgotten epoch.

"We've got enough food and fuel to get back where we started easily enough." Heuvelt's dolorous tone belied the practicality of his statement. "No great loss, apart from time." He sighed. "I suppose Sagasa always needs more—"

"What is *that*?" Ashont pointed through the viewscreen.

"What?" Heuvelt peered. "I don't see anything. Magnify?"

"It's a light," Bianca said. "There's a *light* shining out there!"

"Whatever it's shining out of must be tiny," Clec said. "I'm not picking up any objects in that direction at all. Let me see what I can do with the visual sensors."

That distant yellow point of light leapt forward, growing in the screen, and now they could see the contours of some solid object illuminated by its backscatter, the surface smooth. "Some kind of asteroid?" Bianca said.

"It can't be!" Clec said. "I'd be picking it up on my sensors... here, let me try something, if I move the ship so the object occults one of those distant stars, I can examine the lensing and – wait. It eclipsed that star way too fast. That doesn't make any sense, the object would have to be *huge*." Clec buzzed around like an agitated fly. "That's a planet. Or something the *size* of a planet. But it doesn't show up on our sensors. How does an *entire planet* not show up on our sensors? There's no stealth technology in the galaxy that can do that! If we hadn't seen the light, we might have been caught in its gravity well before we even *noticed*."

Bianca gazed at the absent planet, and a feeling of serenity descended on her like a blanket in the coldest winter. She released an audible sigh. She felt like she'd spent the past twenty years being thirsty and had finally taken a drink.

Hungry, and had finally eaten.

Asleep, and was finally awake.

"We're here," Bianca said.

CHAPTER 29

First they orbited the planet, and did a visual survey, which didn't tell them much: the surface was mostly smooth, and black or dark gray, with occasional large irregularities that might have been structures or the remnant of structures. The planet was either an unnatural object created in a colossal feat of engineering, or a planet with no star that had been transformed for unknown reasons.

There were no lights or signs of habitations, save for the single yellow beacon.

The *Show and Tell* didn't have a shuttle – it was too small – so they had no choice but to descend to the surface on their own. "I'll have to land entirely by eye," Clec said. "We can't use the automated systems, because they don't think there's any land below us at all. If we miscalculate our angle or velocity... well, it won't be good for us."

"Let me pilot the ship." Bianca was perfectly serene.

"Have you ever flown a ship like this before?" Heuvelt asked.

"She hasn't," Sev said. "But she'd never defeated a squad of Letnev shock troopers until the first time she did. If she thinks she can land us safely, she can."

"I can." Bianca sat down in the pilot's chair, looked over the controls, and switched the system to manual. She began a slow descent. "There's no atmosphere, or if there is, it's very thin – I'm not hitting any turbulence at all."

The ship felt like an extension of her body. Flying it was no more difficult than walking down a set of steps. Bianca guided the *Show and Tell* gently in the direction of the light, which proved to be a luminous orb set atop a cyclopean structure made of stone blocks, like a step pyramid.

Bianca set the ship down so gently they barely felt the impact. She smiled beatifically at the crew crowding into the cockpit. "Shall we take a walk?"

"Is this the destination?" Sev said. "I mean, is this the treasure planet? Ixth?"

Bianca shrugged. "It's the place I was meant to go. If I'm meant to go somewhere else after this, that will be revealed. But from what Doctor Archambelle said, no. I don't think Ixth is seventeen days' voyage away from a known wormhole. That seems too easy. So, this may just be a stepping stone."

"Which isn't to say there won't be things to loot here, I trust," Heuvelt said.

"Oh, there may be valuable artifacts," Bianca said. "But the knowledge we stand to gain will be worth far more."

"I am aware it's possible to sell knowledge," Heuvelt said, "but the collectors *I* know are more interested in objects."

"I'll get the blowtorch and the wrecking bar," Ashont said.

Once they were all suited up and ready to deploy the ramp,

Bianca turned to face them. "Maybe I should go in alone, at first? Just in case?" She didn't want to leave her companions behind, but she didn't know what waited for them in this strange place.

"You can take the lead," Sev said firmly. "We'll give you a little space, but you can't possibly think we'd let you go in there alone."

Tears welled in Bianca's eyes, and she threw her arms around Sev. "You're such a good friend." She stepped back, blinking – you can't wipe away tears with a space helmet on – and then straightened her back. "I'll do my best to protect you all, no matter what we find here."

"We know you will," Heuvelt said.

Clec lowered the boarding ramp, and they descended to the surface of a world made of stone. The gravity here was higher than it was on the ship, and Bianca noticed her friends stumble, but it barely registered; the difference in gravity was just another piece of data. The structure topped by the light was only a hundred meters or so away, and Bianca strode toward it confidently, with full faith that her destiny would reveal itself.

Then she stopped, holding up a hand to call the others to halt. "The structure is transmitting… or, no, wait, it's receiving… there's a signal going *into* it."

"A signal from where?" Sev asked.

Bianca turned her head, following the lines of force, and went *hmmm*. "It's communicating with the *Show and Tell*."

"I want to say 'that's impossible,'" Clec said. "Because my encryption protocols are very good. But I am willing to believe a lost civilization of super-intellects can break them,

I guess. It's not as if we have any valuable secrets hidden in our data banks."

"I'd rather an alien entity didn't seize control of my ship!" Heuvelt said.

"We can always do the necessary sabotage to convert the *Show and Tell* to fully manual control," Ashont said. "Bianca has demonstrated she can fly instruments-only. Actually, she barely even had instruments."

"The transmission has stopped," Bianca said. "I guess we keep walking?"

"It is better to act than to wait and be acted upon," Sev said. "Lead on."

Bianca closed the distance to the pyramid by half, but then the beacon lit up in that other spectrum again. "It's transmitting again–" she began.

"Greetings, child of the master, and her companions." The voice was low, rumbling, and broadcasting on their comms channel. "Forgive my intrusion into your ship's systems. I had to ascertain what language I should use to speak to you."

"Who are you?" Bianca asked.

"I am Tyrolian the Gatekeeper. I understand you are known as Bianca Xing, honored heir. May I call you Bianca?"

"I… yes, of course. This is not what I expected."

"I am sure you have many questions. I have answers."

The peace that had flooded through Bianca was overtaken by excitement. She was talking to – what, one of the Mahact? One of their servants? And that title, the Gatekeeper, suggested there was a further destination beyond this one. "We–"

"I have a question," Sev said. "Did you have anything

to do with a crushed spaceship we found en route to this planet?"

The low, rumbling voice laughed. "You are one of the... Letnev, isn't it? Mmm. Your people were still hitting each other with rocks in your caves when my master was at his zenith, shaping galactic affairs. *Your* questions do not interest me."

Bianca cleared her throat. "These are my friends, Gatekeeper. Without them, I never would have made it here."

"Apologies, honored heir. I will address them with greater respect, if that is your desire. But the point stands: my purpose is to assist you in your journey, not to answer the idle queries of your companions."

"It's not idle, though," Bianca said. "*Do* you know about that ship?"

"I did not encounter the vessel personally, as my duties keep me here, on the surface. But some of my, you could say siblings, patrol this system, and yes, they destroyed that ship."

"Why?" Bianca said, but she was afraid she knew. "Because they weren't *me*? Do you kill anyone who comes here except the honored heir?"

"Not at all." The Gatekeeper's tone was soothing. "No one has ever landed here before – no one has been *drawn* to this particular point in space, as you were, and the World of Stone is not easy to discern. We only lit the beacon when we sensed the shape of your mind. But occasionally ships pass through this region, and we allow them go about their business unmolested, so long as they do not interfere with the World of Stone, or the machinery within."

"What made the ship you wrecked any different?"

"That was a scout vessel send by the Argent Flight. They are old enemies of my master, and all the Mahact. They may have been following rumors or whispers about the existence of the World of Stone, or perhaps it was a cosmically unlikely coincidence. My associate disabled their ship before they could reach us. Be assured, Bianca, that we do not take life lightly. But the Argent Flight... they are implacable fanatics, dedicated to continuing a war that ended millennia ago, and they would not hesitate to destroy this place. If they knew about *you*, your death would be the best possible outcome. They have weapons made to destroy the Mahact and their creations, and that destruction is painful."

"Creations like me," Bianca said.

"Indeed. And like myself, and my cohort."

"Maybe we can continue this discussion inside?" Bianca said.

"Yes, it would be disappointing to be killed by a random stray micro-meteor," Heuvelt said.

"Inside?" the Gatekeeper said. "What do you mean – oh. I see. No, there has been some confusion."

The step pyramid began to move, rotating on its base as the stones shifted their positions. The movements weren't drastic, but they changed the shape of the thing in significant ways, and after a moment Bianca was no longer looking at a temple of blocks: she was looking into an immense face made of planes and angles.

The pyramid was no pyramid at all. It was a stone head, bigger than the *Show and Tell*. It opened immense eyes, and they shone with blue-green light.

"I'll stand up," the Gatekeeper said, and began to rise.

"The crew has questions, acting captain," Voyou said.

"You can just call me 'captain,'" Richeline snapped.

"Yes… captain."

"You said 'acting' under your breath, didn't you?"

"Yes… captain. About those questions. A representative asked me to share their concerns with you during our next meeting."

Richeline groaned. Voyou stood at attention before her, because she hadn't told him he could stop, even though she was slumped in the captain's chair at the captain's desk with her head in her hands. The bandage was off her neck, and she was mostly healed, except for a shiny scar she'd chosen not to have removed because, she said, "It serves as a useful reminder about the nature of the chain of command."

"Questions," she said. "They have questions? I have questions. Like how in the light I'm supposed to find an unknown ship in a search area that spans millions of kilometers or more. But fine. What are *their* questions?"

"Just what you'd expect, captain." He managed to swallow the "acting" entirely that time, though it took an effort, and he hoped the *real* captain never found out. He still couldn't really accept that Severyne was dead. His mind simply wouldn't retain the information. Maybe if he'd seen a body… though maybe not even then. Pretending to be dead just to find out what people might say about her afterward seemed like something the captain would do. "We've been following an erratic course for more than two weeks, with no stated mission or goal. We are crewed by loyal Letnev soldiers, of course, and they'll do what they're told, without question, but in addition to troopers, the crew also includes surveyors, linguists, mining engineers, all sorts of planetary annexation specialists who aren't accustomed to this sort of open-ended assignment."

"They'd better *get* accustomed, or they can see how they like taking spacewalks without environment suits on. They should realize that on an 'open-ended assignment' like this I don't actually *need* surveyors and mining engineers."

"I'm sure they do realize," Voyou said. "I imagine that adds to the general anxiety. The half rations don't help. They also want to know when the captain is coming back." Officially, Severyne had been recalled to the home world to update the Baron personally about the state of their annexation efforts, but that was a flimsy sort of lie, and only the most prone to propaganda believed it.

"The captain is dead," Richeline muttered. "Long live the captain. Is there anything *else*?"

"Well. Yes. The crew is also wondering where the 'princess' went. There are all *sorts* of rumors about Bianca at this point – including that she's the one who stabbed you in the neck. One popular notion is that she attacked you and escaped, and you vowed revenge. When the captain refused to let you chase after Bianca, you killed her, and seized control of the ship to pursue your mad obsession."

"That's the plot of *The Lord and the Liar*!" Richeline finally lifted her head. "They think I'm reenacting a two-hundred-year-old *opera*?"

"In the absence of any other narrative, I'm afraid so. If we told them something – anything, really – they'd feel better."

"Tell them we're in pursuit of a terrorist bent on the destruction of the Letnev people. Tell them *she* killed the captain, because she almost certainly *did*."

"Really?" Voyou said. "You want to go on the record, officially, that the captain is dead?"

"Of course she's dead! She must be dead! What else could have possibly–"

A red-bordered emergency call appeared on the screen, and a bridge communication officer said, "We have received an encrypted message for you, captain."

"From the Barony?" Richeline said. Voyou knew she hoped she was being recalled. She was ready to give up this whole mission as a waste. Archambelle was still fanatical about it, but she was mostly being fanatical alone in her quarters these days.

"We're not sure where the message came from, captain – it arrived from an unremarkable quadrant of space, presumably sent from a ship – but it has top-level authorization keys."

A moment of silence. Then: "Send the message to my desk."

A flashing icon blinked on her screen.

Voyou stared at it. "Is that… could it be…?"

"Call Archambelle," Richeline said. "We might as well all watch it together."

The doctor arrived, even more disheveled than the last time Voyou had seen her. She'd been poring over her database of Mahact artifacts and translations, desperately seeking some detail that would narrow down their search parameters, and she hadn't been eating or sleeping much. "What is it? Did you find the girl? Did you find *anything*?"

"Something found us." Richeline activated the message.

The captain's face appeared on screen, half hidden in shadow. "Hello, devoted underlings. I know how much you've missed me. You'd better come and join me, don't you think?"

CHAPTER 30

Heuvelt had seen extraordinary things in the course of his many journeys.

He'd watched twin suns twinkle through the geysers of the living silver fountain on Abadona Eight.

He'd ridden the last train out of the poisoned city of Thammux, and turned in his seat to watch its towers collapse behind him as the local government bombed their own seat of power in a desperate (and futile) attempt to stop the logic plague.

He'd kissed one of the most famous entertainment vid actors in the world in the viewing gallery of a luxury Supernova Tour liner as a star imploded just on the other side of the transparent forcefields.

He and Dob Ell had skied over icy plains beneath red-and-gold aurora, and blasted their way into an icy temple complex devoted to the dead gods of a cold-blooded species rendered extinct by climate change. Once inside, they navigated corridors mosaicked with scenes of reptilian warriors fighting their implacable furry enemies, dodged pit traps and spike traps and arrow traps, and reached the central chamber where a statue of a saurian king ten meters high presided over dust and spiders. (Someone else had gotten there first and stolen the statue's jeweled scepter and orb, but still, what a thing to see.)

He'd seen his whole life, and all its extraordinary wonders and glories, flash before his eyes when Dob Ell came at him, snarling, shame-blade in hand, so in a way, he'd seen all those remarkable things *twice*.

But all those wonders paled in comparison to seeing Tyrolian the Gatekeeper rise. The ground shook beneath their feet, throwing all of them off balance, except Clec (who hovered) and Bianca (who simply compensated, shifting her weight as the ground lurched). The great being raised all four of its arms out of the ground, seams in the planet's surface revealing themselves to be merely the edges of the Gatekeeper's immense fingers and limbs. Those hands *were* big enough to crush a ship, and Heuvelt looked fearfully back at the *Show and Tell*, afraid it would be swallowed by a crack in the ground, but its portion of the planet seemed stable. This wasn't an earthquake, really, as much as it felt like one. It was more like someone climbing out of a hole.

The Gatekeeper's immense chest rose up from the surface, a chiseled blank of stone threaded with lines of shining metal. "There," the Gatekeeper said, resting one set of immense elbows on the ground. "I don't suppose I need to stand *all* the way up. You have some sense of my stature now, and I would hate to inadvertently step on any friends of the honored heir."

"What *are* you?" Bianca craned her neck to look up at the now-distant stone face. "You said the Mahact made you, but… how?"

"The creation of Titans is complex and difficult," the Gatekeeper rumbled. Though his head was far above them now, he still spoke to them through their comms, so the voice was intimate and close. "We can reproduce ourselves, though with great effort, and the process requires long periods of dormancy. The Mahact could create us more easily, but they did not share all their secrets with us. We are living beings, of stone and steel, created to serve the Mahact. I was created to serve a *specific* Mahact: my master, and your maker, honored heir."

"But *why* did he make us? I don't understand what the point of all this is! Why arrange for me to be born on a distant planet, to look like a human, to draw me here – what is the goal? Why am I here?"

Heuvelt winced in sympathy at the anguish in Bianca's voice. He'd often wondered what the point of *his* life was, but he could accept, ultimately, that there was no inherent purpose to existence – he was responsible for making his own meaning. Bianca was different. She'd been created for a reason, and she deserved to know what that was.

"I wish I could ease your mind, honored heir," the Gatekeeper said. "I know only my own part in your journey. I was charged to wait, and watch, and listen. To protect this place, until the honored heir arrived. And, once you arrived, to send you through the gate."

"Where does the gate lead?"

"To the abiding home of the master."

"Who is this master?" Bianca said.

"Kor Noq Weer," the Gatekeeper said.

Bianca didn't say anything for a moment. Then: "I don't know who that is."

"Kor Noq Weer was a great scientist, philosopher, and shaper of destinies," the Gatekeeper said. "His name rang through the stars even at the height of the Mahact empire. He found this planet, near a wormhole, and shaped it to his liking. He created the machinery that closed the wormhole, and that will open it again. He made me, and he made *you*, and I know he considered you the greater creation, simply because of the nature of my orders: to honor and protect you at all costs. Whatever he intends for you, it must be something great."

"Is Kor Noq Weer still alive?" Bianca said. "I thought all the Mahact were dead?"

"I do not know," he rumbled. "I was assigned my duties long ago, and the master was very ill, even in those days. Perhaps he has passed on, but left instructions for you. Or perhaps he waits, dormant, in stasis, to share some final words with you before he passes on. Who can say?"

"I have so many more questions," Bianca said. "What is Ixth like? What do the Mahact *look* like? Was Kor Noq Weer... nice?"

"I will tell you all I know. We can converse while I set the machinery in motion to reopen the wormhole gate."

Heuvelt looked to the sky. There was no evidence of a wormhole yet, and no telling where it would appear. He glanced around at his companions. Clec and Ashont were circling around the immense torso of the Gatekeeper, communicating on their private channel; probably wishing they could pry the valuable ore out of that immense body. Sev was – huh. Where was she? He looked back toward the ship in time to see her disappear up the ramp. He opened a channel to her. "Sev? What are you doing?"

"I'm thirsty and my suit reservoir is empty. I'll be right back."

"Ah, of course." He realized he was speaking to an empty channel – she'd cut the comms as soon as she finished speaking.

Heuvelt didn't trust Sev. He'd confessed this to Bianca once, and she'd only laughed. "I don't blame you. She tried to squish Clec!"

"It's more than that. She has a secretive nature, don't you think?"

"I spent some time on a ship full of Letnev. Believe me when I say Sev is open and welcoming compared to most of them."

"Mmm. I suppose you're right. I find it difficult to trust anyone since Dob Ell. Though Dob was always kind, even deferential, sometimes even fawning, before she betrayed me, so you'd think I'd be more inclined to trust someone abrasive like Sev."

"After all you've been through, of course it's hard to let your guard down," Bianca said. "But if your walls are too high, nothing good can get through them, either."

Heuvelt's walls were nothing compared to Sev's, though, and he still had profound doubts about her. He walked toward the ship, filled with a sudden and irrational terror that Sev would turn on the engines and fly away, stranding them here with the Titan. The fear didn't make any *sense*, but knowing that didn't dispel it.

The interior of the ship beyond the airlock was pressurized, but he didn't bother to take his helmet off – why waste the time? He crept up the ramp, moving toward the galley, where their water stores were kept. Sev wasn't there. He moved quietly down the corridor to her sleeping area. Maybe she had her own supplies stashed away there. He certainly had all sorts of assorted bottles in *his* makeshift quarters.

He walked in to find her crouched behind a pile of crates, speaking into her wrist gauntlet. Her helmet was off, so he could hear her words: "… about to open a wormhole, so if you're anywhere in the vicinity, you need to get here *now*. You'll have to transit the wormhole quickly, because there are these giants made of stone here, and they can crush spaceships as easily as you'd crumple a piece of paper–"

She must have sensed his presence and simply pretended not to, because she spun and knocked his legs out from under him. He went down with a *whump*, landing on his side, and Severyne rolled him face down, then knelt on his back. She was doing something there, messing with his pack, poking at the back of his suit. He tried to open a comm channel to call for help, but only heard dead air – Severyne had torn out his transmitter wires. He tried to rise, but she wrenched his arms behind him, pinning his wrists together, and he couldn't get enough leverage with his knees alone. Maybe he could roll her over, shake her loose, flee the ship, wave his arms–

Things began to get sort of… swimmy. He gasped for air, but air didn't come. She was doing something to his oxygen supply! She was going to kill him – he was going to die – he'd been *betrayed again*, and worse, if she meant him harm, that meant she might try to hurt *Bianca*, and Bianca could fight anything, but only if she knew she *needed* to fight.

Heuvelt's life passed before his eyes again, but curiously, only his life from the *last* time he'd been sure death was imminent – when Dob Ell came at him with the shame-blade.

His life since then was a shorter but rather more depressing span, with a lot more drinking and sulking… but at least the most recent parts of his existence resembled something like the life he'd dreamed of living.

I wish I'd gotten to see Ixth, he thought, and then slipped into the dark.

Once the man was unconscious, Severyne restored his air supply. She didn't think she'd deprived him of oxygen long enough to give him permanent brain damage. *But then again, would I even be able to tell?*

The meddling fool. Bianca was so distracted by the Titan that Severyne decided she could risk slipping back to send another transmission to the *Grim Countenance*, but she hadn't counted on Heuvelt following her.

This situation was annoying. Severyne simply couldn't be found out yet – not before she made it through the wormhole. If Bianca realized Severyne *was* a spy, she wouldn't even have to perform the execution herself: she could just ask Tyrolian to pick Severyne up and make a fist. This situation could be salvaged, though. She opened her comms. "Something's wrong with Heuvelt! I think his suit malfunctioned!"

"What?" Bianca shouted, and Ashont and Clec said "Coming" in unison.

By the time they all crowded through the airlock, Sev had Heuvelt in the reclining chair in the tiny medical suite. A mask over his face fed him oxygen, and his system was filled with sedatives, though Severyne had deleted the logs that would reveal the last part.

Ashont growled "Move," and crouched beside Heuvelt, looking at his medical data scroll past on a screen. "He seems stable. What happened?"

"He was face down, and wasn't moving." Severyne was careful, as always, to avoid outright lies. Bianca was watching her far too closely as she spoke. "His air supply wasn't working properly, but I got the oxygen flowing again, and then brought him here. He hasn't woken up yet, but I think he'll be all right."

"Those suits are all overdue for maintenance," Clec said. "It's my fault. I prioritized ship repairs."

"We all agreed that was the best way to allocate funds," Ashont said. "The suits were still within acceptable range. I'll take a look at his to see what happened."

"I'm afraid I may have damaged his suit," Severyne said. "I was agitated, and I took it off him in a hurry."

Ashont growled at her and stomped off.

"I don't know enough about human health issues." Clec hovered before Heuvelt's face. "Is it normal for them to stay asleep like this? Should I give him stimulants and wake him up?"

Severyne did not reach for the knife hidden in the small of her back, but she was prepared to.

"The body can take time to recover," Bianca said. "I knew a boy who almost drowned, and they saved him but he didn't wake up until the next morning. I think we should let Heuvelt rest. Sleep helps humans heal."

"He'd be just as happy sleeping through a wormhole transit anyway," Clec said. "Those always make him feel ill."

"I need to go talk to the Titan," Bianca said. "Will you all be okay here?"

"We'll prepare the ship for the journey," Clec said. "I hope Heuvelt wakes up before we get to Ixth. He'd hate to miss that."

"Time will tell," Severyne said. Heuvelt might need to suffer a fatal accident later, but if she could keep him sedated until they reached Ixth, and the *Grim Countenance* actually showed up, that might not be necessary. For now, she didn't want Bianca distracted by grief. She might still have crucial work to do. The possibility of encountering a *living* Mahact, even one in stasis, seemed incredibly unlikely. If they did, Bianca was probably the only one of them capable of dealing with such an entity... if anyone could.

Heuvelt's interruption had cut Severyne's transmission short. She'd planned to mention that Mahact name, Kor Noq Weer, to Archambelle, in case it had ever come up in her research.

Oh well. It probably didn't matter.

At just that moment, Archambelle was taking one of her

naps, a brief interval of restless slumber snatched in between long hours spent poring over research.

Quite by coincidence, she'd just read a fragmentary account of one of Kor Noq Weer's more infamous genocidal exploits, the Cleansing of the Barred Spiral.

She was having a nightmare about it, in fact.

CHAPTER 31

The Titan picked Bianca up in its hand and raised her high. The beacon shining on his forehead cast light into the darkness, and she could see other shapes dotting the planet's surface. She clung to the Gatekeeper's fingers and gazed down. The *Show and Tell* looked like a toy from up here. "Are those shapes on the ground more Titans?"

"Some, yes, slumbering and dormant. Others are raw materials for future additions to our ranks. Kor Noq Weer's plans are unknown to us, but we stand ready to serve in whatever capacity his design requires."

Machinery rumbled deep beneath the surface of the World of Stone. Bianca could sense the meshing of great gears, the turning of axles, the thrum of wires, the resonance of crystals. Her expanding senses could feel a change in the sky above them, too. A shimmering. A quickening. A throwing open of locks. "The wormhole will open soon, won't it?"

"Oh, yes."

"Have you seen the other side?"

"I have not. I was created here."

"Then you've never seen Ixth?"

"I have never seen Ixth. I understand it is a place of great and terrible beauty."

She frowned. "Is Ixth where I'm going? Is that where the wormhole leads?"

"My apologies, honored heir. I assumed that was your destination, because you suggested as much. But Kor Noq Weer did not tell me where the gate leads."

"We assumed we were going to the Ixth, but it's just a guess. What if that gate just leads to another stepping stone along the way?"

"Kor Noq Weer is wise, and you must trust in his design."

"I suppose that is, literally, true. I don't have much choice." She paused. "Gatekeeper, did you notice the ship down there sending a transmission a little while ago?"

"I did, honored heir."

"You didn't send it? Through the ship, or something? Like a message to Kor Noq Weer?"

"No, honored heir. I thought one of your friends was sending a message to someone on your behalf."

"No," Bianca said. "Not on my behalf." Her mind was a terrific engine, capable of correlating disparate points of information and drawing conclusions ranked by probability. But she had to pay *attention* to those conclusions for them to do any good. She had to accept them. If she ignored them – willfully ignored them, even – then her capacity for deductive and inductive reasoning was wasted.

Now, unfortunately, some of the probabilities were so high they could no longer be dismissed.

The machinery beneath them fully engaged. A veil of darkness shimmered away, and a shining sphere revealed itself: the four-dimensional point in space-time that marked the end of a wormhole.

"The gate is open," Tyrolian said. "My work is done."

He lowered her to the ground. "Thank you, Gatekeeper."

"To fulfill one's purpose is the greatest pleasure in life, honored heir. I hope you will experience the same joy soon."

Bianca walked to the ship, where her friends – and one person she'd really hoped was her friend – waited.

"We're so close." Richeline was stunned. "We could be there in less than an hour, and if we hadn't gotten that message, we still would have missed it entirely. Voyou, have the navigator set a course."

Voyou sent orders from his gauntlet. He wasn't technically in a position to give orders to the bridge crew, but everyone knew he was the acting captain's unofficial message-carrier, dogsbody, and helpmeet now.

"Giants made of stone," Archambelle muttered. "I've heard of them. Titans, they're called – 'the statues that serve,' sometimes, 'the sleeping giants,' 'the stones that grow.' Some kind of robots, we all assumed. Definitely Mahact. And a *wormhole*. It's just as we thought: a secret passageway to Ixth."

"This will make my career." Richeline was smiling for the first time in weeks, and Voyou thought she looked ghastly. "I assumed this was all a waste of time, but Severyne actually came through. The Baron will make me leader of my own covert operations team for sure after this."

"You think too small," Archambelle said. "Once we have the power of the Mahact at our disposal, the petty wars and covert operations that so excite you will cease to matter. The Barony will have the power to crush our enemies and impose our will on the entire galaxy. Our empire will be eternal."

"It will be good to have the captain back, too," Voyou said.

Richeline glared at him. "Do you find my leadership lacking, Undercommandant?"

What leadership? Voyou thought. She was just following the plan Severyne had provided for her. He bowed his head meekly. "Of course not. I merely respect the chain of command, act– captain."

"See that you respect *my* command first and foremost," Richeline said.

The transit through this wormhole was no different than the first one Bianca had experienced, which was disappointing, somehow – there should have been the bang of drums, the sound of horns, at least a crash of thunder. Instead, there was a silent and nearly instantaneous moment of disorientation, and then they were on the other side.

"We're in a completely uncharted region," Clec said from the pilot's chair. "This star field doesn't appear anywhere in the navigational database. Let me pan around for – oh. Look. There's a planet. At least this one shows up on our sensors."

"I don't think it's really a planet," Bianca said. She could sense, somehow, that the dark shape in the distance was a *made* thing. The World of Stone was a planet shaped to

Kor Noq Weer's whims. This place, on the other hand, was a whim created in the shape of a planet. "More like a giant space station."

Their destination was an immense sphere of metal and ice, dotted here and there with towers as tall as mountains, and one immense black stone obelisk at the pole that made those towers seem like toothpicks in comparison.

"Is this Ixth, then?" Sev said. "It's supposed to be an *actual* planet, right?"

"I'm not sure," Bianca said. "Maybe this is just another–"

She gasped, then doubled over, bracing herself against the console as her whole body shuddered. The full-body muscular contractions were accompanied by a lightheaded feeling, and her blood sang in her veins. "Oh, oh, oh, something – there's something – oh, this makes the yearning feel like nothing at all, this–" She looked up, and now she *could* see the lines of force rising up from the planet, the signals beaming from the towers to the ring of satellites she'd just now noticed, and all that energy streaming – into *her*. "I can feel… this world is like a big machine, some kind of computer, and I'm the user *and* the interface, all at once. I think I can… Look."

She raised her arms, and the lines of force shifted. The tops of all the thousands of towers on the surface burst into jets of sputtering blue flame, and then those flames burned gold.

The surface of the planet was suddenly illuminated, with vast patterns of concentric circles intersected by radiating lines, drawn across the sphere in strokes of light. The new brightness revealed further complex patterning across the surface that resembled circuitry, or a grid of city streets. The towers began to smoothly move, sinking into the surface, but the flames at their tops kept burning, and the circles and lines grew even brighter.

"What did you *do*?" Clec said in awe.

"I am the key." Bianca pointed to the black obelisk. "And that is the door."

"Unless it's the head of another stone giant or something," Sev muttered.

Bianca shook her head. "No. I can *feel* it. That's our way in. And far below, I'll find my heart's desire."

"Which is what, exactly?" Sev asked.

"I have no idea," Bianca said. "I can't wait to find out."

"Fire the torpedoes! Prime the railgun! Launch the fighters!" Richeline screamed. The *Grim Countenance* was a warship with a full complement of small fighter vessels on board, and a squadron of those flew out now, toward the pair of impossible-seeming ships trying to stop them from reaching the wormhole. "Why are their ships shaped like giants?" Richeline said.

"They *are* giants," Archambelle said. "Titans capable of independent spaceflight! They're extraordinary. Imagine what the Barony could do with a fleet of *those*? They could fly to a planet, land on the surface, and lay waste to the enemy. No crew would even be required."

"Trying to put us out of a job, doctor?" Voyou did his best to keep his tone light, but the spectacle on the viewscreen was terrifying. The Titans were a third the size of the *Grim Countenance* itself, and they were reaching out and crushing the Barony fighter ships with their immense hands.

"Oh, stars, what is *that*?" Richeline pointed toward the dim shape of the World of Stone – an anomaly invisible to their sensors. "Is there something climbing *out* of that planet?"

Archambelle leaned close to the screen. "Another Titan," she said. "Bigger. It must have been growing for a *long* time."

"Get us through that wormhole *now*!" Richeline shouted at the bridge crew.

The camera view switched, the wormhole looming before them – until a Titan sailed into their field of view. The *Grim Countenance* was too big for the Titan to simply crush like it had the fighters, but Voyou had no doubt it could do murderous quantities of damage anyway.

"Fire the railgun!" Richeline shouted.

The *Grim Countenance* shuddered. The railgun was meant for disabling enemy warships, and it was basically a simple kinetic weapon: a dense ball of shot, accelerated along a rail that ran the full length of the *Grim Countenance*'s hull, and fired at a small but sufficient fraction of the speed of light. High mass, very high acceleration: immense force.

The shot struck the Titan and sent it spinning away from the gate with a new hole in the center of its chest.

Voyou cheered, and Richeline did too, but Archambelle kept staring at the screen. "The Titan is still moving. Look at that. Arms waving around, legs kicking, thrusters in its feet still firing. Perhaps they don't have anything analogous to vital organs at all. I – wait. Stop. I'm still looking–"

They passed through the wormhole, leaving the few surviving fighter ships behind. Richeline didn't even say anything about them, or their sacrifice. Their pilots must feel so abandoned.

Oh well, Voyou thought. They probably won't have to feel much of anything for very long.

Bianca did the piloting again, guiding the *Show and Tell* toward the monolith. This planet *did* have an atmosphere, but she was deft enough with the controls that the descent wasn't too bumpy. "This atmosphere is breathable for all of our species," Clec said, consulting readouts. "That seems... unlikely."

"Those towers we saw did something to the air. I think I told them what I needed, and just didn't realize that's what I was doing." Bianca guided the ship down, and the irregularities on the surface turned out to be structures of different sizes and shapes, but with no visible doors or windows. The buildings were covered with glyphs, though – Mahact writing, she assumed. She couldn't read the words, but it felt like she *almost* could: like there was a blurry film across her vision, and if she only stopped and rubbed her eyes for a moment, all would be revealed.

She set the ship down on a clear spot, near the base of the monolith. A set of gleaming black-and-gold-flecked steps, just slightly too big for a human to climb comfortably, led up to the top of the obelisk, which must have been five hundred meters high. She turned in her chair. "Ashont, Clec... I think you should stay here with Heuvelt. If he wakes up alone, who knows what he'll think? Even if we left him a message, he'd try to come in after us, and it might not be safe."

Ashont sighed. "Yes. I was thinking the same thing. We can't leave our injured cub behind. Not now."

Bianca patted her furry shoulder. "It will make me feel

safer, knowing you're here to watch over him. We don't know where we are, or what dangers we might encounter. I'll stay in comms contact as long as I can, though I think I'm going pretty deep, so don't worry if I lose connection."

"I'm hearing too much 'I' and not enough 'we,'" Sev said. "I'm going with you."

"My Sev." Bianca touched her hand. "Dear Sev. I knew you'd never leave my side."

"We have exploration packs prepared," Ashont said. "Anti-grav harnesses for those hard-to-reach places, respirators, water, flares, distress beacons. It's a shame Heuvelt isn't awake. He loves all that stuff. There's nothing he enjoys more than climbing into a weird hole in the ground and looking for wonders."

"We'll take lots of pictures," Sev said.

Bianca helped Sev into her pack, then shouldered her own. "It means so much to me, Sev, the way you made my mission your own."

Sev shrugged. "I like to keep busy. The worst part about being locked up in the brig was the boredom. This gives me something to do. Besides. I admit. I am curious about what we're going to find down there."

"I'm sure it will be worth the work and wait," Bianca said.

They passed through the airlock and marched down the boarding ramp. The gravity was lighter here than it was on the World of Stone, and Bianca went bounding up the steps that led to the top of the monolith. Sev came after her, more slowly, but steadily. "How many of these stupid steps are there?"

Bianca glanced at the height of the step before her, then

the height of the monolith. "Two thousand-one-hundred-seventy-four," she said. "But every journey begins with just one, right?"

"I don't mind the first step," Sev said. "It's all the ones that come after. Why don't we use our anti-grav harnesses and fly up there?"

Bianca shook her head. "Come on, Sev. We came all this way. Where's your sense of occasion?"

"You're one of those people who enjoys delayed gratification, aren't you?"

"I'll take gratification any way I can get it," Bianca said. "But sometimes it is a little sweeter when you have to wait."

"Why is that planet *glowing*?" Richeline said. "Archambelle, is Ixth supposed to glow like that?"

The doctor stared at the screen for a long time. When she turned toward the others, her eyes were wider than Voyou had ever seen them.

"I don't know what that is," she said. "But it is not Ixth."

CHAPTER 32

At the top of the stairs they faced the monolith, a blank wall of smoothly gleaming black stone, with flecks of gold that seemed to float deep inside.

Bianca walked across the short landing and pressed her hand against the wall. "I'm here," she said, her breath puffing out against the stone. Some combination of her touch, her voice, and the air from her lungs set ancient machinery in motion, and the stone split vertically right down the middle, each half swinging silently inward, revealing a small chamber beyond.

"Ashont, Clec, we're going in," Bianca transmitted. "It looks like some sort of elevator."

"Keep us updated as long as you can," Ashont said.

Sev and Bianca stepped into the chamber, and a segment of the wall lit up with incomprehensible twisty symbols. "Are those buttons?" Sev said. "Which one do you press?"

One of the glyphs glowed more brightly, and sent tendrils of force through the air toward Bianca, invisible to Sev. "This one." She put her hand against the symbol, and the floor began to drop smoothly down, the ceiling and the spill of light from outside receding until they were lit only by the glow of the symbols on the wall, which somehow moved down with them.

"How did you know that was the right symbol?"

"I know lots of things, Sev. More and more every minute."

Sev went *hmmm*. "Do you think this Kor Noq Weer is really waiting down there?"

"I'm really not sure. There's *something* down there. Something I'm supposed to see. Something I'm supposed to do." She watched spirals of invisible energy swirling all around her. This whole planet was a ship of sorts, she realized; and more than that, it was a shipbuilding facility, and a weapons factory, and more. It was not just a world in itself, but the seed of a greater world to come.

She closed her eyes, and it was as if she moved through the darkened caverns and endless tunnels that riddled the sphere, a bodiless roving point of view. There were incubators here too. The same sort of machinery that had created *her* body waited deep below the ground, on a much vaster scale. Once she offered up a sample of herself, this place could make more of her. Bodies like hers, anyway. Bodies like hers was *now*, with all these new capabilities she barely understood. Enough new bodies to populate this planet. Enough to field an army. But to what end?

"Do you know *what* you're supposed to do yet?"

"Something glorious," Bianca murmured.

They rode the rest of the way down in silence.

"What do you *mean* it's not Ixth?" Richeline said.

Archambelle was chewing on the ends of her hair and staring off into space. "It's a Mahact artifact, I'm sure, but... There aren't many descriptions of Ixth, but there are a few, and it's not like this. Everyone says it's a paradise world, and this... it's some kind of giant space station, can't you tell?"

"The scans definitely indicate something other than a natural planet," Voyou agreed. "Our sensors can't penetrate the surface to a very great depth, but even within those limits we've detected all sorts of tunnels, chambers, and cavities down there. No signs of life, though. Maybe this world is abandoned. The lights are on, but no one's home."

"The dead outpost of a dead race," Richeline said.

"A necropolis," Archambelle said. The idea seemed to cheer her up. "A *city* of the dead. A tomb that we can raid. So, it's not Ixth. We misunderstood, or we were misled. It's still a Mahact world, and it's glowing, and that means it's still *operational*. I'm sure we can find something here to give the Barony the kind of edge we're looking for. Maybe we'll even find directions to reach the *real* Ixth. We won't know until we go inside."

Richeline sighed. "You know the captain's in there already. She must be. If Bianca's the key, the captain is the one who turned her. She might have killed the princess already by now."

"The captain certainly wouldn't wait for us to arrive," Voyou agreed. "She's so decisive."

"I'll bring my research assistants," Archambelle said. "Richeline, call up a full complement of soldiers. We'll need them to..." She gestured vaguely. "Carry stuff."

"I'll bring my best surveying team," Voyou said. "We might as well start making maps of the place."

"Just a small, manageable party of thirty people or so," Richeline said sourly. "It's practically a commando squad. I'll get a shuttle ready."

Heuvelt sat up, gasping, and tore the oxygen mask from his face. Ashont was there, petting him with her immense paws, making soothing sounds, but he shouted over her. "Sev attacked me! She's a traitor, a Letnev spy, Bianca is in danger!"

Ashont immediately slammed the comms panel by the door and shouted, "Bianca, do you read me? Bianca, are you there?"

Only static crackled in reply. Ashont lowered her hand and shook her head. "They descended a while ago. Bianca and Sev. We've lost contact."

"Descended into *what*?" Heuvelt said.

"The depths of the alien planet, or planet-sized space station, maybe, that we landed on while you were unconscious. Ixth, or whatever."

"That's all Sev *wants*, is access to this place, this power! She'll kill Bianca if we don't stop her!"

"Bianca is hard to kill," Ashont said. "But if Sev took her by surprise… hrm. Yes. All right. We'll go in after them. We were just waiting for you to wake up anyway. Clec! Did you get all that?"

"I did," Clec said over the comms. "But we have a bigger problem. A Barony warship, all spikes and cannons, just came through the wormhole, and it's hovering above the planet now."

"Sev made a transmission before she attacked me. She

must have been calling *them*. They were following us the whole time!" Heuvelt rose, cursing as he tore off various bits of diagnostic equipment, to a chorus of squawking machine alarms. "Clec, get our ship out of sight, and then we're going after Bee."

The elevator stopped at last, opening onto a corridor hacked roughly into black stone, lit by fist-sized glowing crystals protruding at random intervals from the ceiling and walls. "It's very rustic down here, isn't it?" Severyne said.

"Who can judge the aesthetics of the Mahact?" Bianca strode along, Severyne at her side.

The tunnels weren't particularly small – they could walk abreast with plenty of room, and the ceiling was a meter above their heads – but Severyne still enjoyed the comforting weight of rock all around her. "This reminds me a little of home," she said.

"I read all about your homeworld," Bianca said. "The Letnev don't even have a word for 'claustrophobia.'"

"I had a bit of trouble comprehending the concept, until someone explained it as the opposite of agoraphobia. *That* I can understand."

"Maybe that's why the Letnev are so obsessed with controlling everything," Bianca said. "It all stems from their basic fear of wide-open spaces."

"You're smart these days, princess, but psychologically assessing an entire culture is a stretch, even for you."

"It's just a hypothesis," Bianca said. The corridor split, one path angling right, the other left. Bianca didn't even break stride, just bore right, and when the path split again, she went left, and when it diverged into three possibilities, she went straight.

"Your yearning is guiding us now?" Sev said.

"Hmm? Oh. Yes. It's a maze down here. This world is remote and hidden away, but it's still possible someone could stumble across it, and I get the sense it's sort of vulnerable, when it's not fully operational. If some explorer or treasure hunter like Heuvelt found it, they could ruin everything. Whatever everything entails. Plus, if enemies ever invaded in force, the layout would frustrate their attempts to take control. This is the safest path. The others are more dangerous."

"A tomb full of traps, then? Marvelous."

Their "safest path" led them to a room with no floor, just a pool of bubbling, hissing liquid, with a few pillars of black stone sticking out of the goo, spaced several meters apart. There was no ledge around the sides, and the ceiling was so far above it couldn't be seen. "Even on the proper route, there are little challenges like this," Bianca said. "Places that are tricky to navigate, unless you have the right capabilities."

"Ah. I see. You jump from pillar to pillar. A bit pointless as a deterrent, since I have an anti-grav harness in my pack."

Severyne began rummaging for it, but Bianca shook her head. "It won't work. There's a dampening field here. None of your tech will work, actually."

Severyne frowned. She tapped at her wrist gauntlet, but it was just a piece of jewelry now. "Oh. Well. Leaping to and fro is all well and good for you, but how do I get across?"

"Do you trust me?"

"I do." Severyne didn't hesitate. She wasn't trustworthy, but Bianca was.

"Great. Hold on tight."

"Wait. What are you doing?"

Bianca picked up Severyne, pack and all, and held her in her arms. Without even taking a running start, Bianca jumped from the edge to the first pillar. She didn't pause there, either, but sprang off to the next, and the next, and the next. A few terrifying seconds later, they were safely on the other side, and Bianca deposited Severyne gently on the floor. "There."

Severyne looked back at the bubbling acid – if it was even something as simple as acid. "Don't get killed in here, princess, or I'll never make my way out again."

"Oh, I don't know, Sev. You're pretty resourceful. You escaped one prison, didn't you?"

"Letnev security has nothing on the Mahact, it seems."

They followed more branches, and Sev did her best to keep track of their route, but it was hard, especially when they spiraled down a corridor that went past several identical doors leading to descending ramps before Bianca picked one that looked just like the others.

They reached a room filled with a greasy-looking green fog, the borders of the mist perfectly, eerily regular. Bianca stuck her head into the fog, sniffed, and pulled back. "It's harmless to you unless you inhale it. Put on the respirator – that's not a machine, just filters, so it should work even with the dampening field. But hold your breath and close your eyes just in case, okay?" Bianca picked Severyne up and ran her through the fog, too.

She carried Severyne when she leapt from a platform into an opaque swirl of cloud and landed, barely bending her knees with the impact, some ten meters down.

She raced with Severyne through a corridor where spikes thrust out of the walls at intervals that seemed perfectly random to Severyne but must have revealed their pattern to Bianca and her time-slowing perception.

She stepped between Severyne and a wall that spat a dozen tiny needles, all embedding themselves in Bianca's back instead. "Pull those out for me, will you, Sev? But put on your gloves, and careful, don't touch the tips. From the smell, it's a toxin that would unravel your DNA, like suffering acute radiation poisoning."

The next obstacle was a long room full of bubbling fluid again, but this time, there was a metal cable about three meters overhead. "I guess I jump up, grab that, and then make my way across hand-over-hand," Bianca said.

"Should I climb on your back and just hold on tight?" Severyne opened her pack. "Actually, there are climbing harnesses in here. We could clip them together, and then–"

"That won't be necessary," Bianca said. "This is as far as you're going."

Severyne thought about acting confused, but she could tell from the look on Bianca's face that the time for all subterfuge was past. "I see. When did you figure it out?"

"I sensed a transmission back on the World of Stone, sent from the *Show and Tell*. Then, moments later, Heuvelt had an accident that conveniently knocked him unconscious." She shook her head. "It was too many data points. I couldn't ignore the obvious conclusion anymore. You are a spy."

"Why not take me out on the ship, then?" Severyne said. "Why bring me here?"

Bianca shrugged. "I know you're dangerous. I saw what you did to Richeline. I didn't want to risk you hurting Ashont or Clec or Heuvelt in those close quarters. I figured I'd take you down here and strand you instead."

"You could have just killed me, and then I wouldn't be a danger to anyone." She shook her head. "But you don't have the will. You'd rather let the Mahact do the killing for you."

"Oh," Bianca said. "You think I'm being weak. No. I wanted to bring you to the very edge of fulfilling your mission, and then watch it crumble before your eyes. I'm being cruel, Sev, because I'm very, very angry, and very, very hurt."

"I see." Severyne smiled. "In that case, I'm very, very impressed."

"I don't care."

"You don't? I have a reputation for being difficult to impress. I'm surprised you didn't hear about that, with all the time you spent with my crew."

Bianca frowned. "Your crew?" It clicked. "Wait. *You're* the captain?" She groaned. "You faked the personnel files, just so you could trick me later? You knew I was hacking your systems all along?"

"I make a point of knowing everything," Severyne said. "Be flattered. The Barony sent the very best to look after you." She dropped her pack and reached for the Argent Flight blade tucked into the small of her back. The knife wouldn't help her now – Bianca could take it from her in the space of an eye-blink, since her only hope at besting the woman was by surprise – but she'd rather die in a fight than sit here waiting to starve.

Bianca staggered away when Severyne brandished the blade, shading her eyes with her hand as if something was blinding her. "What – where did you *get* that horrible thing?"

Severyne looked at the knife, which didn't look any different to her than it had before, but all *sorts* of things looked different to Bianca than they did to everyone else, didn't they? Severyne took a step forward. "This doesn't have to end with you dead, princess."

"Don't call me that," she spat.

"Fine. Miss Xing. I think we can reach a mutually agreeable accommodation. Your death doesn't benefit me. Your life could. What do you say?"

A sudden, blistering wind blew through the room, and it carried a voice that spoke in the tones of a crackling fire: *She says no.*

CHAPTER 33

"We're going to use ropes *and* anti-grav harnesses going down the shaft," Heuvelt said. "I don't want to risk my life to any single form of technology, new or old." They used the harnesses to carry them to the top of the stairs, and once they attained the summit, they drove pitons into the stone landing outside the doors. They attached ropes to those, and dropped them down the seemingly bottomless elevator shaft. There was no telling what awaited them below, but Heuvelt had done blind descents before. He usually enjoyed them. If he hadn't been worried about Sev stabbing Bianca in the back, he would have rather enjoyed this whole experience.

Clec and Ashont readied their ropes, though Clec was merely strapped to Ashont – their fates, as always, so closely aligned they functioned as one. They'd parked the *Show and Tell* a short distance away, in a small square surrounded by taller structures, out of sight and, with luck, at least partly hidden from sensor detection by all the sources of heat and vibration in the walls. This whole planet was a machine, and it seemed to be revving up. Maybe, when and if they climbed out again, they'd still have a ship, instead of a smoking bombed ruin where a ship *used* to be, courtesy of the Barony vessel overhead.

They dropped down the shaft with their anti-grav harnesses, at least until those harnesses abruptly stopped working ten meters from the bottom, sending them all slamming into the wall on their ropes. Heuvelt groaned, but then shouted, "Vindication! The old ways are best!" From there, they rappelled down.

At the bottom they unclipped their ropes and went down the corridor, Heuvelt dabbing the wall with a marker when they reached the first branch in the passageway. He put on a specially tinted monocle and grunted in satisfaction. The mark was invisible to the naked eye, but glowed violet when seen through the lens, and because it was a function of chemistry and optics, whatever tech-dampening field had killed their anti-grav harnesses didn't interfere. He didn't want to get lost down here, but he didn't want to leave the pursuing Letnev a series of trail markers, either. "Which way?" he asked.

Ashont sniffed, then pointed right. "Bianca went that way. Not long ago, either."

"Bless your miraculous nose," Heuvelt said, and they set off.

In the end, a detachment of thirty-six people landed on the new world, because Archambelle had more research assistants than anyone had realized, all carrying various sensors and instruments. The surveying team carried flares, ropes, laser rangefinders, and other useful tools. The soldiers carried guns.

Archambelle touched the glyphs etched all over the walls of the nearest structure. "This is... a sort of life story. Or more like... a series of boasts. An extremely lengthy epitaph? You! Postdoc two! Scan these glyphs!"

"What do they say?" Voyou asked.

"Tales of conquest, enemies crushed, plans enacted, discoveries discovered, inventions invented. There's no mention of this great conqueror's name, though."

"Would the name mean anything to you if you saw it?" he asked, genuinely curious.

"Some names would. Tales of a few individual Mahact have survived. The great ruler Vertar Auran Oublis. The mad renegade Kor Noq Weer. The brilliant scientist Callam Harran Coulis. Others."

"This is rather fancy for a tomb," Voyou said. "Maybe we will find something valuable."

"Let's go!" Richeline snapped. "We can do a proper survey after we secure the princess and find the captain."

Richeline, Archambelle, and Voyou each gave orders to their individual commands, then joined together, the three of them leading the way up the steps to the obelisk. Richeline and Voyou had to help Archambelle up. She hadn't yet recovered from her research binge. "Why don't we just use anti-grav?" Richeline muttered. "Ascend right to the top?"

"We are on *Mahact land*," Archambelle said. "This is a momentous occasion. When I tell my colleagues about this journey, I intend to tell them that I *walked* up all two thousand or however many steps it turns out to be."

"You walked up some of them, anyway," Voyou said. "It doesn't seem like you're walking up *quite* as many as I am, though."

The soldiers, lacking any sense of ceremony, floated up the steps in their harnesses, moving at a slow and stately pace behind their leaders. The surveyors and research assistants didn't have anti-grav harnesses, so they just huffed and puffed and climbed at the rear.

Their party reached the top and looked at the ropes, and Richeline cursed. "Why in the brightness did the Mahact build this giant tower, just to have it descend so far below ground level?" she said. "Because of *ceremony*?"

"The ways of the Mahact are not ours to understand," Archambelle said. "Just to exploit. All right, who's helping me down here? I need to see *everything*."

Kill her, my child, the voice said.

Bianca couldn't take her eyes off the horrible knife in Severyne's hand. The weapon seemed to poison the light around it, twisting and distorting her vision, and it somehow also *stank*, but the stench was in her mind more than her nose. Was it some kind of radiation? Worst of all, the presence of the blade seemed to cut off Bianca from her extra senses: she couldn't detect the flow of energy around her anymore, or even tell which way she was supposed to go – the yearning that had guided her to her maker's side was gone, and she felt bereft.

Strike! the wind blew. *She is slow! Show me what you can do!*

The voice was in her head, and she knew it belonged to her maker, Kor Noq Weer. Rumors of the extinction of the Mahact, it seemed, were greatly exaggerated. His words weren't quite irresistible, but they were certainly *motivating*, and unlocked the paralysis the sight of Sev's strange weapon had caused in her. She had to get that horrible *thing* away from her. If it touched Bianca's flesh, she feared she would simply start to come apart.

Bianca slowed time. That didn't work as well as it should have, either, but even at half capacity her powers were formidable. She darted around Sev, calculating the best way to strike. She wanted to kill the traitor, rip her head off, throw her in the acid – to punish her for the crime of making Bianca think she was her *friend*. Killing her would have been easy. Indeed, moving at this speed, a strike of any force would kill Sev, unarmored as she was. It would honestly be harder *not* to kill her.

Bianca could do hard things, though. She remembered the ring Torvald had given her, meant as a self-defense of last resort. Now it could be an instrument of mercy.

Bianca twisted the ring the way Torvald had taught her, then reached out as slowly as she could, and gently cupped her hand around the back of Sev's neck. The ring sent a jolt of electricity into Sev, and Bianca let time resume its normal flow.

Severyne dropped the horrible knife – it went spinning toward the edge of the chasm – and collapsed in a boneless sort of heap. "Thank you, Torvald," Bianca muttered. She still wasn't a murderer, despite Sev's goading. Maybe she could *continue* not murdering anyone, despite her maker's gleeful urging. She quickly frisked Sev for weapons, but all she found was the sheath she'd kept that horrible knife in.

"What *is* that thing?" She looked at the knife and shuddered. Once, on Darit, she'd turned over a rock and seen a squirming nest of wriggling things, all mandibles and legs and eyes, and she felt the same instinctive revulsion at the sight of that blade.

A weapon made to kill Mahact. Vile thing. Cast it away.

Bianca crept up on it. The hilt wasn't horrible, just the blade, so she gingerly grabbed the hilt and shoved the knife into the sheath she'd taken from Sev. Once that blade was hidden from sight, she was able to exhale, all the tension running out of her, and her powers returning.

Is it gone? the wind demanded. *I can't sense it anymore. Come to me, my child. My heir. Come to me, and we will make the Mahact live again.*

"Is that what we're doing?" Bianca said.

What else? Kor Noq Weer replied.

"What else?" Bianca muttered. She leapt up to grab the cable and swung hand-over-hand across the chasm, toward her destiny.

Ashont was strong and agile enough to jump across the pillars in the acid room, Clec on her shoulder, and she carried a line of strong cable with her. Heuvelt clipped his climbing harness to that line, then pulled himself across the chasm, the fumes stinging his eyes all the way. The acid stench had worried Ashont, but she was able to pick up Bianca's scent well enough on the other side.

They wore their respirators and shut their eyes as they

raced through the room full of green fog. Heuvelt was certain they'd step into a spike-filled pit at some point in their sightless rush, but apparently the Mahact believed in using one trap at a time.

When they reached the platform above the clouds, they lowered Clec on a rope to make sure it was safe, then dropped ropes and rappelled down to the next level.

The corridor full of spikes would have been impassable, but Clec was small enough to crawl along the floor, below their scything passage. She located an access panel – "Even deadly spike traps need to be *serviced* occasionally" – and yanked out wires until the blades stopped moving. Then it was just a question of carefully climbing under, over, and around razor-edged spears. Heuvelt had done more difficult things... but not often.

They saw the needles glistening on the floor of the next room and knew to be wary. They threw objects from their packs – canteens, unlit flares, nutrient bars – across the motion sensors until the walls ran out of ammunition, then jumped over the ankle-deep glittering carpet of deadly projectiles.

After that, they found Severyne, sitting with her back against a wall. She rose slowly to her feet when they entered. "Heuvelt. Are you here to thank me for sparing your life when I could have so easily taken it?"

"How could you betray Bianca?" Heuvelt roared. "I should throw you in that acid!"

"I didn't betray anyone," Sev said mildly. "I'm loyal to my people, the Letnev. Without them, Bianca would never have reached her destiny. She would have pair-bonded with a farm boy named Grandly, had some babies, and died of dysentery or ergot poisoning or whatever they die of on Darit. I'm the real captain of the *Grim Countenance*. That means I'm the one who took her off that planet and gave her the stars. Me, personally, *I* did that, and all I required from her was a share of what she found. She wasn't willing to give me that."

"She told us a different story," Ashont growled.

"Yes, well, her perspective differs in certain key respects," Sev said. "I wouldn't have let the doctor vivisect her. Not as long as she kept being useful, anyway. But look where she led us. This isn't a treasure planet. This is a tomb, and if we're not careful, it could be our final resting place, too. Oh, and it's a *haunted* tomb, by the way – there's a living Mahact down here somewhere, whispering words of murder on the wind. We thought we'd loot this place and take its wonders for our own. We thought the original owners were long gone. Instead, I fear all we did was wake them up."

"I have no interest in anything you have to say," Heuvelt declared. "Where is Bianca?"

"Where do you think, you cretin? On the other side of that bubbling pool of acid."

"Then we're going that way too. Ashont? Help me up?"

"Don't mind me!" Sev called as the panther-woman boosted the human up to the cable above the pool. He clipped his harness to the line and began to work his way across. Ashont growled at her, Clec made a rude noise, and then the Naaz and Rokha followed. "I'll be fine here!" Sev said. "You're going *toward* the mad genetic sorcerer! I hope that works out for you!"

"I," huff, "never," huff, "liked her," Heuvelt said, grunting his way across the chasm.

"I would have bitten her face off," Ashont said behind him. "But she's so awful I'm afraid I'd get face poisoning."

"I hope her crew finds her," Clec said, "and they all fall into the acid together."

"I am beginning to think we should have gone right instead of left at that first branch," Voyou said. He blinked blood out of his eye. It wasn't his blood. It belonged to one of the research assistants, he thought. That one had sprayed *everywhere*.

"The Mahact… left is the more sacred direction in their culture, according to my research, so I thought…" Archambelle was fairly bloody too. She'd lost her right arm from the elbow down when they passed through the room Voyou thought of as the Chamber of a Thousand Blades, but one of the surveyors had a self-tightening tourniquet that had kept her from bleeding out. A tourniquet couldn't help that same surveyor when his head got sliced off in the Room of Electric Whips, though.

"We can hardly go back now," Richeline said. Her eyes were wide, and she brandished a weapon she'd salvaged from the last soldier (he'd died in the Hall of Biting Mirrors, Voyou thought, or maybe it was the Burning Salon; after a while, the deaths all ran together). "That third chamber is sealed, the walls slammed together, there's no getting through anymore."

"I go back and forth on what to name that one," Voyou said. "Do we call it the Chamber of Crushing? Or maybe something simple, like the Pestle? It killed half the troopers in one smush. I'd say it earned a bit of distinction."

"Shut up, shut up, shut up." Richeline's eyes darted in all directions. "You're supposed to be a *surveyor*, so survey us out of this. Do we go left, right, or straight?"

"Hmm. I predict that left leads to horrible death, straight leads to unimaginably horrible death, and right leads to incomparably unimaginably horrible death. But maybe I got those reversed?" He laughed, but even to his own ears, it sounded more like an unhinged titter.

"Forward," Richeline said. "The princess has to be here somewhere."

"Yes," Voyou said. "Somewhere to the *right* of that first branch, if I had to guess. Don't you think so, Doctor Archambelle? Doctor?" He nudged her shoulder, and she fell over. "Oh," he said.

Richeline stared down at Archambelle. "What? We put a tourniquet on her wound!"

Voyou pointed at the small of Archambelle's back, revealed by her collapse. Her white uniform was matted black with blood all across the base of her spine. "It appears she suffered another injury that went undetected. In the Shrapnel Parlor, if I had to guess. I got a piece in my hip there myself. I do hope the shards aren't poisonous."

"We're getting out of here, Voyou," Richeline snarled. "I am *not* dying here."

"You want to die just ahead of here, then?" he asked. "We only survived this far because we always took the rear, and sent other people ahead of us so they triggered the traps first. Now it's just us."

She grinned. It was a horrible grin. She pointed the rifle at him. "That's true. You're right. That really was a successful strategy. This time, *you* go first." He didn't move. "Come on!" She prodded him in the chest with the barrel of the weapon.

"Go ahead and shoot me," he said. "That would be a much more pleasant way to die than being eaten by acid from the feet up, like postdoc number two, or dragged into the ceiling by mechanical arms like that trooper, or slammed between spiked grates like my best cartographer was. Please. I'd shoot myself if I had a gun."

"Coward!" Richeline said. "Fool! You can sit here and wait to die, but I'm getting *out*. I am a professional, I trained for this, I am the best of the best, I am the captain of the *Grim Countenance* and I will not be defeated!" She ran off, choosing the straight-ahead corridor.

"Acting captain," Voyou muttered. Then he heard her scream. Briefly. "Former acting captain," he corrected, and tittered again.

CHAPTER 34

Bianca pushed her way through a set of tall golden doors and entered the central chamber, a suitable resting place for a sorcerer king. The room was octagonal, the walls filled with shelves and niches, and the floor crowded with pedestals, all holding precious objects – the sort of things that Heuvelt would have taken great delight in looting. Jewels in every color, some as big as her fist; a tiny silver bird that hovered in the air above a plinth; model spaceships made of precious metals; golden cups; crowns, necklaces, gauntlets, rings; a full suit of armor, glimmering with forcefields and strange energies; daggers with gems in the hilts; an orrery depicting an unknown solar system; figurines of fanciful animals carved in substances like ivory and jade; and more.

They were like the grave goods buried with ancient kings in some cultures, Bianca thought, to make their afterlives more comfortable. Except… this king wasn't dead. "Kor Noq Weer?" she called.

The center of the room held an immense chest on a raised

platform, with a lid of shining silver metal, filigreed all over in gold. When Bianca spoke, the lid began to slide to one side. She could see the lines of force flowing through the chamber, the machinery that engaged to move the lid, but those lines were much fainter and harder to discern than they had been before.

A figure sat up from his resting place inside the chest – or was it a sarcophagus? He wore robes so purple they were nearly black, intricately patterned around the sleeves, neckline, and cowl with glyphs picked out in shining white wire. His face was shadowed in the deep hood. His hands, hidden in bulky gloves, gripped the sides of the sarcophagus, and he hauled himself to his feet. He was humanoid, though much taller than Bianca herself. Tubes and wires snaked up from the interior of the chest into his sleeves and hood, and he tore them away, letting them drop, hissing and writhing and spurting acrid fluids.

The foot end of the sarcophagus folded down and extended to form a ramp, and he walked down it to the floor... rather unsteadily, she noticed.

He's old, Bianca thought. *He's frail.* "I wasn't supposed to take this long to arrive, was I?" she said. "You thought I would get here a lot sooner than this."

"Plans." The voice was a croak, not at all the strong tones the wind had carried to her before – they must have been generated by some of the strange technology in this place. And here she thought the god-king had actually been *shouting* his encouragements to murder. "Plans seldom work out as intended. That is why we have contingencies. Redundancies. *You* were a backup plan for a backup plan, in fact – and yet, here you are, the one that actually came through. What is your name, child?"

"You don't know?"

"I cannot read your mind. Not without special equipment. I knew you were coming – I sensed your arrival, and the World of Light woke up when it detected your brainwave patterns, designed to interface with its systems, just like my own. I scanned your ship's database to learn your languages, and what sad and rudimentary things they are. But your thoughts, secrets, and memories – those are your own."

"My name is Bianca Xing."

"Welcome, Bianca Xing, to your destiny."

"Why am I here? I don't understand. I came all this way, and I *still* don't know why."

"I'll tell you," Kor Noq Weer said. His voice was getting stronger. "I do, after all, love to talk about myself." He shoved a delicate crystal sculpture off a pedestal, sending it shattering to the floor, and sat down, the effort of standing too great for him, it seemed. "What do you know of the Mahact, child?"

Just what Brother Errin had told her. "They ruled the galaxy, a long time ago. So long ago almost no one remembers them. There was a rebellion, and they were all killed. Or we thought so. We didn't expect to find this place. We were looking for a paradise world, maybe the Mahact homeworld, called Ixth."

"Of course you were. I told the servant who built your incubator to spread those stories, and it seems some fragment of his work survived through the eons. The Mahact did rule, and ruled well, until it all started to fall apart. Our leaders encouraged us all to band together, to crush the rebellion, but I could tell our empire was doomed. The old ways had failed us, or else the upstarts would have never made any headway at all. I knew the Mahact needed new leadership." He put a gloved hand to his chest. "They needed *me*. So I formed my own faction, supported by like-minded people, and clones, and our various servants. I sought to overthrow our leaders and take control of Ixth. I dabbled in forbidden practices in pursuit of those goals."

"What kind of practices could be forbidden to the *Mahact*?"

"Gene warfare, mainly," he said. "Oh, we had no problem using those techniques against our enemies or subjects – destroying or rewriting DNA was part of our standard approach to governance. But it was forbidden to use those powers on the *Mahact*. I did so anyway. I just wanted to hurry along the inevitable collapse of my world's leaders, so I could take over, and rule the galaxy properly. I was making progress. Many victories. Others called them massacres, but, well. Semantics." He sighed, a sound like a death rattle. "But, sadly, there was an accident. A wasting disease meant to destroy my enemies instead infected my allies… and eventually myself. I knew, then, that I could not defeat my enemies. But!" He held up one finger. "I could outlast them. As I said, their doom was inevitable. Just too slow for my tastes. I caused the World of Light to be created, in a remote part of the galaxy, accessible only by a wormhole I controlled, with the aid of my Titans. I installed myself here with all the necessary elements of conquest. Shipbuilding facilities, cloning tanks, weapons. I set in motion various plans to awaken me when a suitable interval had passed, so long that the Mahact were forgotten, and no longer considered a threat. Then I would return, and take control of an unprepared galaxy. Sadly, my plans all seem to have gone awry... except for you. Even your arrival took far longer than expected. My stasis systems were beginning to fail. Another three or four centuries, and I might even have died."

"So, I'm just, what? A living alarm clock?" Bianca said. "I'm here to wake you up?"

"You serve multiple purposes, as all good components do. You were designed to blend in with the local population in terms of gross morphology, adapting to suit whatever society you found yourself in, while remaining Mahact on the inside. You would be able to travel in disguise, as it were, gathering intelligence about the state of the galaxy – indeed, you would have a relentless drive to learn all you could about culture, politics, technology, and military matters. Did you not find it so?"

"I just thought I was a curious person."

"I *made* you to be curious. I also gave you the ability to defend yourself, to win, to conquer – and instilled in you a profound urge to reach this place. Your body and mind are, if I may say, the height of my art. Once you'd gained the necessary data, you would come to this place, a world closed to everyone else, and awaken the World of Light. I was already stirring, alerted by certain arcane systems to the fact of your quickening. I've just been waiting for your arrival."

"What if I'd been born after you were already awakened by some other process?" Bianca said. "What if I'd followed my yearning all the way out here, and found you already gone, departed centuries before?"

Kor Noq Weer laughed. "Then you would have been disappointed, I suppose."

"I don't think I could possibly be any more disappointed than I am right now." She crossed her arms. "I don't understand, though. You're still dying. Am I supposed to continue your work after you pass?"

The Mahact rose, and spread his arms. "Sweet Bianca Xing. *I* am not going anywhere. I could not clone my damaged body, no. So I used all of my art to create something new: a body possessed of Mahact capabilities, hybridized with alien DNA to create a more robust whole – one immune to the wasting disease that targets my people. That body you're walking around in belongs to me. I designed it. And now, I intend to take possession."

She fell back a step. Were those dim lines of force changing direction? Flowing into her? No, oh no. "You can't do this."

"Of course I can, Bianca. Your brain is specifically designed to accommodate the architecture of my thoughts, and the World of Light, my greatest invention, is an engine that will allow me to transfer my consciousness into your form. My mind, in that exquisitely engineered body! I will be strong again. Fast. And capable of moving unnoticed among the denizens of the galaxy, in your alien guise. Everyone will look at me and see a harmless human girl. It's delicious, isn't it?"

"What will happen to *me*?" Bianca imagined herself trapped in his desiccated husk of a body and shuddered.

He chuckled, wet and soft. "Have you ever reformatted a

hard drive, Bianca? Repainted a wall? Those are not perfect analogies, but close enough. I'll retain your memories, all that useful intelligence you gathered, but your personality will be erased. Except, perhaps, for the odd ghost and shadow of data bleeding through. The occasional fleeting memory. Perhaps an occasional dream, of what it was like to be Bianca Xing, before she ceased to exist."

Bianca set her feet. "What makes you think I'll allow this? You said it yourself. I'm fast. I'm strong. You can't force me to, to hook myself up to some machine."

"Hook you up? Bianca. The whole World of Light is the machine. And as for the process…"

It's already started, his voice said, but this time it came from inside her own mind, like an intrusive thought.

Kor Noq Weer rose and stripped off his gloves, revealing fingers twisted into claws. He spread his arms wide. "The vessel is prepared. Come to me. We need only embrace to complete the transfer."

"No." She gritted her teeth. "Never."

"It doesn't have to be an embrace. Any sustained touch will do. My hands around your throat, for instance."

"I won't let you take my body from me!"

You have no choice, Kor Noq Weer said. *You are part of the machinery. A mere component. You are programmed to obey. You want to reach for me – you yearn for my embrace. Don't you?*

She did. She wanted to fold herself into those outstretched arms, just like she'd wanted to travel to the dark place at the center of that triangle of stars, just like she'd wanted to descend to the heart of the World of Light. It was more than a desire. It was a drive. She took a step toward her maker, and then another, and another.

He started to close his arms around her.

Bianca's yearning to accept his embrace was powerful, but it wasn't impossible to resist. Not anymore.

Not since she'd put the sheathed blade she took from Sev in the small of her own back, the smartcloth of her dress helpfully forming a pocket the perfect size and shape to hold it. While the blade was covered, it didn't make her sick or disoriented, but its proximity did somewhat dull her connection to the machinery of the World of Light and the intensity of her compulsion to obey her maker.

As she stepped into Kor Noq Weer's arms, she reached behind her and drew the knife. She had to grit her teeth against the sickening vertigo that seized her when she exposed the blade, and even so she stumbled into the Mahact sorcerer. His body was light, frail, a bag of sticks, and they went down together in a heap. He hissed, sensing the blade, but wrapped his arms around her more tightly, his claws scrabbling for any centimeter of bare skin, so he could complete the transfer.

Bianca wriggled around until she freed one arm, then jammed the knife into Kor Noq Weer's chest. She had no idea if the Mahact even had hearts, but it seemed likely there was *something* vital in there. She pulled the knife out, though exposing the blade made her guts seize up and her vision blur.

She stabbed again, and again, and again, even as Kor Noq Weer screamed in her mind: *No! No! You're mine, you're mine, you're mine!* One of his bare hands closed around her throat and started to squeeze, but it was just a spasm, and a moment later his grip went limp and his ancient claw fell away.

The lines of force around Bianca snapped, the delicate whorls and toruses and arcs of energy vanishing from her senses. The deep machinery she felt thrumming all around and through her shuddered, and stalled, and then died. The resulting silence was the silence of an undiscovered tomb.

The last of her strength ran out of her, and Bianca collapsed atop Kor Noq Weer. *I am me*, she thought. *I am still me.*

The lights in the chamber went out. A moment later, so did the light of Bianca's consciousness.

Everything went dark in the chamber where Severyne sat, the crystals dimming and plunging the room into darkness. A moment later, everything went silent, the thrum and hum and vibration of the engines deep inside this planet-sized machine subsiding.

Interesting. Severyne rummaged in her pack until she found a chemical light. The Letnev had excellent night vision, of course, but they needed at least the occasional stray photon to work with, and there were none here. But maybe, since the machines had stopped… She strapped on an electric headlamp instead, and, wonder of wonders, it turned on, shining a beam that illuminated the acid pit. *That* kept bubbling. No power source necessary there beyond its own chemical reaction, apparently.

Hmm. If the planet was turned off, though, how long before the breathable atmosphere dissipated?

Severyne checked her anti-grav harness… and it worked too. Whatever jamming technology the mysterious Kor Noq Weer had in place had definitely stopped working.

She carefully made her way back through the tomb,

retracing her earlier journey, using the harness to float over obstacles as necessary. The crew of the *Grim Countenance* should have come to rescue her by now, but of course she had to do everything *herself*, didn't she? Richeline would catch the rough side of her temper once Severyne got back. Speaking of, she'd better steal the *Show and Tell* quickly, just in case Heuvelt and his merry band came crawling out of the depths again.

When she reached the first corridor, the one that led to the long shaft up to the surface, Severyne heard *singing* from the branch Bianca hadn't taken. The Letnev weren't much for music, apart from martial tunes, and this was a soldier's marching song. She considered, then crept a little way down the passage, until she saw a light.

The bearer of the light must have seen hers, too, because it stopped. "*Captain?*" a voice cried out in disbelief.

"Oh, it's you, Voyou." She sniffed. "You went the wrong way, I see. Where's everyone else?"

"They didn't make it, captain."

"What, Richeline and Archambelle too?"

"I… yes, captain. I was there when they died. Archambelle first, Richeline soon after."

"Hmm. Did Archambelle get dissolved in acid or anything?"

"No, captain. It was blood loss. Her body is back in–"

"Well go and *get* her," Severyne said. "We can do without Richeline's remains, but this whole idea was Archambelle's, and the inquiry will go much easier for us if we can demonstrate that her wild ideas got her killed." Severyne paused. "That was an order, Undercommandant."

"Yes, captain!"

Severyne waited for a while, gnawing on a protein bar, until he came floating back, dragging Archambelle's corpse. She dangled, slack, in her own anti-grav harness, tethered to Voyou's waist by a rope. Now that he was closer, she got a good look at his face. "You've got blood all over you."

"Yes, captain."

"How many people were in your little expeditionary force?"

"Thirty-six, captain."

"And you are the sole survivor?"

"Yes, captain."

"You know, Voyou, you may be due for a promotion. Come on. Let's get out of here."

"Is… did you… what about the princess?"

"Bianca Xing is dead."

Voyou didn't speak as they returned to the main corridor and reached the bottom of the long shaft. There was no light shining at the top, now, just more darkness. This place had seemed like a necropolis before, but now it was dead in truth.

"How did Bianca die?" Voyou said.

Severyne grunted. They began to rise up the shaft in their harnesses, holding onto the dangling ropes, just in case. "I didn't *see* her die, directly, but she must have. This whole world came to life when she arrived, somehow activated by her very presence. Now it's all dark. I suppose it's possible she's alive, but her death is the most likely explanation for why a planet-sized machine would turn into a chunk of dead metal."

"When your tracker died, we thought you did too, but you

were still alive," Voyou said, seemingly to himself.

"What are you going on about?"

"Nothing, captain. So, the mission is a failure, then?"

"The point of the mission was to ascertain whether Bianca Xing could lead us to valuable Mahact artifacts. My report will say no: she led us to a hole full of death traps, and it killed everyone who came near it, and then shut itself down when Xing died. I suspect Archambelle's one-armed corpse will have a chilling effect on the enthusiasm of her colleagues. The Barony may send engineers here in case there's something they can salvage, but I doubt they'll have much luck. That's if the Titans on the other side don't seal the wormhole and cut this place off again. Frankly, I hope they do. I hate it here."

"Oh, darkness, the Titans – what if they're waiting for us on the other side? They nearly tore the *Grim Countenance* apart when we arrived!"

"We'll deal with that if it happens," Severyne said. "Don't we have enough current problems without worrying about future ones? The Titans were tasked with preventing anyone except the princess from passing through that wormhole. I doubt their orders require them to stop anyone who comes *out*. My expectation is, as long as we leave them alone, they'll leave us alone, too."

"I hope you're right, captain."

"Oh, Voyou," Severyne said. "Haven't you realized yet that I'm essentially *always* right?"

CHAPTER 35

Heuvelt shouted, "Bianca! Bianca, where are you?"

Everything had gone dark and silent a little while ago, but their tech started working again at the same time, and Ashont could still smell Bianca's trail, so they soldiered on. That trail led them here, to an impressive set of golden doors, standing ajar. Heuvelt squeezed through and shone his light around the inside. Ashont and Clec came in after, and Clec rose up near the ceiling in her harness, shining lights down and illuminating the cluttered space.

Bianca was on the floor, her arms wrapped around what appeared to be a bundle of filthy rags. Heuvelt rushed to her and pulled her into his lap. The rags proved to be the corpse of some unknown creature composed mostly of rotten meat and dust.

He looked for Bianca's pulse, and breathed out in relief when he found one, but it was rapid and thready, her breath shallow and uneven. He pulled up one of her eyelids, and her pupil didn't respond to light. Heuvelt was no physician, but he knew that was a bad sign. "Bianca? Are you all right? Bianca?"

"She appears to be comatose," Clec said.

"We have to get her out of here, back to the *Show and Tell*."

Ashont put a heavy paw on his shoulder. "We will. Of course we will. But Heuvelt... you have to prepare yourself–"

"She'll be fine," Heuvelt said. "She just had a shock. She'll come out of it."

"She was linked to this place, in some way beyond our understanding," Clec said. "Now that this place has stopped functioning–"

"She. Will. Be. Fine. Help me get her out."

"You don't want to look around quickly, to see if there's anything worth pillaging?" Ashont asked.

"I'd be afraid anything we took from this place would sprout needles or teeth or stingers and kill us in our beds," Heuvelt said. "Besides, I didn't get into treasure hunting for the *treasure*. I was born with treasures aplenty, and they never fulfilled me. One needs money to live, of course, but what does one live *for*? Adventure! Excitement! To challenge oneself and test one's limits!"

"I'm fine with just the money," Ashont said.

"Me too," Clec said.

"So I'm just going to grab up some of these jewels and figurines," Ashont said. "In deference to your pure love of the work for its own sake, though, Clec and I will gladly keep your share of any profits."

He looked down at Bianca. She seemed stable enough. "Now that you mention it," Heuvelt said, "I do have room in my pack for a bauble or two. Why don't you hand me a couple of those crowns?"

They hooked an anti-grav harness onto Bianca and made their way out. They paused in the chamber where they'd left Severyne. "Do you think she made it out of here?" Ashont asked.

"I think that woman could survive anything short of a direct railgun strike," Heuvelt said. "I just hope she isn't crouched in a corner with a knife, waiting to gut us."

She was not. They made it to the top of the long shaft and emerged onto the planet's surface, where the air was noticeably thinner, and the wind furious. *This must be what it feels like when an atmosphere starts to shred away*, Heuvelt thought.

There was no sign of the *Grim Countenance*, or any Letnev at all. Severyne must have given up the whole expedition as a bad job. Heuvelt wondered what his legal status with the Barony was now. Probably, not good. Ah, well. He was used to it, really, by now.

"I hope Sev didn't bomb our ship on the way out," Clec said.

"Thank you for that cheerful thought," Heuvelt said.

Their ship was unmolested, though the ground beneath it was beginning to tilt. It seemed the structural integrity of the false planet was beginning to fail, chambers and tunnels collapsing now that load-bearing forcefields had flickered off.

They got Bianca on board and hooked into their rudimentary medical suite. While Clec and Ashont took the shuttle up and headed toward the wormhole – mercifully still open – Heuvelt looked at the suite's readings.

He'd feared – expected, really – to see no brain activity at all, but instead he saw quite the opposite: Bianca's brain was incredibly active, but in a disordered and erratic way. The medical suite recommended immediate medication to stop the life-threatening seizures Bianca was having. Except she wasn't having seizures. She wasn't moving at all, apart from the occasional flutter of her eyelids.

They passed through the gate. There were two Titans hovering on the other side, including one with a large, rough, circular hole through its center mass.

The Gatekeeper's voice spoke over the ship's public address system. "Honored heir. You have returned. What did you find? Do you have new orders for us?"

"Clec, transmit on the open channel," Heuvelt said. He cleared his throat. "Gatekeeper, the heir was hurt on the other side of the wormhole. She is unconscious. We're... quite worried about her."

A moment's silence, and then, "I see. Our remit is to protect the heir. Bring her here."

They piloted the *Show and Tell* toward the World of Stone. "I don't suppose you destroyed a passing Barony warship a little while ago?" Ashont asked the Gatekeeper.

"Their vessel emerged not long ago, and departed at great speed. We saw no reason to interfere with their exit."

"I can think of a few reasons," Ashont said.

They made a rather rougher landing than Bianca had managed, and once they settled down the surface of the planet began to shift, the ground rising up around them, curving above them, and enclosing them in a dome like a vast hangar. "They're pumping breathable atmosphere into this space," Clec said.

"Bring her outside," the Gatekeeper said.

Ashont and Heuvelt got Bianca onto a floating stretcher and carried her down the boarding ramp. The domed hangar was brightly lit, like an operating theater. A small Titan, only a meter or so taller than Heuvelt, and glittering like onyx, waited for them. The Titan gestured toward a stone plinth rising out of the floor. "Place her there," it said.

They put Bianca down, and the Titan gazed at her, then touched her temples with its fingertips. Those hands could have crushed her skull easily, but they moved with impossible gentleness. "Ah. There is a battle within her. Another mind is attempting to take over her body."

"What?" Heuvelt said.

The Gatekeeper's voice rumbled in the air. "It seems Kor Noq Weer did not intend his heir to receive his estate, but instead, to provide a vessel for his mind."

Heuvelt frowned. "He wanted to steal her body?"

"He created her body, human. He merely wanted to take ownership of what he made."

"How do you feel about that?" Heuvelt said.

"I believe it is monstrous," the Gatekeeper said. "If I could prevent such a possession, I would – and since I was tasked to protect the heir and aid her in her journey, there would be no conflict with my orders if I did. But, there is nothing I can do to stop this. She must fight on her own. The psyche of a young woman, pitted against the mind of one of the most powerful Mahact to ever live. I do not know who will prevail."

"I believe in Bee," Heuvelt said. "She'll open her eyes again."

"She may," the Gatekeeper said. "The question is, who will be looking out of them?"

They stood. They watched. They waited.

Bianca was back on Darit, but something terrible had happened. The Halemeeting hall was a burned shell, the ruins still smoking. The burgher's house had collapsed in on itself, the walls covered with strange mold. The trailrunner was overturned in the street, legs kicking randomly, sparks shooting from the joints.

She blinked, and she was somehow back at her family farm, only where the house should have been there was a black obelisk instead, solid and sealed. The caprids were all dead in a heap and covered in flies. A stench of burning metal came from the direction of Old Torvald's junkyard, and a black cloud covered that whole quarter of the sky.

Also, the sun was the color of blood, and all three moons were on fire. "That's a bit much," Bianca said. "Where are you, maker?"

The obelisk split open, and Kor Noq Weer emerged. He was wearing the armor she'd seen in his chamber, flickering with blue light, resplendent and mighty. But he stumbled when he approached, and wove an unsteady path toward her. The obelisk vanished behind him, replaced by her family home, cozy and undamaged, smoke rising from the chimney.

"You're barely even here," Bianca said. "Look at you. You didn't get your whole mind into me. You're like... we have these insects, bees, they're fat and yellow and black, good little pollinators. They have stingers, but they're really meant for killing other insects, not hurting people or animals. When the bees sting a person, the barbs get caught, and the poor little creatures end up disemboweling themselves when they pull away, leaving the stinger behind. That's you. You're just a broken-off piece of poison."

Those stingers can get infected if they aren't removed, though, can't they? He spoke in her mind, even though, in the truest sense, they were already in her mind. *You stopped the transfer, it's true, but there's enough of me here to make sure you never wake up again.*

"What's the point of that?"

Kor Noq Weer's face was hidden – she'd never seen it, she realized – but even so, she knew he was looking at her with contempt. *The point is* revenge, *of course!*

"You tried to take my body, but you couldn't. In a way, you should be proud. You made me. You made me so well even *you* couldn't defeat me."

You are a tool that turned in my hand. An experiment gone wrong.

"Perhaps we can reach some mutually agreeable accommodation," Bianca said, echoing something Sev had said to her. The woman had broken her heart, but still, her approach was worth a try. "You can guide me, advise me, and we can work together to fulfill our mutual–"

I would sooner die than negotiate with a lesser being.

"Would you rather spend a subjective eternity bickering here in my mindscape?"

I will grind you down. I am eternal. I am implacable. I am stone.

"And I'm flexible," Bianca said. "You made me that way.

I'm far more adaptable than you are, Kor. I can change myself to solve whatever problem faces me – I can change my body. I can change my brain. I can change my *mind*. And in here, that means..." She glanced up at the sky, and the flames wreathing the moons snuffed. The clouds rolled back, and the smoke blew away over the sea. "I can change the *world*."

Kor Noq Weer ran toward her, but she made the ground split open with a glance. Mechanical arms reached out of cracks in the earth, grabbing his limbs, pulling him down, and he shrieked in outrage. She cocked her head, remembering what the Gatekeeper had said about his illness, and his hood fell away, revealing flesh that melted and bubbled, necrotized and sloughing off. More mechanical limbs – the hidden treasures beneath Darit's surface – grabbed at him, pulling him down, tearing off pieces of his rotting body in the process.

Bianca understood that this was all analogy. She was altering the landscape of her own *mind*, capturing and isolating the rogue psyche that was trying to take control. He'd made her too well. Maybe at his height she would have been unable to resist him, but he'd overestimated his own strength. Even so, she wasn't sure if she could fully eradicate him, but she could bury him deep.

You cannot destroy me. His whole body had been pulled underground now, and only the sockets where his eyes had been held guttering lights. *I am too vast, too full of knowing, my stratagems span eons, my wisdom is eternal–*

"I'll hold onto whatever bits of you are useful, don't worry." She snapped her fingers. The chasm snapped shut, crushing his skull, scattering fragments across the newly solid soil.

Eternalllllll, his voice whispered on the wind, but the words trailed off, and faded.

Bianca sat down cross-legged on the solid ground of her own mind, and looked for a while at the moons in the sky. She felt a yearning now, too, but it was different than the one Kor Noq Weer had planted inside her.

Now what she yearned for was home.

A little while later, back on the World of Stone, Bianca opened her eyes.

CHAPTER 36

Torvald looked at the components scattered on his workbench and whistled. It was the damnedest thing: that morning, a whole bunch of pieces of inert technology in his scrapyard just all of a sudden *woke up*. Mysterious boxes started beeping. Inscrutable cylinders began to hum. Fans turned, and solenoids clicked, and indicators lit up. As best he could figure, some kind of remote power station had come online, and dormant systems were sending messages across the planet again. He wondered if the Letnev surveyors had stumbled on some ancient control center deep in a dead mine and gotten it up and running again. *I wish Bianca was here*, he thought. *She'd have a good old time figuring out what all this junk does.*

His alert system beeped. Someone was at the gates – he'd disabled the automatic opening system, because not all his visitors were welcome anymore. He sure hoped it wasn't another tax collector. He'd already given them pretty much all his best aluminum. The Barony had an endless hunger for resources, and Torvald had yet to see what they offered in return.

He went out into the scrapyard and pressed the remote that made the small door in the gate swing open.

"Open the big doors!" a voice called. "I'm bringing something in!"

Torvald frowned. That voice sounded familiar, but... He made the larger gates swing wide.

There was a spaceship parked beyond the gates, one that looked a little like a bug wearing saddlebags, but that wasn't what drew his eye. There was some kind of three-meter-high *robot* standing there, only it was made of black stone that glittered–

A woman ran toward him. She wore a red dress with a skirt that fluttered, and there was some sort of tiara glittering on her head.

She was just a few steps away before he recognized her, and shouted, "*Bee!*"

She flung herself into his arms, squeezing him and laughing in his ear. "Torvald! That's 'Queen Bee' to you, old man."

He took a step back, but kept his hands on her shoulders as he looked her up and down. "You look different, your local majesty, but I can't quite say how."

"A lot of things have changed," she said. "I'll tell you all about it." The immense stone figure stepped forward, and Torvald craned his neck. "What's this?"

"This is my friend, Natrion the Vigilant. He looks out for me. Doesn't like to be far from my side."

"I'm pleased to meet you," Torvald said. The immense figure nodded. Maybe more than just a robot, then.

Torvald touched Bianca's tiara, straightening it a little from where it went askew during their hug. "Did you turn out to be a space princess after all?"

"More sort of a king," she said. "But I abdicated the throne. The world they offered wasn't much to my liking. Too big. Too ugly. Too dangerous. I closed it up behind a broken wormhole, where it can't do any harm." She cocked her head, and her eyes got a little faraway, like she was listening to words Torvald couldn't hear. "But there's another world that *does* interest me. Darit."

"Since when? You couldn't wait to get away from here."

"I just never appreciated it properly before." She gazed around the scrapyard. "Sometimes you have to go away from a place so you can come back and see it with fresh eyes, I guess." She linked arms with Torvald and began to lead him toward the ship, the tall fella following at their heels. "Tell me," she said. "Have the Letnev been bothering you much?"

"More than I'd like."

"I have some ideas about how to encourage them to move along. Undo their annexation. Bother someone else for a while."

"Bee, are you talking about fighting the Barony? That seems like a tall order, even with your big friend's help."

"Oh, a couple of his siblings came with me too," Bianca said. "They're in space, hanging out beyond the orbit of the moons. They're a little bigger than Natrion here, and they'd draw too much attention if they came down to say hello. We have other resources as well. Darit has all kinds of fascinating things buried under the surface. It was a valuable colony world, once upon a time, with rich mines, and it has planetary defenses to suit. Most of them still work, I think. I can see all the connections now, all the lines of energy and force. It's just a question of altering the flow. I think I can even increase the radii of the habitable zones, connect the settlements better, so you don't have to bundle up in tundra gear to get from place to place."

Torvald whistled. "Did you have something to do with all this machinery waking up again, Bee?"

She looked over at him, and her eyes twinkled. "I always did have something of a knack for tech, didn't I? That's gotten a lot stronger lately. Just like the rest of me."

"Even so... the *Barony*..."

"It won't be easy," Bee said. "But it turns out my original destiny was to conquer the whole galaxy. I figure it shouldn't be *that* hard to liberate and protect one little world."

RETURN TO
THE VOID IN...

THE
VEILED
MASTERS

ACKNOWLEDGMENTS

Thanks again to Marc Gascoigne and the whole Aconyte team, especially Lottie Llewelyn-Wells and my editor Paul Simpson, and to the Twilight Imperium creative team too. And look at that cover by Scott Schomburg! Thanks to my agent Ginger Clark and the whole Curtis Brown team too.

In my personal life, especially in these pandemic days, my wife Heather Shaw and son River help keep me steady. I also rely on Ais, Amanda, Emily, Katrina, and Sarah – I hope I get to see them all in person a lot more soon. My fellow writers are always there for me, and Molly Tanzer especially offered great insight and support on this project.

And thank you, readers, for joining Bianca on her journey. I'll see you next time. (You may not have seen the last of Severyne, either.)

ABOUT THE AUTHOR

TIM PRATT is a Hugo Award-winning SF and fantasy author, and finalist for the World Fantasy, Sturgeon, Stoker, Mythopoeic, and Nebula Awards, among others. He is the author of over twenty novels, and scores of short stories. Since 2001 he has worked for *Locus*, the magazine of the science fiction and fantasy field, where he currently serves as senior editor.

timpratt.org // twitter.com/timpratt

TWILIGHT IMPERIUM

Welcome to a galaxy of eternal conflict. Explore an epic space opera while proving your superiority over those who would dispute your claim. Use your military might, clever diplomacy, and economic bargaining to control the galaxy.

Explore an incredible universe
with Fantasy Flight Games.
fantasyflightgames.com

WORLD EXPANDING FICTION

Do you have them all?

ARKHAM HORROR
- ☐ *Wrath of N'kai* by Josh Reynolds
- ☐ *The Last Ritual* by S A Sidor
- ☐ *Mask of Silver* by Rosemary Jones
- ☐ *Litany of Dreams* by Ari Marmell
- ☐ *The Devourer Below* edited by
  Charlotte Llewelyn-Wells
- ☐ *Cult of the Spider Queen* by S A Sidor
  (coming soon)

DESCENT
- ☐ *The Doom of Fallowhearth* by Robbie
  MacNiven
- ☐ *The Shield of Daqan* by David Guymer
- ☐ *The Gates of Thelgrim* by Robbie MacNiven
  (coming soon)

KEYFORGE
- ☐ *Tales from the Crucible* edited by
  Charlotte Llewelyn-Wells
- ☐ *The Qubit Zirconium* by M Darusha Wehm

LEGEND OF THE FIVE RINGS
- ☐ *Curse of Honor* by David Annandale
- ☐ *Poison River* by Josh Reynolds
- ☐ *The Night Parade of 100 Demons*
  by Marie Brennan
- ☐ *Death's Kiss* by Josh Reynolds

TWILIGHT IMPERIUM
- ☐ *The Fractured Void* by Tim Pratt
- ☑ *The Necropolis Empire* by Tim Pratt

ACONYTE

**EXPLORE OUR WORLD
EXPANDING FICTION**

ACONYTEBOOKS.COM
@ACONYTEBOOKS
ACONYTEBOOKS.COM/NEWSLETTER